# Beyond This Place

To: my loveable Daddy
have the best
Christmas ever!
Love Hilary
Christmas 1989

# Books by A. J. Cronin

ADVENTURES IN TWO WORLDS

BEYOND THIS PLACE

THE CITADEL

DESMONDE

GRAND CANARY

THE GREEN YEARS

HATTER'S CASTLE

THE JUDAS TREE

JUPITER LAUGHS

THE KEYS OF THE KINGDOM

THE NORTHERN LIGHT

A POCKETFUL OF RYE

SHANNON'S WAY

A SONG OF SIXPENCE

THE SPANISH GARDENER

THE STARS LOOK DOWN

A THING OF BEAUTY

THREE LOVES

# A. J. CRONIN

# Beyond This Place

Little, Brown and Company   Boston   Toronto

LIBRARY OF CONGRESS CATALOG CARD NO. 84-80911

A

FLD

*Published simultaneously in Canada
by Little, Brown & Company (Canada) Limited*

PRINTED IN THE UNITED STATES OF AMERICA

# Part I

# Chapter 1

ON Wednesday evenings Paul's mother took the tram from her work in the City Hall to the mid-week service at Merrion Chapel and he usually walked over from the university, after his five o'clock philosophy class, to meet her as she came out. But on this particular Wednesday, his interview with Professor Slade kept him late and, with a glance at his watch, he decided to go straight home.

It was June, and the lovely expectant evening had imposed a spell upon the begrimed buildings of Belfast. Framed against the amber sky, the roofs and chimney stacks of the northern Irish city lost their prosaic outlines and became mysterious, resplendent as a city in a dream.

As Paul came up Larne Road, the quiet side street of semi-detached brick houses where, on the ground floor of No. 29, he occupied with his mother a three-room apartment, a surge of elation took hold of him. He felt suddenly the breath-taking beauty and promise of life. Standing for a moment at his door, an unassuming young man, bareheaded, in a worn tweed suit, he filled his lungs with the soft, still air. Then, briskly, he turned and put his latch-key in the lock.

The canary was singing in the kitchen. Whistling to the bird, he removed his jacket, hung it on a hanger in the hall, and, in his shirtsleeves, put the kettle to boil and began to see about supper. A few minutes later the nickel alarm clock on the mantelpiece struck seven, and he heard his mother's step in the

3

outside porch. He greeted her gaily as she came in, a spare and enduring figure, bent a little to one side by her indispensable "hold-all" bag, clad in respectable black.

"Sorry I couldn't get across, Mother," he smiled, "but Slade's given me the job. At least, I'm almost sure of it."

Mrs. Burgess studied him. The strand of drab grey hair escaping from beneath her weather-rusty hat enhanced the impression of weariness, of Christian fortitude and resignation, created by her lined features and intent, near-sighted eyes. But her expression melted gradually under his frank and cheerful gaze. It was, she thanked God, a good face, not particularly handsome — again she voiced gratitude to the Deity for sparing him the perils of excessive comeliness — but open and straight-featured, a trifle finely drawn, no doubt from over study, cheekbones too prominent but with a healthy complexion, clear, very light grey eyes, and a broad forehead set off by close-cropped brown hair. He was well set up too, a good figure, blemished only by an accident at football which caused him to turn in his right foot slightly when he walked.

"I'm glad it's settled, Son. I knew you'd have good reason for not coming over. Both Ella and Mr. Fleming missed you."

She rolled her cotton gloves into a ball and, casting a practiced glance over the table, brought from her satchel some cold ham wrapped in greased paper and a bag of his favourite wheaten scones. They sat down, and when she had asked the blessing, began their simple meal. He saw that, despite her restraint, she was deeply pleased.

"It is a stroke of luck, Mother. Three guineas a week. And for the whole nine weeks of my holidays."

"It'll be a nice change after all your study for your final."

"Yes." He nodded. "Teaching summer school is just like a vacation."

"God is very good to you, Paul."

4

He subdued his smile and remarked:

"I'm to send off my birth certificate to Professor Slade tonight."

There was a pause. Head bent, she took her spoon and removed a tea-leaf floating in her cup. Her voice was a little indistinct.

"What do they want with a birth certificate?"

"Oh, a pure formality," he answered lightly. "They won't engage students under twenty-one. I'd some difficulty in persuading Slade that I came of age last month."

"You mean he wouldn't take your word?"

He looked across in sharp surprise.

"Mother! That was a little uncalled for. The man's only obeying the regulations. My application, accompanied by my birth certificate, has to go before the Board."

Mrs. Burgess did not answer. And, after a brief silence, Paul launched into a half-humourous description of his interview with the professor, who was also principal of the summer school at Portray. When he had finished his third cup of tea he rose from the table. Only then did his mother stir.

"Paul," she detained him, unexpectedly, "I'm . . . I'm not sure, after all . . . that I like this idea of you going to Portray."

"What!" he exclaimed. "Why, for weeks we've both been hoping I'd go."

"It means your being away from me." She hesitated and again looked down. "You'll miss our week's holiday with the Flemings. Ella will be disappointed. It'll be too much for you."

"Nonsense, Mother. You worry about nothing." Light-heartedly, he dismissed her misgivings, and before she could protest further, moved along the passage to fill out the application in his own room.

This was a small study-bedroom, at the front of the house, its bright wallpaper hung with passe-partout photographs of football and hockey groups. On the mantelpiece were a number of cups and other trophies which he had won from time to time at the university sports. Under the window stood a bookcase containing a selection of novels and more solid works, mostly classics, indicating an intelligent and well-balanced taste. In the alcove opposite, draped by a green baize curtain, was the narrow cot in which he slept, and upon an unvarnished table against the wall, his university lecture sheets were neatly laid out beside his study-programme. Everything bore silent witness to the quality of Paul's character, the soundness of his young body, the sensitive vigour of his mind. If one looked for a fault this might have been found in the excessive order of the room, suggesting a certain primness of disposition, an over-striving for perfection which could perhaps have derived from those corrective and "elevating" influences constantly exerted by his mother.

He sat down at the table, uncapped his fountain pen and, with his shoulders squared, elbows well tucked in, expertly completed the form. Reading it over to assure himself that it was correct, he nodded his head, and returned to the living room.

"Will you get it for me now, Mother? The certificate. I want to catch the nine o'clock post."

She raised her head. She had not begun to clear the table but was still seated where he had left her. Her face seemed flushed, her voice pitched in an unusual key.

"I scarcely know where it is. It's not a thing you can put your hands on at a moment's notice."

"Oh, come, Mother." His glance flew to the bow-fronted chest where she kept all her papers, a few family trinkets, her Testament, spectacles, and other private oddments. "It must be in your top drawer."

She gazed back at him, her mouth slightly open, half exposing her cheap, badly fitting dentures. The flush had faded, leaving her lustreless cheeks more than usually pale. Rising, she

6

took a key from her purse, and unlocked the top drawer of the chest. With her back to him, she searched methodically for five minutes, then she shut the drawer and turned around.

"No," she said, in an expressionless manner, "I can't find it. It isn't there."

He bit his lip in annoyance. He was a dutiful and affectionate son, bound by the strictness of his upbringing, yet at this moment he failed completely to understand her attitude. In a controlled tone he said:

"Really, Mother, it's an important document. And I need it."

"How was I to know you needed it?" Her voice trembled with sudden resentment. "These things get lost. You know the struggle I've had, left a widow all those years, bringing you up, with a hundred things to think of, and a bigger load on my shoulders than ever mortal woman had before, worrying half the time whether I could keep a roof over our heads, let alone educate you properly. I can tell you I've had enough to do without bothering about a few papers, especially since half the time I've had no proper place to keep them in."

This outburst, altogether foreign to her controlled nature, took him aback, left him even more perplexed at her lack of reason. But the severity of her expression — a warning signal to which he was well accustomed — forbade further argument. In a quiet tone, he said:

"Fortunately it's possible to get a duplicate. By writing to Somerset House in London. I'll do it tonight."

She made a gesture of negation. Her voice was calmer now.

"It's not your place to write, Paul." Reading his doubtful glance she added. "Don't let us make a fuss about nothing. I've not had too easy a day. I'll write for the certificate, on the City Hall notepaper, tomorrow."

"You won't forget?"

"Paul!"

"I'm sorry, Mother."

"All right, dear." Her smile, wavering slightly, lit her harassed features with a pale gleam. "Now, light the gas. I'll clear up, and we'll settle down for the night."

# Chapter 2

DURING the next two days Paul was fully engaged. Queen's University was breaking up for the long vacation and there were numerous obligations connected with the end of term. By general request he acted as pianist at the annual student sing-song. A mislaid library book proved difficult to trace. There was a last minute chemistry "practical," and he suffered the usual tension in awaiting the results. But when the lists were posted he had taken a satisfactory place. In general, as a good scholar, an agreeable companion, and an excellent athlete, Paul was well regarded by the members of his class. But his popularity was tempered by an undercurrent of opinion, prevalent mainly amongst the medical students — a reprehensible lot — which belittled his extreme propriety of conduct and found in his abstention from the less inhibited undergraduate diversions, an attitude that was regrettably straight-laced.

Once or twice, during his preoccupation, Paul's thoughts reverted to the recent scene with his mother and, watching her, he wondered if she were not showing signs of strain. She seemed on edge, paler than usual, given to moods of queer abstraction. Of course, despite a temperament naturally masterful, and doubly fortified by austere conviction, she had always been a highly strung woman — he recollected how, in their early days in Belfast, a sudden knock on the door would make her start

8

and change colour. But this was different: now a consuming anxiety seemed pressed upon her brow. On the evenings of both Thursday and Friday she went out after supper to spend an hour with their pastor and oldest friend, Emmanuel Fleming of Merrion Chapel, returning quieted but wan, with a lurking apprehension in her reddened eyes.

On Thursday morning he asked her directly if she had received an answer from Somerset House. She replied:

"No."

Several times thereafter, he was on the point of questioning her further but an odd compunction, springing from the subjugation she had wrought upon him, deterred him. There could be nothing wrong, nothing. Yet he was puzzled, and began to seek an explanation of her queer behaviour in his own past history. The facts, however, were all ordinary and open.

The first five years of his life he had spent in the North of England, in Tynecastle, his native town: a blurred background fixed by the sound of the rivet hammers, and the long early morning blast of the "hooter" summoning the men to the shipyards. Threading this dim impression was the glowing recollection of his father, a gay and incomparably friendly figure, who on Sundays took him by the hand to Jesmond Dene to sail little boats, made from folded blue cartridge paper, in the pond, who, when he was tired, seated him upon a park bench in the shade and, exercising a fascinating natural talent, made sketches of everything around, people, dogs, horses, trees, wonderful drawings, which charmed and tickled his childish fancy, and who, as if this were not enough, when the Sunday passed and weekdays came, brought him home in the evening coloured marzipan fruits, strawberries with green husks, yellow bananas, pink-cheeked peaches, delicious to admire and to eat, made by the national confectionery firm which employed him as a travelling representative.

After his fifth birthday they had moved to the great Midland city of Wortley: a greyer and less happy memory, mingled with smoke and rain and moving about, the glare of steel foundries and the moody faces of his parents, climaxed by the departure of his father on a business trip to South America. Ah, the pang of losing his dear debonair companion, the suspense of waiting for his return, then — as though fulfilling the premonition of that childish yearning — the unimaginable grief on hearing of his death in a railway disaster near Buenos Aires.

Thereafter, a melancholy wayfarer, not yet six years old, he had come to Belfast. Here, through the good offices of Emmanuel Fleming, his mother had found work in the accounts division of the City Health Department. The salary was small, but at least it was secure and had enabled the widow to keep a respectable roof above their heads and, by a miracle of economy and self-denial, to educate her son for the teaching profession. Now, after these fifteen years of her strenuous endeavour, he was within reach of graduating from the university.

Looking back, it seemed to Paul that the very intensity of his mother's effort had constricted their life in Belfast to the narrowest limits. Except for her frequent attendance at chapel she never went out. Paster Fleming and his daughter Ella apart, she had no intimates. She barely knew their next-door neighbours. At the university he had never been able fully to indulge his sociable nature, for always he had felt that his mother frowned upon his friendships. Often he chafed at this restriction, yet, deeply sensible of what he owed to her, chastened, too, by repeated exactions, he suffered it.

In the past he had credited his mother's protectiveness mainly to her extreme and watchful piety. But now, in the light of her present conduct, he wondered if there were not another cause. An incident came sharply to mind: a year ago, he had been honoured by an invitation to play in the international Rugby game between Ireland and England. Nothing surely could have been more gratifying to a mother's heart. Yet she had positively refused to allow him to accept. Why? Then, he could not guess. Now, dimly, he divined the reason. Indeed, considering the pattern of her existence, in its guarded quiet, its shrinking from all contacts, its secrecy, its passionate dependence upon the Almighty, he saw it, with a start of apprehension, as the life of one who has something to conceal.

On Saturday, which was her half holiday, she came in from her work at two o'clock. By this time he had made up his mind to have the matter out with her. The weather had turned to rain, and, after leaving her umbrella in the hall, she entered the living room where he sat turning the pages of a book. Her appearance really startled him: her face was quite grey. But she seemed composed.

"Have you had lunch, Son?"

"I had a sandwich at the Union. How about you?"

"Ella Fleming made me some hot cocoa."

He glanced at her quickly.

"You've been there again?"

She sat down wearily.

"Yes, Paul. I've been there again. Asking and praying for guidance."

There was a pause, then he straightened himself, tensely grasping the arms of his chair.

"Mother, we can't go on like this. There's something wrong. Tell me, did you get that certificate this morning?"

"No, Son. I didn't. I didn't even write for it."

The blood rushed to his face.

"Why not?"

"Because I had it all the time. I lied to you. It's here now, in my bag."

The heat went out of his anger. He gazed at her, startled,

11

as she fumbled in the satchel on her lap and brought out a folded blue-grey paper.

"All these years I've fought to keep it from you, Paul. At first, I thought I'd never do it, it was sore and difficult. Every step on the stairs, every voice in the street made me tremble for you. Then, as the years went on, and you grew up, I fancied with the help of God I had won through. But it was not His will. I had feared the big things, but it was a little thing that did it, just that trifle of your teaching in the summer school. But maybe it had to come sooner or later. So the pastor says. I begged him to help me to put you off some way. But he says No. He says you are a man now, that you must know the truth."

Her agitation had increased with every word and despite her resolution to be calm she ended with a kind of moan. Her hand quivered as she held out the paper to him. In a daze he took it, looked at it, and saw immediately that the name there was not his name. Instead of *Paul Burgess* he read, *Paul Mathry*.

"This isn't right . . ." He broke off, gazing from the paper to her, a chord, deep in his memory, faintly touched by the name "Mathry," vibrating almost painfully like a plucked harp-string in a long-deserted room. "What does it mean?"

"When we came here I took my maiden name of Burgess. I am Mrs. Mathry, your father was Rees Mathry, you are Paul Mathry. But I wanted to forget that name." Her lips twitched. "I wanted you to be out of sight and sound of it forever."

"Why?"

There was a pause. Her eyes fell. Almost inaudibly she answered:

"To save you . . . from a horrible shame."

Conscious of the rapid beating of his heart and of a hollow sickness in his stomach, he waited, motionless, until she should continue. But this seemed beyond her. She threw him a despairing glance.

12

"Don't force me to go on, Son. Mr. Fleming promised me he'd tell you everything. Go to him. He expects you now."

He saw that it was torture for her to proceed, but he too was suffering and he could not spare her.

"Go on," he said palely. "It's your duty to tell me."

She began to weep, in choking sobs which convulsed her narrow shoulders. Never before had he seen her in tears. After a moment she took a quick, painful breath, as though gathering all her strength. Without looking at him she gasped:

"Your father did not die on a trip to South America. He was trying to get there when the police arrested him."

Of all things that he had expected this was the last. His heart missed a beat, then bounded into his throat.

"For what?" he faltered.

"For murder."

There was a mortal stillness in the little room. Murder. The petrifying word echoed and re-echoed down the rolling convolutions of his brain. He felt limp. A cold perspiration broke all over his body. His question came in a trembling whisper.

"Then . . . he was hanged."

She shook her head, her pupils filmed with hatred.

"Better for us if he had been. He was sentenced to death . . . reprieved at the last minute . . . he is a life convict in Stoneheath Prison."

It was too much for her. Her head drooped sideways, she swayed and fell forward in her chair.

# Chapter 3

PASTOR Fleming's house stood in the busy heart of Belfast near the Northern Station — an ugly, narrow dwelling painted slate-grey, like the chapel, which it adjoined. Although he felt physically exhausted, fit only to hide in some dark corner, a gnawing urgency had driven Paul to trudge through the wet streets, flaring with lights and rowdy with Saturday-night revellers, to see the minister. His mother, recovered from her fainting attack, had retired to bed. He could not rest until he knew more; until he knew everything.

In answer to his knock the hall light was turned up and Ella Fleming admitted him.

"It's you, Paul. Come along in."

She showed him to the parlour, a low-ceilinged room, with dark red curtains and horsehair furnishings, warmed by a small coal fire.

"Father is busy with a parishioner. He won't be long." She forced a small, suitable smile. "It's turned damp outside. I'll make you some cocoa."

Ella's panacea for most ills was a cup of cocoa — a true parochial gesture — yet, though he had no wish for the innocuous beverage, he was too spent to refuse. Was it his imagination which saw in her too inconsequential manner, her slightly tightened lips, an awareness of his predicament? He sat down in a deadened fashion, while she brought a tray from the kitchen, stirred the sugar in with the cocoa and poured the hot water.

She was two years older than he, yet with her trim narrow-waisted figure and pale complexion, she had a somewhat girlish air. Her eyes, of a greyish green, were large and expressive — her best feature. Usually they were shining and soulful, but on occasion they could fill with tears, and spark with temper too. Always attentive to her appearance, she wore tonight a neat dark accordion-pleated skirt, black stockings, and a loose, white, freshly laundered blouse, cut round at the neck.

He accepted and drank the cocoa in silence. Once or twice she

14

lifted her eyes and looked at him questioningly over the knitting she had taken up. She was naturally talkative, with a flow of bright conversation, and keeping house for her widowed father had given her a certain social assurance. But when he failed to respond to a few desultory remarks, her well-marked brows drew together, she seemed to resign herself to silence.

Presently there came the sound of voices in the passage followed by the click of the front door. Ella rose at once.

"I'll tell Father you're here."

She went out of the room and a moment later the minister, Emmanuel Fleming, appeared. He was a man of about fifty, with thick shoulders and big clumsy hands. He wore dark trousers, heavy workman's boots and a black alpaca jacket turning whitish at the seams. His beard, clipped to a point, was iron grey, but his wide light blue eyes gave him the look of a child.

He immediately came forward, grasped Paul's hand with extra warmth, then with meaningful affection took him by the arm.

"You're here, my boy. I'm very glad. Come along and we'll have a little chat."

He led Paul to his study, a small austere room at the back of the house, uncarpeted, the bare boards stained, sparsely furnished with a yellow oak roll-top desk, some bent wood chairs, and a glazed bookcase. A presentation green marble clock, a hideous affair, supported by gilt angels, weighed down the flimsy mantelpiece, which was edged with a velvet ball fringe. Having seated his visitor, the pastor took his place slowly at the desk. He hesitated for some time, then began, in a tone of affection and sympathy.

"My dear boy, this has been a frightful shock to you. But the great thing to remember is that it is God's will. With His help you'll get over it."

Paul swallowed dryly.

"I can't get over it till I know something about it. I must know."

"It's a sad and sordid story, my boy." The minister answered gravely. "Had we not better leave it buried in the past?"

"No, I want to hear it. I must hear it or I'll never stop imagining . . . " His voice broke.

There was a silence. Pastor Fleming rested his elbow on the desk, shading his eyes with his big hand, as though engaged in inward prayer for help. He was an earnest and well-meaning man who had laboured long and unsparingly "in the vineyard of the Lord." But he was limited in many ways and often, with great despondency, saw his best efforts and intentions go astray. He was a lonely soul and knew many moods of self-reproach. Even his love for his daughter became an accusation to him — for he realized her imperfections, her pettiness, her vanities, yet was too fond of her to correct them. It was his tragedy that he longed to be a saint, a true disciple who would heal by his touch, make his flock radiant with the word of God, which he himself felt so deeply. He wanted to soar. But alas, his tongue was clumsy, his feet were bogged — he was earth-bound. Now, when he began to speak, his tone was troubled, his grave, pedantic phrases seemed measured by the sombre beat of the clock.

"Twenty-two years ago, in Tynecastle, I married Rees Mathry to Hannah Burgess. Hannah I had known for some years, she was one of the dearest of my flock. Rees I did not know, but he was a well-mannered, engaging young man, of Welsh extraction, and I liked and trusted him. He had an excellent position as the Northern counties' representative for a big wholesale firm of confectioners. I had every reason to believe them happy, especially when a son was born to them. It was I, dear boy, who christened you Paul Mathry."

He paused, as though weighing his words with the utmost care.

"I will not deny that there were occasional slight rifts in the harmony of the home. Your mother was strictly religious — a true

16

Christian — your father, to put it charitably, held more liberal views and this naturally produced a clash. Your mother, for instance, was firmly set against the use of wine and tobacco in the house — a prejudice your father could never fully understand. Again, your father's work took him away from home for at least one week every month, which had, perhaps, an unsettling influence upon him. Also he made friends, many friends I may say — for he was a handsome, likeable fellow — of whom one could not always approve and who consorted with him in pool rooms, saloon bars, and other unsavory haunts. Still, I had nothing serious against him until the terrible events of the year 1921."

He sighed and, removing his hand from his brow, pressed his thick fingertips together, his eyes pained and remote, as though they looked back sadly across the years.

"In January of '21 the firm which employed your father made some staff changes, in consequence of which your parents moved with you to the Midlands. For that matter, a few months previously, I myself had been transferred to this parish in Belfast, but I still kept closely in touch with your mother by correspondence. And I must confess that your life in Wortley was, from the first, unsettled. Your father seems to have resented his removal to a district which appeared to offer him less scope. Wortley, although surrounded by a pleasant countryside, is a grey unprepossessing city and your mother never liked it. They could not find a suitable house and occupied a succession of furnished rooms. Suddenly, in September, to be precise, on the ninth of that month, your father announced that he had reached the end of his patience. He proposed to throw up his job and emigrate straight away to the Argentine — there would be a better chance for all of you in the new world. He booked three passages on the liner *Eastern Star* due to sail on the fifteenth of September. On the thirteenth he sent you and your mother to Liverpool in advance, to await him at the Great Central Hotel. Late on the night of the

17

fourteenth he left Wortley by train to join you. But he did not join you. At two in the morning, when he reached the Central Station the police were on that platform. After a violent struggle, he was arrested and lodged in Canon Street Jail. Dear God, I can still remember the stunning shock of it — the charge was wilful murder."

There was a long, tense pause. Paul, hunched in his chair, like a hypnotised figure, scarcely breathed until the minister resumed.

"On the night of September eighth, a particularly horrible and sordid crime had been perpetrated. Mona Spurling, an attractive young woman of twenty-six, employed in a florist's shop in the vicinity of Leonard Square, was brutally done to death in the flat which she occupied at 52 Ushaw Terrace in Eldon, a near suburb of Wortley. The time of the crime was quite definite, for it occurred between eight o'clock and ten minutes past that hour. Returning from her work at seven-thirty, Miss Spurling had apparently partaken of a light meal, and had then changed into the flimsy negligee in which she was found. At eight o'clock a couple named Prusty in the flat below heard sounds of unusual violence coming through their ceiling, and urged by his wife, Albert Prusty went up to investigate. He knocked loudly on the door of the flat above but received no answer. He was standing on the landing in some perplexity when a young vanman named Edward Collins came up the stairway to deliver a package of laundry. Just as Collins joined him the door opened, a man came from the Spurling apartment, brushed past them, and dashed down the stairs. They hastened into the sitting room, where they found Miss Spurling, her head almost severed from her body, stretched on the hearthrug in a pool of her own blood.

"Immediately, Mr. Prusty ran for the nearest doctor in the neighbourhood. He came at once, quite uselessly, since Miss Spurling was already dead. The police were sent for, the local police surgeon, and a detective-inspector by the name of Swann.

At first it seemed that the murderer had left no traces, but within a few hours three clues came to light. Inspector Swann discovered in the bureau a pencil-sketched picture post card posted only a week before from Sheffield, which bore the following words: *Absence makes the heart grow fonder. Won't you meet me for supper at Drury's when I return?* It was signed *Bon-bon.*

"Also he found a note, charred, partly destroyed, and unsigned, but bearing the date stamp of September eighth, which said: *I must see you tonight.* Finally, lying on the hearthrug beside the body was a peculiar money bag, of the type known as a jug-purse, made from a soft and unusually fine leather, caught at the neck by a metal ring. It contained some ten pounds in silver and notes. Promptly, from particulars given by Edward Collins and Albert Prusty, a description was issued of the wanted man, offering a large reward for information leading to his apprehension.

"On the following day a local laundrywoman came to the police station with one of her ironers, a girl of seventeen, named Louisa Burt. It appeared that Louisa, a cousin of Edward Collins, the laundry vanman, had accompanied him to Ushaw Terrace on the night of the crime, and while waiting in the alley-way — she was averse to climbing the stairs — had been bumped into and almost knocked down by a man running out of No. 52. In her deposition she gave a description of this individual. The police had now three witnesses who had seen the murderer."

Pastor Fleming broke off and turned upon the young man his troubled, guileless gaze.

"It is not pleasant to touch on certain matters, Paul, but they are, alas, only too relevant to this tragic history. In a word, Mona Spurling was not a moral woman — she knew many men in a loose way and of these one in particular was her regular associate. No one knew who the man was, but the other assistants in the flower shop affirmed that Mona had recently seemed worried and low-spirited, that she had been overheard at the telephone in

conversations of an angry and recriminatory nature, using such
phrases as: 'You are responsible,' and 'If you leave me now I'll
give the whole show away.' Finally, the post-mortem examination of the body revealed the unhappy fact that the murdered
woman was pregnant. The motive was now established: clearly
the woman had been done to death by the man accountable for
her condition. Perhaps he was already tired of her. When threatened with exposure, he had written to make an assignation, and
had killed her.

"Armed with this evidence the police brought their full resources into action to find the wanted man. Reproductions of
the sketched picture post card signed 'Bon-bon' were prominently
displayed in all the newspapers, and anyone having knowledge
of the sender or the card was invited to communicate at once
with the Wortley police. All railway stations and ports of em-
barkation were closely watched and for almost a week the most
intensive search went on. Then, late on the evening of the thirteenth of September, a bookmaker's clerk named Harry Rocca
sought out the Chief Constable and, in a state of considerable
agitation, volunteered to make a statement. He confessed outright to an intimacy with the dead woman and, in fact, admitted
having been with her on the night before the murder. Then he
proceeded to lay information that he knew the sender of the post
card — a friend with whom he often played billiards who had a
marked talent for sketching. Some months before he had introduced this man to Mona Spurling. Moreover, when the reproductions of the post card appeared in the daily press his friend
had come to him with a worried air and asked him to back him
up, saying: 'If anyone asks where I was on the night of September eighth, make out I was playing pool with you at the Sherwood
Hotel.'

"That, of course, was enough. The Superintendent of Police,
accompanied by Inspector Swann, immediately proceeded to the

address which Rocca gave them. There they learned that the person they wanted boarded the Liverpool night express from the Leonard Street Station only an hour before. The arrest, at Liverpool, followed inevitably. The man, Paul, was your father."

Again there was silence. The minister moistened his lips at the carafe which stood on his desk. His brows drawn, he went on.

"It so happened that Albert Prusty, the main witness, was confined to bed by an acute attack of asthma — he was, by trade, a tobacconist who manufactured cigarettes and the nicotine dust periodically caused him this complaint — but the two other witnesses were immediately taken to Liverpool by the Superintendent and Inspector Swann. There, from a dozen assembled persons, they unhesitatingly picked out your father as the man they had seen on the night of the murder. There was, indeed, a terrible certainty in their recognition. Edward Collins exclaimed, 'So help me God, that is the man!' while the younger girl, Louisa Burt, carried to the verge of hysteria by the responsibility of her position, burst into tears. 'I know I am putting a rope round his neck,' she cried. 'But that's him.'

"Popular feeling ran high against the prisoner — to escape the fury of the mob he was taken from the southbound train at Barbridge Junction and conveyed in a closed vehicle to Wortley Jail. But God knows, dear Paul, I have wrung your heart enough. The trial began on the fifteenth of December at the Wortley Assizes before Lord Oman. With what anguish did we endure these fateful days! One after another, the prosecutor called the witnesses to give their damning evidence. Search of your father's trunks had resulted in the discovery of a razor which medical experts for the Crown proved to be the instrument of the crime. A handwriting expert testified that the charred, half-destroyed note of assignation found in the murdered woman's flat had been written, left-handed, by your father. He had many times been seen in the florist's shop, buying himself a boutonniere, laughing and chatting

21

with Miss Spurling. So it went on. The attempted flight to the Argentine, his vicious resistance of the police, all bore heavily against him. Most damning of all was his fatal attempt to establish a false alibi with Rocca. And when he took the stand, he was, alas, a poor witness on his own behalf, contradicting himself, losing his temper, yes, even shouting at the judge. He could not properly account for his movements at the hour of the crime, asserting that he had spent part of the evening in a cinema. But this pitiful excuse was riddled by the prosecuting counsel. Amidst the darkness only one faint gleam shone in his favour. Albert Prusty, while admitting that your father resembled the man who ran from the flat, would not swear that he was the actual person. However, it came out that Prusty's eyesight was bad, and in cross-examination it was plainly seen that he entertained a grievance at not being taken to Liverpool with Collins and Louisa Burt.

"The summing up of the judge went dead against the accused. The jury retired at three o'clock on the afternoon of December twenty-third. They were absent only forty minutes. Their verdict was 'Guilty.' I was there in the courtroom — your mother was too ill to attend — and I shall not to my dying day forget the frightful moment when Lord Oman, assuming the black cap, pronounced sentence and commended your father's soul to the mercy of God. Struggling and raving as the warders bore him away, your father shouted, 'There is no God. Damn your mercy and His. I want neither.'

"Ah! The Lord God is not lightly mocked, Paul. Yet perhaps it was to answer such a blasphemy that the Almighty did show mercy to the sinner. Although no one dared expect it, on the eve of the execution — mainly, I believe, because the Home Secretary of that time was a man of great humanity — your father's sentence was commuted to life imprisonment and he was removed to Stoneheath Prison."

With the falling cadence of the pastor's voice a final stillness fell upon the room. Both men kept their gaze averted one from the other. Paul, now so deeply sunk in his chair that he seemed crushed into it, wiped his forehead with the handkerchief crumpled in his damp hand.

"He is still alive?"

"Yes."

"No one has seen him . . . since he went in there?"

The minister sighed deeply.

"At first I tried to keep in touch with him through the prison chaplain but he met my advances with such resentment — I might even say ferocity — that I was forced to discontinue them. As for your mother . . . well, my dear Paul . . . she felt that she had been used most cruelly. Moreover, she had you to consider. In your interest she judged it better to obliterate this awful chapter from your young life. That she has not altogether succeeded makes no difference. You are fine enough to stand the shock of this revelation and that is why, rather than dupe you with half truths, I have made it to you in full. But now it is done, I want you to cleanse your mind of it. You are your own man, and your life lies ahead. You must go forward as though all that I have told you had never been, forward, forward, not only with faith but in forgetfulness."

# Chapter 4

A WEEK had passed since the interview in Fleming's study. It was Sunday afternoon and the Merrion Scripture class was over. The last of the children had gone, and Ella stood waiting for Paul at the door of the hall, wearing her best blue costume and the neat straw hat she had herself trimmed with navy ribbon. He got down stiffly from his desk and moved between the empty benches towards her. Although he took the class mainly to please his mother, usually he enjoyed the experience, the sharp-witted urchins from Merrion Street amused him, but today, his brain dazed, his head ringing from another sleepless night — heaven alone knew how he had gone through with it.

Ella addressed him tactfully.

"I'm sure you don't feel like music, Paul. But it's fair now, if you'd like us to take our walk."

In the ordinary way, before their regular Sunday stroll, he sat down at the little organ and, in his good-humoured style, played for her: he had more than average talent, and knowing her taste — which was not his own — would play Handel or Elgar, anything likely to meet her restricted choice. But today such a performance was beyond him. For that matter, he had little wish to go walking, but since he felt she had suggested it to distract his mind — he offered no objection.

She took his arm, with a faint possessive pressure, and he accompanied her along the street in the direction of Ormeau Park. They were early, yet a fair number of promenaders were abroad, the women exhibiting their finery, the men looking respectable and self-satisfied in their Sunday suits — a note of sabbatarian orthodoxy which for once jarred on Paul. As they passed through the gates of the park he muttered in a strained voice:

"I'm not in the mood for this parade."

She looked vexed at this, but kept silent. Although her nature had no profound capacity for emotion, her affections had long been centered upon him. Her acute sense of the conventions did not permit her to reveal this, and Paul himself, though he accepted her as an intimate friend, though his mother from time to time dropped fondly encouraging hints, had drifted into the relationship with careless good nature, not realizing the utter incompatibility between his free and generous character and the narrow

24

stereotyped piety which marked her every action. Nevertheless, Ella regarded the matter as settled — all her plans for the future were based upon the certainty of their marriage. She was highly ambitious both for herself and for him, recognizing that his cleverness matched well with her own talent for "managing." Already she saw her good influence advancing his career until he stood finally in a high academic position, moving with her in the most distinguished circles.

In these circumstances, the recent disclosure had been a severe injury to her pride. She saw also how great had been the shock for Paul. Yet if she was willing to get over it why should not he? The damage was not deadly, the whole thing lay buried in the past, with a little care no one need ever remotely suspect it. Such was her attitude. And now, finding him still pressed into the dust, a touch of grievance, even of annoyance, began to qualify her sympathy. Although she controlled it admirably she had a pretty temper — not violent, but vixenish — and at this present moment, as he spoke again, it was costing her a struggle to subdue it.

"It seems as if all these years I've been living under false pretenses." In a shamed manner he tried to give form to his tormenting thoughts. "I can't even call myself Burgess any more — my name is Mathry, Paul Mathry . . . if I don't use that name I'm a liar and a cheat. If I do use it, everywhere I go, I'll imagine I see people pointing me out, whispering about me . . . that's Mathry, son of the man who . . ."

"Don't, Paul," she interrupted. "You're making it too hard for yourself. No one need ever know."

"Even if they don't, I know." He strode on, his hurt gaze fixed on the gravel drive before him. "Yes, what about me . . . myself . . . what am I going to do about it?"

"You must forget about the whole thing."

"Forget?" he repeated incredulously.

"Yes." Her patience was wearing thin. "It's perfectly simple.

You must put all thought of . . . this man Mathry right out of your head."

He turned to her with haggard eyes.

"Disown my father?"

"Is he someone to be proud of?"

"Whatever he's done, he's paid for it, shut up for half a lifetime . . . poor devil."

"I was only thinking of you," she answered sharply. "And kindly do not swear in my presence."

"I didn't say anything."

"You did." She could contain herself no longer. The blood rushed into her face. She snapped at him. "You used a bad word that no lady would tolerate, I think you're behaving inexcusably."

"How do you expect me to behave?"

"With a little more civility. You don't seem to understand that this affects me just as much as it does you."

"Oh, Ella, for God's sake don't let us be childish at a time like this."

She drew up suddenly, overcome by her sense of injury, by the desire to exert her influence over him. Her face had taken on a greenish colour, her eyes were moist, with the whites upturned.

"I'm afraid . . . in your present mood . . . there's no point in our walking any further."

There was a pause. He gazed at her numbly. His thoughts were far away.

"Just as you please."

Disconcerted at being taken at her word, she bit her lip to keep back angry tears. Then, since he made no effort to detain her, she gave him a pale smile, full of reproach and outraged goodness — the martyred smile of an early-Christian virgin when they tore her bosom with hot pincers.

"Very well. I'll turn and go home. Goodbye, for the present. I hope you're in a better frame of mind when next we meet."

She swung round and moved off with her head in the air, a shamefully ill-used figure. For a few moments he gazed after her, regretting their unaccountable misunderstanding, yet relieved, deeply relieved, to be alone. When she was lost to view, he moved off slowly in the other direction.

He could not endure to return to Larne Road. There he would find his mother awaiting him with anxious, unbearable solicitude. He shrank from the hushed voice, the putting out of his slippers, the mute coaxing to a safe and peaceful evening in the home.

How strange was this new attitude to his mother! But stranger still, and more illogical, was the feeling, forming unconsciously within him, towards his father. Here, in truth, was the criminal, the cause of all his misery. Yet Paul could not hate him. Instead, during these last tortured, sleepless hours, his thoughts had flown towards him with a singular pity. Fifteen years in prison — was not that punishment enough for any man? Recollections of his early childhood, vague yet poignant, surged upon him. What tenderness he had received, always, from his father — not one harsh memory marred the picture. Tears suddenly blurred his vision.

He had now reached Donegal Quay, the poor dockside district of the city. Unknown to himself, the strange impulse growing within him had brought him here. Head down, he tramped on, across the railway tracks, threading his way through the confusion of bales, sacks, and carboys which littered the cobbled wharfs. An evening mist was stealing in from the sea, mingling with the brackish emanations from the harbour pool, turning the tall pier derricks to spectral shapes. The foghorn of the outer breakwater began to sound its deep melancholy note.

At last, brought up by a barrier of merchandise piled between the sheds, he sat down on a packing case. Immediately opposite, a small rusty freighter was making preparations for departure on the tide — he recognized her as the *Vale of Avoca*, a cross-channel

27

cargo boat plying between Belfast and Holyhead. Occasionally she carried a few steerage passengers and at the gangway a small group of men and women, potato pickers bound for the Lincolnshire farms, stood with their belongings, taking goodbye of their friends.

Seated there, in the mist, which swirled around him in wraith-like forms, with the foghorn sounding, sounding in his ears, Paul stared at the vessel with a growing intensity. With his holidays begun, his plans for the summer school broken off, time stretched before him mercilessly. A sudden excitement, strange and pre-destined, passed over him. Impulsively, he took out his notebook and scribbled two lines:

> *I am going away for a few days. Do not worry.*
> *Paul*

He tore out the page, folded it over, and wrote his mother's name and the address on the back. Summoning a boy from amongst the onlookers, he gave the note to him with a coin to ensure delivery. Then he stood up, advanced steadily to the shipping company's kiosk, and for a few shillings purchased a ticket for Holyhead. They were already casting off as he crossed the gangplank. A moment later a heavy rope splashed; then, with a throbbing of her old engines, the freighter lurched and shuddered to the outer seas.

# Chapter 5

IT was six o'clock next morning and raining heavily when the *Avoca* berthed at Holyhead. Stiff and chilled, Paul stepped ashore and crossed the tracks to the railway station. There was scarcely time for him to swallow a cup of tea in the refreshment room before the southbound train was signalled. He paid the half-awakened waitress and hurried to take a place in the corner of a third-class compartment. Then the engine shrieked and started off.

It was a lengthy journey, through Shrewsbury and Gloucester, with two changes at junction stations where, having no coat to protect him, he got thoroughly drenched. Yet with this physical discomfort, more and more his spirit hardened. As though in keeping with this darker mood, gradually the pastoral character of the country altered to a wilder, bleaker note. Stony moors and straggling heaths supplanted the square, hedged fields. Tall monoliths, grouped in circles, weird and prehistoric, struck upon his vision. To the west, from out the pine woods, a livid ridge of mountains rose, capped with grey clouds and veined by tumbling cataracts. The engine laboured as the wind came blasting from the sea, and at a curve of the line Paul saw cold waves beating against high cliffs.

At last, towards four o'clock in the afternoon, the train drew into a small moorland station — it was his destination. The single platform was almost deserted as, with the blood pounding in his ears, he surrendered his ticket to the solitary porter. He had meant to ask the man to direct him to the prison, but somehow the words thickened on his tongue; he passed through the white wicket in silence. However, once outside, he saw in the distance, across the red earth and rain-drenched heath, crouching behind its castellated walls, the great grey bulk of Stoneheath. He set off along the narrow road which wound across the moor.

The nearer he drew to that grim citadel, the faster his pulse raced. His mouth was dry, his chest constricted, he felt sick and empty: except for a cup of tea and a sandwich he had eaten nothing all day. At an incline on the path he leaned against the bole of a stunted birch tree to gain his breath. Now a patch of greenish opalescent sky had opened on the western horizon, and against this delicate screen he could, from the slight eminence, discern acutely the details of the prison.

There it rose, a great blank windowless square, pierced by a low portcullis, with watch towers hovering like eagles at each corner, sheer as a rock, stern as a medieval fort. Two rows of warders' houses stood outside, with sheds and other workshops, and all around was the desolation of the moor. An unscaleable wall, with spikes on the coping, enclosed the whole domain in which, like enormous wounds, three red stone quarries caught the eye. In one of these some gangs of prisoners were working, seen at that distance like grey ants, guarded by four warders in blue, each promenading slowly, yet menacingly, with a gun. Under Paul's rigid gaze the little drab figures bent and strained and toiled, and over the place was a silence like eternity.

A sudden step behind him, startling as the crack of doom, made him spin around. A shepherd had come up the hill, followed by a shaggy sheep-dog. The man had a close and secret aspect, as though tainted by this gloomy wilderness, and when he halted beside Paul and leaned upon his crook, a native suspicion was in his eye.

"Not a pretty view," he remarked at length.

"No." Paul spoke with an effort.

The other nodded in slow agreement.

"It's a plague spot if ever there was one. And I should know, I've lived here forty years." He paused. "They had a riot last month — five of the convicts and two of the warders got killed — and it looked just the same then as it does now. Quiet and blind. Ay, even as we're talking here, a guard in that tower has a pair of field glasses levelled on us, watching every move we make."

Paul suppressed a shiver, and forced himself to ask the question uppermost in his mind.

"When do they have visiting days?"

"Visiting days." The crofter looked at him with open derision. "There are no such days in Stoneheath."

Paul felt his heart contract. Quickly, he exclaimed:

"But surely . . . on certain days . . . the prisoners' relatives are allowed to see them?"

"They have no visitors," the other said briefly. "No, not ever." His weathered face, never given to merriment, twitched grimly. "It's as hard for us to get in there as it is for them to get out. And now good evening, young sir."

He whistled to his dog and, with a final nod, was gone.

Alone and re-enveloped by the stillness, Paul remained absolutely motionless, all his sanguine expectations dashed to the ground. No visitors . . . never! He could not see his father . . . could not even speak one word with him . . . what he had come to do was quite impossible. Indeed, at this moment, confronted by the chilling reality of the prison, he knew that the hope he had entertained and his impetuous, sentimental journey to this benighted spot were both unutterably futile.

The landscape darkened and, as he still lingered, a bell in the prison began slowly and heavily to toll, breaking the everlasting silence as though tolling for the dead. Then he saw the convicts cease their work and, marshalled by their keepers, move in slow line towards the prison. Presently the portcullis was raised to engulf them, then lowered. At that, the last of the green transparency departed from the sky.

Something broke within Paul's breast. Torn by grief, pain, and a terrible frustration, he gave a wild inarticulate cry. Scalding tears burst from his eyes and ran down his cheeks. He turned from the accursed heath and made his way back blindly to the railway station.

31

# Chapter 6

UPON the outskirts of the city of Wortley, at the corner of Ayres Street and Eldon Avenue, there stands a tobacconist's shop, bearing the faded sign: A. PRUSTY, IMPORTER OF BURMA CHEROOTS. This emporium, old-fashioned, yet with a solid and well-established air, has two windows, the one carrying a sober display of cigars, snuff, meerschaums, and the better grades of cut tobacco, the other an opaque blank — except for a small gilt-circled peephole shielding the bench at which the proprietor makes by hand the cigarettes, Robin Hood Straight Cut, for which he is locally renowned.

Towards noon, on this June day, Mr. Prusty was, in fact, seated at his bench, in apron and shirtsleeves, rolling out his special brand with a rapid and delicate touch. He was a skinny little man, past sixty, with a blunt porous nose and a choleric complexion. He was bald, except for a single tuft of white hair, and a large wen grew like a plum on his bare scalp. His straggling white moustache was fumed with nicotine and his fingers showed the same bright yellow stain. He wore steel-rimmed pince-nez.

Perched on his stool and peering through his peephole, Mr. Prusty had for some minutes been following with inquisitive suspicion the movements of a bareheaded young man who, pacing up and down outside, had several times approached the shop, as though about to enter, only to hesitate at the last moment and turn away. In the end, however, he seemed to muster all his will power. Pale but resolute, he crossed the street with a rush and came through the door. Mr. Prusty, who kept no assistant, slowly got off his stool.

"Yes?" he inquired brusquely.

"I'd like to see Mr. Albert Prusty. That's to say . . . if he's still alive."

The tobacconist gave his visitor an acidulous smile.

"So far as I know he's alive. I am Albert Prusty."

The young man, like a diver plunging into any icy sea, took a deep determined breath.

"I am Paul Mathry." It was over. Once he had articulated that name a flood of relief suffused him, his tongue seemed no longer paralysed. "Yes, Mathry. Spelled M-a-t-h-r-y. Not a common name. Does it convey anything to you?"

The cigarette maker's expression had not changed. He answered irritably:

"What would it convey to me? I remember the Mathry case if that's what you mean. I'm not likely to forget the most unpleasant time in my whole life. But what the devil has it to do with you?"

"I am Rees Mathry's son."

A bar of silence throbbed within the low-ceilinged shop. The old man looked Paul up and down, took a pinch of snuff from the canister on the counter before him, then slowly inhaled the pungent dust.

"Why do you come to me?"

"I can't explain . . . I had to come." In broken phrases Paul made an effort to define the circumstances which had occasioned his trip to Stoneheath. He concluded: "I got in here this morning . . . there's a train out at nine this evening that connects with the midnight Belfast boat. I felt if only I could learn of something . . . oh, I scarcely know what . . . perhaps some extenuating circumstance, I'd go home easier in my mind. I came to you . . . because you were the one favourable witness in all the case."

"What do you mean favourable?" Prusty objected in a provoked voice. "I don't know what you're driving at?"

"Then . . . there is nothing you can tell me?"

"What the devil could I tell you?"

"I . . . I don't know." Paul sighed. After a pause he squared his shoulders and turned towards the door. His voice was steady. "Well, I'll go now. I'm sorry I troubled you. Thank you for seeing me."

He was half way out when a testy command drew him up short. "Wait."

Paul came back slowly. Again Prusty stared him up and down, from his strained young face to the mud-spattered ends of his trousers, and again the tobacconist took snuff.

"You're in a devil of a hurry. You pop up from nowhere after God knows how long, and rush in and out as though you'd come for a box of matches. Damn it all! You can't expect me to go back fifteen years in fifteen minutes."

Before Paul could reply, the shop bell sounded and a customer entered. When he had been served with an ounce of navy cut and was on the point of departure, another of Prusty's clients appeared, a stout man who, having selected and lighted a cigar, seemed disposed to stay and gossip. The tobacconist came over to Paul and addressed him in an undertone.

"The lunch hour is my busy time. We can't talk now. Not that I've anything to say — far from it. But as I close at seven and your train doesn't leave till nine you can come up to my flat around half seven o'clock. I'll give you a cup of coffee before you go."

"Thank you!" Then a flicker passed over Paul's eyes, dilating his pupils. "At your flat?"

Prusty nodded with a queer grimace, a narrowing of his near-sighted eyes.

"The same address. 52 Ushaw Terrace. It's still there. And so am I."

He went back to his customer and Paul left the shop. As he walked down the street, drugged with weariness — he had spent the previous night on a hard chair in the station waiting room —

and weak for want of food, Paul recollected that he had passed a Y.M.C.A. on his way out from the centre of the city, and boarding a yellow tramcar, in five minutes he had reached the hostel. Here, after a hot bath, he brushed his clothes and tidied himself; then sat down to a good dinner of soup, a hot cut from the joint, and rice pudding.

It was now only two o'clock. As Paul quitted the dining hall, greatly restored, he pondered how he should use the time remaining before his appointment with Prusty. Suddenly an idea entered his mind. He made an inquiry at the desk, and after a ten minute walk along the congested pavements of Leonard Street, crossed to Kenton Place and passed through the portico of the City Public Library.

Under the high echoing dome, he sought out the newspaper reference section.

"Could you give me the name of the most reputable Wortley newspaper?"

The youngster behind the desk looked up pertly.

"Are any of them reputable?"

Then quickly, in the tone of one whose function it is to instruct strangers, he added: "Probably the *Courier* is the best. It's quite dependable."

"Thank you. Could I see the files for the year 1921?"

"For the entire year?"

"Well, no." Despite his show of confidence, Paul coloured. "The last four months of 1921 would be sufficient."

"Will you complete a form, please."

"Of course."

Paul picked up the chained pencil, filled in the slip and handed it over.

"You are not a resident of Wortley?"

"No."

The clerk hesitated, flicking the form with a fingernail.

"Strictly speaking, you are not entitled to the use of the reading room."

Paul's face fell. But immediately the other relented, advanced a brisk suggestion.

"You probably have relatives in the city?"

"No."

"Surely you can give some address?"

"Well," Paul paused, "I've just come from the Y.M.C.A. in Leonard Street."

"That'll do nicely." The young librarian smiled affably. "I'll put it down." He pressed the bell on his desk. A few minutes later an attendant brought out a heavy leather-bound folio and placed it upon an adjoining table.

With an agitated touch, Paul began to turn the dry, yellowish sheets, and the dark cords of his emotion drew taut again as he came, suddenly, upon the first mention of the crime: yes, there it was: DASTARDLY OUTRAGE AT ELDON. YOUNG WOMAN BRUTALLY MURDERED.

He controlled himself, and clenching his teeth, set himself to read. He read steadily, with bent head, while the hands on the dome clock moved forward, read from the beginning to the end. In essence it was the story he had heard, but told with a more dramatic force. When he came to the arrest, sweat broke out upon his brow. As, word by word, the drama of the trial unfolded itself, a groan broke from his lips. The speech of the prosecutor, Matthew Sprott, K.C., cut him like a whip.

" 'This atrocious murder,' " he read, " 'carried out by a cool and abandoned ruffian in circumstances of savage ferocity which beggar description, is barely paralleled in the annals of crime. The blackguard who committed a crime of this order has sunk to the lowest depths of human degradation. Hanging, gentlemen of the jury, is far too good for him!' "

Then, in a special supplement, at the end of the last sheet he found a page of photographs: reproductions of the victim — a pretty, simpering young woman, with a padded, fluffy chignon, wearing a beribboned blouse; of the witnesses; of the contemptible informer, Rocca, a weak-faced, weedy creature with sleek hair plastered in a middle parting; of the fatally incriminating post card with its fatuous phrase: "Absence makes the heart grow fonder"; of the weapon — a German razor manufactured by the firm of Frass. There were no omissions, even the ship was there, cleaving the waves, the S.S. *Eastern Star*, on which the criminal had meant to flee. And, in the centre of the page, standing in the dock to receive his sentence, between two officers of the law, the condemned man. Paul gazed at the photograph with stricken eyes: his father's face, bearing a hunted, a strangely sunken look, like an animal finally cornered for the kill, filled him with a culminating anguish.

Quickly, quickly, he closed the file of newspapers. He felt deprived of the last hope to which, fondly and perversely, he had clung. "Guilty! Guilty!" he muttered to himself. "Beyond the shadow of a doubt!"

He glanced at the clock and saw, with dull surprise, that it was nearly eight o'clock. He rose and carried the file back to the desk. The librarian who had issued it to him was still on duty there.

"Shall you want this again?" he inquired. "If so, we'll keep it out for you."

Through the trances of his senses, Paul noticed that the young fellow was looking at him with friendly interest. He was about nineteen, small and slim, with a wide humorous mouth, grey intelligent eyes, and a snub nose which gave to his face a lively, rather perky expression. Paul wondered a little shamefully if he had witnessed his display of feeling.

"No, I shan't want it again."

He stood for a moment, as though expectant of a reply, but although the clerk's eyes remained upon him, he did not speak. Paul turned and went out of the library into the noisy streets.

# Chapter 7

NOW that he knew everything, his first impulse was to abandon his appointment with Albert Prusty, to spare himself a senseless repetition of the pain he had recently endured. Yet in the end, with the strange fatalism which since the moment of revelation had guided all his actions, he bent his steps in the direction of Eldon.

He walked slowly: twilight was falling as he began to traverse the flagstones of Ushaw Terrace. It was a narrow thoroughfare with a tall row of stucco houses on either side, each with a porch and carriage step, bespeaking a bygone gentility. Though still respectable, conversion of the once stately dwellings into flats had robbed the neighbourhood of dignity, rendered it drab, even gloomy. Paul could not restrain a shudder as he approached the actual house where the murder was done, but setting his jaw, he passed through the entrance, mounted the damp-smelling stone staircase, and halting on the second landing, rang the bell.

After a short interval Mr. Prusty admitted him, through a dark hall, to the untidy front parlour, where, on a small gas ring a bubbling pot of coffee diffused a rich aroma.

The little tobacconist wore carpet slippers, an old velvet smoking jacket and, as though to point this eccentricity, a somewhat battered fez. But his manner was hospitable, and, bustling about, he poured the coffee, added brown sugar, then offered his guest a cup.

Paul sipped the thick black beverage, bitter-sweet and full of grounds. It was hot and refreshing. Meanwhile the tobacconist withdrew the straw from a long cheroot, sniffed it appreciatively, rolled it at his ear, and lit up.

"I do for myself here," he remarked, inhaling with a sigh of content. "The wife died six years ago. I hope you like the coffee . . . I import it."

Paul mumbled an answer. Overcome by the strangeness of his position, he glanced about the room, furnished in worn red plush, and, caught by the ornate brass chandelier, his eyes finally came to rest upon the ceiling above his head.

"Yes," said Prusty, interpreting his expression. "I was in this very seat when the banging came through, such a fearful banging it made me rush up. God! I'll never forget the sight of her . . . lying there, half-naked, a tasty dish . . . but with her throat slit from ear to ear!" He broke off. "Don't look so scared, man. There's no one there now . . . it's empty. I have a key . . . the landlord lets me keep it . . . if you'd like to see the room."

"No, no." Paul shook his head. Then, pressing his forehead, he apologized. "I've had about as much as I can stand. All this afternoon I went through the case in the *Courier*."

"Ah, yes," Prusty meditated. "It was well reported there. They were even fair to me. And I made a poor enough show. Sprott, the prosecutor, made a regular fool of me. All because I would not swear the man who came out of that flat . . ." he gave his cheroot an upward tilt, "was Rees Mathry."

"You did not recognize him . . . as my father."

"It was dark in the hallway. I didn't have my glasses. Oh, I daresay I was wrong. . . . Ed, the lad from the laundry, and all the others were so positive. But," he preened himself with a kind of crusty vanity, "I'm a stubborn man. I was not sure, and for all the badgering of that upstart Sprott I would not swear to it. Have you ever been in the witness box?"

"No."

39

"God, when they have you there, they tie you in knots. Half the time you don't know what you're saying. The other half they won't let you say what you want to say. Now there was one strange thing I never got the chance to mention. I used to discuss it with my wife and Dr. Tuke — he was the doctor I called to see the body. Oh, he never figured in the case, they had their own medical experts and what not, but he was interested and we often talked it over afterwards."

The tobacconist impregnated his lungs with smoke, and reflectively stirred his coffee.

"When I went in the sitting room and saw that murder had been done, instinctively I rushed to the window and threw it open. I wanted to catch another glimpse of the man that ran away. And, by God, I did. Down there in the street, by the light that came from the window, I saw him pick up a bicycle that stood against the railings, jump on it, and pedal off like mad. Now the colour of that bicycle was green . . . I'll swear to it . . . a green bicycle. Strange, eh?" Prusty, who seemed to enjoy dramatizing himself, paused significantly. "Especially when you consider that all his life Mathry never had possessed even an ordinary bicycle." He waved a deprecating hand. "Of course they made out that he had simply lifted the machine to make a quick getaway. But if so, who owned that green bicycle, and where the devil did it vanish to — they dredged the canal for miles around, but never found it?"

There was a heavy pause.

"Another thing," Prusty went on, deliberately, "that peculiar leather purse found beside the body. It was not the murdered woman's. It was not Mathry's. Then whose was it? That was a point. . . . It was a point that bothered a brainier man than me. The fellow who had charge of the case from first to last. Swann."

"Swann," echoed Paul blankly.

Prusty nodded with a sudden seriousness.

"Detective Inspector James Swann." Instinctively the tobacco-

40

nist glanced about him, as though fearful of being overheard. He drew his chair closer to Paul. "I'm no humanitarian, I don't like to stick my neck out for anyone. But being who you are — I do think you ought to know about Swann."

The change in the other's manner struck through Paul's apathy. He sat up as Prusty resumed in a low and guarded tone.

"Swann was a nice chap, and smart too. But it wasn't only that — When he was on his beat, for instance, and any of the young lads got up to mischief, he wouldn't run them in, he'd just talk to them like a Dutch uncle — you see what I mean, he was regular decent. Unfortunately he had one weakness, and a bad one . . . the drink." Prusty stared at the glowing end of his cheroot and shook his head. "By God, it was strange, very strange."

Paul felt the back of his scalp contract. He was now listening intently.

"I knew him well, for he used to come to the shop twice a week for his half ounce of shag. And of course I saw a lot of him during the case. When it was all over and things had settled back to normal I began to notice a change in him. For one thing he was hitting the bottle harder. He'd never been talkative, but now it was difficult to get a word out of him. He wasn't so cheery, either, he seemed to have something on his mind. I often chaffed him about this, asked him if he was in love, and so on, but he always passed it off. Then one day, it would be about a twelve-month later, he came in looking extra grim . . . he was maybe just a little tight. 'I'm going to take a big step, Albert,' he says to me. 'I'm going to see Walter Gillett.' "

Prusty paused to sip his coffee.

"Now Walter Gillett was a lawyer with a first-class reputation, who did a lot of work about the police courts, and naturally I asked Swann why he was going to see him. But Jimmy shook his head. 'I can't say anything just now,' he answered in an odd way. 'But maybe you'll hear all about it soon.' "

**41**

Again the tobacconist lifted his cup and sipped. Paul could barely contain himself.

"Well," Prusty continued, sombrely, "I did hear something soon. The very next day, Swann turned up for point-duty at Leonard Square, stupid drunk. He fouled up the traffic, gave the wrong signals and caused a serious accident — a woman was run over and nearly got killed. Naturally there was a tremendous outcry. Swann was tried, dismissed from the force, and, as he no doubt deserved, sentenced to six months hard labour."

"Prison!" Paul exclaimed. "Then . . . what became of him?"

"He was finished," said Prusty. "When Swann came out he tried a number of jobs — private inquiry agent, hotel porter, cinema commissionaire — but he never stuck at anything for long. He was a changed man, to be honest, what with drink and one thing and another, he went to pieces. I can't say how he is now for I've lost track of him these last couple of years."

"But why?" Paul gasped. "Why did all this happen? Had he gone to see Gillett?

"Ah!" Prusty answered meaningly. "Ask me another?"

He drained the last of his coffee, and spoke in a still lower voice.

"I seldom saw Swann after he came out. But one night he dropped into my shop. He'd been drinking heavy for days — and he was pretty far gone. He stood there, swinging and swaying, never opening his mouth. Then he said to me, 'Do you know what?' 'No, Jimmy,' I said, humouring him. 'Well,' he says, 'it's this. Don't ever try to tell tales out of school.' And he began to laugh, to laugh and laugh, he staggered out of my shop laughing, and by God it wasn't a laugh you'd want to hear."

"What else did he say?" Paul cried out.

"Nothing . . . then or later . . . not another word. But, so help me God, right or wrong, I had the feeling in my bones that he'd come to this pass through the Mathry case."

There was a long stillness. Paul, conscious of a tight feeling in his breast, remained rigid in his chair. Then, gradually, as he sat there, his head went back, his gaze became fixed upon the ceiling above. Nothing was clear to him, the clouds of obscurity pressed upon him more densely than before, yet through the muddled darkness he felt again that strange incitement, urging him forward.

"It's getting late." Prusty had thrown his cheroot end in the fire. He was gazing at the clock. "I don't want to hurry you, but if you're not careful you'll miss your train."

Paul stood up to go. In a steady voice, he answered:

"I can't take the train tonight. I must find out . . . what Swann and Gillett have to say."

# Chapter 8

THE next morning came fresh and fine. Paul awoke early at the Y.M.C.A. where, on the previous afternoon, after leaving Mr. Prusty's shop, he had secured a room. When he had breakfasted he wrote and posted a brief letter to his mother which he hoped would relieve her mind; then with a sense of purpose, he set out for the centre of the city. The tobacconist, who nowadays rarely left his suburb, was ignorant of the present whereabouts of Swann and Gillett, but by rummaging through his papers had at least been able to furnish the number of the lawyer's office in Temple Lane, together with an address near the Corn Market where, to the best of his knowledge, Swann had resided some two years ago.

Paul reached 15 Temple Lane at half-past nine and was fortunate enough to find a man in a green baize apron, who had apparently just opened up the premises, polishing the brass plate on the outer door.

"Is this Mr. Walter Gillett's office?"

The janitor interrupted his polishing. He was a horsey-looking customer, bandy-legged and with a small bloodshot eye. He answered civilly enough.

"It was."

"He's left this address?"

"Correct."

There was a pause.

"You wouldn't know where he is now?"

The janitor summed up Paul with a sidelong glance.

"I wouldn't say I don't."

"Where can I see him?"

"Well," said the man, with another sidelong glance. "I doubt if you could see him. Still, there would be no harm in trying." He rubbed his nose reflectively. "Would it be worth as much as a bob to you?"

From his depleted supply of cash Paul paid over a shilling.

The janitor spun the coin expertly, and wiped his mouth with the back of his hand.

"He's in Orme Square. Quite near here, in the old town, by the City Church. Go down to the end of Temple Lane, turn right and keep straight on. Look around and you'll see his name up. You can't miss it."

Paul had not anticipated so easy or so early a success. He felt the man staring at him as he hastened away, down the long lane of bow-fronted offices.

He found Orme Square without difficulty. It was, as the janitor had said, quite near the City Church. It was, in fact, the City Churchyard, a pleasant old burying ground entered through an ancient black and white half-timbered gatehouse, shaded by tall elms. At first Paul did not fully grasp the significance of the directions that had been given him. Then it dawned on him — Gillett was in the churchyard, dead. He flushed, suffused for a moment

44

by an angry impulse to return and exact satisfaction from the man in the baize apron. But instead he went into the churchyard, and after about half an hour he came upon the object of his search — a white marble tombstone tucked away in the corner of the burying ground. He scanned the brief epitaph:

*Sacred to the memory of Walter Gillett.*
*Born 1881 — died 1930.*
*Deeply regretted and highly esteemed.*
*A credit to his community.*
*Every man's work shall be made manifest.*

Three times, in a mechanical fashion, Paul repeated that final phrase under his breath, realizing that with Gillett gone, now more than ever must he try to find James Swann. He spun round resolutely and walked rapidly away.

Presently he was knocking at the door of a basement house which stood in a row behind the Corn Market. A respectable middle-aged woman in a blue check wrapper came out into the area beneath him.

"I am looking for Mr. Swann . . . Mr. James Swann." Paul made an effort to keep his tone matter of fact. "I understand he lived here some time ago."

"Yes," the woman admitted. "He had a room here for many a month. But he's gone these two years back."

"Where did he go?"

The woman considered. "I had nothing against the poor man . . . he paid his rent when he could. You wouldn't be seeking him for anything wrong?"

"Oh, no," Paul said quickly. "Quite the contrary."

"Well, then . . . he went to a lodging-house in Ware Street. I don't know the number, but it's kept by a man called Hart."

Ware Street was not more than half a mile away, a long poor thoroughfare traversing a congested area of the city, lined with

cheap shops and hucksters' barrows, choked with traffic, reverber-
ating with the noise of passing trams. By consulting the city directory in a branch post office, Paul succeeded in locating the Hart
lodging-house.

This was a brick tenement situated in a squalid court, hemmed
in by tall, smoke-grimed buildings and approached by a narrow
entrance. The bell-pull had been torn from its socket, leaving
a ragged hole, and there was no knocker on the dilapidated
door. Paul rapped repeatedly with his knuckles on the blis-
tered panels. Presently, there appeared a boy of twelve with a
dirty face and swollen neck glands wrapped up in a strip of red
flannel.

"There's no one home," he announced in a husky voice, before
Paul could speak. He explained that he was sick, had been kept
home from school and, when questioned, declared that all the
men who lodged in the house were at work, mostly at the foundry.
He knew of no one by the name of Swann. His mother, who
looked after the place, would be back at four o'clock.

Having told the boy that he would return, Paul retreated
through the alley and regained the garish expanse of Ware Street.
He could not remain idle, his nerves were taut for action. An impulse, which had been gathering within him since the previous
night, drove him once again to the public library.

It was now afternoon and the same clerk was on duty. As Paul
came through the swing doors he was idling, rather dreamily, at
the desk, but when he raised his head and perceived Paul he
straightened, and watched him with gathering attention as he
traversed the length of the reading room. He accepted in silence
the slip that was handed to him.

"That *is* my address now," Paul felt compelled to explain. "I'm
staying for a few days."

The clerk nodded and pressed the bell for the attendant. When
the man had gone he opened a drawer beneath his desk.

"On your last visit you left some notes in the file. Here they are."

Paul stared at the sheet of paper — he had begun to make a précis of the case but had soon abandoned it. His instinct told him that despite the other's detachment he had undoubtedly read these notes, had taken pains to examine the newspaper file, and perhaps even guessed his identity.

"I don't really want the sheet," he said, then added, "but thank you for saving it."

The young man gazed at him in a peculiar manner with those bright, bird-like, interested eyes.

"Those things should be torn up."

Paul watched him destroy the sheet. At this point the attendant reappeared burdened with two heavy folios — bound copies of the *Courier* for the year 1922. Paul followed him to a nearby table, sat down, and opened up the first volume.

Diligently, running his finger down each column, he scrutinized every page. It was tedious work and made his eyeballs ache. But he persisted, passing to the second folio when he had gone through the first. When he had completed his examination he sat back in his chair, frowning, rubbing his forehead with his hand. The clock beneath the dome showed that it was past four o'clock. Mindful of his appointment, he rose to return the files.

"Did you find what you wanted?" The clerk made the inquiry sound like part of the regular routine. Yet, somehow, Paul sensed a lively curiosity in that simple question.

"No, I didn't."

There was a pause. He knew the other would not speak again. He had only to walk away to terminate the encounter. However, in some strange way, he felt that the young librarian by the mere act of withholding speech, and by a slyly calculated invitation in his eye, had given him, almost impudently, yet with the best in-

47

tentions, an opening, and all at once he was swept by a desire to confide in him.

"I was looking for the report of a case where a police inspector named Swann was tried and convicted in the year 1922."

The clerk was surprised, but he concealed it.

"That shouldn't be difficult. If I come across it in one of the other files I'll put it aside for you." He paused. "Are you . . . interested in the gentleman?"

"I'm trying to locate him."

"Any idea of where to look?" The question came smartly.

"He's probably still in the neighbourhood. By all accounts he's down and out."

"I see."

There was a silence. Paul stood a moment, then, confused now by his lack of reticence, he thanked the other in a few awkward words, put on his hat, and went out of the library.

He kept on walking in the direction of Ware Street, and at five o'clock reached the Hart lodging-house, to find that the landlady had returned. She was a stout woman in a merino skirt, with a check shawl across her shoulders, and upon her head, skewered by two black imitation jet hatpins, a man's cloth cap.

"Yes," she admitted, "I remember Swann, well enough. Down on his luck, he was. Got sick and couldn't hold his job at the works. Too much lifting of the elbow, if you follow me. I wasn't sorry when he left."

"When did he leave?"

"Ah, about six months ago."

"You don't know where he went?"

"Now you're asking me. To Bromlea I think it was, to work on the new building scheme."

"That's quite near, isn't it?"

"Near enough . . . about three miles out."

"Did he leave you his address?"

"Swann wasn't the man to leave no address. You'd never get a word out of him nohow. But wait a minute, let me think. He did say he was expecting a letter and for me to send it on if it came, which it never did. The question is, did I write it down." She turned to the boy who stood listening in the back hall. "Fetch me the book from the room, Josey."

A moment later the boy brought her a battered dog-eared ledger. Moistening her forefinger, she began to flick over the pages.

"Ah, what's this, now? Didn't I tell you."

Drawing near, with a sudden surge of hope, Paul peered at the place she indicated. There, scrawled in pencil on the dirty page, was the address he sought:

> *James Swann,*
> *c/o Roberts,*
> *15 Castle Road,*
> *Bromlea.*

Quickly, he copied it in his notebook, thanked the woman and made his escape. As he hastened down the narrow alley, now lit by a single feeble lamp, he felt that the day had been far from wasted. He was really on the track of Swann, had even glimpsed a picture of the man — wretched, down at heel, sinking lower and lower, drowning his sorrows, labouring with his bare hands for the necessities of existence. It was too late to go to Bromlea tonight. But he would go tomorrow. Yes, tomorrow he would find Swann.

# Chapter 9

ON the following evening, precisely twenty-four hours later, Paul was again on his way back to the Y.M.C.A. A steady rain had been falling since early afternoon, but he walked on, unconscious of his sodden shoes and saturated clothing. All his high hopes were gone, all his great expectations dashed and shattered. He had been to Bromlea, had visited the address given him by the lodging-house keeper, talked with the building contractor for whom Swann had worked, combed the district from end to end, and all without the least avail. Swann was gone, vanished without trace.

Despondently, Paul entered the hotel and slowly climbed the stairs to his room. Dropping a coin in the meter slot, he lit the gas fire in the little cubicle. Then, as he straightened himself, he noticed a telegram on the mantel. He tore it open and read:

DREADFULLY ANXIOUS RETURN AT ONCE SUMMER
SCHOOL APPOINTMENT AWAITING YOU LOVE FROM ALL.
                                    MOTHER

Crouching before the tiny fire, while the steam arose from his damp suit, he re-read the message. Yes, it was natural that she should beg him to return and indeed, in his present mood, he wondered if this were not the only course for him to pursue. Absence had softened his feeling towards his mother. Apparently she had spoken to Professor Slade, more probably she had asked Pastor Fleming to do so — and the position at Portray was still open to him. The phrase "love from all" made him smile a trifle bitterly, so patently did it include the affection of a forgiving Ella.

When he had dried out he turned off the gas and went downstairs to get a meal. Then, in the lobby, as he was about to enter the dining hall, he saw the door-boy coming towards him.

"There's a young fellow to see you. He's in the visitors' room."

Surprised, Paul followed the boy to the musty little lounge, furnished with stiff cane chairs and a potted palm, modestly screened by a bead curtain, and set apart for the reception of guests. As he pushed through the clicking beads he perceived with a start, seated on one of the cane chairs, the clerk from the library.

Paul advanced hesitantly.

"Good evening."

"You didn't expect to see me."

"No, I didn't."

The young librarian accepted this directness with a quick, lively smile. Detached from his official position he was perkier than ever, with a naïve and ingratiating frankness that was disarming yet, to Paul, in his present mood, almost an embarrassment.

"I've something to say to you." His glance briskly swept the empty room. "I suppose we can talk here without being overheard."

Paul stared so hard the other gave a short chuckle.

"I realise you don't quite get me yet, but I'm quite a decent sort. My name's Boulia . . . Mark Boulia."

He held out his hand, Paul gripped it, then sat down. The situation was beginning to give him a sensation of queer expectation. Mark studied him quizzically before he resumed.

"That first day at the library I watched you — I couldn't help it, you were so obviously . . . in difficulties. I felt sorry for you, and friendly too. You know how it is, how you take to a person at first sight. Afterwards I went through the file." He made, not without self-satisfaction, the statement of fact. "I know who you are and all about you."

51

All this Paul had surmised. He kept silent, listening intently as the other went on.

"Yesterday you were looking for some further references. You didn't trace them. But when you had gone, I did. In one paper, only one, the *Clarion,* a liberal paper with practically no circulation, I found a comment on the Swann trial. Oddly enough it was a protest against the extreme harshness of Swann's sentence."

Paul's face was pale, unreadable, yet with a dark fire burning in his eyes. At last he said:

"Why are you telling me this?"

Mark shrugged, drew down his lips in a half-humorous smile. "Because you wanted to find Swann."

Paul shook his head slowly. "It's no good."

"Why not?"

"Not after fifteen years."

"Don't be too sure." Mark's eyes sparkled, his air turned slightly jaunty. He waited just long enough to make his words important. "As a matter of fact, I have found him."

Paul felt his mouth turn dry. He stared unbelievingly at this odd individual who nodded with alert composure.

"It wasn't too difficult . . . after what you told me. I took a flyer and checked the relief lists, also the registers of the work house, and of all the city hospitals. Swann is in Belvedere Infirmary."

# Chapter 10

THE ward where Swann lay was long and narrow, with white-washed walls and a sloping ceiling containing a row of fanlight windows. This was the pauper ward of the infirmary, a bare and dismal dormitory. The bed, completely screened off, was raised upon wooden blocks, and on the floor there lay an oxygen cylinder equipped with a long inhaler. The indefinable smell of sickness, of organic dissolution, had even imposed itself over the pungent odour of carbolic.

Propped on two pillows, Swann lay with his limbs extended, his eyes upturned to the ceiling. His frame showed that he had been a big man, but now he was much emaciated and his sunken face — the drawn cheeks exaggerating the length of the nose — showed yellow against the white coverslip, with a curious bronze mottling of the skin. His fingers, limp on the counterpane, had thickened ends. His shallow, listless breathing barely disturbed the contour of his ribs.

It was the afternoon visiting hour and, beside the bed, Paul stood with Mark Boulia. They had arrived ten minutes ago and Mark, not without tact, had made Paul known to the sick man. Paul had then made an impassioned plea. And now, overcome by the significance of the moment, he waited tensely for Swann to speak.

Swann did not hurry, he had his own thoughts. But presently, without moving, he let his eyes fall on Paul and after a pause, remarked in a faint, hoarse tone:

"You're like him."

He then returned his gaze to the fanlight and was silent for a long time before resuming in that same spent voice.

"It's queer I should see you now. After what happened to me I swore I'd keep my mouth shut — I was a fool ever to open it. But you're Mathry's son. And I'm done for anyway. So here goes."

A short pause — Swann seemed to be looking deep into the past.

"When I was assigned to the Eldon murder case I was keen as mustard — a bit different to what I am now — and I remember like it was yesterday when the big clue came in. A bookie's tout named Rocca turned up at headquarters. . . . Yes, flash Harry Rocca . . . a weak-kneed rotter if ever I saw one, and in such a state of panic he could scarcely talk. But he did talk, and what he said was this — he'd been friendly with the murdered woman over a period of twelve months, had gone home to sleep with her often, and had spent the night with her on September seventh. But he'd had nothing to do with the murder, he couldn't have, because on September eighth and ninth he'd been in Doncaster, at the races, and had a dozen witnesses to prove it. He'd come forward voluntarily to clear his name.

"Well, this didn't help us much, we knew that Spurling had a pretty wide circle of admirers, but we thought we'd detain Rocca anyhow. When he heard that he was to be held he turned green and really spilled the beans. He told us about his pal, Rees Mathry, who had been sweet on Spurling. He told us how worried Mathry had been about the publicity we had given the hand-sketched post card. Above all, he told us about Mathry's attempt to fake an alibi. Now this news was wonderful for us — after being stuck for nearly three weeks we had a red-hot trail to follow. And the things got hotter when we found that the man we were after had just left for the port of Liverpool. We telephoned Liverpool at once and Rees Mathry was picked up."

Swann paused, moistened his lips.

"Unfortunately for him, Mathry was a quick-tempered man, he resisted his arrest, made the fatal mistake of striking an officer. Add on the fact, as I've just said, that he was taken in the very act of leaving for South America, and you had a very damning situation. And straight away he made it worse. Naturally, at his preliminary examination the first question asked of him was: 'Where were you between eight and nine on the evening of September eighth?' Not knowing that his friend had given him away, Mathy answered: 'Playing billiards with a man named Rocca.' That seemed to put the clincher on it."

Swann let his head fall back, and a queer look came into his lack-lustre eyes.

"I must tell you about my boss, the Superintendent — now he's the head of the Wortley police, Chief Constable Adam Dale. The son of a Cumberland farmer, he'd worked his way up from the bottom, was strict on discipline, loyal to his men, a first-rate officer, and he never took a bribe in his life. He loved his work and used to boast to me that he could spot a criminal a mile away. And from the beginning, he'd spotted Mathry."

Fired by his own words, the sick man strove to raise himself upon his elbow.

"Now for me it wasn't so easy. Although the evidence seemed so conclusive, I pointed out that Mathry had booked the tickets to South America in his own name, that he had likewise engaged rooms at the Liverpool hotel for himself and his family quite openly, without concealing his identity — a thing inconceivable in the case of a man who was afraid of pursuit and who wished to cover up his traces. Besides, in spite of the chain of damaging evidence, Mathry impressed me favourably. He made no attempt to deny that he knew Spurling, acknowledged he had sketched and sent her the post card. And he maintained he was only out for a bit of mild amusement. Now that flirtatious, slightly silly message on the card, 'Absence makes the heart grow fonder' bore this out exactly. Again, the injuries to Spurling were so terrible they could only have been inflicted by a powerful individual, and Rees was slightly built. His character was lightweight too, and this struck me as a conceivable explanation of his attempt to arrange the alibi with Rocca. Nervous and worried, more and more alarmed by the publicity given his stupid post card, he might have felt the need of somebody to back him up. A foolish step — but one that fitted the pattern of his story.

"I put all this up to the Chief but he would not listen, he was convinced — and quite honestly, mind you — that he had the right man."

Swann sank down on his pillows and rested for a moment before resuming, more quietly:

"The official mind works in regular channels — nobody knows that better than me — and the routine set in motion by Chief Constable Dale followed the standard and, of course, perfectly proper practice. He wanted to find a weapon among Mathry's belongings accountable for the victim's injuries. He wanted to discover blood stains upon Mathry's suit. He wanted witnesses who could identify Mathry as the man seen at the scene of the crime.

"Almost at once, in one of Mathry's trunks, the Chief Constable found his weapon. This was a razor, a large old-fashioned German blade, slightly rusty from disuse. Mathry freely admitted it had been in his possession for years — he had inherited it from his father. He had often been tempted to scrap it, but for sentimental reasons he hadn't. Now, if Mathry had used this blade to do the deed was it likely that he would have carefully and considerately preserved it for us to find? No, no, without exception the first action of a murderer is to rid himself of the weapon. Yet Dale was near jumping with pride and satisfaction when he showed the razor to me.

"'Didn't I tell you,' he declared. 'We have him now.'

"It was sent to the experts to be examined for blood stains, along with a large package of Mathry's clothing. Meanwhile, the examination of the witnesses was proceeding, who on the night of the crime had seen the murderer coming from the flat . . . Mr. Prusty, Edward Collins, and Louisa Burt. Prusty was a short-sighted man, Collins a soft youth who seemed reluctant to testify. However, the witness Burt was quite a different character. Now this young girl, on a dark and rainy September night, in a street with hardly any lights, got one second's glimpse of the criminal.

Yet she professed herself able to supply the most exact details of his appearance. I can still see her round, earnest face, as she came gushing out with her statement.

"'A man about thirty-five,' said she. 'Tall, thin and dark, with pale features, straight nose, clean shaven. He wore a check cap, a drab-coloured raincoat, and brown boots.'

"At first, Dale was pleased with this description. However, after the arrest of Mathry, the band played a different tune — for Mathry was neither tall, dark, nor clean shaven, but of medium size, fair-complexioned, and he had a brown moustache. Also, his clothing was quite different. However, Burt was equal to the occasion. She protested she had been confused, had spoken in a hurry when she made her first statement. Quite calmly she shelved the big, clean-shaven character in favour of a shorter man with a moustache. And Collins, who, immediately after the event, had flatly told me he would not be able positively to identify the man now came into line with Burt. The light check cap became a soft dark hat, the raincoat a grey ulster. In short, the description was adjusted to one which, though it was vague, might well have fitted Mathry."

Swann rested again, his pale lips drawn back, as he fought to get his breath.

"The next step was to take these important deponents to view the prisoner. The Chief himself accompanied them, and I was in the party also. Eleven policemen in plain clothes were lined up in a room with Mathry. It's the standard identification parade and some think it's a fair test. At any rate, the two witnesses were positive in their identification. Mathry was removed to Wortley, formally charged with the murder of Mona Spurling."

The sick man turned weakly on his side and gazed directly at Paul.

"Yet I still couldn't think that his number was up . . . the case against him was too perfect and I felt that somewhere it must crack. But I hadn't bargained on the advocate who was counsel for the prosecution. You might think that the Chief Constable — honest, dogged Dale — was mainly responsible for what happened to Mathry, but no, no, when it came to the bit, it was this Sprott, this brainy man who really did the trick. He's now Sir Matthew, he's risen near the top of the tree, and he'll likely go further, but then he was unknown, and desperately anxious to succeed. The minute I heard him I saw that he meant to hang Mathry.

"Well, it began. The prosecution called all its experts. They didn't call Dr. Tuke, the doctor who had first seen the body. They had, besides the police surgeon, Dobson, a professor named Jenkins, who testified that the Frass razor could have caused the injuries which had proved fatal to the victim. He was not prepared to swear that there were blood stains upon the weapon or on the prisoner's coat, but he had found traces of bodies which might have been mammalian corpuscles. Next came the handwriting expert who swore that the charred note found in the victim's flat was written by Mathry 'in a disguised left hand.' When Collins and Burt went into the box they surpassed themselves — Burt, especially, with her young innocent face and big earnest eyes made a tremendous impression on the jury. She stood there like an angel, and swore: 'That is the identical coat,' and 'That is the very man,' and again — referring to the identity parade — with real pride: 'I was the first to put the finger on him!'

"Then came the speech for the Crown. For three hours Sprott let himself go, without a pause, without a single written note. The words flowed out of his mouth and put a spell upon the court. When he painted the picture of the crime, by God, he laid it on heavy — the guilty man hugging the razor in his pocket, brutally attacking his defenceless paramour, the mother of his unborn child, then fleeing headlong to hide himself in a foreign land

. . . I tell you it was masterly. The jury, open-mouthed, hung on every word.

"The speech by the prisoner's counsel was useless beside this performance. The financial resources of the defence were negligible, counsel was an oldish man, draggingly slow, with a thin voice, and he was uninstructed on many points. In particular he seemed quite unaware of evidence likely to be favourable to Mathry.

"Well, it was soon over. Guilty. The prisoner's protests of innocence went through me like a knife. But he was dragged away and everybody was well pleased. The £500 reward offered for conviction was paid out to Collins and Burt. God knows they had earned it."

The sick man's strength seemed at last to fail him, he lay back, and, in an exhausted voice, declared that he could not continue.

"Come again in a day or so. You'll hear the rest then."

There was a long, a terrible silence in the narrow room. Silently, Boulia got up, poured some water into a glass and put it to Swann's lips. He swallowed, without moving. All this time, Paul sat dazed, his head supported in his hands, a storm of emotion sweeping him. A string of questions trembled wildly upon his tongue. But he knew he could not put them, that the session for today was ended — Swann had closed his eyes, completely limp, beyond all further effort. As Mark tip-toed from the room Paul rose unsteadily, pressed the sick man's hand between his own, then followed through the door.

# Chapter 11

COULD it be that an innocent man had been buried alive for fifteen years? Uncertain and confused, swayed this way and that,

Paul scarcely dared frame that frightful question. Swann had as yet offered no concrete proof, only an attitude of mind. The thing seemed inconceivable. Yet the mere possibility of such a monstrous injustice inflicted upon his father was enough to drive Paul frantic. He must not think of it. Determinedly he strove for command of his emotions. He realized that now, above all, he must be calm, practical, and resolute.

His first step was to write home asking for a parcel of fresh clothing, his next to find a permanent lodging which would afford him more freedom of action than the Y.M.C.A. After some searching he discovered a cheap attic on the fifth floor of a rooming-house in Poole Street — a frowsy but respectable thoroughfare in a loop of the Sherwood Canal mainly given over to inferior boarding houses, which lay south of the traffic-infested channel of Ware Street. The landlady, Mrs. Coppin, a spare little woman with a penetrating voice, showed him upstairs, gave him soap and a coarse clean towel. The advance payment on his room almost exhausted the small store of money he had brought from Belfast, and, when he had washed, he set out to find some means of supporting himself.

Wortley was a humming city, a vast hive of activity, embedded in flat farming country, but, like its neighbours Coventry and Northampton, its industries were highly specialized, devoted mainly to the manufacture of china, cutlery, and leather goods — trades demanding a technical training and skill which Paul did not possess. Also, he had no union membership card, no references which he cared to produce, and of course he was not yet fully qualified as a teacher. When two days had gone by without result he scanned the "situations vacant" columns of the newspapers with increasing anxiety.

But on the following morning a stroke of real luck came his way. As he came out of his attic room and walked along the crowded pavement of Ware Street to the cabman's shelter, where he had discovered that he could lunch for a few pence on a sausage roll and coffee, he observed, pasted on the window of a large store known as The Bonanza Bazaar, a notice:

PIANIST WANTED.
Apply Mr. Victor Harris, Manager, within.

After a moment's hesitation, Paul entered the shop. It was one of those emporia selling all sorts of everyday goods, from hardware and cosmetics to underwear and children's toys, lavishly displaying its merchandise upon a series of open counters — a local replica of the transpontine five-and-ten-cent stores. The manager, a man of about thirty with marcelled hair and a smoothly efficient manner, took a brisk look at Paul, then led the way, in his striped double-breasted suit, his flowered tie blowing in the breeze of the electric fans, to a section of the store where an upright piano stood amongst a display of sheet music. Taking a piece at random, he placed it on the instrument and said briefly:

"Play!"

Paul sat down and ran his fingers over the keys. He could read perfectly at sight, even difficult music, and this popular waltz before him was simplicity itself. He played it through, repeated it with some variations of his own, then picking up several other sheets, he played these over too. Before he had finished, the girls at the adjoining counters were listening and Mr. Harris was beating time approvingly on the counter with his rhinestone ring.

"You'll do." The manager nodded his decision. "You're hired. Three pounds a week and a sandwich lunch. Only see you keep going. No slacking or you're out on your ear. And use the loud pedal. Make the customers buy."

He gave Paul a patronising smile, showing the gold in his

61

teeth, then, with a frown towards the other assistants for wasting their time, he moved easily away.

Paul kept on playing all day. It was no sinecure. He began freshly enough, but as the hours wore on his muscles ached from sitting, unsupported, on the hard piano stool, and when the ill-ventilated store filled up, the crowd milling and pushing around him, breathing down his neck, jogging his elbows, almost sitting on the keyboard, became unbearably oppressive. His mind, too, was in a turmoil, torn by thoughts of his father, by half-formed plans and projects, by the need for deciding upon a definite course of action.

Towards one o'clock Harris swaggered out for lunch and after a few minutes the girl in charge of the cafeteria brought over coffee and a plate of sandwiches to Paul. Glad of a respite, he got up, stretched himself, and, with a smile, asked her name. She told him, flatly, Lena Andersen. But although he had thought to exchange a word with her, she moved off immediately to another part of the shop. There was nothing uncivil in this reserve; yet beneath the surface of her manner he sensed a constraint which, through his troubled mood, stirred his curiosity. And later, when she returned to the cafeteria across the way, almost instinctively he glanced towards her before beginning once more to play.

She could not have been more than twenty years of age and seemed to him a Scandinavian type — tall, with blond hair, and long limbs. Her features were regular and, though marred by a fine white scar running down from her high cheek-bone, would have been attractive but for a deep melancholy concentrated between her brows. Indeed, in repose, her face was unusually sad, her expression distant, intent, and serious. Several times that afternoon, despite himself, Paul's gaze was drawn towards this tragic young Amazon. He noticed that she wore her uniform quietly, with good taste. Although she appeared on good terms with the other assistants, she kept herself apart, and was restrained with all but a few of her regular customers. What sort of person was she? He tried her with a glance, inquiring and friendly, but it passed unanswered. Instead she lowered her gaze and turned away.

The afternoon dragged on. He closed his eyes while his fingers hammered out on the keyboard a melody already so sickeningly familiar he knew it by heart. Six o'clock came at last and, with a sigh of relief, he was free. Hurrying from the store, he made his way directly to the infirmary, and after some difficulty, again gained admission to Swann. The sick man seemed worse, and in a low and brooding mood was disinclined to talk. Indeed, it was as though he regretted having spoken so freely on the previous occasion. But as Paul sat patiently by his bedside, not pressing him in any way, he gradually relented. He did, then, turn his head, gazing at the young man with a kind of pity.

"So you came back?" he said at last.

"Yes," Paul answered in a low voice.

"I warn you . . . if you go on with this it'll change your whole life . . . as it did mine. And once you've put your hand to it, there'll be no turning back."

"I won't turn back."

"Then how do you propose to begin?"

"I thought if I typed out a statement and you signed it, I could take it to the authorities . . ."

Swann could not laugh — but a short, sardonic tremor passed across his pale lips.

"What authorities? The police? They're already fully informed — and quite satisfied with the situation. The Public Prosecutor, Sir Matthew Sprott? From personal knowledge of that gentleman, I advise you not to meddle with him." Swann paused, taken by a long fit of coughing. "No. The Secretary of State, in Parliament, alone has the power to open up the matter, and you wouldn't get within a mile of him with your present evidence. The delirious ravings — that's what they'd call it — of a dying, discredited ex-policeman would carry no weight whatsoever. They'd simply laugh at you."

"But you believe my father is innocent."

"I know he's innocent," Swann answered, with a trace of brusqueness. "In his summing up the judge called the Spurling murder a vile, brutal, monstrous crime, for which the extreme penalty of the law was too light a punishment. And yet they reprieved Mathry. Why, I ask you, why? Maybe they weren't quite sure, after all, that the man they'd convicted was guilty and so, out of the generosity of their hearts, they didn't swing him up quick, they gave him slow death instead — life imprisonment in Stoneheath."

Paul sat, silent and appalled, while the sick man struggled to regain his breath.

"No," Swann said presently, in a dry, totally different tone. "There is only one way to force them to re-open the case. *You must discover the real murderer.*"

Taken unawares, Paul felt a chill traverse his spine. Hitherto he had considered only his father's innocence, the thought of the actual assassin had scarcely entered his head. It was as though a new and formidable shadow had fallen across his path.

"The man Rocca," he ventured, after a prolonged silence. "What about him?"

Swann shook his head contemptuously.

"He had nothing to do with it — hadn't the guts. He only wanted to save his own skin. But speaking of skin," the sick man's lips drew into a grimace, "we come back to the purse that was found by the body. Believe it or not, that unidentified purse was made of the finest leather in the world . . . tanned human hide."

A moment of absolute silence.

"So you see," Swann resumed in that same vein of bitter satire, "you've only to lay your hands on a character perverted enough to possess such an article, link him up with a few other pieces of evidence that got mislaid — and you have the killer." Again that sardonic facial tremor. "After fifteen years . . . it should be relatively easy."

"Don't!" Paul said. "For God's sake. I need your help . . . all you can give me."

Swann's expression changed. He gazed at Paul almost despairingly.

"Well, if you must . . . let me tell you more about the two main witnesses — who identified the wrong man, not the right one — Edward Collins and Louisa Burt.

"When Burt and Collins came to headquarters to claim their reward I was on duty. Now as I've told you I had my serious doubts about this pair — not so much Collins, who was a soft mark with good enough intentions, as Louisa Burt, who, for a seventeen-year-old girl, seemed to me . . . well, a character worth watching. I put them in a side room to wait and while they waited I was next door working at my desk and, because of an acoustic arrangement we had, was able to hear everything they said. I wrote it down too. At first they didn't say much. Then Collins, who sounded scared, said: 'Will we get the money?' 'We'll get it, Ed, don't worry,' Burt answered, cool as you please, and she added: 'We might do even better.' 'What do you mean?' he said. She laughed. 'I've got something up my sleeve that might surprise you.' That seemed to bother Collins. He didn't speak for quite a while, then, in a kind of parrot voice, as though he'd repeated it often before, he said: 'Mathry was the man, wasn't he, Louisa?' 'Shut up, will you,' she came at him. 'It's too late to back down now. We didn't do no harm. With all that evidence they would have done for Mathry anyhow. And after all he didn't get hung. Don't you understand, you fool, it don't pay to

65

go against the police. Besides, things may come out of this better than you ever dreamed. I've 'ad a notion them last few days,' she went on in a kind of far-away voice. 'I'll live like a lady yet, Ed, maybe like a queen, with servants to wait on me and wash the dishes and empty the slops. Just let me take my chance and I'll spite the whole world and never iron another shirt.'"

Swann paused for breath. When he resumed he looked straight at Paul.

"That was the end of the conversation. But I'd heard enough to confirm my worst suspicions. Burt, out of her own mouth, had given the show away. She had seen the murderer and come out with his description. When this didn't quite fit Mathry, she obligingly shifted her position. There would be a lot of probing and cross-questioning at headquarters and it suited her to fall in with it — for everything pointed to Mathry being the guilty man. Then she wanted to stand well with the authorities, to be the little prima donna, right in the front of the picture, and of course to get the reward. It was her influence that swung Collins. Maybe she actually persuaded herself it *was* Mathry she saw . . . it can happen with that type. And then, when it was all over, headlines, publicity, praise, the whole peepshow, and she had time to think, she began to wonder about all the things that hadn't come out at the trial and to ask herself if, after all, it wasn't somebody else she had seen, a vaguely familiar figure, that she'd noticed around Eldon on her way to and from the laundry. Suddenly it came to her . . . a possibility of who this man might be . . . a chance . . . and with it a sense of golden opportunity.

"I ought to have gone to the Chief, but I didn't . . . I'd badgered him too much in the early stages of the case for him to want to listen to me now, besides, he'd reprimanded me for slackness the week before and we weren't on the best of terms. So for a while I chewed on what I knew; then, in the end, I went for advice to a lawyer named Walter Gillett. Now Gillett was a man I liked and trusted, and I'm sure he liked me too. What do you think he told me to do? To keep clear of the whole business. He knew I was in bad standing in the force. Maybe because he knew I was drinking he didn't fully credit the new evidence I gave him. He said: 'Jimmy, for God's sake don't bring a hornet's nest about your ears.' And what did I do? My mind was in such a state of tension and confusion, I went on a blind, came on duty soused and . . . well . . . you know the rest. After I came out of quod I didn't give a damn for anything. . . ."

Swann's words had gradually grown less and less audible. Now interrupted by a long spell of coughing they ceased altogether. He made a gesture that indicated there was nothing more he wished to say.

Rigid and motionless, Paul broke the silence.

"Are they still here . . . Burt and Collins?"

"You'll never get hold of Collins — he married years ago and emigrated to New Zealand. But Burt is still here . . . yes, Burt . . . little Louisa Burt, my God, what a character . . . she is the key to the whole enigma." Swann paused. "There's just one chance in a million you might get something out of her."

"Where can I find her?" Paul exclaimed.

"She works for a highly respected family . . . another proof of how she can gull decent people."

From beneath his pillow Swann took a scrap of paper on which were written certain particulars. In silence he handed it to Paul.

"There!" he said, in a flat voice. "Though it won't do you any good. Now let me be. I've done enough for you and I'll do no more. I feel damned bad and want to get some sleep."

He stretched himself on his side and drew the bedclothes to his chin, a gesture which indicated that the interview was over.

Paul got to his feet. His voice was charged with feeling. "Thank you," he said, simply. "I'll come again soon."

With a last glance at that wasted and impassive figure, he swung round and left the ward. As he went down the stairs his heart was bounding with a new hope. Swann had helped him beyond all his expectation. Yet somehow he could not escape the impression that the sick man was still holding something back, something he was unwilling, afraid almost, to reveal. He told himself he must discover it on his next visit to the infirmary.

# Chapter 12

ON the following evening, after work, Paul met Mark by appointment outside the Bonanza — the library assistant had telephoned him earlier in the day. Boulia seemed pleased to see him, and when they had shaken hands, he exclaimed eagerly:

"We're making a start tonight?"

"Yes," Paul said. "What about something to eat first?"

"No thanks. I had a snack at five. But how about you?"

"I'm all right."

"I've hardly been able to wait, since I phoned you," Mark broke out excitedly, as they moved off along the thronged pavement. "Tell me about Burt."

Paul was silent. Boulia's mercurial temperament, his tendency to treat the matter light-heartedly, as a gay and thrilling adventure, made him question the wisdom of having asked him to accompany him. Yet the real and generous help given by the other had more or less imposed this obligation on Paul. And so, after a moment, he answered:

"Burt is employed as a domestic servant, hasn't turned out too well, I gather. This is her evening off. I've a fair idea what she looks like and where to find her."

"Good work," Mark exclaimed, and added, "How did you leave Swann?"

Paul shook his head, glancing at him sideways, Boulia lost his effusiveness.

"Worse?" he murmured.

"I called at the hospital lunch time. He was too ill to have visitors."

After that, they walked through the park in silence, passing the bandstand, shuttered for the winter and strangely spectral in the dusk, skirting the ornamental pond, reaching the higher northern slopes above the Municipal Art Galleries and the Natural History Museum. They were now on Porlock Hill, one of the best sections of the city, spaced with handsome mansions, laid out in broad terraces and bordered by avenues of tall chestnut trees. Adjoining this fine residential area there was, however, a queer survival of an older period — a cramped little colony of back streets and cobbled alleys composed of converted mews, a number of small shops, and one public house: The Royal Oak.

"That's it," Paul said, as the sign became visible. "I needn't warn you to be careful. If you don't know what to say, just say nothing."

They crossed the lane towards the yellow light shining from the leaded windows, and pushed through the swing doors of the tavern.

The saloon was old and dingily genteel, upholstered in tarnished plush, with frayed lamp shades, reproductions of racehorses upon the walls, and a cracked gilt mirror behind the curved bar. It had begun to fill up for the evening, mainly with the local tradespeople and a few belated artisans, as Paul led the way to one of the fumed oak tables and, having ordered two glasses of ale, cautiously surveyed the room.

"Not here yet." He turned to Mark. "We may be out of luck tonight for all I know."

He had no sooner spoken when the doors swung again and a woman entered and walked, with the air of a habitué, to a corner booth. Paul guessed at once, with a queer tightening of his throat, that it was Louisa Burt. She seemed about thirty, rather heavy about the hips and bust, wearing a costume of cheap plaid material, with yellow gloves and a fancy handbag. She was, indeed, so completely ordinary, so obviously a domestic servant on her evening out, that Paul, though his heart was beating fast, sat momentarily confounded.

She settled herself, ordered a small gin and, after fussing with the contents of her handbag, explored the saloon with her eyes. Paul, meeting her gaze, smiled slightly. She immediately turned away, as if insulted, but two minutes later, though with an offended air, she was again looking in their direction. This time Paul rose and crossed over to her booth. Nothing could have been more foreign to his character than this approach, but, with a new maturity, he did it perfectly. Easily, yet with the correct note of ingratiating politeness, he said:

"Good evening."

There was a pause.

"Are you addressing me?"

"Yes. If you're alone perhaps we might join you."

"I'm not alone, not really. I'm waiting on a friend."

"Oh!"

"Of course he might be detained tonight, working late. He's a very important man."

"Then he probably will be detained. And his loss will be our gain. Have a drink?"

"No, not really. I'm not in the habit. Still, if you insist."

Paul signalled across his shoulder to Mark, who came over to the booth carrying Paul's tumbler and his own.

"May I introduce my companion?"

"Pleased to meet you I am sure. I forgot my visiting cards but my name is Miss Burt."

As they sat down beside her she drew back slightly, arranging her skirt in a ladylike manner; then, crooking her little finger, she emptied her glass.

"Now it's my treat, Miss Burt," Mark said. "What will you have?"

"Well nothing was further from my thoughts. Gin."

"Mother's ruin." Mark smiled pleasantly.

She did not smile back. Her eyes, of a light dolly blue, kept moving over them in shallow, yet appraising inquiry. Her face was pale and of a coarse texture, with large pores, thickly powdered, on her snub nose. Her plump childish cheeks, curiously indrawn at the corners of the mouth, gave her thin moist lips a strange sort of smirk, persistent, yet watchful, and utterly incongruous, since her expression was quite devoid of humour. She had practically no forehead.

"Well, here's luck," Paul exclaimed, when her drink arrived. He raised his measure of beer.

"You know," Mark went on, "there's nothing beats a nice convivial evening. Amongst friends you understand. Cheers you up. Makes you feel good. Breaks the old routine."

"I got to be back at nine tonight." She preened herself warningly, and with all the conscious dignity of sex. "I couldn't walk out nowhere. Not tonight."

"Ah, well," Paul said easily. "We'll have better luck next time. We'll be properly acquainted then."

She digested this, stared from one to the other.

"You are perfect gentlemen, I must say. Some does rush you, something cruel." Her eyes came back to Paul, not without interest. "Haven't you been with me before, somewheres?"

"No," Paul said. "I'm afraid not."

71

"That's a pleasure that's still in store for him." Mark laughed agreeably.

Keenly alert, Paul kept the conversation flowing, playing on Burt's vanity, deferring to her affectations, accepting with admiration her explanation that she was "lady housekeeper" in charge of a large mansion on Porlock Hill. After several drinks she began to lose something of her watchfulness, her air of gentility intensified, and suddenly a flood of self-pity welled into her glassy eyes.

"It's nice to meet two perfect gents. Not like some I could mention, only I wouldn't, being a perfect lady myself, though I do say it as perhaps shouldn't. I was brought up very strict, you understand, educated by the nuns in a French convent. Oh, it was lovely there in the seminely, so quiet and peaceful, and the nuns was such dears, they made a regular pet of me. It was Louisa this, and Louisa that, all the time I can assure you, especially from the reverend mother — she couldn't do enough for me, from breakfast in bed to hand-stitched lace on all my negligees. Of course, me being half French myself made a difference, they all knew what I would have been if only I'd had my rights, and p'raps they guessed the terrible time what was in store for me." She broke off, searching their faces humidly. "Does that surprise you?"

Paul shook his head gravely, thinking at the same time, "Dear God, what a natural-born liar!"

"If you only knew." She clutched at Paul's arm. "What I've went through! My father was in the army, not the Salvation, the reg'lar army, a colonel. He used to beat my mother, the brute, especially when he came home boozed, late Saturday nights. I wanted to run away. The footlights always was my great ambition, to have all them people watching and admiring me. Oh, if only I'd had my chance."

"And didn't you?" Mark prompted, sympathetically.

She shook her head, her heavy lids veiling a sullen gleam. "Something happened. I only done right, mind you. I only told the truth, the whole truth, and nothing but the truth, so help me God. And what did I get for it? A few quid, what went in six months."

"That's always the way," Paul agreed, with assumed bitterness. "You do somebody a good turn and get no thanks for it."

"I didn't want no thanks!" she burst out. "I only wanted to be recognised proper . . . have my place. I didn't expect to have to be a serv . . . I mean a lady housekeeper for the rest of my born days."

Paul had the wit to keep silent but Mark, in his excitement, leaned forward.

"Why don't you tell us about it?" he pressed. "Perhaps we could help you."

There was a sharp pause. Paul bit his lip and lowered his gaze. Burt looked at Boulia, suddenly seemed to recollect herself. The angry flush faded from her plump cheeks. She glanced at the clock above the bar, finished her drink, and got to her feet.

"Do you see the time? I got to go now."

Masking his chagrin, Paul helped her gather up her things, paid for the drinks, and escorted her through the swing doors.

"It's such a lovely night." He glanced up at the stars. "Perhaps we could see you home?"

She hesitated, then, somewhat grudgingly, consented.

"Well . . . only to the gate, mind you."

They left the cobbled alley and set out along the dry, deserted, suburban road, Burt picking her way, on high heels, between Boulia and Paul. More than ever Paul exerted himself to please. Presently they reached a broad avenue, screened by a double row of topped lime trees and flanked by red tiled villas standing in their own gardens. Opposite the end house Burt drew up.

"Well," she said, "this is it."

"What a lovely mansion," Paul said.

"Yes." Burt was flattered. "I'm with the Oswalds . . . most refined people."

"Well, naturally." Paul spoke persuasively. "May we see you next Wednesday?"

Burt hesitated, but only for a moment.

"All right," she said. "Same time, at the Oak."

"Splendid."

Paul removed his hat, and with great politeness held out his hand. As he did so, the front door of the villa opened and an elderly gentleman came out, bareheaded, smoking a cigar, and carrying a few letters. He strolled towards the gate and opened it, evidently making for the pillar box at the end of the road. In the darkness it was impossible fully to discern his features, but Paul saw that his expression was abstracted and benevolent, his hair silver grey. As he passed the little group he noticed Burt and, in a pleasant voice, remarked:

"Good evening, Louisa."

"Good evening, sir," she answered, in a humble voice, a change of tone to respectful servility which was almost comic.

When he had gone, leaving behind an agreeable odour of cigar smoke, Burt, in some discomfiture took leave of her two companions. Entering the drive, she followed the service path on the left, and was lost behind a screen of laurel bushes. As Paul and Boulia turned away they heard the slam of the back door.

For a full five minutes, while they tramped down the avenue, there was a silence between them; then in an apologetic tone Boulia said:

"I'm sorry, Mathry. She was just beginning to talk . . . when I sent her back into her shell."

Paul compressed his lips on a sharp reply.

74

# Chapter 13

WHEN Paul went up to his attic room it was nearly eleven o'clock. He could not sleep. Pacing the confined space between the rickety wash-stand and the truckle bed, scarcely hearing through the thin walls the inevitable nocturnal noises of his fellow lodgers — the Parsee medical student, playing his radio on the floor below, James Crocket, the accountant's clerk brushing his boots and whistling mournfully next door, old Mr. Garvin, the retired auctioneer, creaking downstairs to refill his ewer — he struggled with the excitement to which the evening had strung him.

At last he undressed and got into bed. He slept badly for his thoughts were still seething, his nerves keyed for action. He was glad when the first grey streaks of dawn reached over the chimney pots and filtered through the dingy bedroom panes.

All that day, at the store, he was strained and preoccupied. When Lena Andersen took him his luncheon from the cafeteria he ate the sandwiches without his usual appetite. Perhaps she noticed this for, with a serious and impersonal air, she remarked:

"Don't you like the ham?"

He came out of his abstraction, glanced up, and forced a smile.

"I do. I just don't happen to be hungry today." He added: "You're much too good to me. I know Harris said I could have a snack. But you bring me a regular spread."

"It's not a proper lunch. Sandwiches aren't too good for anyone. But I suppose you have your dinner in the evening?"

He did not contradict her. Despite the burden of his mood, he was pleased by the way in which she stood and talked with him, not easily, but with a sort of painful tenseness, almost against her will. Perhaps his wordless gaze, to which custom had

75

given a certain intimacy, had caused her to break silence. It was as though each had sensed the other's loneliness and had, because of that, been moved to speak.

"You're in digs, by yourself, I suppose."

"Yes," he agreed. "Are you?"

"Oh, no. I'm very lucky." A quiver of pride came over her face. "I have a nice place — two rooms in a friend's house in Ware Terrace."

"That's quite an establishment."

She nodded simply, looking away. Her eyes, of a dark hazel, seemed to express the desire and the burden of life.

"I can do it. I work hard, you see. Often I go out in the evenings to public banquets. It's good pay."

"Don't you ever go dancing, or to the movies, like the others?" he asked curiously.

"No." She shrugged her shoulders. "I don't bother about that."

She stood, gazing ahead absently, then she took his empty cup and with a faint half-smile went back to the cafeteria.

The duration of Lena's conversation with Paul had not passed unnoticed by some of the sharp-eyed waitresses and, since business was slack, when she returned to her counter, one of the younger girls, named Nancy Wilson, nudged her neighbour. She was a pert, dressy little character, a product of Ware Street gutters, who wore a red patent belt with her uniform, openwork stockings, and button boots with cloth uppers.

"D'you see that?" She made a sly movement of her head. "Miss Andersen had a long music lesson today."

"Doh, ray, me!" sang out a second girl.

"Oh, Lena!" another called over, with a broad smile. "Was you arranging to have your piano tuned?"

A general titter of laughter went up and Nancy Wilson attempted to cap the joke.

76

"Be careful, Lena," she exclaimed sweetly. "Once bitten, twice shy."

There was an uncomfortable silence. The girls suddenly became busy again and several gave Nancy a quick angry glance. Lena, who had given no sign of having heard, picked up her charge-list and began to add up the figures. Usually she had a good-natured answer for any sort of banter. But on this occasion she said nothing.

Although Paul wondered what was being said, the incident soon passed from his mind. He was, indeed, existing in a state of unbearable expectancy, unable to concentrate upon anything but his next meeting with Burt, counting the days until the week should pass.

At last Wednesday arrived and Paul's keyed nerves were more tautly strung by the sense of impending action. Somehow he managed to get through the day. He had arranged to meet Mark outside the Bonanza at seven o'clock, and at closing time he was amongst the first to leave. Since Boulia had not yet arrived, he took up his stance under an electric standard on the opposite pavement, eagerly glancing up and down the street. The other assistants had now begun to emerge, singly and in pairs — chattering and with linked arms — from the half-shuttered doorway of the store. Towards the end of the procession Lena came out, alone, wearing a raincoat and a small brown felt hat, that looked anything but new, pulled low over her bright hair. Despite her commonplace dress, as she moved off, with her hands in her raincoat pockets, there was something in her graceful, high-breasted, well-proportioned form which pleased and arrested the eye. Paul watched, and suddenly he saw her wave her hand as, in the crowd, an elderly woman appeared, short and stout, carrying several parcels. The newcomer greeted Lena with manifest affection and they moved off in the direction of the Ware Cross.

77

The brief scene gave to Paul a passing sense of warmth but now, abruptly, he looked at his watch which, to his surprise, indicated twenty minutes past seven. What on earth was delaying Mark? Renewing his glances up and down the busy thoroughfare Paul sought with growing impatience for Boulia's advancing figure. Now it was half past seven and still there was no sign of him. Anxiety was added to Paul's impatience, every minute he kept looking at his watch. At last he could wait no longer and, with a worried frown, started off at a fast pace in the direction of the library. In ten minutes he was there, saw that Mark was still on duty, and hurrying to the desk, he exclaimed:

"What's the matter? Aren't you coming?"

Boulia had flinched perceptibly at the sight of Paul. He hesitated, then, with a nervous glance behind him, answered in a low voice.

"I'm on duty. I can't make it."

Paul stared at the other in amazement. His tone, his manner, even his appearance, were so completely altered. His flippancy, all his natural carefree air, was gone, he seemed subdued, even cowed, indeed, his eyes kept darting about the reading room in a thoroughly intimidated fashion.

"You might surely have let me know," Paul protested, with justifiable annoyance.

"Not so loud," Boulia muttered. He came close to Paul, spoke in a hurried undertone. "I'm sorry to let you down, Mathry, but the truth is . . . I'll have to drop out of our arrangement. I went into it without thinking, just for a lark, but it isn't such sport as it looks."

"What's happened?"

"I can't tell you . . . but listen," Mark's voice fell to a lower key, "take my advice and drop it, too. I can't say more, but I'm serious, never was more serious in my life."

A strained silence followed.

78

"At least I'll see you again?" Paul said slowly.

With averted eyes, Mark shook his head. His words came stiffly.

"I've been transferred out of the city . . . to the public library at Retwood. I have to leave the end of the week."

Again there was silence, rigid and prolonged. Paul drew in a slow, comprehending breath. He had not, in truth, built too heavily on Mark's co-operation. Yet now even that was gone. He was alone again . . . must face the future single handed. And more, he glimpsed, for the first time, in the young librarian's change of front, the sudden crumbling of his morale, something of the dark and unseen dangers which he himself must face.

A score of questions rose to his tongue. But he perceived that Boulia was on edge for him to go. So he held out his hand, and said simply:

"I'm sorry if I've got you in a mess. Thank you for all you've done. Good luck. I hope we'll meet again."

The next minute he turned sharply and went out of the library to the nearest telephone booth. Perhaps it wasn't yet too late. With urgent fingers he fumbled through the tattered dog-eared book that hung on the brass chain, at last found the number he was seeking, and placed two coins in the slot. After a delay that seemed interminable he got through.

"Is that the Royal Oak?"

"This is the Royal Oak Inn. Jack speaking."

Paul thought he recognized the voice of the waiter who had served him the week before.

"This is one of Miss Burt's friends calling. I had to meet her tonight at seven. Will you give her a message? Tell her I've been delayed but that I'm coming over straight away."

"I'm sorry," the waiter's voice came back, "Miss Burt isn't here."

"Didn't she come in this evening?"

79

"She came in as usual and stopped for half an hour. She left around eight."

Paul dropped the receiver back upon its hook, reflected for a moment, then left the booth. In three minutes he was in the Square where he took a tram direct to Porlock Hill. His watch showed half-past eight when he arrived at the end house in the Avenue.

The front of the house appeared to be in darkness, but there was a light in one of the side windows upstairs. Paul opened the gate and entered the drive; then, nerving himself, he walked round by the service entrance and knocked on the back door. Immediately a dog barked inside, then the door was opened by a thin, placid-faced woman of about fifty, in a black house-keeper's dress.

"Could I see Miss Louisa Burt, please?"

The woman looked Paul up and down.

"She's gone to her room with a headache."

"Couldn't she come down for a minute?" Paul pressed. "I'm her friend."

"I'm sorry." The housekeeper shook her head. "Followers are not allowed here. It's one of the rules of the house."

She closed the door with a conventional murmur of regret. Discouraged, he nevertheless told himself he was not beaten. He must see Burt at all costs.

The night was dry and crisp, with a darkness made soft and luminous by the stars. The hint of frost, which had polished the sky, made the fallen plane leaves crackle underfoot as Paul retraced his steps to the front of the house. Here, through a large illuminated window, over which, perhaps because of the beauty of the night, the curtains had not yet been drawn, he made out the master of the house, the man whom he had already seen walking to the mail-box, and an elderly woman with an amiable, kindly expression, who was obviously his wife. Another

80

couple, apparently guests, were in the sedately furnished drawing room. All wore evening dress.

Sheltered by the laurel bushes Paul stood watching the scene, so dignified and gracious, remote from the dark and painful passions warring within his breast. He saw that a bridge table was set out beside them. From their leisured progress, the laughter and conversation, it would be late before they finished and he resigned himself to a lengthy wait.

Suddenly, in the shadows, he heard a heavy step behind him. He swung round, and found himself confronted by a police officer.

# Chapter 14

"WHAT are you up to?"

At the officer's words an icy wave rushed over Paul, and for an instant he almost bolted. But he took a grip of himself.

"I wanted to see someone in the house."

"Is that how you make a call — hiding among the bushes in the dark?"

"I wasn't hiding."

"Yes, you was. I been watching you ever since you arrived. Loitering with intent, I call it."

"No, no," Paul protested. "I can explain everything, if you'll only listen."

"Explain to the sergeant at the station," the other interrupted. "You'd better come quiet."

With a hard face, Paul stared at the uniformed figure before him. This, of all conceivable misfortunes that could have befallen him, was the worst. But there was nothing for it but to submit. He set off beside the policeman in silence.

It was a long march back through the lighted, crowded streets to the centre of the city. Significantly, Paul realized that he was not being taken to the nearby local station. At last they passed through an archway lit by a square blue lamp, and entered the charge room of the Wortley Police Headquarters.

The room was small and bare, brightly illuminated, with a grated window, two doors — one with a small square grille — and two benches against the walls. Standing at a high desk, with the collar of his tunic undone, writing laboriously like a schoolboy over his copy book, was a stout, red-faced sergeant, whose name, conspicuously stamped on the charge-sheet, was Jupp. He had the stolid air of a country innkeeper, and his square head, with its sparse hair oiled and neatly parted in a cowlick, shone beneath the green shaded electric light.

He kept Paul waiting before him for five minutes while he dotted the last "i" and crossed the last "t" to his satisfaction; then he looked up, turned a fresh page, and exclaimed:

"Well, now, what's all this about?"

In routine, almost perfunctory fashion, Jupp took down the particulars offered him by his subordinate, twirling the waxed end of his moustache, glancing at Paul queerly from time to time, out of the corners of his eyes. Finally, he pointed the butt end of his pen towards the bench.

"I've an idea the Chief would like to see you. Sit there till I tell you."

Paul did as he was bid. By this time he was convinced that he had not been picked up by accident, that his presence here was part of some broader design. He sat on the bench for perhaps half an hour. During that time two seamen were brought in, both drunk, looking as though they had rolled in all the gutters of the city, and a raddled creature with a stony face and a broken feather in her hat — a street-walker charged with soliciting. All three were removed, through the grilled door on the left. When

the door opened there came through, quenched but not obliter-
ated by the odour of disinfectant, the faint sour smell of soiled
humanity.

At last Paul received a signal from Sergeant Jupp. He rose and
followed him down a passage to the right. Then a baize covered
door was opened, and Paul found himself in a comfortable office,
furnished with leather armchairs, a wide mahogany desk, and a
large glass-fronted cabinet filled with silver cups and trophies.
Displayed upon the walls were numerous framed "annual groups"
of the force, photographs of police football and athletic teams,
also an interesting show case of antique truncheons. A thick red
carpet covered the floor.

But Paul felt no response to the cheerfulness of the room, his
attention was riveted upon the man who sat behind the desk.
He recognized him at once from the photograph he had seen, and
he knew himself to be in the presence of the Chief Constable of
Wortley, Adam Dale.

"Sit down, my boy. There. You'll find that a comfortable seat."

The quiet voice, warm with unforeseen friendliness, came to
Paul as such a shock; he sank into the easy chair before the desk.
He could not take his eyes from Dale.

The Chief Constable was now a man of fifty-five, and had
reached, perhaps, the very acme of his physical powers. He had
an enormous frame, a massive neck, and arms as thick as an
ordinary man's thigh. There was no fat upon him, it was all
bone and solid muscle, the features carved in granite, the slant
of the face bones, jutting out and downwards from the brow,
intimidating in its strength. The forehead was sound, not unin-
telligent, but the chin, rock-like, and implacable, gave battle to
the world. The eyes were grey as ice.

"I've wanted to see you for some days now, lad," Dale resumed
in the same calm, considering manner, "and this seemed as good
an opportunity as any to bring you before me."

83

Paul braced himself in his chair.

"I haven't done anything."

"I trust not. We'll talk of that later. First of all, I want you to understand that I know who you are and all about you. Wortley may seem to you a large city. To us it's only a small village. We're aware of what's going on in it. We hear most things. That's all part of our business. And I had information regarding you just after your arrival." He fingered a telegraph form in the japanned box on his left. "An appeal from Belfast, sent out by your good friends there, asking us to trace you and keep you out of harm. I know where you lodge, what you work at, all that you've been doing."

The Chief Constable picked up an ebonite ruler and turned it thoughtfully in his tremendous hands, which in his early days as a Cumberland-style wrestler had pinned many an opponent to the mat.

"Now look here, lad . . . I've a fair idea of how you feel towards me. You're full of hatred. I'm the brute who sent your father up for life, who nearly brought him to the gallows. That's your side of the case. Well, let me tell you mine. It's this. I only did my duty. In the face of overwhelming evidence, I had no choice in the matter. Your father was just one of hundreds that have gone through my hands. In fact I'd forgotten all about him until you came along."

Again Dale paused, and turned upon Paul the steady battery of his eyes.

"I am here to safeguard the community. Society divides itself into two classes — those who do right and those who do wrong. It's my job to prosecute the wrong doers and protect the right. Have you got that clear? For if so, I want to put a straight question to you." He paused and pointed the ruler at Paul. "Which side do you belong to? Just ask yourself that. If you set yourself up against the forces of law and order you'll wind up in serious trouble. See where it's got you already. You're found hanging around the grounds of a big house after dark, without the consent, or even the knowledge, of the owner. Next thing you know you'll be inside. Mind you, I prefer no charges. But we work here on the sound policy that prevention is better than cure. So I'm just warning you, trying to show you for your own good where this sort of mischief is likely to end."

There was a pause during which Paul sat rigid and silent. At first he had meant to speak with all his soul, to pour out his side of the case, to argue, expostulate, and explain. But some inner force, a sense of secret foresight held him back.

"It's not my place to give you advice," Dale's tone, unmistakably sincere, had a reasonable, persuasive note. "But take my tip and go home to Belfast and your mother. You've a decent job waiting for you there and — I understand — a decent girl too. Give up raking around the seamy side of life. D'you hear me? I've children of my own, you know — I'm human. And I'd hate to see you get hurt. That's all. You can clear out of here now. And if you're wise you'll never be back."

He made a gesture of dismissal, cordial rather than curt. Without a word, Paul rose and left from the office, traversed the corridor and the charge room unmolested, and emerged to the cool night air. He was free. Sweating all over now, he walked rapidly away. The Chief Constable's outspoken candour had shaken him. There was no mistaking the other's honesty and sincerity of purpose. Yet through the tumult and disorder of his thoughts he felt, running deep and swift, an undercurrent of resentment. He had committed no wrong. In this free country no one had the right to dictate to him, he could not and would not surrender to Dale's demand. Instead, the very nature of that demand, and the circumstances which had preceded it, awoke in him a hot defiance, a longing for a stronger course of action which for some days had been developing in his mind.

His need of advice upon this matter was immediate, and despite the lateness of the hour, he thought, a trifle desperately:

"I must see Swann . . . at once. It's true he told me to go slow . . . but then . . . he didn't know this was going to happen. If I'm to be blocked here . . . in Wortley . . . I must, yes, I must take a more direct approach. After all, it was he who told me I would only get redress at the highest levels."

Striding through the echoing streets, he quickly reached the infirmary.

But there, when he made his request at the entrance lodge the aged porter, first running a ragged finger nail over the register, raised his spectacled eyes, and mildly shook his head.

"Swann . . . James Swann. I'm sorry, lad. He's off the list for good. He passed away quite peaceful . . . at four o'clock this afternoon."

Late that evening, after prolonged reflection, Paul made his decision. He wrote and mailed a letter to Westminster, in London.

# Chapter 15

THE Liberal Member of Parliament for Wortley enjoyed his brief visits to his constituency, especially in November, when the partridge shooting was at its best. George Birley came of local country stock and his success in London, where, by marrying Lady Ursula Ancaster he had allied himself with one of the most influential Liberal political families in the land, had not dulled his affection for his old friends and his favourite sport. He was a popular figure in Wortley and, at fifty, ruddy, clean-shaven, genial, a great hand at a story, fine judge of a cigar, always well turned out — with a tendency to check suitings in his leisure hours — ever ready to help a friend, to subscribe to a local charity, he had become a kind of symbol for native worth unspoiled by success.

True, his career in Parliament had not been especially noteworthy. He took his seat regularly, voted faithfully in the divisions, played golf annually for the Commons against the Lords. Every public man has his detractors, and there were some who said that Birley had neither the brains nor the qualifications for his position, that a good fellow was not necessarily a good statesman, that he was afraid of his noble spouse, and, indeed, of all the lordly Ancasters, that his hail-fellow-well-met heartiness was merely an inverted snobbery, that were it not for his lady wife and her high connections in the cabinet and elsewhere, George might not, for so long, have had his place in governing the nation.

On this particular morning Birley was in an excellent humour. His journey to Wortley by the early express had been comfortable, and now, seated at breakfast in the suite they always kept for him at the Queen's Hotel, he had partaken of a healthy portion of eggs and bacon, with grilled kidneys and a mutton chop on the side, and was at toast and marmalade and his third cup of coffee. The *Courier* on his knee, had been pleasant to glance through: the party shaping well in the Cotswold bye-election, no strikes in the offing, the stock market still rising. There had been frost over night, just enough to crisp the ground, and now the sun was breaking through. In ten minutes his car would be at the door, in an hour he would be snuffing the rich earth of his boyhood, tramping through the county furrows, with three other good fellows, good shots also, though perhaps not quite so handy on the trigger as himself. He had a new cocker, too, just broken to the gun, that he thought would do well.

A waiter entered, an oldish man with whiskers, very correct

and deferential. George liked the atmosphere of the hotel, standing for the good old-fashioned traditions, opposing all that new-fangled nonsense which he hated.

"There's a young man asking for you, sir."

Birley looked up from his paper and frowned.

"I can't possibly see him, I'm going out in ten minutes."

"He says he has an appointment, sir. He gave me this letter."

Birley took the letter which the waiter tactfully handed him — his own letter, with the House of Commons heading. His frown deepened. What a nuisance! He had fixed this days ago, in response to a rather vague communication soliciting an interview, then forgotten all about it. Still, he was a man who prided himself on never going back on his word.

"All right," he said. "Bring him up."

A moment later Paul was shown into the room. Birley, who was now lighting a five-shilling cigar, shook hands with him in an affable manner; motioned him to a chair at the table.

"Well!" he exclaimed heartily, through a cloud of smoke. "I've been expecting you ever since you wrote. Will you have a cup of coffee?"

"No thank you, sir." Paul was pale, but his firm expression and well-set-up shoulders made a distinctly favourable impression on Birley, who always liked to help a respectful, up-and-coming youngster.

"Let's come to the point, then, young man." Birley used the tone of friendly, half-humorous patronage at which he was adept. "I'm rather pressed you know. Have an important conference outside the city. Taking the express back to London tonight."

"I guessed you mightn't have much time, sir." Tensely Paul took a paper from his inside pocket. "So I prepared a typewritten statement of the facts."

"Good, good!" Birley approved blandly, at the same time raising a restraining hand. He objected strenuously to reading statements — why, otherwise, would he maintain two secretaries at the House? "Tell me in a few words what it's about."

Paul moistened his lips, took a swift deep breath.

"My father has been in prison fifteen years for a crime he did not commit."

Birley's jaw dropped, he stared at Paul with bulging eyes, as at something suddenly offensive. Paul, however, gave him no time to speak, he went on steadily with all he wished to say.

At first it seemed as though Birley would stop him. Yet though his face lengthened progressively, though he kept darting at Paul these queer glances of distaste, he did not. He listened. And his cigar went out.

The recital lasted exactly seven minutes, and when it was over Birley sat like a man caught in a most unpleasant trap. He cleared his throat.

"I can't believe this is true. It sounds like a complete cock-and-bull yarn to me. And even if it isn't . . . it's very ancient history."

"Not for the man in Stoneheath Prison. He's still living every minute of it."

Birley made a peevish gesture.

"I can't accept that. And I don't believe in stirring up a muddy pond. In any case it's no affair of mine."

"You're the Member of Parliament for Wortley, sir."

"Yes, damn it. I'm not the member for Stoneheath. I represent decent people, not a bunch of convicts."

He rose and strode up and down the room, furious at the blight put upon his day. If only he hadn't given this young fool an appointment. He couldn't stick his head into such a hornet's nest. No man in his senses would touch it with a barge pole. And yet, even while he glared at Paul, sitting quite still at the table, he experienced an uneasy qualm. Suddenly, with a fretful glance at the clock, he temporized.

"All right, then. Leave me that damn statement of yours. I'll go through it sometime today. Come and see me again this evening at seven."

Paul handed over the typewritten document with a suppressed expression of thanks, then rose and quietly left the room. Outside, he filled his lungs with the morning air. If only he could induce the Member to act, in Parliament, the very fountain head of government, the whole matter must be opened up. As he hurried towards the Bonanza he was hopeful that he had made some impression on Birley.

The day passed with intolerable slowness. Conscious of the fateful processes of thought now taking place in Birley's mind Paul kept glancing at the clock with anxious eyes. Several times Harris, the manager, came over and stood watchfully behind him as though hopeful of seeing him slack off. But at last the hour drew near. Just before closing time Paul went to the washroom, plunged his head in cold water, freshened himself up. He was at the Queen's at quarter past seven and after a short wait was shown upstairs.

But on this occasion, as he entered the room, there was no affability in Birley's manner. The Member for Wortley stood with his back to the fire, his suitcase packed and ready, a heavy travelling ulster flung across the table. By way of greeting he barely nodded, then he favoured the young man with a long, unsociable scrutiny. Finally he spoke.

"I've gone through that paper of yours . . . every word of it. Read it in the car going down the country. Read it over again coming back. I must say you've put it together cleverly. But there are always two sides to a case. And you've only stated one of them."

"Only one of them can be true," Paul countered quickly.

Birley frowned and shook his head.

"Things like that simply don't happen with us. They might in some rotten foreign country . . . but not here. Haven't we the

90

best system of legal justice in the world? We lead there, as we do in everything else. What could be fairer than trial by jury? Good God! It's been going on for over seven hundred years!"

"That might be an argument against it," Paul answered in a low voice. "I've thought about this a great deal, sir. It's natural, in my circumstances. Don't you think that juries are sometimes composed of stupid, ignorant, and prejudiced persons, who can't understand technical points, have no knowledge of psychology, are easily swayed by circumstantial evidence and the emotional rhetoric of the public prosecutor?"

"Good God!" Birley exclaimed. "Are you slinging mud at the Lord Advocate next?"

The passionate resentment which now, day and night, worked in Paul, a dark and bitter ferment, forced him to answer.

"A paid official whose career depends upon his ability to take away the life of the man placed before him in the dock deserves as little respect, in my opinion, as the common hangman."

"You forget that we need the common hangman."

"Why?"

"Hell and damnation!" Birley exploded. "To hang our murderers of course."

"Must we hang them?"

"Of course we must. We have to protect the community. If it wasn't for the fear of the rope any blackguard would cut your throat on a dark night for a five-pound note."

"In countries that have abolished the death penalty, statistics show that there has been no increase in crime."

"I don't believe it! Hanging's the best precaution. And it's a humane death, better than the guillotine or the electric chair. It would be an act of the greatest folly to do away with it."

Under the deep stress of his feelings, Paul lost all sense of caution.

"That's what Lord Ellenborough, the Chief Justice of England said, not so many years ago, when Samuel Romilly tried to get hanging abolished for thefts of more than five shillings."

The blood mounted to Birley's head. He spluttered:

"You damned young idiot! You can't pin that sort of thing on me. I'm a Liberal. I'm all for humanity! And so is our system. We don't want to hang people. Good God, you ought to know that from your own experience. A man can always be reprieved."

"Your legal system, the best in the world, first convicts a man of murder and condemns him to hang; then, when it questions its own judgment, reverses itself, and sends him to a living hell in prison for the rest of his life. Is that an act of mercy? Of humanity? Is that justice?" Paul rose to his feet, his face white, his eyes blazing. "That's what happened to my father. He's in Stoneheath because of a system of criminal procedure which relies on circumstantial evidence and on witnesses who are unfit to testify, a system which permits manipulation of facts by the prosecution, calling of experts who are no more than paid 'yes' men for the Crown, and the employment of a public Prosecutor whose sole purpose is, less to secure justice, than, by every means at his command, to hang the prisoner in the dock."

Ignoring Birley, and swept away by his obsession, Paul went on in a suppressed voice.

"Crime is the product of a country's social order. Those who make that social order are often more guilty than the so-called criminals. Society should not deal with offenders on the same principles which made them hang a starving boy a hundred years ago because he stole a loaf of bread. But if we're determined to exact an eye for an eye, and a tooth for a tooth, then at least we should expect some efficiency from the law. Instead, what do we get? In capital charges especially? Methods as antique as that ghastly relic, the black cap, as inexcusable as the gallows on which, after the polite burlesque of prayers, the last scene of vengeance is enacted." Breathlessly, Paul rushed on. "It's time

92

for a newer, better system, yet you want things never to change, to remain exactly as they were 'in the good old days.' Maybe you'd like to go back even further, to the feudal system, when, incidentally, trial by jury began. Well, you're entitled to your views. But, at the same time, you're the representative of the people, you're my representative in Parliament. Even if you don't believe the statement I gave you it's your duty to see that it gets a proper hearing. If you don't, I'll go out myself and shout it in the public square."

Suddenly realizing what he was saying, Paul stopped short. His legs turned weak and he sat down, covering his eyes with his hand. In the long silence which followed he dared not look at Birley. He felt that he had utterly destroyed his chance of success.

But he was wrong. While obsequious pleading left him unaffected, Birley could be genuinely won by a display of spirit. He admired courage and often took a liking to those who, in his own phrase, "could speak up to him." He did feel, also, that there might be something in this strange, unpleasant case. Moreover, in questioning his sense of duty, Paul had touched him on the raw. Birley was only too conscious that his increasing self-indulgence and the pattern of life laid down for him by his autocratic wife, had in these later years occasionally made him shirk the more disagreeable functions of his office.

He took a few paces up and down the carpet until his temper should cool. Then he said:

"You youngsters seem to think that you have all the virtues. That's your trouble. You can't see good in anyone else. Now I don't set up as a plaster saint. But in spite of all the adjectives you've thrown at me I do stand for some things. And one of them is fair play. Now I don't like this business of yours one little bit. But, by heavens, I won't fight shy of it on that account. I'll take it and I'll bring it to the open, right on the floor of the House of

Commons. Yes, by the Almighty, I give you my solemn oath, I'll land it right into the lap of the Secretary for State himself."

Paul raised his eyes. So unexpected was this declamation, so staggering the victory, he felt the room spin dizzily about him. He tried to stammer out his thanks but his lips would not move, the room whirled faster than ever.

"In the name of God!" Birley hastily tugged a large travelling flask from his pocket, bent over and forced some of the spirit between Paul's teeth. "There! That's better. Keep your head down."

He stood watching the colour come back to Paul's cheeks with a new air of patronage, meanwhile treating himself to a series of generous nips from the flask. The intensity of Paul's reaction dispelled the last of his anger, restored to him a comfortable sense of his own authority. And later on, when he had cleared up this nonsense about injustice, what a good story it would make at the Club! — "collapsed at my feet, the young idiot," he heard himself say. But time was getting on.

"Are you all right now? My train leaves at eight o'clock."

Paul got to his feet, blindly accepted the hand which Birley held out to him, and a few minutes later was in the street, with a singing in his ears, and even wilder singing in his heart.

# Chapter 16

NEXT day, Paul left an order with the corner news stand for the Wortley *Courier*, to be delivered to him every afternoon. This paper reported verbatim the previous day's proceedings in the House of Commons. And although he knew there could be no immediate result — in the press of Parliamentary business Birley must await his opportunity — Paul read it eagerly every evening after returning from his work.

Buoyed by hope, he faced up to his present circumstances and cheerfully made the best of them. At his lodgings he widened his nodding acquaintance with the only other boarder of his own age — James Crocket, the accountant's clerk. Crocket, a sedate and rather stodgy character, regular as clockwork in his habits, favouring high stiff collars and made-up bow ties, was caution itself in returning Paul's advances; but one Saturday morning, as they came out of their rooms together, he speculatively produced two tickets from his pocket-book.

"Would you care to have these? I got them from the governor. He's a Fellow of the Society."

Paul examined the tickets.

"Don't you want them for yourself?"

"My young lady isn't well," Crocket answered, "so unfortunately we can't go. It's very nice. The public isn't admitted Sundays — only the Fellows and their friends."

Unwilling to hurt Crocket's feelings, Paul accepted the tickets with a word of thanks and dashed off to the store. In his change of mood he found himself playing without boredom. From time to time he gazed at Lena Andersen across the aisle, trying to break through the barrier of her reserve. It was not by any means an easy matter — lately, following that period when she had spoken to him more freely, her earlier reticence seemed to have returned and sometimes, in her eyes, there was a stubborn, questioning pain. It hurt him, this apparent withdrawal from the friendship he offered and, at lunch time one day — it was Saturday — a sudden impulse took hold of him.

"Lena," he exclaimed, making his tone especially light. "Why don't you and I take a small outing to ourselves . . . tomorrow afternoon?"

As she did not answer he continued: "A chap in my digs gave

me two privilege tickets for the Botanical Gardens. It won't be wildly exciting, but it might break the monotony of our young lives."

Her expression had changed perceptibly, and for a moment she stood very still.

"What is it?" Puzzled and vexed, he attempted a joke. "Afraid the orchids will bite you?"

She smiled faintly. But her stiff facial muscles barely relaxed and that look of fear, a fear of the world and of human beings, remained in her eyes.

"It's very kind of you," she said, with her head averted. "I don't often go out. . . ."

He could not understand her confusion, so completely out of proportion to his casual invitation. And the store was filling up again.

"Think it over," he said, swinging the piano stool round to the keyboard. "You can let me know if you'd like to come."

Lena went slowly back to her counter, strangely excited. During these past six months, since coming to Wortley, she had not once encouraged or accepted the slightest attention from any man. There had been difficulties, of course, unpleasant ones, too. Harris, for instance, had pestered her when she had first come to the Bonanza, but her rigid indifference had gradually shaken him off. Then, not infrequently, she was accosted and followed in the streets as, like a young Juno, she strode home in the evenings — occasions which caused her a sickening revival of her dread, making her hasten on, with a rigid, frozen face. But this, today, was altogether different, perhaps on that account more likely to be dangerous. Had she not made for herself a rule of life, placed upon her emotions an inflexible restraint?

And yet, as the afternoon wore on, she told herself that there could be no great harm in accepting Paul's invitation. Obviously it meant nothing to him — for that matter his attitude towards her was invariably no more than frank and friendly — he had not once given her an intimate glance, had never even touched her hand. Oh, she must not carry to excess a resolution taken under great stress and anguish of mind. When business slackened and she had an opportunity, she crossed the aisle and told him she would be glad to go, if he could call for her at two o'clock.

Thus, after lunch, on the following day, which was fine and sunny, Paul found himself strolling along Ware Place. The locality, though near the store, was quiet and respectable. Many of the tall soot-stained houses had painted window boxes, a feature which brightened up the old-fashioned street. As he reached No. 61 the door opened and Lena, wearing a dark Sunday coat and hat, come down the short flagged path between the green iron railings to the street. In the doorway, behind, was the elderly woman he had seen that evening outside the store and who, after a moment, seemed suddenly to decide to come out to the pavement and make herself known to Paul.

"I'm Mrs. Hanley." She smiled, holding out a hand crippled by arthritis. "I've heard about you from Lena."

She was about fifty, grey-haired, of less than medium stature, and so bent by rheumatism she had to tilt her head back to look at Paul. Despite her stiffness, she had a brisk and cheerful air, enhanced by the bird-like brightness of her eyes.

"I'm told you are a great musician," she remarked, still searching his face with those bright eyes.

Paul laughed outright.

"I pound the piano a little. I'm no more a musician than the organ grinder who turns the handle of a hurdy-gurdy."

"Anyway, I'm glad you're taking Lena out. She doesn't get about half enough. I don't want to keep you — just wanted to say 'How do you do.'" As though satisfied, Mrs. Hanley withdrew her gaze from Paul and gave Lena a tender, encouraging smile. "Have a good time."

She hobbled back to the house, helping herself up the steps by the railings.

When the door closed, Paul and Lena set out together. The red tram took them along Ware Street — steeped in Sunday quiet — across Leonard Square and out into the suburban grandeur of Garland Road, where red brick villas stood behind banks of laurels and prickly monkey-puzzle trees. The Botanical Gardens lay on the outskirts of this district, and at the terminus they descended and entered the big ornamental gates.

"Might be worse." Paul smiled to Lena, after a brisk survey of the pleasant rolling lawns, the avenue of shapely chestnut trees leading to a distant lake, and the numerous ornamental green-houses spaced within the extensive domain. "There won't be much to see outside this time of year, but let's take a walk before we do the green-houses. Incidentally, Lena, may I tell you that today you are looking extremely nice."

She made no answer to this casual compliment. Yet it was perfectly true, and he had been conscious of it ever since she had appeared, just as he was conscious now of the interested glances which she attracted from the people who passed them as they strolled towards the lake. He had never seen her in anything but her uniform and her worn everyday coat, never properly realized what natural grace and individuality she possessed. She was a different person today — so unusual, too, with her warm complexion and thick honey-coloured hair, her graceful figure and easy carriage. Her eyes, which he had never observed before in clear daylight, were of a dark, flecked hazel. Most striking of all was the complete unawareness of her manner, a simplicity of bearing and expression which was both dignified and touching. A sudden curiosity to know more of her took hold of him.

"Tell me about yourself, Lena . . . about your family . . . your home."

A moment passed, then, gazing ahead towards the silver shimmer of the lake, between the tall leafless trees, in a few brief phrases she told him that she had been born in the East coast fishing town of Sleescale — probably her Swedish forebears had settled there many years before. Her father, widowed when she was a child of seven, had been part owner of a herring trawler and, as such, he had shared in all the misfortunes of a waning industry. The seasons grew gradually worse and sometimes the boats would bring in only a few crans between them. But for the produce of their farm they would often have fared badly and this small property, set on a stony headland overlooking the North Sea, proved in the end insufficient to hold the family together. When the father died her two brothers sailed to seek their fortune on the great wheat plains of Manitoba — and they had now succeeded in acquiring a promising tract of land in Canada. While she, before they left, had secured a satisfactory position, relieving any anxiety they might have felt on her behalf. At the age of eighteen she had come to the resort town of Astbury, which lay some twenty miles east of Wortley, to work in the reception office of the County Arms Hotel.

There was a pause when she concluded.

"So you are the only one of your family left?"

She inclined her head.

"Didn't you like Astbury?" Paul asked, after a moment.

"Very much."

"But you left?"

"Yes."

There was a definite pause. He felt that she could have told him more, a great deal more, but she did not do so.

"Then you came to live with Mrs. Hanley?"

"Yes." She turned and looked at him directly with an unusual depth of feeling in her wide-pupilled eyes. "I can't tell you how good she has been to me."

99

"Does she rent out rooms?"

"Not really. But she lets me have two at the top of the house. Her husband is away at sea a good deal — he's chief engineer in a tanker."

It seemed odd that she should abandon a promising career as hotel receptionist in favour of her present position in a cheap cafeteria. Yet that was her affair, and since, despite the frankness of her gaze, her manner had become withdrawn, he relinquished the subject and, rising, escorted her towards the glass-houses where, tier upon tier, above the thick steam pipes in the warm, humid air, masses of exotic blossoms were banked.

As they went round the beautiful collection, Paul, who had no more than a cursory interest, was struck by the reaction of his companion. For once the cloud of sadness that hung over her was lifted. Taken out of herself, she began to talk with animation and an unsuspected delicacy of feeling. She noticed many things which escaped his observation, and what she lacked in learning she made up for in common sense. Her appreciation was natural, without affectation. When they stood before a young orange tree in the arboretum which bore both fruit and blossoms, she gazed at it in silence, with an unguarded air of wistfulness and wonder as though its fragrant beauty had pierced her through and through. It seemed as if she could not bear to leave that lovely tree. Watching her, he saw two tears form like crystal beads beneath her lashes. Unexpectedly, his heart swelled and he too became silent.

They had tea in the Japanese pagoda which served as a restaurant. It was a draughty little place, full of chilly bamboo, the tea was weak and tepid, the seed-cake fit only for the sparrows which hopped expectantly about their feet. But their sense of comradeship loosened their tongues, made them forget the inadequacies of the meal. She was a restful companion, a sympathetic listener, ready to be interested in the things that interested him, and always with a sensible remark which showed him that she had understood his meaning.

"You haven't asked why I'm at the Bonanza." he spoke suddenly, unexpectedly, after a pause, "Perhaps you think that's where I belong?"

"No," she answered, with downcast gaze, and added: "I imagine you have a reason for being there."

"I have."

She raised her eyes.

"Some kind of trouble?"

He nodded.

"I hope it's going to be all right," she said in a low voice.

Something in the simple words touched him. Her profile, serene and sad, like that of a young Madonna, her lashes casting a soft shadow upon her cheek, was lit by the lingering twilight.

Presently they left the Gardens and set out on the journey back to Ware Place. Now Lena's expression had grown more pensive, she seemed to be debating some question in her mind. Once or twice she glanced at him as though about to speak. But no words passed her lips.

He did not speak either for, on his part also, he was conscious of a return to reality. Outside Mrs. Hanley's house he drew up and held out his hand.

"It's been a wonderful afternoon," she said slowly. "I enjoyed it very much. Thank you for taking me."

There was an interval during which her glance travelled indecisively towards the windows. He wondered if she were about to ask him to come in. But she did not do so. The silence became oppressive, and still she hesitated, her eyes searching his face, her breath coming faster as though that inner desire to communicate with him had suddenly become intense.

"Paul . . . " It was the first time she had used his Christian name.

"Yes?"

She glanced at him, then away, affected by a painful tenseness, an actual physical distress.

"Oh, it doesn't matter. Never mind."

Whatever it was that she wished to say, she simply could not say it. Instead, hurriedly, she murmured:

"Goodnight."

Then she turned and walked quickly up the flagged path, between the railings, to the house.

Paul stood for a moment, even after the door had closed, perplexed by this disappointing ending to the afternoon, a little depressed, and vaguely disturbed. At last he moved off, retracing his steps through the quiet Sunday streets.

It was about six o'clock when he got back to his lodgings. Upstairs, in his room, the *Sunday Courier* lay upon the table and, when he had lit the gas and washed, he opened it with his usual anticipation.

At first he thought he had again drawn blank. But, at the foot of the last column, his eye was caught by the name he had been seeking. It leapt at him from the printed page. His heart turned over with a great joyful throb then, as his eyes dimmed, it slowly sank, like lead, within him.

The paragraph was quite short.

In the House of Commons, Mr. George Birley (Wortley, C.) raised the question of the case of Rees Mathry now undergoing a term of life imprisonment in Stoneheath Prison. Was it not a fact, asked the right honourable gentleman, that the new evidence which he had brought forward might demand a reconsideration of the case? Moreover, in view of the fact that Mathry had already served fifteen years in prison was the man not now due to be pardoned?

Replying, Sir Walter Hamilton (Secretary of State)

stated that the answer to both questions was in the nega-
tive. In the first place, having carefully considered the right
honourable gentleman's submissions, he saw no reason whatsoever to interfere with the normal processes of justice, and
in the second, the prison record of the man Mathry was
so bad, involving several floggings for flagrant insubordi-
nation, he had thereby forfeited any right to pardon. The
matter should be considered as finally and completely
closed.

Paul laid the newspaper on the table. He did not look up as
Mrs. Coppin came into the room, gave him a swift glance, placed
a special delivery letter on his plate. It had just come in.

Paul opened the letter, read it through steadily. It was from
George Birley, amplifying and confirming the statement in the
*Courier*. Birley had kept his word, had done everything in his
power, only to be met by an unconditional refusal. Further action, he wrote, would be utterly useless. He softened the blow as
best he could, urged "his young friend" to put the whole unhappy affair out of his head forever. It was a good letter,
well-meaning and unquestionably kindly. It nearly broke Paul's
heart.

# Chapter 17

NEXT morning, after a sleepless night, Paul automatically drank
a cup of coffee, then passed through the slushy streets to the
Bonanza where he sat at the piano and began doggedly to hammer out cheap music. The white lights, which in bad weather
were kept on continuously in the store, dazzled his heavy eyes

but he noticed a bunch of marigolds standing on his piano, four or five yellow flowers in a small earthenware jar — Lena, obviously, had bought them and placed them there.

Such was Paul's bitterness he made no acknowledgement of this modest reminder of their outing, nor could he guess how long Lena had struggled with herself before she made it. But when she brought his lunch he mumbled a few words of thanks.

His manner troubled her and, after a moment, she forced herself to look at him directly.

"Has anything gone wrong?"

"Yes," he answered, in a strained voice. "Everything."

At that point, before she could question him further, she was called back to the cafeteria. As she moved away, Paul caught Harris watching out of the corner of his eye, making play with the quill toothpick. Presently the manager strolled over, with an odd expression, a mixture of malice and hostility. His tone was conversational.

"So you and the lady friend made a little expedition yesterday?"

"Expedition?" Paul's eyebrows contracted.

"Sure. The girls told me you was out together. Though I must say it surprised me." Something between a sneer and a smirk spread over Harris's face. He leaned over the piano. "I thought I'd warned you about Andersen. Don't you know what we all know?"

Paul did not answer.

"Don't you know she had a child? And not married, either. Yes, a little bastard, that was deaf and dumb, and died in some kind of a fit — if you can believe it. Quite romantic! Talk it over, next time you go gadding out with her. She might give you the details while you're holding hands."

In the pause which followed the sneer became predominant,

104

then Harris nodded meaningly and, with the toothpick cocked between his teeth, walked away.

Paul remained perfectly still, eyes fixed on the manager's retreating back. Oh, heaven, what a dirty slimy beast. So that was the reason of Lena's fits of sadness. Poor girl! He could not have believed it of her. Pity flowed into his heart, yet this pity was strangely cold, and somehow it quenched the small warm flame that had been kindled there. All the puritan in him, the sabbatarian strain that was the product of his upbringing was jarred and outraged by this revelation. He could not but feel that, with her quiet expression, her virginal serenity, she had imposed on him. To have kept silent upon such a matter was surely the limit of deception. He turned his face away, deliberately avoiding her eyes. God, was there no end to the misery of this day?

That afternoon, as he sat plugging his way through the latest tango, wave after wave of bitterness swept over him. Poor Swann had been right — all hope of official help was futile, he must see this thing through on his own. And, by heaven, he would see it through. His jaw set with nervous intensity. He was not defeated. He had only begun to fight. Whatever the risk, he must make a fresh approach to Burt — now she represented his only chance. If the authorities had rapped Mark Boulia over the knuckles, they had no grounds for doing so with Burt. It was just possible that she had not been warned.

In the evening he went straight back to his lodging, took a plain paper pad and an envelope, and wrote:

DEAR LOUISA,

I was very upset at missing our previous engagement but it was not my fault. I hope you forgive me for since we met I've been thinking of you every day. That being so, will you meet me next Wednesday at the Oak? My friend won't be with me. Be there for sure Louisa, round about seven o'clock. Looking forward to the pleasure of your society, and assuring you that I won't disappoint you as I unavoidably did the last time.

I am,

Yours,

PAUL

Two days later he received this reply:

DEAR SIR,

I would like to meet you only be careful and don't come round the gardin nor the back door no mores. Just be at the same place as arranged and I will try and be there. With my best respecks no more no less at the present time.

L. B.

A stifled cry of satisfaction rose to Paul's lips. Burt was still unsuspecting, the opportunity remained open to him. He could scarcely wait for Wednesday to come. During the past forty-eight hours he had worried constantly lest Birley's action might compromise him further with the authorities. Now, with a sense of relief, he felt convinced that the insignificant paragraph in the *Courier* relating to his father had passed altogether unnoticed in Wortley.

In this belief, unfortunately, he was quite mistaken.

# Chapter 18

THAT same morning, at the precise moment when Paul received Burt's letter, a man of forty-five, slightly portly, but with the clean-cut features of an actor, stood after breakfast in the morning room of his house, gazing through the window towards the wide lawn cut with ornamental flower beds and flanked by rhododendron shrubberies. From the adjoining room came the chatter of his two daughters as they made ready for the St. Winifred's School pony show and, occasionally, in a lower key, interposing some gay remark, the beloved voice of his wife, Catharine. But despite these cheerful signs of family unity, Sir Matthew Sprott's mood was irritable.

The entry of a maidservant who began silently to clear the well-appointed table, disturbed his train of thought, and with that testy glance which he reserved for underlings, he went out into the hall. Here the little party stood ready, his wife pulling on her long gloves, looking particularly charming in a little fur toque with a necklet of the same soft brown fur, the girls neat and natty in jodhpurs and velvet riding caps, carrying the gold mounted switches he had given them last Christmas. The elder was sixteen now, slim, dark and serene like her mother, while the younger, who favoured him, with her short plump figure and ruddy colouring, had only just turned twelve.

His expression lightened as his two children pressed about him, urging him to accompany them, while his wife, watching the scene with a quiet smile, added persuasively:

"It would do you good, dear. You've been too hard at it lately."

She was a slender, delicate woman with a pale oval face, and an expression of great sweetness. At forty, with her fine face bones and unthickened figure, she still looked girlish, but she had the fragile air of one who, all her life, had struggled constantly with ill health. Her pure white skin bore a transparent texture. Her fingers were long and tapering.

Gazing at her with unconcealed affection, Sprott hesitated, smoothing his lips with his forefinger — a habitual gesture. Then he softened his refusal with a joke.

"Who is to earn the pennies if I go gallivanting off with you?"

He opened the front door for them. The closed car was already waiting in the drive with Banks, the chauffeur, in attendance. Soon they were comfortably settled, tucked in with the rug. When they moved off Catharine turned to wave to him through the back window of the limousine.

Slowly, he came back through the library, towards his study, frowning a little, pausing to stare absently at the finest of his pictures. It was a rich and commodious home — over the past ten years he had set out deliberately, guided by his wife's inherent good taste, to achieve the highest in refinement and luxury. He prized his fine things, the petit point chairs, the Aubusson rugs, the Rodin and Maillol bronzes, his two Constable landscapes. These material possessions were, so unmistakably, the proof of his success.

He had risen, solely by his own efforts, from the humblest and most contemptible stratum of society — in his own phrase "from less than nothing." An orphan child, he had been brought up by an aunt, a gaunt woman who, in shawl and wooden clogs, begrimed every day with coal dust, eked out an existence as a pithead screener in the impoverished colliery district of Gadshill, near Nottingham. From the beginning, despite these crushing surroundings, the squalor of the one-room dwelling in the miners' row, the kicks and cuffs bestowed upon him, Matthew Sprott had been dominated by one desire — to succeed. The motto "I will get on, get on, get on," was engraved, indelibly upon his heart.

As in the evolution of most self-made men there was, in his early rise, the usual pattern of feverish application and fortunate chance. He was a clever lad, and the Gadshill schoolmaster, a man who loved the classics, gave him education at nights, free. At fourteen, rather than enter the pit, he ran away to Wortley, became office boy, then clerk, in the legal printing and stationery firm of Marsden & Company. Here he got his first view of the machinery of the courts; spurred by that impressive sight, in his spare time he studied hard, and was given the opportunity to enter the office of old Thomas Hailey, a reputable county solicitor, as an articled clerk.

Sprott chose the law, not from predilection, not because he felt himself morally adapted for it, but because he sensed it offered ultimately the likeliest chance to power. "I will get on, get on, get on," the words throbbed endlessly, like whirling wheels, within his brain. He set out to make himself indispensable to his aged principal. He had, of course, no notion whatsoever of continuing in Hailey's office as a mere assistant, and at the end of five years, when he passed the final examination of the Law Society, he walked out of the office and set up for himself, leaving in the lurch his principal, who was in poor health and quite dependent upon him. What did that matter? Matthew Sprott was the new Under Sheriff of Wortley.

He was now a law agent, practicing, it is true, in the lowest court, charged only with the prosecution of minor crimes, holding inquiries in cases of suspicious deaths, attending upon the judges at assizes, executioning writs, preparing the panel of jurors and ensuring the safe custody of prisoners — an inferior position, yet allied to the Crown, which was the first step towards his main ambition. While carrying out his official duties with exemplary vigour he privately continued his studies in civil, public, and constitutional law. When he was ready, and had scraped together the requisite fee, he applied to have his name removed from the Roll of Solicitors, entered the Inner Temple and was finally called to the bar.

He was not blind to the magnitude of the task he had undertaken. He had little money and few connections and for many months he haunted the courts, a briefless advocate. Then a registrar's appointment at the Inns of Court was offered him. He accepted it, but only as a stopgap, a springboard from which to make himself useful to those in power. Gradually he became

109

known as a man of intelligence and immense industry, with a specialized knowledge of criminal law. Better still, he was a good speaker, with a gift of repartee, cutting or jovial, as the occasion demanded, and a notable power, amounting almost to genius, of playing upon the emotions of the jury. In 1916, when the parliamentary elections came round he enlisted under the banners of the local Conservative candidate, Sir Henry Longden, sparing no effort, declaiming from the hustings at all hours. When Longden was elected, Sprott presently received his reward. He was appointed by the Crown Recorder to the City of Wortley.

Back again in his native county, though his salary was modest, his jurisdiction as principal legal officer was vastly increased. And for five years Sprott slaved in Wortley: to such purpose that at the quarter sessions he became a terror to the debtors, delinquents, and wrong-doers of the city. He cultivated, assiduously, the people who could be of use to him — and, indeed, when it suited him he could be the best company in the world. Yet, despite all his efforts, preferment did not come to him. He had married during this period and often his wife was hard pressed to keep him from despair. Would he never "get on, get on, get on?"

Suddenly, when he seemed doomed to a life of provincial officialdom, there occurred a heaven-sent opportunity. A murder case, which had excited the popular interest, was due for trial at the County Assizes and, on the eve of the opening date, the distinguished counsel briefed by the Director of Public Prosecution was stricken with a serious fever. All other counsel on the circuit were engaged. Rather than postpone the trial, it was decided to entrust the conduct of the Crown case to Matthew Sprott.

This was the turning point of his career. While that inner voice whispered to him exultantly: "Get on, get on, get on . . . this, at last, is your chance," he flung himself, with every weapon at his

110

command, into the prosecution of Rees Mathry. His intention was to focus attention upon his own powers, to stun, to over-whelm with his brilliance, come what may, to convict the pris-oner. And he succeeded.

Before eight months had passed he had resigned his recorder-ship and, while retaining his provincial home — an easy matter considering the admirable express railway service between Wortley and London — gone into chambers in the Temple. Two years later he took silk, and partly because of his early training, partly also because of his remarkable forensic skill, he was more and more frequently briefed in capital charges as Prosecutor for the Crown, a position which he filled so admirably that, in 1933, he received a knighthood. Now, at forty-five, comparatively young and full of energy, his ambition further swollen by success, he felt himself poised, as it were, for even higher flights. His policy of maintaining his residence in Wortley had borne fruit — he had been asked to stand as Conservative candidate for the city, replacing George Birley — a safe seat — at the coming elec-tion. Once in the House, the Attorney Generalship was not far away. And then, in time, might he not become Lord Chief Jus-tice, perhaps even in the end achieve the highest pinnacle of all — Lord High Chancellor, sitting in the House of Lords, the su-preme legal officer in the realm.

Of course, in such a homeric upward struggle it had been es-sential to employ a certain ruthlessness. Sprott had no illusions regarding the qualities necessary for success — life was a stern battle wherein only the fittest could survive. As authority came to him his frown grew hard and heavy, his tongue cut like a lash. Obliged to ingratiate himself, at all costs, in high political circles, he had learned, to a nicety, when to discard a person who had served his purpose, when to pass a man whom he had wheedled and flattered, with an absent stare. And above everything, he had acquired the faculty of always maintaining himself one pace ahead of his rivals, constantly proving his worth, demonstrating his ability, by a formidable display of power.

Naturally, he had made enemies and he was not unaware of the reputation he had gradually acquired. It was said of him that he was a timeserver and a toady to the great, that with every upward step he had planted his foot squarely in the face of the man who stood beneath him. He was accused of having done certain people serious injury. In particular it was whispered that in the exercise of his official duties as Prosecutor for the Crown he brought to bear too strongly his great native talents for directing the course of justice.

Here, as he moved restlessly about his study, the prosecutor's frown deepened. He admitted at last the cause of his present irritation. Yes, that question raised so suddenly in the House of Commons had occasioned him the bitterest chagrin. Of course George Birley was a fool, and he had been severely reprimanded by the party leaders. Moreover the Secretary of State had at the very outset quashed the wretched affair with the utmost firmness. Nevertheless, the implications had been in the highest degree disagreeable. Within a restricted circle there had been considerable comment — the thing had even come to the ears of his dear wife, causing her to question him, mildly, the other evening when they were alone together.

Although not given to oaths, Sprott swore softly under his breath. The only truly disinterested passion in his life was his affection for his family, especially for his wife. She had not brought him money or position, being no more than the daughter of a Wortley doctor, and in marrying her for love he had been for once inconsistent to his own behaviour pattern. Yet her gentle companionship, the sustaining admiration and pervading sweetness of disposition had more than rewarded him. He had no friends and the knowledge that he stood well with her, that she was always on his side, had sustained him in many a difficulty. It was the rankling mistrust that his reputation might perhaps suffer some slight slur in her eyes which at this moment finally decided him.

With a decisive gesture he took up the telephone, and put through a call to Police Headquarters at Wortley Central 1234.

# Chapter 19

TEN minutes later Chief Constable Dale put on his heavy silver-braided uniform coat and, in answer to the summons, set out across the Park towards Grove Quadrant.

Rather than take his official car he preferred to walk. The deference which was accorded to him when he traversed the West End — the brisk salutes of his own officers, the respectful glances, even the scurry of activity which the mere sight of his figure produced amongst the Park sweepers — in a grim way always gratified him.

At Sprott's house in the Quadrant he was shown, by an elderly maid in dark mauve uniform, into the small private study on the right of the hall. The woman told him, in the hushed voice used by superior servants, that Sir Matthew would see him immediately. Dale, in reply, gave her a brief nod. He well knew he would be made to wait, and he did not like it.

He eased himself into a leather armchair and, resting his portfolio on his knees, gazed around the room, which was panelled in natural pine, thickly carpeted, lined by many books in finely tooled bindings. With a twinge of envy he reflected that he might have done as well, even better, if he'd only had the schooling. As things were he had to put his pride in his pocket — he couldn't quarrel with his bread and butter.

113

"Ah, there you are, Dale." Sprott entered the room, extending his warm hand, showing no trace of the ill-humor which had recently affected him. "Can I offer you some refreshment?"

"No thank you, Sir Matthew."

Sprott sat down.

"You're well, I hope."

"Quite well."

"Good." The public prosecutor paused for a moment and stroked his lip. "Dale . . . did you notice that bit of nonsense in the House . . . about the Mathry case?"

Dale was startled. But he concealed his surprise.

"I did notice it, Sir Matthew."

"Of course the whole thing is absurd . . . political mudslinging. Still," Sprott shook his head, "we have to watch out these days that none of it sticks to us."

Dale slowly revolved his heavy uniform cap in his huge hands, still somewhat at a loss.

Sprott continued to meditate.

"That young fool . . . the son . . . what's the name again . . . Mathry . . . is he still in the city?"

Dale shifted his eyes and contemplated his thick-soled boots.

"He's still here. We've had our eye on him for some time."

"Yes," said Sprott. "He seems a troublesome sort. Oh, you know what I mean — the type that follows you around, tries to see you at all hours, shoves the usual petitions into your hands . . . the complete crank with a grievance. As if we weren't used to it."

There was a curious pause. Then, tapping his front teeth thoughtfully, Sprott added:

"The question is . . . what to do about him."

For a full minute the Chief Constable held his tongue. He perceived now why the prosecutor had telephoned to him and

114

a curious sensation of doubt, touched by a vague malice, took hold of him. Deliberately, he raised his eyes.

"Do you wish to prefer a charge against him?"

"By no means," Sprott protested. "After all, misguided though he may be, this young man is scarcely a criminal. And we must be merciful, Dale. Mercy, it is twice blessed, it falleth like the gentle dew upon the plain beneath. I hope I am quoting correctly." He looked straight at the Chief Constable. "However, it might be that you could induce our misguided young friend to leave this fair city of Wortley."

"I've already told him to clear out."

"Words, my dear Adam, as I know to my cost, mean so very little. I make no suggestions whatsoever. Nevertheless, you may find it possible, in your own way, to bring him to a more reasonable frame of mind."

Sprott rose to his feet and, with his back to the fireplace, authoritatively addressed the Chief Constable.

"I don't wish you to misunderstand me, Dale. I have taken the trouble, despite the immense amount of work upon my desk, to go through the records of the Mathry case."

"Ah!" thought Dale to himself with that same strange interior tremor.

"We have nothing to reproach ourselves with, simply nothing. We stand confirmed in the highest quarters. Nevertheless, the situation presents certain dangers. At the present time, with elections, both civic and national, falling due in a few months, the merest suggestion, no matter how unfounded, of a miscarriage of justice would be serious for all concerned. You know that I am standing for Parliament in the Conservative interest with, I trust, reasonable hopes of success. But my concern is not a selfish one. I am thinking not simply of my own future *and yours* . . . the effect on the people at this juncture, if such a diabolical falsehood were nursed into a scandal by mischievous parties, would be to undermine confidence in the whole judiciary, and in the government as well. That is why it is essential for this idiotic affair to be suppressed."

When he had concluded, Sprott again directed towards the Chief Constable that fixed and penetrating regard, then he held out his hand to terminate the interview. As Dale stepped out on the broad pavement of the Quadrant, there was no longer a flickering question in his mind. Somehow the thought had changed its form, was now fixed, a thorn piercing his natural honesty. With a frigid face he muttered stubbornly to himself:

"There can't . . . no, there can't be anything in it."

Yet his voice rang bleakly in his ears, and with his natural combativeness aroused, he resolved to temper Sprott's injunctions. He would watch young Mathry, but would not molest him unless he contravened the law.

# Chapter 20

THE night of Wednesday came dank and dark, with a cold drizzling rain. As he set out for Porlock Hill the tension of Paul's mind and body gave to his movements a deceptive calm. He reached the Royal Oak shortly after seven, and having first surveyed the surroundings of the tavern, he crossed the street and peered through an uncurtained window of the saloon. Everything appeared normal, and with a quick movement, he went inside, advanced to the table Burt usually occupied, and sat down.

He glanced round. The place was about half full — two domestic servants were talking and tittering with their young men, a middle-aged married couple sat drinking beer in stolid silence, two old cabbies were playing dominoes, surrounded by their watching cronies, a square-headed man in a dark suit who looked like a butler was absorbed in a pink sporting paper. Paul decided he had nothing to worry about — no one was paying the least attention to him.

Then, as his eyes returned to the door, he saw Burt come in and walk towards him.

He got to his feet, holding out his hand in welcome.

"Louisa!" he exclaimed. "It's good to see you again."

She gave him a restrained smile, and a ladylike pressure of her gloved fingers, then arranged herself affectedly at the table. He noticed that she was rather more done up than before, with a string of blue glass beads round her neck and an embroidered handkerchief, smelling strongly of scent, tucked under the bangle on her wrist.

"I didn't ought to have came," she remarked reproachfully. "After the way you disappointed me before. I believe you was out with another young lady."

"No, indeed," he protested. "You're the one I'm interested in."

"So you say. You fellas is all alike." She patted the puffs of hair over her ears, and nodded an intimate greeting to the waiter. "The usual, Jack. Bring the bottle."

Paul leaned forward. "The difference is that I'm serious." He forced an admiring smile. "You look a treat tonight."

"Get away with you!" Flattered out of her pique, she spoke almost archly and took a sip of her gin. Then she looked at him sideways.

"Don't think I don't know what you're after. But I'm a respectable girl."

"That's why I'm attracted to you."

"Mind you, I'm no prue though I am a lady. If I like a fella I would go with him. Provided he saw me prop'ly. You do have a regular job, don't you?"

"You bet I have. And you know I'm gone on you." He pressed his knee against her leg under the table.

"So that's it." She giggled unexpectedly. "Well . . . a little of wot you fancy does you good. I know a place we could go . . . maybe later. A sort of hotel, very classy, we could have the big room. But not for all night, mind you. I have to be back by eleven."

"Of course," he agreed. "By the way, I hope you had no difficulty in getting here?"

She straightened.

"What makes you say that?"

"Why, you mentioned it yourself in your letter . . . about being careful."

"Yes . . . so I did." She sat back and took another drink. "It's just that the housekeep . . . that Mr. Oswald is shocking particular about some things. He's very high principled. You've surely heard of him? One of the biggest charity contributors in Wortley. Gives hunders and hunders away to the hospitals every year, and in the winter puts up free coffee stalls for nothing . . . they call it the Silver King Canteen. He's a toff all right for all he's so strick. And he's always treated me like a lady, else I wouldn't have stopped."

"Then you've been there some time?"

She nodded complacently.

"I wasn't more nor eighteen when they took me in. You don't believe me?" she inquired, archly crossing her plump knees and arranging her skirt.

"Of course." He wondered if she were lying about her age. "It's just that you look so young."

"I do, don't I."

"I'm surprised you never married."

Under his flattery she gave a conceited little smirk.

"The Oswalds would like me to. It's a fact. They keeps on

118

saying what a good thing if I got married and settled down with somebodies, say like Frank their handyman, or Joe Davies the milk roundsman. Oh, they're steady fellas all right but both of them's over fifty. Now can you imagine me and them? Well, I might one of these days, you never can tell. But at the present time, catch me! I like a bit of fun. Do you blame me?"

"No, no," he agreed, squeezing her hand. The pattern he had suspected was emerging clearly: the philanthropic Oswalds had befriended this unfortunate and erratic girl, had done their best to keep her on a steady course, even to the point of suggesting marriage with a sober and reliable man. But despite all this, there existed in her mind a deep-rooted grievance, a grudge against life. And suddenly he saw how he could use this to his advantage, to secure the very thing he sought. Controlling the excitement that rose within him he murmured: "It seems odd to me that anyone as smart as you shouldn't have a better job."

"You're right," she nodded sulkily. "Mind you, I wouldn't of took up the domestic, that is the housekeeping line except that I was talked into it." As she spoke her self-satisfaction faded, her eyes filled with tears of self-pity. "The truth is, dearie, I've had a dirty deal. And after all I've went through."

He affected disbelief. "Nobody could have been hard on a nice girl like you."

"That's what you think. And all because I done something what was right, something noble you might call it."

Holding himself in check, he absently refilled her glass, murmured sympathetically:

"People often suffer for a good action."

"You said something there. Oh, it was right enough at first. They put me in all the papers . . . photographs and everything . . . on the front page . . . just like I was a queen."

119

While she looked at him sideways as though gauging the effect of her words, he laughed, with just the correct note of incredulity. She reacted immediately.

"So you think I'm a liar, eh? That only shows your ignorance, as to the person you're addressing. It may interest you to know that at one time . . ." she broke off.

"Ah, I knew you were joking." He smiled and shook his head.

Her face went red. She looked over her shoulder, then brought her head close across the table.

"Is it a joke to nearly get a man hung?"

"Oh, no," he exclaimed, in shocked admiration. "But you never did that?"

She nodded her head slowly, then tossed off her second gin.

"That's the very thing I done."

"Was it for murder?" he gasped.

She nodded again, with pride, holding out her glass while he tilted the bottle.

"And but for yours truly, they'd never of got him. I was the big noise in the case."

"Well!" he exclaimed in an awed tone. "You could knock me over with a feather. I never dreamed . . ."

"Let that be a lesson to you —" she sunned herself in his open adulation — "as to the lady in whose society you find yourself. And I could surprise you a lot more if I wanted."

"Go ahead then."

She gave him a sly and amorous glance.

"That would be telling, Mr. Curious. Still, I've took to you. A perfect gent if I say so to your face. And it's so long ago . . . it can't reely hurt. Well, here's how . . . chin, chin, and all the best. Now, suppose yours truly had somethink up her sleeve that could reely of blew the lid off. For instance . . . ever hear of such a thing as a green bicycle?"

"A green bicycle?"

"That's right, dearie. Bright green." She broke into a titter. "Green as grash."

"Never knew of such a thing."

"That's what they all said in court. Laughed they did, when some old bird swore he saw the man ride off on one. But *I* could of made them laugh a different tune. I knew my way around when I was a kid . . . I was always on the streets I was. *I* knew about green bicycles."

As she hesitated, Paul laughed incredulously.

"I believe you're making all this up."

"What!" She flushed indignantly. "You won't make me a liar. Just at that time there was a cycling club in Eldon, mostly made up of fellows what called themselves the Grasshoppers. And, just for swank, to go with the name, every member's bike 'ad to be a special bright green colour."

"The Grasshoppers?" He spoke with assumed indifference. "Then the man that owned the bike you speak of must have been a member of the club."

"Exactly. And a bit of a spark as well," Burt answered, with a knowing wink. "The kind that might 'ave 'ad fancy tastes . . . and a fancy sort of purse . . . say one actually made out of a human being's skin. Do I shock you?"

Paul tried desperately not to show too much interest. Surreptitiously he refilled Burt's glass.

"Indeed you do."

"Now I ask you, dearie, what kind of a person would 'ave that sort of purse?"

"A crazy person?"

"Ah, go lay an egg. What about a medical stoodent, as dissected bodies for anatomy?"

"My God," Paul exclaimed. He had never dreamed of making such a deduction, yet he saw at once that it was unmistakably correct. He recollected now that at Queens's a few of the bolder

121

anatomy students often removed portions of epidermis from the dissecting rooms and had them tanned as souvenirs.

There was a vibrant silence — Paul simply could not speak. Delighted with the effect she was producing, Burt gave a prolonged titter and took a fresh sip of gin. She was already swaying slightly on her seat.

"I could make your hair stand on end if I wanted. For instance . . . the fella they got their hooks on was married. All the girls that worked in the florist's shop where he dropped in occasional like, they knew it, including Mona — that's the young woman what got done in. Now from what I knew about *her*, I can tell you straight she'd never of got herself mixed up with a married man. She was too cute, too much out for a good match. . . . In other words the gent that she was mixed up with, what got her in trouble . . . was single. Furthermore, she'd been in trouble, in the family way, if you'll pardon the expression, for a good four months. Now the fella they accused 'ad only known her a matter of six weeks. 'E couldn't 'ave 'ad nothink to do with the condition she was in. The very thing they blamed him for was impossible."

Paul raised his hand to his eyes to mask the emotion which overwhelmed him. In a hoarse voice he muttered:

"Why . . . why was this never brought out?"

Burt laughed.

"Don't ask me. Ask them what ran the show. They 'ad a lawyer there what tied everybody in knots from first to last."

The Public Prosecutor! At every turn he was confronted by this man, this high official who, though still remaining remote, invisible, nevertheless seemed omnipresent, the crux of the mysterious case, the power which had crushed his father, ruthlessly, into the living death of Stoneheath. For the first time in his life Paul knew hatred and with a burning question on his lips he leaned towards his companion.

122

But at that precise moment a startling change came over Burt's face. Her plump cheeks turned a sickly yellow and her eyes, over Paul's shoulder, were stricken with a sudden panic.

"Excuse me." Burt spoke in faltering tones. "I've suddenly come over giddy."

"Have another drink," Paul said. "Here, let me do it."

"No . . . isn't it silly . . . I got to get out."

"No, no . . . don't let's go yet."

"I got to."

Paul bit his lip perplexedly. It was maddening to be interrupted like this, just when he had brought Burt to the point of making the most vital disclosure of all. Come what may, he must hang on to her. He bent forward, spoke in a lowered voice:

"What is it?"

"A copper."

Half-turning Paul stared at the square-headed man at the neighbouring table. Perhaps, unconsciously, he had all the time been aware of that figure in the dark suit, deeply, almost too deeply, immersed in the racing news. The man had not once, in the past twenty minutes, changed by an inch the position of the folded pink paper which half concealed his immobile face. But now, imperceptibly, he lowered it, revealing himself as Sergeant Jupp.

Paul took a grip of himself, turned back to Burt.

"I'll come along with you. It is a bit hot in here. A breath of air will put you right."

Before she could protest, he called the waiter and paid for the drinks. Nervously, stealing glances at the adjacent table, she gathered her belongings, got into her coat. At last she was ready. They stood up. Immediately, Sergeant Jupp got up too, tucking the folded pink newspaper into his pocket and, gazing at nothing with a noncommittal air, walked out of the bar before them.

Paul's nerves were jangling like a peal of bells. As he walked out with Burt, would a hand be laid once again upon his shoulder, hauling him off again to Police Headquarters on some trumped-up charge? No, by God, he would not submit to that. His eyes darted ahead. He could see the policeman standing on the pavement, waiting, facing the swing doors. Grimly, taking the wilting Burt's arm, he kept on his way.

"Just a minute."

Paul drew up, faced the sergeant, who came closer, with a blank expression.

"I've been watching you in there. You're annoying this young woman."

"You're a liar."

"Oh, am I?" he turned towards Burt. "This fellow's been interfering with you . . . hasn't he?"

There was a hollow pause. Then, with a gasp, Burt shrilled:

"Oh, he has . . . askin' me to go with him . . . and all that, when I didn't want to."

"All right. Clear out of here quick."

As Burt took to her heels Jupp gave Paul a meaning glance.

"You see. Now look here, Mathry, we're not going to run you in. But the Chief wants you to know this is your second warning and he hopes you're wise enough to take it."

Instead of relief, Paul felt a blinding anger sweep over him. This assumed indulgence was harder to bear than actual injury. He did not wait. It was useless to follow Burt now. Breathing a little quickly, he swung abruptly into the shadows and turned the corner of the street.

After crossing three minor intersections he took a side road into the busy thoroughfare of Marion Street. Here he slowed his pace and mingled with the stream of people moving along the wide pavement towards Tron Bridge and the centre of the city. Mostly they were women, slowly promenading, singly, or in pairs with linked arms, along the wide and dusty tree-lined

124

boulevards, offering their glances of invitation under the blue downpour of light which fell at long intervals from the overhead electric standards.

As he went forward, his jaw still set, recovering his breath in quick gulps, Paul's sense of outrage grew. He had escaped the immediate danger but his contact with Burt was irreparably broken. She would never recover from this scare. A savage exclamation broke from Paul's lips. The sense of being hampered, spied upon, and threatened at every turn fanned the dark embers which continually smouldered in his breast.

When he got to Poole Street he pulled off his clothes and fell, dog-tired, into bed. Would they seek him here? He did not think so. The actual occasion had passed and although it would be marked against him, he doubted if they would use it as a pretext to apprehend him. Rightly or wrongly he guessed that the purpose of the Chief Constable was still to frighten him away from Wortley. But if they did come he would not really care. He closed his eyes and slept heavily.

# Chapter 21

NEXT morning when he awoke it was to a clearer perception of what he had gained on the previous evening. Interrupted though the interview had been, he had nevertheless obtained from Burt several vital facts, of which not the least were those relating to the green bicycle and the skin purse. Reflecting deeply, Paul now realized that if the owner of the purse had been a medical student he must by this time, almost certainly, have qualified as a doctor. By checking the Medical Directory against an old list of the members of the Grasshoppers' Club it would be possible to determine his identity.

Spurred by this fresh hope, Paul jumped out of bed. It was after eight and fifteen minutes past his usual time for getting up. He shaved, dressed, rushed through his breakfast and hurried to the store. At the Bonanza he found Harris waiting for him inside the main entrance. This was unusual, the manager did not normally appear till ten.

"You're late," Harris said, stepping forward and blocking the way.

Paul looked at the big clock at the end of the store. It showed six minutes past nine. There were no customers in the shop yet, only the assistants, and most of them, including Lena, had their eyes on the manager. Lena, in particular, seemed strangely troubled.

"I'm sorry," Paul muttered. "I'm afraid I overslept."

"Don't answer me back." Harris was working himself into a temper. "Have you an excuse?"

"What for?" Paul stared at the other in dull surprise. "I'm only six minutes behind."

"I asked you if you had an excuse."

"No, I haven't."

"Then you're sacked. We've no use in this store for police suspects."

Giving Paul no opportunity to answer, he swung round and walked back to his office. As he traversed the aisle the assistants busied themselves at the counters — all but Lena, who still stood, pale and undecided, at her desk.

With a raw hurt in his breast Paul turned and went out of the store. As he walked along Ware Street he had a vague suspicion that he was being followed.

At first, in a restless fury of resentment, he strode rapidly and without purpose through the busiest thoroughfares of the city, losing himself in the crowds that thronged the pavements. Then gradually his mood grew calm and cold. Freed from the tyranny of that insufferable piano, at least he was at liberty to put his deductions of the previous evening to the test.

He stepped into a telephone booth and by consulting the directory discovered that the National Cyclists' Union had an office at 62 Leonard Street. In ten minutes he reached the building, passed under the sign of the gilded, winged wheel, and stood at the inquiry desk in the map-hung foyer.

The secretary, a middle-aged woman, received his inquiry without undue surprise, and taking a handbook from the counter, flipped the pages expertly. But her search was unproductive.

"We seem to have no present record of such a club. Was it affiliated?"

"I don't know," Paul confessed. "And it may now have been disbanded. But I do particularly want to trace it. Please help me. It's most important."

There was a pause.

"I haven't the time myself," she said. "But if it's important I might let you look over our back records. It should be listed there."

She showed him into a small annex beside the office and indicated a rack of yellow and green paper-backed books.

Left alone, Paul went through all the handbooks and annual reports for the past twenty years. This meticulous research occupied him a full three hours. There was no record whatsoever of the Grasshoppers' Club.

Discouraged, but undeterred, he reflected grimly, with all the logic he could command, if such a club had actually existed its members must undoubtedly have procured their machines from some local store. Abruptly, he left the N.C.U. and set out on a systematic tour of all the cycle agencies in the city.

But there, again and again, he was disappointed, meeting

only blank negation, indifference, ridicule, and in certain instances, actual abuse. No one had ever heard of the organization he sought and some were inclined to suspect him of playing a stupid practical joke. He had begun by thinking in high excitement that if only he could find a member of this old cycling clique who was by this time a medical practitioner, his quest was ended. Now he told himself despondently that the whole thing must be a myth, a fantasy created by Burt's disordered and perverted imagination.

At four o'clock in the afternoon, tired and cast down, he had reached the outskirts of Eldon in search of the last address on the list of cycle agencies, which proved to be a small garage bearing the name Jed Stevens. It was little more than a petrol station with two hand pumps, but outside a shed in the yard he perceived a few second-hand bicycles laid out for sale or hire. Nothing could have seemed less promising; yet after a momentary hesitation, almost automatically, he crossed over and approached a man in overalls who was hosing down the concrete pavement.

By this time the form of Paul's inquiry had become blunt, almost peremptory. But as he waited for an answer equally terse he was surprised to discover in the features of the garage proprietor a note of consideration. Without replying immediately he cut off the water at the nozzle, and looked at Paul reflectively.

"The Grasshoppers," he repeated to himself. "Come to think of it, I've heard my father speak of them."

"You have?"

"Yes. In Dad's time this was purely a cycle shop — it's since he died I've added the garage — and I believe he used to do repair jobs for a club of that name. Sturmey-Archer bicycles they used . . . all painted green."

"Then you must know who were the members."

"Not me." The proprietor smiled. "I was just a kid at the time."

128

"Surely your father kept some record . . . receipted bills . . . an address book . . . something."

"Not him. Cash over the handlebars was always his motto."

"But there must have been a list of members . . . printed minutes . . . reports of meetings. . . ."

"I very much doubt it. According to my impression, it was an informal sort of affair, made up of a group of young fellows more out for a lark than anything else, a bit of a craze you understand, and it didn't last long."

There was a pause. Raised to a peak of excitement only to be dashed down again, Paul fought off an onrush of bitterness and frustration.

"When you have time, I wish you'd look for any papers your father might have left. And if you find anything at all bearing on the club, please let me know. I'll be most grateful."

In a controlled voice he gave his name and address; then accepting a trade card which the other offered him, with a word of thanks he turned on his heel and set off for the city.

And now, fatigued by useless effort, broken with disappointment, he lost his way, and found himself unexpectedly in Grove Quadrant, a residential district given over to stately houses. Vaguely, as he trudged along, he noted the names upon the entrance pillars. The Towers, Wortley Hall, Robin Hood Manor: they all had a grand and opulent sound. Suddenly, above a letter box fixed upon an imposing double gate, his eye was caught by a small brass plate which bore simply the owner's name. It was *Sir Matthew Sprott*.

Halted, transfixed by that name, Paul stared at the shining plaque, and at the garden, the mansion and fine domain beyond, his cheeks so pale they seemed drained of blood. This was the prosecutor's home — he had come now to identify Sprott in terms of that single word: prosecutor. And in finding himself, without warning, in such close proximity to it there rushed over him, in a flood tide, all that secret sense of accusation which, fostered by Swann, already had gathered and grown within his breast.

Here was a man of paramount intelligence, a legal expert, skilled to the highest degree in the technique of deduction and elucidation. How had it come about that he had ignored evidence of the first importance — the green bicycle, the skin purse, above all, the duration of the murdered woman's pregnancy? Was the omission deliberate? Could such a one wilfully ignore facts favourable to the accused and by concentrating solely upon prejudicial evidence, playing the part of devil's advocate, use all his power and personality to crush a feeble, incompetent opposition and secure a conviction which he knew to be false? Was that the law?

At the mere thought a chaos of emotion, of rage and rancour, rose chokingly in Paul's throat. He trembled to think that, from this very entrance, the prosecutor could suddenly appear, that he might meet him face to face. All at once he wanted to escape, but his limbs were leaden, he could not move and held on to the railings for support. But at last, with a great effort, he dragged himself away, and found refuge in a crowded street at the foot of the hill.

Back in his room he flung his coat on the bed and began, nervously, to pace up and down. At least he had proved that there was vital substance in Burt's story. But his inability to act upon it galled him beyond endurance. He wanted action, drastic and immediate. As the minutes passed his restlessness increased. Just as he felt he could endure it no longer, there came a knock upon the door. Hurriedly he threw it open. Lena Andersen stood before him. She wore her loose raincoat and was hatless. The keen night air, or perhaps her rapid passage through the streets, had brushed back her blond hair from her forehead and brought a fine blood into her cheeks. Poised uncertainly upon the threshold, her eyes

130

were wide and startled, her brows marred by a concern she seemed unable to conceal.

"Paul . . . I'm sorry to disturb you . . . I had to come. This afternoon at the store . . . someone called to see you."

"Yes?" he questioned, in a strained voice. At the sight of her, so unexpected, his gaze instinctively had brightened. But, immediately, insidious as poison, came the recollection of all that Harris had told him. He could not bear to think of her in this new, discreditable light. He had an unwelcome feeling that in her affected simplicity she had sought to make a dupe of him. Unconsciously, his manner chilled, became harder, as he said: "Will you come in?"

"No. I have to get back at once." She spoke impulsively. "It was so unfair of Mr. Harris this morning."

"I daresay he had his reasons."

She watched him, still agitated. Above the buttoned collar of her raincoat he could see the pulse beating in her white throat.

"Have you found another job?"

"I haven't tried."

"But what will you do?"

Her unguarded anxiety wrung his tortured spirit. But he shrugged.

"Don't worry. I'll get along all right. Who was it wanted to see me? Someone from the police?"

"No, no," she said quickly, with a tremulous lip. "It was a queer little man. Mr. Harris was very rude to him, wouldn't take a message, or give him any information. But afterwards I managed to get a word with him. He's a Mr. Prusty, of 52 Ushaw Terrace. He wants you to call and see him tonight."

"Tonight?"

"Yes. No matter how late. He said it was terribly important."

"Thank you," Paul said quietly. "You've done me a real good turn."

131

"It's nothing. . . . I don't want to interfere . . . but if there's any way I can help. . . ."

Her sympathy, restrained yet spontaneous, swept him with an overwhelming desire to confide in her. But again he would not yield to it. Instead, he forced a conventional smile — a weak grimace that twitched his cheek.

"Haven't you enough troubles of your own?"

She glanced at him strangely, inquiringly almost, her chin pressed down upon her breast.

"If I have, won't I understand yours better?"

She waited, almost anxiously, waited for his reply. As he kept silent she compressed her lips, as though to suppress a sigh.

"At least . . . take care of yourself."

For an instant her eyes held his; then with a swift movement, she turned and was gone.

Immediately a coldness filled him, a sense of deprivation mingled with anger at his own weakness in wishing her to remain. He was tempted almost to rush to the landing and recall her. But the striking of the hour on the Ware clock deterred him. He counted: nine strokes; and at once took up his hat and coat. As he went downstairs he asked himself why should Prusty wish to see him? This sudden overture ran quite contrary to the tobacconist's cautious disposition. With knitted brows, trying to find an answer to the puzzle, he set out for Eldon at a rapid pace.

# Chapter 22

THE weather had changed at last and the night was cold and wintry. Beneath a leaden sky the streets lay quiet and deserted, the city seemed sealed in a frozen stillness. Presently it began to snow. The dry flakes milled around in the air, then fell, spent and soft, upon the pavements. With muffled footsteps Paul passed the shuttered cigar store and pushed on towards Ushaw Terrace.

The tobacconist was at home, wrapped in a thick woolen comforter. He peered at Paul across the threshold, then, with a wheeze of recognition, widened the narrow aperture of the door. Paul entered, having first kicked the snow from his boots upon the stairs. The parlour was still as dim and dusty as before, still redolent of cigar smoke, and still the gas fire sent its glow across the sheepskin rug. It was close and stuffy after the outer chill.

"Winter's come early," Prusty said, darting sharp glances over his pince-nez. "I feel it in my tubes. Sit down. I'm going to have supper."

He poured out a cup of his indispensable coffee for his visitor and gruffly insisted on sharing with him a meat pie, bought from the baker's and made hot in the oven. Despite this hospitality Paul had a strong suspicion that he was less welcome than before. The tobacconist kept examining him with surreptitious glances, and by a series of questions, roundabout, yet all bearing shrewdly towards the point, he managed to acquaint himself pretty fully with Paul's doings in the past few weeks.

When he had done so he made no immediate comment, but his air was sombre as he selected and lit a cheroot, coughed spasmodically, then bent his bushy brows upon the fire.

"So that's it." He meditated frowningly. "No wonder I felt the whole thing was waking up again. For all these years it's been buried . . . now it's like as if, when you put your ear to the ground, you heard a faint stirring in the grave."

There was a silence. The parlour, darkened by the falling snow, seemed suddenly full of shadows.

"As yet it's all under cover," Prusty went on steadily. "But there's signs and symptoms . . . ay, there's omens and portents

. . . for better or worse I cannot say, but I feel it in my bones, there's a resurrection coming. I feel it even in this room." He cast his eyes upwards. "And in the room above."

At the note of strange foreboding in Prusty's voice, Paul suppressed a shiver, and stared up at the ceiling.

"Is it still unoccupied?"

The tobacconist nodded his head. "Blank empty. As I told you, since the murder it's never been occupied for long."

Paul stirred uneasily, preyed on by disturbing thoughts, by the urgent need to press forward at all costs.

"There's something on your mind. Is what I've been doing responsible?"

"Ay, it's got around," Prusty agreed. "In whispers and in echoes. And it's penetrated to some queer places. That's the reason I asked you to visit me."

Interlocking his fingers tightly to restrain another tremor, Paul leaned forward in his chair to listen.

"Last Friday a man called to see me, here, at this flat. I was out, at my business, but Mrs. Lawson, the woman who comes in twice a week to clean up for me, was in. She's a plain, sensible woman who doesn't scare easy. But by all accounts the very sight of this man frightened her near out of her wits." Prusty glanced towards Paul. "Do you want me to go on?"

"Yes."

"The man was of no particular age. He might have been young and he might have been old. He looked strong yet he looked sick. His clothes didn't fit him. His face was hard and dead white. His head was cropped, down to the bone. Mrs. Lawson took her oath he was a convict."

"Who could it be?" Paul's lips were dry.

"God knows . . . I don't. But I'll lay you odds he came from Stoneheath. He left no name. What he did leave, before he bolted, was a message."

With grave, deliberate movements Prusty took from his waist-coat pocket a tiny paper spill which he unrolled and handed over. Showing faintly brown on the yellowish tissue slip were some minute words. Paul read them again, and again.

*For God's sake don't let them throw you off. Find Charles Castle in the Lanes. He'll tell you what to do.*

What did it mean? Who had written this desperate message? By whom had that despairing cry been uttered? Paul sat upright in his chair, petrified by a wild conjecture. It could not be! And yet, by some undreamed-of chance, it might be true. What if this scrap of paper had come from his father's hands — conveyed through secret and underground channels, delivered furtively, by a fellow prisoner who had been released?

An electric thrill traversed Paul's spine. In this terrible appeal he saw a new inspiration, a command, urging him onwards. With a convulsion of his breast, he rolled the paper up, and questioned Prusty.

"Can I keep this?"

The tobacconist, disclaiming responsibility, made a resigned gesture.

"I'll be glad to be rid of it. I didn't bargain to be mixed up in that kind of business."

The room was now almost dark. The gas fire cast no more than a ruddy glow upon the hearth. Outside, the darkness had intensified, and the snow was piled thickly against the window panes. Immersed in his reflections, throbbing with fresh hope, Paul sat motionless.

Suddenly, and without warning, there came the sound of a footstep upon the floor above.

Paul stiffened, and for a moment thought he must surely be mistaken. But no, the footstep was repeated, again, yet again, with a hollow, a mournful regularity. Impinging like this, upon the present current of his thoughts, this strange manifestation took on a dire significance. He sat up, his hair bristling, his eyes fixed upon the ceiling overhead. Prusty also had drawn himself erect, and was staring upwards with equal consternation.

"You said the flat was empty," Paul whispered.

"I swear it is," Prusty answered.

With unusual agility Prusty sprang from his seat, rushed through the lobby and out of the flat. At the same time there came the slam of the door above, succeeded by footsteps descending the stairs. Paul's impulse had been to follow Prusty but now an exclamation, as of relief, from the outside landing, arrested him, half way to the hall. He stood listening, his nerves vibrating, his ears strained towards the dimness beyond. He heard first a word of greeting in an unknown voice, then Prusty's voice, now pitched in a normal key. Then came some quiet conversation and finally, from each, a friendly "goodnight."

A minute later Prusty returned, wiping his forehead. He shut the door, lit the gas chandelier, then turned to Paul with a slightly sheepish air.

"It was our landlord," he explained. "The top roof is leaking . . . some slates blown off. He was up to see about it." Prusty drew his comforter tighter around his shoulders. "Sitting in the dark makes a man fancy things. I let my imagination run away with me."

Paul stirred slowly.

"You didn't imagine that scrap of paper."

"No," said Prusty. "And when I heard that noise, and found myself dashing upstairs . . . my God, it felt as real as it did fifteen years ago. Ah, well! Won't you have a drop more coffee?"

Paul, however, declined. He could not sit still. These faded words on the scrap of paper were burning into his skin, through the lining of his pocket, like molten metal. No longer did he concern himself with the green bicycle and the leather purse, which

136

only a few hours ago had seemed so vital to the case. This latest clue had driven all else from his mind.

As he hurried back to Poole Street his thoughts were feverish and confused. Were his own actions in any way responsible for this heart-breaking message? Or had Birley's abortive effort sent faint whisperings filtering mysteriously to the fastness of the prison? Paul heaved a short, sharp sigh — this suspense was more than he could bear. But now at least he had a direct and powerful lead — he would follow it to the end.

# Chapter 23

"I'M sorry, but you're a week overdue with your rent."

It was Paul's landlady, as he finished dressing early the following morning.

"I'm a bit short, Mrs. Coppin. Will you let it wait till next Saturday?"

Standing in the doorway, her soiled wrapper clutched across her flat bosom, she scrutinized him doubtfully. She realized that he had lost his job, and although she was not heartless, the struggle for existence had made sympathy a luxury she could not well afford.

"I can't be put upon," she said finally. "I'll give you till tomorrow evening. If you haven't got work by then, I'm afraid you must go. And I'll be obliged to keep your things."

He had no intention of seeking regular work, and not more than ten shillings in his pocket. Yet he did not wish to victimize her. When she had gone he opened his suitcase, considered his few possessions, including his silver watch and chain. If she sold them they would perhaps pay what he owed her. Beyond what he was wearing, he took only his papers relating to the case, stowing them carefully in the inside pocket of his overcoat. Then, with a last look round the room, he went out.

The Lanes, which he reached towards ten o'clock, was the name given to one of the oldest parts of Wortley, an abbreviation of Fairhall Lanes, the site, in mediaeval times, of an encampment and tilt yard, which had later degenerated to a fair ground. In the late nineteenth century the process of deterioration had been continued by the erection of cheap workers' tenements — a manifestation of the Victorian industrial era. The result, today, was a slum, the worst section of the city, a network of narrow, twisted streets, hemmed in by tall dilapidated buildings. And all that day Paul combed these streets trying, without success, to locate the man named Castles. When evening came a soft rain began to fall. Resolved to stop at nothing, he made his way to the heart of the district, where for ninepence he was admitted to a "one-night" workmen's lodging-house.

It was an even poorer place than the Hart house which he had once visited, consisting merely of a long upstairs room, with bare boards, approached by a broken wooden staircase. The beds were strips of sacking, stretched out like low hammocks on two long master ropes which ran the entire length of the dormitory. At one end was a dirty kitchen where, clustered round the stove, a crowd of ragged men armed with frying pans and "billies" were pushing and elbowing in a cloud of rancid steam for places to cook their supper.

With a glance towards this crowd Paul stretched himself, fully dressed, on his hammock, and pulled up the thin worn grey blanket.

"Don't you want no dinner, mate?"

Paul turned. In the adjoining hammock an undersized man with a shrunken, humorous face was lying on his elbow with two soiled paper bags before him. He wore a torn overcoat, burst canvas tennis shoes, mudstained and stuffed with brown paper, and a jaunty check muffler. While his bright beady eyes remained on Paul his bony fingers dipped into one bag, took out a cigarette end, split it, and shook and shredded the tobacco into the second bag with practiced rapidity.

"I'll cook for both, mate, if you happen to have a bit of grub about you."

"Sorry," Paul said. "I had something before I came in."

"Ah, you're lucky, mate. Me, I could eat an ox," he added, with his death's head grin. "Horns and all."

When he had finished he closed the full bag and carefully tucked it away next his skin under the shirt. From the shreds that remained he rolled a cigarette and stuck it behind his ear. Then he rose, a little human weazel, and with a knowing glance at Paul and a nod towards the notice which said NO SMOKING, shuffled briskly towards the latrine.

When he returned Paul leaned towards him.

"I'm looking for a man called Castles. Have you ever heard of him?"

"Charlie Castles? I've heard of him. Who ain't?"

"Where can I find him?"

"He's away for the present. Like enough on a job. Should be back in a few days. If he ain't lagged again. Hang around and I'll give you a knock down." He paused oddly. "You know who he is, don't you?"

Paul shook his head.

"No."

In a nervous fashion the other laughed.

"Then you'll find out, mate."

"Tell me," Paul said.

"Well," the little man shrugged. "He's a wrong un all right . . . welsher on the racetracks . . . fence for stolen property in his spare time. He's done years in quod. Robbery and assault and that

139

like . . . in fact he's just new out on parole after a long stretch. A regular old lag. Mind you, he was up in the world once. But now he's pretty low."

"I see," Paul said. "What prison was he in?"

"Stoneheath."

Paul drew in his breath sharply.

The din in the dormitory increased — shouts, curses, bursts of laughter. Someone began to play a mouth-harmonium. It was nearly midnight before some sort of silence prevailed. Paul slept brokenly.

Next morning, at six o'clock, everyone was wakened by the untying of one master rope, a process which automatically unslung all the hammocks. Those who tried to continue their sleep, when spilled to the floor, were nudged to activity by the doss-master's boot. As Paul filed out with the others into the raw dawn his neighbour of the night before hung on to him, guiding him to the nearest coffee stall where he stood, stamping his burst slippers, blowing on his cupped hands with an air of humorous expectancy.

"How about a mug of grits, mate? You cough up. I've nothing less than a fiver."

Breaking one of his few shillings, Paul stood the other a roll and coffee.

Jerry was his name. Jerry the Moke, to his pals. He admitted, with his shrunken grin, that he was a regular "scrounger," had not been in regular work for years, but he knew every dodge for scraping a living. His most usual occupation was that of "fag-lifter" — he scoured the city gutters for smoked cigarette ends and sold the mixed pickings for as much as three and six a pound. But in bad weather the pickings ran low and this morning he was going to try for a day with "the boards." He offered to take Paul with him.

"You come along, mate. With these good duds you'll be sure of a board."

140

At first, Paul was about to refuse. Yes, why not? To find Castles he must keep in touch with his odd companion. In these surroundings he might remain hidden from the police. And with almost nothing in his pocket he had to keep himself alive. He moved off with the other in the direction of Dukes Row.

At the head of the alley, outside a dilapidated yard bearing the sign LANES BILLBOARD AND ADVERTISING COMPANY, they took their places behind the men already lined up alongside the wooden palings. After about an hour the gate was opened and the first twenty men, including Paul and his companion, were admitted.

Inside the yard stood a row of sandwich-boards, each freshly pasted with a red and yellow poster for the Palace Theatre. Imitating the others, Paul went forward, to one of the double boards, lifted it upon his shoulders, moved towards the big gate. The line then re-formed, Paul fell into step and plodded along behind Jerry the Moke.

All day long the line weaved and wormed its way through the busiest streets of the city. The boards were heavy and awkward, with a tendency to snap back on the shoulder muscles. But at five o'clock they were back at Dukes Row, where each man was paid two shillings and ninepence for the day's work. As they came together out of the yard Jerry remarked:

"Now we can feed." With his beady smile he took Paul straight to the nearest eating-house.

Every day that week Paul went out with the boards. It was humiliating work — to attract attention, the men had to wear some odd article of dress, and one morning Paul was sent out with the others in a battered top hat. Towards noon, as he paraded along Ware Street, he saw one of the Bonanza assistants, Nancy Wilson, coming towards him. Quickly, he lowered his head, but not before she had recognized him, a look of startled surprise appearing in her face.

He did not care. With the money he received he was able to

141

exist: ninepence went to pay for the nightly doss, and the rest was spent in the purchase of food. Since it was more economical to use the lodging-house kitchen, on Jerry's advice Paul bought a second-hand frying pan from the man who bossed the place. The cheapest meat when fried with onion made a filling supper.

The lodging-house harboured a strange, abandoned, shiftless company, the dregs, the very scourings of Wortley. None of the men had steady work, even the best of them were dependent upon the vagaries of casual labour. If a string of barges came up the canal for unloading; if there was a new sewer to be dug; if a blizzard laid snow thickly upon the streets; then in Jerry's phrase, they ate and drank. There were others who followed stranger and more devious trades: the rag-pickers, the "bottle and bone" men, the cowp-hunters and midden-rakers — silent figures, in odorous rags, who scoured the garbage bins of the city, half-stooping, their eyes upon the ground, perpetually in search of the treasure of a bottle, a discarded piece of china, a scrap of rusted metal. The street entertainers were a queer crew also. There was a contortionist who amused the others by eating a sausage with his toes; a blind fiddler — a bad-tempered old man, who, every night, when he had laid aside his blue spectacles and the stick with which he pathetically tapped along, read the *Courier* comfortably in bed; and a vocalist who specialized in theatre queues, a fervid Dubliner whose favourite supper was "taters and point" — hot potato dipped in salt herring. Finally, there were the cripples — the legless man who slid over the pavements on his hands and hips, the fake paralytic — the sickly youth trading on open sores, and the beggars, open and unashamed. Many were corrupt and vicious. Some were far gone in disease. Herded together in the low, ill-ventilated dormitory, seedy and unwashed, snoring, starting in nightmare cries, they gave off in the hours of darkness a foetid odour, which mingled with the stench of the latrine.

And how quickly the blight of this place infected Paul, filled him with a sense of desperation and despair. He began to feel that he would never solve the mystery and, under the growing burden of inaction, to long for some decisive action which would cut, once and for all, the tangled cords which held him. More and more savagely the joke of injustice galled his youthful spirit, he brooded palely through sleepless nights, his thoughts returning with growing bitterness to the main instrument of his father's suffering, the figure of the prosecutor, Matthew Sprott.

Towards the end of the week, the Lanes Advertising Company stopped sending out its sandwich boards. Turned away at the yard, Paul glanced at Jerry, who unconcernedly shrugged his meagre shoulders.

"They often run out on us. Post the boardings instead. We'll try the station."

Together they went to the railway station and, for the next two days, hung around on the chance of carrying a bag, always watching out for the porters, who resented this infringement of their rights. The few tips he received kept Paul going until Saturday. On the evening of that day as they entered the doss-house Jerry drew up short and pointed to a stranger, a tall, sinewy man of about forty with a pale, narrow face, unshaven chin, and small eyes, dressed in a brown suit, with a derby hat on his head and a dark scarf hanging loose on his waistcoat.

"There you are then, mate." Exclaimed Jerry, in a low voice. "That's Castles . . . and watch out how you use him."

# Chapter 24

LATER that night, in a small back room which Castles had rented in an adjoining street, Paul faced this man whom he had so anxiously awaited. Despite his unprepossessing appearance and coarsened voice he was, as Jerry had inferred, educated and of obvious intelligence. There was, indeed, in his appearance, a lingering flavour of the law. His long lean cheeks had a clerkly air and in his dead, yellowish eye, chilling and saturnine, there was the look of one who had drafted many a well-phrased deed. But whatever he once was, or might have been, now, clearly, he had fallen far into the seamy shadows of the underworld.

"You're wondering about me," he said, cutting so suddenly into Paul's thoughts that the young man coloured with confusion. "Don't. I no longer exist." His dead eyes could express nothing, but the pale lips twisted downwards in scornful inquiry.

"What do you want with me?"

Again there was silence; then, still without speaking, never taking his eyes from the other, Paul handed him the spill of paper which Prusty had given him. Castles unrolled it, glanced at it carelessly, then, with a sort of bitter indifference, handed it back.

"So that's what brought you."

"Who sent me that message? Was it . . . was it my father?"

Another pause, brief, but loaded with suspense.

"I daresay it could have been," Castles answered in a flat voice.

"Then . . . you know him?"

"Perhaps."

"In Stoneheath?"

"In that accursed place . . . yes . . . if you must know, we had adjoining suites. We used to tap-talk at night . . . when he wasn't in solitary."

Paul drew his hand across his hot brow.

"How is he?" The words came with a gasp.

"Bad." Castles took a bag of shag tobacco from his overcoat pocket, slipped off a rice paper from a pack and, with one hand, rolled himself a cigarette. "In fact, couldn't be worse."

For all his courage something like a sob broke from Paul's breast.

144

"Have you nothing to tell me? No hope of any kind to give me?"

"Is there any hope in Stoneheath?"

The pounding of Paul's heart seemed to fill his ears like the beat of a funeral drum. Yet there must, oh, there must be something behind this man's inscrutable and sinister reserve. He bit his lip fiercely.

"Why was I told to find you?"

"Your old man knew I was getting out. Thought we ought to meet. He slipped me this bunch of drivel."

Paul took the papers the other handed to him — little more than soiled scraps covered with a pencil scrawl. But though he read and reread the almost illegible words, slowly his eagerness died. They were no more than outcries from the darkness, protestations and complaints, continually repeated, proof of suffering which cut Paul to the heart, yet offered no further evidence, nothing of material value. Dully, he raised his eyes to Castles, who all this time had waited with cold yet exemplary patience.

"Then you can't help me?"

"That depends," Castles said slowly, drawing deeply on his cigarette, "on what kind of help you want."

"You know what I want," Paul exclaimed passionately. "To dig out a poor devil who's been buried alive for fifteen years."

"Once you're in that grave, you never get out."

Wildly, Paul exclaimed:

"I will get him out. He's innocent . . . and I'll prove it. I'll find the one who really did the murder."

"Never." Castles spoke disdainfully. "After fifteen years you haven't a dog's chance. Whoever did it could be a thousand miles away. Changed name. New identity. Maybe dead. It's hopeless." He waited to let his words sink in, and over his yellow eyes, fixed steadily on Paul, there flowed an opaque film. "Why don't you go after the legal killer . . . who really did Mathry in?"

"Who do you mean?"

145

"The man who prosecuted him."

As though he had been stung, Paul drew himself erect. He caught his breath.

"For God's sake . . . who are you?"

There was a heavy pause. Then slowly, with that indifference that hid him like a mask, the other answered:

"It's no secret — I'm in the records . . . convicted embezzler. At least, that's how it began. I only needed a little leniency . . . time to pay the money back. I begged for it . . . in open court. Instead I got seven years' penal servitude."

A long stillness followed. Then Castles resumed:

"So you see we're in the same boat, you and me. No doubt that's why Mathry thought we ought to get together. We owe everything to that one man. And we're so soft we haven't done a thing about it."

"What can we do?" Paul cried hopelessly.

He bowed his head between his hands, crushed by the weight of his disappointment. And still the searing voice went on.

"You've never met the gentleman?"

"No."

Castles laughed shortly.

"Don't take it to heart. We're down where we belong, you and I, but a cat can look at a king." A strange light flickered in his clouded pupils. "What you need is a bit of cheering up. Why don't you let me give you a little entertainment?"

"Entertainment!"

"Why not? You don't read the papers properly, or you'd know there's been a prime show in town for the past ten days . . . two first-rate performers. Oh, they play Wortley regularly, but this is one of their biggest attractions. And the joke is . . . it's all free!"

His voice had gradually taken on an inflection which chilled Paul to the bone. There was a pause. Paul waited.

"The High Court is in session, Lord Oman presiding, Sir

146

Matthew Sprott prosecuting . . . wouldn't you like to see them?"
Staring at the other, Paul did not answer.

"It's such an opportunity . . . the last day of the trial." Castles
was mocking him again, in that same deadly manner. "Surely
you'd like to come with me tomorrow afternoon . . . and see how
they do it?"

"Do what?"

"You know what," he said, affecting ingenuous surprise. "Of
course you do! Mind you, this one won't be so exciting. Just a
wretched little bawd who's knifed her lover. Still . . . the black
cap is interesting . . . quite smart . . . and always fashionable."

"No," Paul said violently.

Castles's face hardened. He pierced Paul, through and through,
with his yellow eyes.

"Are you afraid?"

"No, I'm not afraid . . . I don't see why I should go."

"I say you are afraid." The cold and cutting words came faster.
"I thought at first you had guts. But I see I am mistaken. You say
you want a showdown. Well, for God's sake, why not have it!
Don't you realize that there are two kinds of people in the world
today? The ones who take what they want. And the ones that
don't."

His nostrils dilated, his face was bloodless. "What sort of a
game do you think you and I are in? Do you think we're playing
for fun? I know what you're up against! But you . . . you'd let
them all tramp over you . . . you want it both ways . . . you
want to run with the hare and hunt with the hounds. Well, so be
it! If you don't want me to help you, go your own way, and I'll
go mine."

His voice dropped, he rose and threw his cigarette butt in
the empty fireplace. Paul stood watching him, wounded and
aroused, torn by indecision. It was the word "help," thrown out
by Castles, which finally swayed him. Obscure and inscrutable

though it might be, he could not reject this proffered aid.

"I'll go," he said. "What time shall I meet you?"

"No!" Castles shook his head. "It's no use pretending. We're finished."

"What time will I meet you?" Paul repeated.

Castles turned slowly, buttoning his coat.

"Do you mean it?" He searched Paul's face intently. "Very well. Outside the High Court. Two o'clock. Tomorrow." He swung round and held the door open.

# Chapter 25

ON the following afternoon, which was grey and damp, Paul met the ex-convict as arranged. The High Court was a noble edifice of fine grey stone, built in the Palladian style, with moulded pillars set into the tall portico. At the entrance in a central niche, a marble figure with bandaged eyes stood holding the scales of justice.

Castles, who was shaved and respectably dressed in a drab suit with a white collar and black tie, apparently knew his way about. He led Paul through a side archway and up a broad circular staircase to a heavy mahogany door, guarded by an official to whom, without a flicker of his impassive face, he handed two stamped admission cards. When the officer had inspected the cards he laid his finger on his lips, to ensure silence, then ushered them through the door into a narrow public gallery where they squeezed into two vacant seats.

Below, lay the crowded court — the robed judge on his dais at one end, the jury box to the left, the witness stand to the right, the well of the court, filled with figures in wig and gown, and in the centre, the dock, where a young woman in a cheap Nottingham shawl stood between two motionless bareheaded policemen. Grey and sombre though it was, all this broke upon Paul's vision with blinding force. Gripping the gallery rail, he leaned forward, his gaze bent upon Lord Oman. His lordship was an aged figure, of more than average stature and stooping slightly, as though beneath the weight of honours. His face, the colour of port wine against his snowy ermine, was haughty, fixed in implacable severity. On either side of the beak-like nose his heavy jowls hung down, dangling like the dewlaps of a bulldog. From beneath the brooding thatch of eyebrows, his eyes looked out, senile yet formidable.

A pressure on Paul's arm made him turn to Castles, who now pointed towards a figure rising at the front of the court.

"Don't bother about Oman, he's in his dotage." The words grated on his ear. "There, getting ready to speak . . . your real friend . . . Sprott."

Paul felt a faint sweat break out upon him as he looked in the direction indicated, and observed the compact form of the prosecuting counsel in curled wig and sombre black robe. His hard, close-bitten cheeks and rounded chin showed clean-cut in the twilight of the court, he pursed his mobile lips and sent his fine eyes darting, like an actor, searching out his audience, as, after a due pause, he began to address the jury in a final, measured recapitulation of the case.

Sordid and wretched, the facts were of the simplest. The accused was a woman of the streets, a prostitute of the poorest class who, since the age of seventeen — she was now twenty-four — had followed her trade in a mean quarter of the city. She had, inevitably, a "protector," the man who "watched for her" at the street corner, who lived with her upon her pitiful immoral earnings, who, in fact, preyed upon her and often beat her brutally. One night, without provocation, when she was drunk, in a surge of revulsion and remorse, she had stabbed him with a kitchen

149

knife, then turned the weapon, but ineffectually, upon herself.

It scarcely seemed as if this miserable story would bear elaboration, but Sprott dwelt upon it, and all its sordid aspects, in dramatic detail, and with withering admonition, indicating to the jury that no thought of extenuating circumstances should cause them to compromise their verdict. If the accused had, of deliberate intent, slain her paramour, then unquestionably she was guilty of murder. It appeared to Paul as if the prosecutor were revelling in the fair execution of his duty, drawing from his own exposition of the vicious degradation of the accused, an almost histrionic satisfaction, using his utmost powers to crush and to condemn.

When he concluded, with a final dramatic gesture, a thrust with the actual knife showing how it had pierced the victim's heart, he sat down amidst a deathly stillness.

"Take a good look at him," Castles's hoarse voice was keyed to a whisper. "That's how he worked on Mathry."

Even without this prompting, staring rigidly at the prosecutor, Paul was conscious of a surge of extraordinary emotion, so violent and intense it turned him sick and brought a cold dampness to his brow. In his past life he had experienced instinctive manifestations of dislike — certain natures are mutually antagonistic, and at first sight a wave of animosity passes between them. But this present feeling held more, far more, than that ordinary aversion. Dark and predestined, it welled from the very depths of his being. He thought of all that this man had said of his father, the merciless and unwarranted vituperation which he had heaped upon him. He remembered, from the photograph, the trapped and hunted look upon his father's face as he bore the cross-examination of the prosecutor, of this man, now lounging at ease here, before his eyes. Oh, it was true that familiarity must breed contempt, and constant usage dull even the finest sensibility. Nevertheless, there was, in the studied deportment of this agent of the Crown, something so impervious, so bereft of ordinary humanity, it roused in Paul's breast a wild thirsting for revenge.

Suddenly there was silence. The speech for the defense was over, the judge had concluded his summing up. With a shuffling of feet, the jury retired, the court quickly cleared.

"Four o'clock," Castles remarked, drawing back his pale lips. "Just in nice time for them all to have tea."

"How can you?"

Castles shrugged with cynical indifference.

"It's all in the day's work for them . . . Oman and Sprott, Unlimited. I wonder how many they've knocked off between them in the last fifteen years. Want to go out?"

"No," Paul answered between his teeth, and turned away.

His neighbour on the other side was eating sandwiches from a paper bag with the air of a habitué — a hollow-chested little man with scanty hair plastered across his waxen scalp. He leaned over confidentially.

"You two came in a bit late. You missed the best of the sport. Sprott wasn't too bad in his final address but you ought to have heard him this morning. Gave it to her hot and strong. Scrapings of the gutter . . . panderin' to the dregs of humanity . . . he didn't half make her cry. All over bar the shouting now. I give the jury another ten minutes. She'll swing all right. By the looks of that foreman — I bet his wife nags him — there won't be no recommendation to mercy. Excitin', ain't it? I'd rather see this than a football match, any day."

A pasteboard ticket to see the show. Were they all like that, Paul wondered. The hot air of the gallery sent a flush of nausea over him. The jury were back now, and the judge, all of them.

"Guilty!"

Of course . . . the little man, the expert, had predicted it. But not the scream from the poor wretch, cowering beneath her shawl, in the dock, nor the fit of coughing, the prolonged and racking

151

paroxysm which followed. His lordship, frigidly annoyed, was forced to wait until it ceased. Then the black cap — Paul watched with staring eyeballs as the crape was laid upon the judge's head and, as the words came forth, "to hang by the neck till you are dead," fifteen years were rolled away, he felt all that his father must have felt, he writhed in torment, tried to cry out and could not, fought for breath, came to himself clutching the hand-rail of the gallery.

"It's all over," Castles said, agreeably. "Not bad for a matinee."

In a daze, Paul accompanied him down the staircase, out through the wide forecourt. Already the newsboys were calling out the verdict. As they came into the street Castles paused.

"Shall we go somewhere for a bite?"

He seemed trying to estimate Paul's reactions, cold and curious, as though he watched an insect pinned beneath a magnifying glass. Yet there was more in it than that . . . behind that death-mask brow Paul sensed the presence of emotions, darker even than his own.

"I couldn't eat anything."

Castles put a hand on his companion's arm.

"Why don't we go back to my place for a drink? I think we need it."

"All right." In the seething welter of his emotions Paul cared neither what he did, nor where he went.

They walked off together.

# Chapter 26

WHEN they got to the back room in the Lanes Paul sank into a chair while Castles carefully pulled down the blinds, took a bottle from the cupboard and poured out two drinks.

"We've earned this," he remarked, as he handed Paul the glass. "It won't hurt you. I got it from the right place."

The stimulant warmed Paul's stomach and steadied his nerves. In his distress he felt he needed it, and because of that need gave no thought to the effect which it might have upon his present mood. Never in his life had he known such a dark and hopeless bitterness of soul. He emptied his glass at a gulp and made no protest when, tilting the bottle, Castles refilled it for him.

Placing his drink upon the mantelpiece the ex-convict stood for a moment observing the young man, out of the corner of his eye. Stealthily, he moistened his lips, conscious that the crisis was at hand. Yes, that unique combination of chances he had so often longed for was at last before him. He must not miss the opportunity afforded him by that thin spill of papers thrust into his palm with a muttered injunction during exercise in the yard, a few days before his release. Mathry, the prisoner in Stoneheath, meant nothing to him — in any case, he was finished and done for, a lifer without the slightest hope of remission. To Paul he gave not a thought, except to regard him as a heaven-sent instrument of revenge.

At the time of his "disgrace" Charles Castles had been trust officer for the large Midland Counties Insurance Company. A bachelor, with sporting tastes, he lived well, went out occasionally with the local hunt, regularly patronized the neighboring race-meetings. To such a man, astute and venturesome, it was second nature to gamble "on a good thing." Thus, when information of a most private nature reached him of an amalgamation planned between his own organisation and the small Haddon Hall Fire and Life Assurance Company — a jointure which would prove immensely favourable to the minor concern — he sensed this as the opportunity of a lifetime, and borrowing from the Midland Counties funds under his control, he bought fifty thousand shares of the Haddon Hall stock.

The purchase was achieved discreetly, yet the amount involved was so large that a rumour began to circulate, and after some time reached the ears of the authorities. To Castles's dismay, an examination of his books was demanded by the sheriff, who was then Mr. Matthew Sprott. Immediately Castles went to Sprott, whom he had often met socially and, having freely acknowledged his culpability, asked him to stay the investigation for a mere ten days. Quite correctly, the sheriff refused. Under his direction Castles was rigorously investigated, prosecuted, found guilty, and given the maximum sentence. In the interim the Haddon shares had tripled in value. But instead of making seventy thousand pounds, Charles Castles received seven years' penal servitude.

To a man of his disposition it was unforgettable — always, with a deadly and increasing venom, he hated Sprott, sought unceasingly for revenge without danger to himself. And now . . . after all these years . . . had come Mathry's son . . . an idealistic young idiot, hell-bent on the melodramatic folly of "clearing his father's name." Good God, the mere thought of it was enough to make a cat laugh. In the circles wherein Castles now moved, all that pertained to police activity was a matter of common knowledge and so it was not long before he had full word of Paul's inexpert striving. How easy, thereafter, for one of his subtlety of mind to seize the advantage.

Castles could resist no longer. With a tremor, almost of intoxication, he yielded. Composing his features to their mask-like blankness, he advanced towards Paul.

"I must admit you took it well this afternoon," he said, seating himself on the arm of the other's chair. "You made yourself go through with it, didn't you?"

Paul gave no answer.

"Perhaps I was unfair to you last night." An inflection of grudging acknowledgement crept into Castles's voice. "After all, things have turned out bad for you. With everything gone wrong, and the police badgering you, I don't blame you for losing heart." He paused and shook his head. "You're battering your head against a stone wall. That's why I wanted you to see that precious pair today. Oh, not so much Oman — he's an old, broken-winded hound now, though he still likes to follow the scent of blood. It's Sprott I really mean." As Castles articulated the prosecutor's name his face darkened, and despite his effort to maintain a note of irony, his tone turned hard as stone.

"He's the master mind of the system, the most cursed reactionary in the city of Wortley. I couldn't tell you all he's done — always indirectly, always under cover. He's the one who put your father into the hell of Stoneheath. *And so long as he's around you'll never get him out.*"

In the silence which followed, a vision of the prosecutor, supremely self-assured, rose before Paul's sight, and a strange fever began to throb within his veins.

Castles continued, his calmness apparently restored, as though thinking aloud.

"Yes, the others were merely stupid — Dale, for instance, is a blockhead, hidebound by his own professional prejudice. He probably convinced himself that he was right. You could not lower yourself to hate him. Oman, the judge, works by rule of thumb. But Sprott, ah, Sprott is different. Sprott's mind is brilliant. Sprott must have ripped through the pitiful tissue of evidence and known it, at a glance, to be utterly inconclusive. Yet Sprott went ahead, absolutely regardless, with every subtle word at his command. Sprott condemned your father to worse than hanging, to a living death, for fifteen years. He is the one who did it. Yes, he is the one."

Under this relentless logic, the fever in Paul's blood was mounting beyond endurance. He saw the case in clear perspective, and like a haggard shaft of light, there broke upon him anew the knowledge of the prosecutor's responsibility. Almost by accident,

155

Castles let his hand rest, caressingly, upon the young man's shoulder.

"I understand how you feel. I'm sorry for you. How can you get at such a man? He is entrenched."

Paul raised his head, turned his burning eyes upon the other.

"There must be some way of reaching him."

"No, Paul . . . there isn't." Castles spoke in a tone of commiseration. Then he hesitated, concealing a sudden contortion of his features. "At least, there's *one* way . . . but of course, it's impossible."

Paul's eyes were dark and glittering in his white face.

"Why impossible?"

Castles considered, in a strange manner, then seemed to dismiss his thought.

"No. You're too young. You couldn't go to Sprott . . . to his house . . . and square your account with him. . . ."

As Castles said this he glanced at Paul swiftly and his breath came faster, too fast indeed for one whose mood was so detached and calm. But Paul was now beyond perceiving this betrayal of the passion which shook the other. He muttered, with twitching cheek.

"Why shouldn't I go and face up to Sprott? I can do it."

"Can you?" Castles questioned with that same strange intensity.

Paul stared back at him, in a dim perception of his meaning. The blood was pounding in his ears, hammering through his head, like the beat of a hundred hammers.

"Can you?" repeated Castles in a more insistent voice.

Paul nodded his head.

"It's the only way left for you to get justice. To take the matter into your own hands. No one will blame you. All the facts will come out. If you do it . . . they can't hush up your father's case any longer. Everyone must hear about it. Just think of it. A complete exposure of everything they're trying to hide. What fools they'll look . . . if you do it. The whole thing attributable to them . . . from first to last. And Sprott, the agent, the conniver of the injustice, out of the way, finished, done for . . . if you do it. He richly deserved it . . . that's what they'll say. They won't hold it against you . . . they'll say you were justified . . . if you do it . . . if only you do it. . . ."

Paul got to his feet, goaded beyond reason by these words, by all that he had witnessed at the trial, by the process of demoralization which for the past ten days had been brought to bear upon him. Flashes of light were darting through his brain. He poured himself another drink and swallowed it down.

"Here," said Castles in a hoarse whisper. "In case they try to stop you . . . take this."

It was a black Webley automatic. Paul experienced no surprise. Castles did not speak. Nor did he. Castles opened the door. Paul went out. Descending the steps, he could feel the heavy weight in his pocket bumping against his thigh. He entered the darkness of the street.

Alone in the room, his hand pressed against his side, Castles leaned for a moment against the doorway, as though gasping for breath, his mouth contorted, his cheeks strangely hollow. Then, with fingers that trembled slightly, he rolled and lit a cigarette, looked at his watch. A train for the North left in ten minutes. It was not wise to delay. He pulled on his overcoat, then stood hurriedly extracting the most he could from the cigarette. His thoughts, known only to himself, caused his lips to draw back from his pale gums. With a violent gesture he crushed the cigarette beneath his heel, swung round, and went out.

# Chapter 27

THAT same evening, when Sir Matthew Sprott left the robing-room of the Courts, he stood on the portico, debating how best to employ the two clear hours of leisure before his seven o'clock dinner. A snooker match was being played at Burrough's Hall, Smith against Davies. But although he liked the game and, as a skilful amateur, had his own full-sized table at home, he decided that the session must, by now, be nearly over. He resolved to go down to his club in Leonard Square, the Sherwood.

There was still a gleam of sunset in the west as he strolled along, a reddish afterglow which made the sky quite lurid, and in particular lit up one small purple cloud, low on the horizon, no larger than a man's hand. The prosecutor's eyes were caught and held, strangely, by this cloud, which lay, dark and brooding, like an omen of calamity, in the sky. Abruptly Sir Matthew shook himself. During these past weeks he had not been quite himself. Perhaps he had been overworking, planning ahead too arduously for the coming election. Although he often boasted that "he had not a nerve in his body," lately he had been inclined to worry, absurdly, over trifles. Why, for instance, should he take so much to heart these trivial dreams which had recently plagued his wife?

Sprott winced visibly as his thoughts reverted to this vexatious matter. These fantastic scraps of nonsense, apparently so meaningless — what was one to make of them? They had, however, a single point in common. All of them concerned him, and in every one he met with some preposterous misfortune. He was in court and had forgotten his brief; he rose to address the jury and broke down in his speech; he was rebuked in scathing terms by the presiding judge; then, as he left the court — and this image came most frequently of all — everyone rose to mock and disparage him. It was, indeed, this ending to the sequence which gave his dear wife the greatest pain, which had caused her to confide in him.

The heavy colour of the sky was in Sprott's face as he turned, solitary and morose, into the Square. However he might pretend to despise the new psychology, he was forced to acknowledge that this subconscious mischief now affecting his beloved Catharine came as an echo of that long-past Mathry case. And a flame of anger leaped in his breast as he realized how disproportionate a havoc had been wrought by this little stinging gnat, arising, so outrageously, from the swamps of the past.

He had lied when he told the Chief Constable he had gone through the papers of the case. That had been quite unnecessary, his memory was faultless, and he remembered it in every detail. How indeed could he forget, even after fifteen years, that which had given him the first great impetus towards his present eminence?

Even now he could see Mathry's face, as the prisoner stood before him in the dock, a handsome "dago" face, the type of face that women always liked, to their sorrow and undoing. Yes, he had played upon this point, he freely admitted it . . . and upon other points, weaknesses if you like, evident in the prisoner's character, reducing him, when he entered the witness box, to utter and complete confusion. Well, why not? Was it not his duty to make his presentation as strong as possible, to gloss over its deficiencies, accentuate its strength . . . in short to win his case?

Sir Matthew had by this time reached Leonard Square, its gracious central green bedecked with pigeon-haunted statues of past civic dignitaries, and, with an effort, he tried to shake off his annoyance. Entering the dignified portals of the club he gave up his hat and coat, found a corner in the lower lounge and ordered tea. While this was being brought, he looked about him.

The Royal Sherwood was an exclusive institution which drew its members from the old county families and the Midland aristocracy. Sprott was not a favourite here; indeed, before he had at last forced his way into membership he had been blackballed three times — an achievement that had singularly gratified his vanity. Since he felt that people envied him his success, for this reason he was inclined to glory in his unpopularity, in his power to break down all opposition. Often, as he stood before the pierglass in his robes while Burr, his middle-aged, snuff-coloured clerk, obsequiously handed him his wig, he would smile complacently at his own reflection, and remark: "Burr! I'm the most hated man in the city of Wortley."

This evening, however, his attitude was strangely chastened, and as he viewed the sprinkling of members in the lounge, he wished that one of them might come and speak to him. Beyond a few distant nods he had received no acknowledgement of his entry. In the opposite corner four men were playing bridge, amongst them a member of his own profession whom he knew slightly, Nigel Grahame, a King's Counsel. Once or twice they glanced in his direction and, instinctively, he had a strange suspicion that they might be speaking of the Mathry case. No, no, that was impossible — he must really take a grip of himself. Yet why didn't Grahame recognize him? As he slowly drank his tea, he bent his gaze upon the other man.

Grahame, in his opinion, was a queer individual, an exponent of odd and unaccountable beliefs. Son of a country rector, he had, as a boy, achieved the distinction of winning an exhibition to Winchester College. From this famous school, which had stamped him with its own particular mark of scholarship and manners, he had proceeded to Oxford University. A year after he had been called to the bar, his father died, leaving him a small income of two hundred pounds a year. After the funeral he had immediately gone abroad and for the next five years had lived an unsettled existence. Part of the time he spent as tutor to an Austrian boy suffering from tuberculosis and compelled to spend his days in the high altitudes of the Tyrol. For the rest, Grahame wandered about Europe, mainly on foot, with a knapsack on his back, wintering in the Juras, spending his summers on the Dolomites. He loved to walk among the mountains — in one day he had tramped from Oberwald to Innsbruck, a distance of fifty-two miles.

Naturally this apparently aimless life had caused his friends anxiety, but in the following year Grahame returned to Wortley, apparently sound in mind and body, and with complete uncon-cern, as though he had left only yesterday, addressed himself to his own profession. Gradually, he acquired a practice which, while not extensive, was in the highest sense distinguished. It was said that he owed much to his manner and appearance — tall and spare, with pale, regular features and dark, ascetic eyes, he was always immaculate, courteous, and reserved. Yet behind these superficial attributes there lay a particular integrity of pur-pose which formed the unseen structure, the very keystone of his reputation. He was fanatically honest. It was even whispered of him, often with a sidelong smile, that he would not accept a brief unless he knew it to be just.

This, in itself, was enough to cause Sprott to sneer. What rot indeed! How could the world go round if everyone behaved like a saint upon a gridiron. Yet, despite that disparagement, there was about Grahame, something untouchable and unfathomable, which had always baffled and disturbed Sir Matthew.

He recollected well, for instance, that occasion when, at one of his larger dinner parties at Grove Quadrant, knowing Grahame to be interested in art and wishing also to display his own posses-sions, he had taken him away from the other guests to show him his Constables. Grahame had behaved with perfect courtesy, yet all the time Sprott had sensed this strange fellow's indifference to his treasures — as though, almost, they were counterfeit. And, at last, provoked by this feeling, he had exclaimed:

"Well, my boy . . . as a connoisseur, don't you envy me?"

Grahame had smiled pleasantly.

"Why should I . . . when I can see pictures, at least equally good, just across the park in the Municipal Gallery?"

"But damn it all, man . . ." Sprott had burst out, "in the Gallery they're not *your* pictures."

"Aren't they?" Grahame's smile had deepened, causing the prosecutor a strange disquiet. "Don't the greatest masterpieces belong to us all?"

A recurrence of this aggravation suffused Sprott now, and as, at this moment, the group of card players broke up, a perverse impulse made him signal to Grahame.

Almost imperceptibly Grahame hesitated, then he crossed the lounge.

"Join me," Sprott threw out the invitation with spurious heartiness. "I'm alone."

"I've already had tea." Grahame smiled politely.

"Then sit down a minute. You and I don't see enough of one another."

Maintaining his polite, rather deprecating smile, Grahame seated himself on the arm of an adjoining chair.

"That's right," said the Prosecutor, helping himself, with a show of appetite, to a fresh muffin. "I don't bite, you know. In spite of all the tattle in this club."

"I assure you," said Grahame, in slight embarrassment, but with perfect good manners, "so far as I am aware . . ."

Sprott laughed, easily, but somewhat louder than he had intended.

"Weren't you discussing me a minute ago, over there, with those others? You can't deceive an old hand like me." Sprott knew he was going over the score, but something within him drove him to continue. "I haven't exercised my powers of deduction all these years for nothing."

There was a pause while the prosecutor raised his cup and drank some tea.

"You see, Grahame, a man doesn't reach my position without a multitude of back-biters collecting on his doorstep, waiting their chance to cry, 'Wolf!' It only takes an irresponsible half-wit like George Birley to start them off. Don't you agree?"

"I saw merely the briefest account of the matter in the *Courier*," Grahame spoke slowly. "I have given it no consideration whatsoever."

"There never was a more bare-faced snatch for publicity. They never knew what was coming till Birley stood up in the House. The Secretary for State was furious. That same night one of the Ancasters was giving a reception. Birley's wife was there and she said publicly, 'I always knew George was an idiot. But I thought he had enough wits not to shoot his own side!' Did you ever know such imbecility? I'm told they won't let him stand at the election."

There was a short silence. Grahame kept his eyes lowered. At last he said:

"Perhaps his motives were sincere. In any case, don't you think it's better to be a fool than a knave?" He glanced at his watch. "Now if you'll excuse me. I must be off." He got up and civilly took his leave.

With darkened face Sprott poured himself another cup of tea, but it tasted bitter in his mouth. The interview had afforded him no satisfaction, and in Grahame's abrupt departure he created for himself an added slight. At this, his expression hardened, and there swept over him a wave of resentful anger. Had he not, in the past, overcome far greater difficulties, survived much deeper malice?

Instinctively, he thought of his triumphs, his shoulders straightened, his lower lip protruded, and something of his "jury" manner descended upon him. He regretted the momentary phase of weakness through which he had passed. Was he losing his fire? Would he give up now, on the threshold of Parliament, when greatness lay within his grasp? No . . . a thousand times, no.

In a hard mood he rose and left the club. The porter who showed him out made a pleasant remark about the weather. Sprott, with studied incivility, made no answer. He stepped into a taxi, and curtly ordered the man to drive to Grove Quadrant.

At his home, he let himself in, and to his surprise, found his wife coming towards him in the hall. She kissed him, helped him out of his coat.

"Matthew, dear, there's a young man waiting for you in the library. He's been so patient . . . won't you see him before dinner?"

He raised his eyebrows. It was on the tip of his tongue to tell her that for anyone to be allowed to trespass upon his privacy was quite contrary to his orders. But, because he adored her, he said nothing. He inclined his head and walked towards the library.

# Chapter 28

IT was a handsome room, this library, with a thick cream carpet, many books, and some fine etchings on the walls. Motionless as a statue, Paul had been waiting there for about ten minutes. The prosecutor's wife had herself shown him in, a pretty woman of about forty, rather pale and delicate, wearing a soft grey dress. He could see that she thought he was from her husband's office.

"I hope you have no more work for Sir Matthew," she had remarked with her quiet smile.

Then she had asked him if he would take a glass of sherry

and a biscuit. When he refused she smiled again, and went out.

It was very quiet in the room. Then, upstairs, somebody began to practice the piano. One of Chopin's preludes, number 7, played slowly and with some mistakes. It was a child playing and he could hear talking and laughing. The sound of that piano jarred cruelly upon him. He thought of this man with his beautiful home and his attractive wife and laughing daughters. He thought of the other man in his damp stone cell. He couldn't bear it any longer. And then he heard the sound of a car. He knew it was Sprott. He sat up straighter than ever. He felt ready for him. The front door opened and shut. There were voices in the hall. A minute later the library door opened.

Paul sat perfectly still as Sir Matthew came in. He looked at him, but didn't speak. For a moment there was absolute silence. Then Sprott drew himself up.

"What is the reason for this intrusion?" He was very angry. At the same time there was something else in his eyes. Paul could tell immediately that he knew him. "You've no right to come here. This is my private residence."

That remark revealed everything to Paul — the crack hidden away behind the grand façade. He thought: this man has no right to condemn. His brain suddenly became crystal clear. He said slowly:

"When a matter has been waiting for a long time it becomes urgent."

The veins thickened on the other's forehead. He did not attempt to approach Paul, but still stood near the door. He summoned all his dignity, was again the actor, delivering appropriate lines.

"I won't disguise the fact that for some months now I have been notified of your presence, your movements, in this city. You are the son of a life-term convict trying to stir up trouble over a case that was judged fifteen years ago."

165

"There are doubts about that case," Paul said. "There is fresh evidence which should be heard."

For a moment Sir Matthew's anger got the better of him, even overlaying that secret shadow of mistrust.

"Don't be a fool," he said. "After fifteen years it's a legal impossibility. Because of your infernal meddling a petition to reopen was placed before the Secretary of State, and he refused categorically."

"But you need not refuse," Paul said. "You were the prosecutor. Your main duty is to see that justice is administered. And you would feel yourself compelled to take some step, if you were convinced that my father was innocent."

"But I am not convinced," Sprott almost shouted the words.

"If you would listen you would be convinced. The least you can do is to hear the fresh evidence in your official capacity."

Sprott was so enraged he could scarcely speak. His face seemed full of blood. But with an effort he took hold of himself. At least, his anger chilled. He spoke in an icy tone.

"I really must ask you to go. You simply do not know what you are asking . . . the technical difficulties, the legal machinery, the repercussions involved. You are like a stupid child who wants to pull down a great building because he thinks that one brick, in the foundations, has been badly laid."

"If the foundations are rotten the building will come down."

Sir Matthew did not condescend to answer this. His features were now fixed in a heavy sneer. But as he looked sideways at the young man, head thrust forward, small eyes slanting across his face, Paul could see again that vague misgiving, that secret fissure in the façade, and he knew, finally, that if only because the prosecutor must at all costs hide that crack, he would never, under any conditions, move to reopen the case. Still . . . he must give him one last chance.

"When a prisoner has served fifteen years of a life sentence

. . . isn't it the humane practice . . . for him to be pardoned?"

Sir Matthew, with those protruding, slightly bloodshot eyes, was still looking sideways at Paul. He said cuttingly:

"The Secretary of State has already pronounced upon that point."

"But you haven't," Paul persisted in a suffocating voice. "A word from you in the proper quarters would carry great influence. One word . . . a hint of this new doubt which has arisen . . ."

The prosecutor shook his head, irrevocably, even savagely, disowning all responsibility. With a movement of his arm, behind him, he opened the door.

"Will you go now?" He spoke with that same fixed sneer. "Or must I have you shown out?"

Paul saw then, once and for all, that it was useless. This man would never do anything, would not even stir to utter a plea for pardon. Encased in his official pride, nothing mattered to him but his own dignity, his own position, his own future. Whatever the cost, this must be preserved.

At that thought an uncontrollable rage came over Paul, rage and desperation, it flowed all through him like a drug. Castles was right! His father, Swann, he himself, every human obstacle or obstruction — all had gone down before this man's insatiable pride. Only one thing remained to be done. He stood up. His joints felt stiff, his limbs didn't belong to him. He started to walk towards the burly figure at the door.

"For the last time." His voice was barely audible. He could scarcely breathe.

"No."

He had his hand in his pocket. All the time he was talking he had been holding the gun. It didn't feel cold now . . . the heat of his hand had made it warm . . . as if it were part of him. His finger was on the trigger, he could feel the strength of the spring.

He didn't even have to take the gun out of his pocket. He had it pointed towards Sprott, the actor, the hollow man. The prosecutor suspected nothing. He stood there, not looking at Paul, with that snarl of outraged dignity stamped on his face. Paul was abreast of him now, not more than two feet away. He could see the round bulge of Sprott's well-fed stomach. The gun aimed there, point blank. He was not in the least afraid. He shut his eyes, holding himself tense, his lips slightly parted in a sort of ecstasy, as though all his being were suffused and elevated by a supreme physical desire.

Then, all at once, a convulsive shudder shook his body, in a pang of re-birth, agonizingly, he came back to reason, to himself. No, oh my God, no, he thought in a stabbing flash of light. They had called his father a murderer. Would they make him a murderer too? His grip on the gun relaxed. He opened his eyes, looked at the prosecutor blindly. He was panting, as though he had been running. He could not speak. But as he met those hostile eyes, a faint smile trembled across his lips, all his face shone with a strange illumination. While Sprott stared at him lividly, he walked straight past him, out of the house.

There, in the cool darkness under the stars, a fountain of tears gushed from his eyes. In a low triumphant voice he whispered brokenly to himself:

"I didn't do it. Oh, thank God, I didn't do it."

# Part II

# Chapter 1

THREE weeks before, when Paul was dismissed by the Bonanza manager, Lena had witnessed the incident with a heavy sensation of dismay. This lessened somewhat when she called on Paul that same evening. She had talked with him, conveyed a message which seemed to cheer him, she believed that in some way she had helped him. But as the days passed and she did not see him again, life became strangely drab and empty. At the end of the week another pianist, a young woman, was engaged by Harris, and the notes of the piano drifted anew towards the cafeteria. Alas, without avail: the music was good but it wasn't the same. And the heaviness did not lift from Lena's breast. She felt herself slipping back into a state of abject depression such as she had not known since the time of the calamity which had broken up her life.

In telling Paul that she had been happy in her position at the County Arms Hotel two years ago, she had spoken nothing but the truth. Astbury was a charming old town, noted for its ruined abbey, many black and white Elizabethan houses and some interesting Roman barrows, situated on the prettiest reach of the River Trent, something of a resort during the spring and summer months. And the hotel was of a superior class, run by a retired Army officer named Prentice and his wife, patronized mainly by anglers and tourists from the South. The place and the work suited Lena — her prospects were good, she felt that she was liked by the other members of the staff.

Every other Saturday she had a half day off. It was pleasant to take an excursion by train to Wortley and to spend the afternoon looking through the big department stores, filled with so many things that to a country-bred girl were novel and exciting. At five o'clock she had tea, all by herself, at the Green Lantern, a cheerful little café which she had discovered off Leonard Square. Then, flushed and bright, with her few parcels, she caught the six o'clock train to Astbury. The distance from Astbury Station to the County Arms was considerable, over two miles; the road, which bordered the river, was winding and wooded. But this did not trouble Lena who was a splendid walker, and at home, had been accustomed to tramp for miles across the moors that surrounded Sleescale.

One Saturday evening in the late summer, Lena set out, in her usual spirits, with a cheerful "good-evening" to the ticket-collector, to walk from the station to the hotel. The moon lay behind banks of cloud, the road was in darkness. It was a hot and heavy darkness, with stirrings in the unseen woods, and the sultry hum of night insects in the air. A stagnant, jungle darkness. Even Lena seemed to feel its strange oppression, to fear she was being watched. She recollected that on the train there had been a gang of rowdies. Contrary to her usual custom she kept glancing back across her shoulder. When a dry stick snapped on the path behind her she hastened her pace, nervously, almost to a run. Suddenly, as she approached the loneliest bend of the road, out of the darkness, an arm was thrown about her neck. She let out a cry but a hand, thrust brutally against her mouth, stifled it. She struggled fiercely, with all the strength of her young body, but uselessly. There were five in the gang that had attacked her, five powerful young roughs. She was thrown heavily and in falling, struck her head against a stone. Mercifully she lost consciousness.

Certain acts are unmentionable — they belong to the degradations of the brutes and are best left in their primaeval slime. But there is a certain fateful continuity in crime, an interdependence of chance and circumstance which links events that may be years apart. This horror that happened to Lena Andersen, because it bears upon the Mathry case, because indeed, had it not occurred, the Mathry case might never have been solved, has to be recorded here. When she came to herself, Lena groaned, tried as best she could to comprehend, rose, fell again, then, with a gashed cheek and swollen eyes, staggered to the shelter of the hotel.

The immediate shock occasioned by the outrage shook the entire community. Search parties were organised. But the assailants were never discovered. They were strangers, probably part of the hooligan element from Nottingham that invaded the district at the time of the Mosley Fair.

Major and Mrs. Prentice behaved towards Lena with exemplary kindness. When the first shock had passed, and she was able to get about, they pressed her to take a long holiday at their expense before resuming her duties at the hotel. But neither course was acceptable to Lena. She could not bear the overt solicitude and covert glances, the too obvious attentions showered constantly, and with the best intentions, upon her. She knew that her career at the County Arms was finished. Besides, for another reason, she wanted to get away. Though she told no one, holding the knowledge to herself with stoic reticence, she had discovered, with a shudder, that she was to have a child.

At this time one of the guests at the hotel was a man named Dunn, a taciturn and rather ill-favoured person, who came regularly to Astbury, bent on luring with small flies the silvery salmon which in the autumn were reputed to run up the river. Dunn, amongst other things, was a student of human nature and between his notably unsuccessful forays against the salmon, he studied Lena.

Although he flattered himself that he could not be impressed, he observed with unspoken admiration her silent, dogged courage, her desire to make the best of a dreadful business, above all the quiet endurance with which her wounded, independent soul suffered the prevailing effusive hysteria. He thought, as he dreamed by the river and exposed the bald patch on his scalp to the sun, that he would like to write a book about Lena, but he was not a writer of books and he feared he would make sad work of it. Still, he had the perception to divine what Lena's bruised spirit was seeking after — to escape utterly, to lose her own identity, away from everyone who had ever known her. Without fuss, he arranged for her to get away to Wortley, to a woman by the name of Hanley, an old friend whom he knew to be reliable.

Dunn was not a rich man and he had a wife and family to support. Nevertheless, the peculiar qualities of his character led him to stand by Lena in her trouble when she had been forgotten by all those sweet people who had gushed with the milk of human kindness and run to put cushions behind her back on the front verandah of the hotel.

He arranged for her confinement, which proved difficult and dangerous. The child, born deaf and dumb, was not normal, lived for only a few weeks then mercifully died. But it was months before Lena, prostrated physically and mentally, was able to crawl back to her lodging with Mrs. Hanley.

Dunn did not offer to find Lena a job. Now that the worst was over, he wanted her to get her feet on the ground again. When, finally, she was engaged at the Bonanza Cafeteria he did not tell her it was unsuitable. He merely nodded in approval. And often, on his way to work, he would stop in for a coffee, to view the progress of his protégé. Beneath his habitual detachment he watched the situation with interest, the struggle for regeneration taking place in this wounded, stoic soul. It amused Dunn to find that her unfailing remedy for the moods of sadness which so often weighed upon her was hard work.

This was the antidote which she now applied to her present melancholy. When she got home from the store she put on her overall and set to, in noiseless determination, scrubbed and polished the floor, laundered the window curtains, blackleaded the grate and burnished the brasses, worked on her two rooms until they shone.

At the weekend she looked round helplessly: there was nothing more to do, not a speck of dust which she could attack. Restively, she went downstairs to Mrs. Hanley's domain and set to work to bake a cake. Afterwards, she sat in the landlady's parlour, listening to the latest letter from Mrs. Hanley's husband Joe who had sailed from Tampico and was to dock in Tilbury the following Monday. But her attention wandered sadly from the engineer's news.

"What's the matter, Lena?" Mrs. Hanley asked. "You don't seem yourself. You've been overdoing it."

"It's nothing." She forced a smile.

"No, you're a bit off colour. I scarcely feel like leaving you. It's a shame Joe has to stand by the ship for the refit . . . all his month's leave too."

"I'll be all right. And you'll have a nice time in London."

"Well . . . I've always wanted to go. And the company pays our hotel for the whole four weeks. Still . . . promise me you'll take care of yourself."

"I will . . . I'll slack off tomorrow. It's my Saturday off."

But Saturday did not noticeably improve Lena's state. On the next afternoon, when she had seen Mrs. Hanley off at the station, a painful loneliness descended upon her and, strangely, her steps wandered from the path which normally constituted her Sunday outing. With a start of confusion and self-reproach, she found herself at the entrance to the Botanic Gardens.

"Well," she thought, frowning at her weakness, "since I came, I may as well go in. At least it's free today."

She passed through the wide gates and set off along the trim paths in a direction quite opposite to that which she had taken with Paul. For an hour she fought her inclination, but at the end, as she was about to leave, she entered the orangery. Inside the tall ornamental glasshouse as she drew near the slender orange tree which they had viewed together, her heart was beating heavily. Hastily, she pressed her face against a branch, heavy with waxen, perfumed flowers. A single tear, salt and bitter, splashed upon her hand as she turned away.

That night, while she undressed she suddenly caught sight of herself, her unclothed body, in the little mirror on the dresser, the marks of her pregnancy showing clearly, bluish cicatrices, on her white skin. She grew rigid then, sick with self-disgust, without warning she struck herself a hard blow on her scarred cheek.

"Don't be a fool," she whispered to herself. "It's no good . . . ever."

She switched out the light, and closed her eyes tightly in the darkness.

However, all her resolution was insufficient to beat down all of the feeling which swelled within her. It was stronger than she and at last she yielded to it with a shamed surrender. On the following night, immediately she left the store, she went to Paul's lodging in Poole Street and asked if she might see him.

Mrs. Coppin inspected her with narrowed eyes.

"He's gone," she answered shortly.

Lena's heart missed a beat. But she persevered.

"Where did he go?"

"I've no idea. It may interest you to know that the police came inquiring for him." "I had to keep his suitcase for the rent," she added.

There was a pause. A thought formed in Lena's mind.

"If I pay you, can I take away his things?"

Mrs. Coppin reflected. The value of the goods she had distrained was slight, she had never expected "to see the colour of her money" from them. In a case like this, one did not ask questions — the opportunity was too good to miss. She made an acid murmur of assent and leaving the door ajar, went back into the house.

Flushed, and with a secret air, Lena took home the battered brown suitcase she had redeemed. It contained only a few worn articles of clothing. She washed and ironed the shirts, darned the socks, sponged the shapeless flannel trousers and pressed them with her hot iron to a fine edge. She even placed a few shillings in the pocket. While she did this she experienced a further alleviation of her feeling, but when everything was neatly folded and restored to the suitcase, she was no better off than before. More and more, she became convinced that some misfortune had overtaken Paul.

Then, at the Bonanza, she had word of him. Next morning, as she went in, Nancy Wilson was relating an incident with great gusto to the others. Everyone was clustered round, even Harris stood near, listening — it was such a tid-bit of news.

"I tell you." Nancy spoke dramatically. "You could have knocked me down with a feather. There I was, going to the pictures with my young man, when I saw him, carrying a billboard. At first I scarcely recognised him he was that changed — thin and shabby, ragged in fact, without an overcoat to his back. 'Wait George, just a minute,' I said to my young man, 'there's somebody I used to know.' And I stood and watched him while he tramped in line with the other dead beats. It was Paul all right. He suddenly caught sight of me across the street and he turned and slunk away."

A chorus went up from the little audience. Lena felt herself turn weak.

"You ought to have seen him." Nancy rolled her eyes. "He's regular down and out."

"I knew he was no good." Harris concluded the session, with an air of superior knowledge. "I got the tip from the police. Come on now . . . back to your counters."

It was then that the last of Lena's defences broke. She knew her own folly, knew also that she was laying up a store of future misery. Yet she could not help herself. She began, frankly, to search for Paul. Every morning, as she went to work, and every evening when she returned, she chose roundabout ways, combing all the poorer streets of the city, her eyes alert for his dejected figure. In her free time she waited for hours around Leonard Street Station. She tried the other stations too. But he was not there. In all her eager efforts she knew only failure, days and nights of bitter disappointment.

# Chapter 2

WHEN Paul moved off from the prosecutor's house, blindly traversing the silent streets, the night was cold and clear, with a biting wind, and a keen touch of frost in the air. Almost overcome by the weakness of reaction, one idea was uppermost in his mind. And when, presently, he reached the canal he drew the gun from his pocket and, with a sob of relief, hurled it far into the oily water. A dull splash echoed in his ears. Numbly he watched the dark circles ebb in the moonlight. Only when the last ripple had gone did he turn away.

At that moment the clock on the Ware steeple struck eleven. The heavy strokes brought him back more fully to himself and suddenly, through the turmoil of his thoughts and the overpowering lassitude which bore upon him, he realized that he was penniless. He drew up, wondering where he could spend the night. Gradually it became apparent that only one course was open to him. He would have to do what Jerry and the others at the lodging house dreaded beyond all else. He had to sleep out. There was a place known as the Arches, the only corner of the city, short of the graveyard, where — by some strange unwritten law — the homeless might "doss out" undisturbed. As Paul slowly resumed his way towards this wretched spot he felt that the last frail bulwark of his respectability was gone. Now, surely, he was beyond the pale.

The Arches lay not far from the canal; two dark cuttings under the span of the Midland Railway Bridge. And when he arrived other unfortunates had already settled themselves for the night. Pulling up his coat collar, he sank down in the chilly shadows with his hands in his pockets and his back against a round iron pillar. It was bitterly cold. Trying to suppress his shivers, Paul drowsed in fitful snatches. Morning came in a grey and sullen haze, with the heavy thunder of an early train upon the bridge above. So cold and cramped he could scarcely rise, Paul got to his feet and stumbled off. In a sick fashion, his stomach ached for food, but he had not even the price of a farthing roll. Instinctively he moved off in the direction of the Lanes Advertising Company then, finding the gates closed, bent his steps towards Leonard Street Railway Station. Here, he hung about the outer approaches all day, roundly abused by the regular porters, and in the end earned ninepence. It was not enough for both supper and a bed. In a nearby workman's café he ordered sausage and mash, an ill-cooked, greasy meal which lay like lead on his stomach and gave him a griping pain as, once again, he dragged back to the Arches.

Next morning it was raining hard. He could not face the station again and wandered off through the streets in search of shelter. Already he was filled with lassitude; yet there seemed nowhere in this great city where, without payment, he could sit down. Finally he came upon a billiard saloon and, upstairs in the smoky atmosphere, lit by green-shaded lamps, he found a refuge. But it was only temporary — when he had apathetically watched a few games and gave no sign of playing, the attendant quietly approached him and asked him to leave.

Out in the street again all he knew was that he had to keep moving, to what destination he did not care.

In the late afternoon he found himself on the tow-path of the branch canal, a dismal, inky channel flanked by factories and pottery kilns. Here a bargee hailed him, and asked him to take the rope while his craft negotiated the hand-operated lock. On the barge was a motherly-looking woman frying bacon and eggs on the open cabin stove. Perhaps she had a shrewd idea of Paul's condition. When he had pulled them clear, before the boat got under way, she handed him a thick bacon sandwich, hot from the pan.

This sign of kindness, the glance of pity that the woman gave him, shook him painfully, and he was taken by a sudden overwhelming desire to abandon everything, to go home, back to a normal life of decent human comfort. But with a trembling lip, he fought the impulse down. He would never give up, never. Rain-drenched, he made his way back to the city and the Arches.

And now there began for Paul a period of such clouded suffering that when, from time to time, the realization of his state broke through the mists into his consciousness it caused him a start of haggard disbelief. Dependent always upon the chance of a casual coin, there were days when he went entirely without food. For brief intervals his memory would fail him, he would wander in a sort of stupor. In this nightmare state in which he moved, he forgot who he was, and when he remembered he had an irrational desire to go up to strangers and explain his identity to them. At other times he saw the people in the street merely as blurred forms and, blundering into someone, would murmur an apology before moving on. Through it all he had the notion — less an illusion than a conviction — that he was being followed and it was always the face of Jupp, the police sergeant, who watched from the shadows, watched and waited, expressionless yet hostile, for the inevitable end. Vaguely, he asked himself why he was not arrested. His clothes were soiled, his boots leaking, he had not shaved for days. His hair, uncut, fell across his collar, his eyes had no expression. He wondered dizzily if it were possible to starve to death in this great and thriving city.

Of course there was charity — and at last, too broken to be proud — he came to this last resort. One evening as dusk approached he dragged himself to the eastside corner of the Corn Market. Here, in a small triangular space between the tramway tracks, a plain wheeled wagon stood, a sort of caravan, with a tin chimney and a flapboard, already surrounded by a waiting, destitute throng. At five o'clock exactly, the flapboard was let down, forming a counter and disclosing in the interior of the caravan, a modern kitchen unit. An attendant in a white apron stood behind the counter and as each man advanced he handed him a bowl of soup and a hunk of bread and dripping. When Paul, in his turn, received his portion, the scalding soup flowed into his veins with a reviving glow. He ate the bread and dripping hungrily, then walked silently away.

Amidst the flitting obscurity of his life, in this struggle, needless yet savage, for survival, this Free Canteen became the one fixed point, the focus, as it were, of his existence. Every night, in fair weather and in foul, he silently joined the waiting figures. The men never talked, they simply waited. And when they had been fed they slid away, back into the shadows, in equal silence.

Then, after about a week, on the night of Wednesday the white-aproned attendant was joined by a man of about fifty, tall and erect, dressed in black, almost clerical, with dark eyes and a faint, yet kindly smile. Paul recognised him at once as Enoch Oswald,

181

became aware for the first time that he had been frequenting the Silver King Canteen. Indeed, when Mr. Oswald removed his black wide-brimmed soft hat his hair under the naphtha lights gleamed silver white, a feature so striking it had earned him the name by which he was familiarly known to the outcasts who received his bounty.

Bareheaded, wearing that remote, friendly smile, he came slowly down the breadline, stopping a moment at each man, not looking at him, never speaking, but pressing into his palm a newly minted shilling. As Oswald stood beside him, Paul, though his head remained bent, was throbbingly conscious of his presence. At first this emotion was purely one of gratitude. But gradually another feeling took possession of him, a deep, despairing longing, born of his own hopelessness, to enlist the aid of this truly good man who, in his passionate urge to extend a hand to the neediest of creatures, surely could not fail to help him. Betrayed by Castles, bogged in the quicksands of human treachery, lost and hunted, he had need, before God, of such succour and support.

The desire to speak, to reveal himself, and his predicament, became overmastering. What a chance, he thought breathlessly. More and more, through hours of painful brooding, he had come to realize that only through Burt could he pierce the mystery of the murder. Burt knew — of that he was certain. Burt was at hand, alive and real — the rest was shadowy, lost in the obscurity of the years. And here, at his side, was the single person who, beyond anyone, from his position and influence, could compel the wretched woman to speak. Surely, in the circumstances of his destitution, which had brought them face to face like this, there was something providential and predestined.

A kind of vertigo took hold of Paul. In his enfeebled and nervous state, the suddenness of the opportunity was too much for him. He was taken by a spasm of the larynx, words died in his throat, he failed to open his lips. When his head ceased to spin and he came to himself, his benefactor was gone. Savagely he cursed himself for his weakness. He dared not go openly to the Oswald home. But from the attendant he learned that the "boss" visited the canteen every Wednesday night, and through his disappointment, he realized that in the following week, his chance would come again. The silver coin remaining in his hand was like a talisman.

The next few days were hard to bear. Towards the end of that week the weather turned colder. Recurrent fogs swept up from the fens and settled like a blight upon the city. In this grimy twilight the smoky air was charged with sulphur fumes. Paul developed a hacking cough. In his lucid intervals, he acknowledged to himself that he could not go on.

Then, Wednesday came again, and hope revived in him. He went early to the Corn Market and took his place amongst the first arrivals at the Canteen. Night fell swiftly. The naphtha flares were lighted, the hatch thrown down. Suddenly, as he waited in the breadline, he became conscious of someone standing beside him. It was not the inspiring presence of the Silver King. After a moment, he raised his head. He saw it was Lena Andersen.

# Chapter 3

YES, he was there, she was actually beside him, but the change in him was so great it moved her deeply.

"Why, Paul . . . it's you." She pretended the meeting was an accident.

Deadly pale, he averted his eyes and did not answer.

"It's quite a surprise." She stumbled on. "Why don't we walk down the street together?"

After a pause he said:

"I have to wait here."

"But why?"

He knew she would not understand if he told her. He answered flatly:

"As a matter of fact, this is where I have supper. If I lose my place I shall be out of luck."

The blankness of his manner, as he made this admission stabbed her anew. She said:

"I'm just going home. Come and have supper with me."

He turned his strained eyes towards her. There was a solicitude in her gaze which intensified the perpetual ache that lay about his heart.

"You mustn't get mixed up with me," he muttered.

Her gaze, undeterred, remained upon him.

"Come, Paul . . . please come."

He hesitated, torn between his weakness and his determination to await the Silver King. A wave of dizziness swept over him. At last he mumbled, glancing downwards at his frayed trousers and cracked boots.

"I can't walk through the streets with you like this. Leave me now . . . I want to stay here for half an hour. I'll come to your place later."

"You promise." She breathed quickly.

He nodded. For a moment she considered him anxiously; then, giving him a final glance, she slowly moved away.

His head drooped, he did not follow her with his eyes, yet somehow from the unexpected sight of her, in the great sea of nameless, unknown faces, hope had been renewed, as though perhaps at last things might turn for the better.

It began to rain, the slanting pitiless rain of an English winter. Instinctively Paul turned up the collar of his jacket and, as the distribution of bread and coffee had begun, edged slowly forward in the line, alert for the appearance of Enoch Oswald.

Tonight, however, the Silver King was long in coming and when Paul reached the hatch, he had not yet arrived. In acute suspense, Paul scanned the approaches to the market then, turning to the attendant he said:

"The boss is late tonight."

"Not coming till tomorrow," answered the other, slapping down a tray of fresh cups. "Next!"

A cruel disappointment struck at Paul. He was counting so much on this meeting, that now, even its postponement by so brief an interval was enough to unsettle him. The pressure of the line behind forced him forward. He did not take either his coffee or his bread. He remained motionless for a moment, then, with an indeterminate glance at the Market clock, moved off, without purport, dragging his feet along the greasy pavement.

But Lena had not gone home, she had remained in shelter across the street and, at the corner of the square, she joined him.

"Come, Paul."

"In point of principle," he began vaguely, "that is to say, in the realm of pure logic . . . well, I really don't know. . . ."

She was thoroughly alarmed now. Her hesitation vanished. She put out her hand and took his arm. He submitted while she led him away. He did not speak a word all the way to Ware Place, but she could see his lips moving, from time to time, as though he were talking to himself. Once or twice he looked behind him, over his shoulder.

When he entered the house and climbed the stairs, she was paler than before, but her manner was firm. On the landing, outside her little living room she faced him.

"You'll have supper in a minute." Although she was trembling within, her expression was steady. "But first you must have a change."

She showed him the bathroom, turned on the hot tap, brought

185

him soap, towels, his own shaving things, and a change of clothing. He considered the pile of clean garments with a strange fixity.

"Whose are these?"

"They're yours," she said quickly. "Now don't ask questions. Just get ready."

While he was in the bathroom she lit the fire in the living room, went into the cupboard kitchenette, placed two saucepans upon the stove, hurriedly set the table. When he came out shaved, wearing the flannel trousers and an open-necked shirt, her preparations were almost complete. In silence she placed a chair at the table, motioned him to sit down, and set a bowl of soup before him.

He held the bowl in both hands, before recognising the spoon on the table cloth before him. He dipped the spoon in the thick broth and raised it shakily to his lips. When the bowl was empty, she gave him a plate of meat stew. He ate in silence and with such abstraction, he did not see her watching him. He was painfully thin, but worse than that, was the fixity, the stiff deadness of his face in repose. When at last he had finished he sighed and raised his head. He spoke in a low voice.

"I haven't had a meal like that for weeks."

"Do you feel better?" she asked, getting to her feet to hide the tears that rushed, unbidden, to her eyes.

"Much better." And he got up as though to go — he seemed to be obsessed with the idea that he must move on.

Abruptly, she turned his chair to the fire. When he understood that it was for him he sat down, his hands locked together, eyes bent upon the leaping flames. Occasionally, with a kind of anxious wonder, his glance strayed round the room, absorbing the novelty and comfort of those four surrounding walls.

Observing him, while she cleared the table, Lena's lips set determinedly. The situation, in the absence of her landlady, was painfully difficult, yet she did not shrink from it. When she had finished washing up, she unrolled her sleeves and quietly went out. Ten minutes later she returned, and came over to where he still sat staring at the flames.

Suddenly aware of her presence he started, and got to his feet.

"Well . . . it's about time I went."

"Where?"

"Back to my hotel."

"And where is that?"

He tried to force a smile, but something went wrong with the muscles of his face. His shoulders drooped, he hung his head.

"Under the Arches, if you want to know. If you're not there on time you don't get under cover." A short laugh shook him. "It's damp when the rain gets down your neck."

"No," Lena said. "You're not going."

"But I must." He spoke with sudden agitation. "Don't you understand? I can't keep walking the streets all night. Give me my coat. If I don't get my place there, where am I to sleep?"

"Here," said Lena. "This is where you'll sleep. You can have Mrs. Hanley's spare room. And the sooner you're in bed the better."

She swung round and led the way to the half landing where she threw open the door of the room she had already prepared for him. The red curtains were drawn, the lamp was lit, the gas fire glowed, the covers of the comfortable bed had been turned down.

He rubbed his eyes slowly with the back of his hand as though unable fully to apprehend this cheerful warmth.

"Really," he said in a stilted, dazed fashion, "supper . . . and a bed. How can one adequately express . . ."

"Oh, Paul," Lena murmured, in a breaking voice, "don't try to say any more . . . just go to bed and rest."

"Yes," he agreed. "That's it . . . rest."

187

As they stood there, a sudden gust outside blew a spatter of rain against the window panes. Instinctively Paul shivered and, at the thought of that cold wet outer darkness, a childish sob rose in his throat. Holding his face averted so that she should not see the twitching of his cheek, he entered the room and closed the door behind him.

# Chapter 4

THE daylight was glinting into the room when Paul awoke. He lay quite still for a few minutes, getting his bearings; then, hearing sounds next door he got up, dressed quickly, and went into the kitchen. Lena was there, placing breakfast upon the table. As he entered she flushed suddenly, a deep wave of colour that flooded her face and neck. She had scarcely slept all night, thinking of Paul, so near to her at last, yet at the same time reproaching herself for the liberty she had taken in her landlady's absence. Nevertheless, despite the difficulty of her position her instinct was to keep him here, away from the streets, at all costs, at least until Mrs. Hanley returned. She poured out coffee, gave him a boiled egg and toast, watched him begin to eat. He did not talk much and she judged it wisest to restrain her own remarks. Finally, having finished her breakfast, and without any further comment, as though taking his presence for granted, she went off to the Bonanza.

When Lena had gone Paul returned to his room and he remained there, overcome by a profound lassitude, most of the forenoon. After all that he had endured, this sense of shelter, of transitory safety, gave him an opportunity to think. And, freed of the misery of the Arches, properly clad and fed, he felt his courage return, his brain began to function more lucidly, he decided he must, after all, make an effort to see Mr. Oswald at his house.

Just on four o'clock he left the flat. It was a long way to Porlock Hill and he was forced several times to sit down on a bench, when crossing the Park. But in about an hour's time he reached that neighbourhood which he had avoided for so long.

Suddenly, as he made to cross to Porlock Drive, he encountered a man at the corner of the street who stared at him curiously in the fading light as he passed, then stopped, turned, and came back. It was Jack, the waiter at the Royal Oak.

"It's you," Jack exclaimed in some surprise. Then: "I have something for you."

The words penetrated Paul's apathy. He stood passive, as the other pulled out a battered wallet, and began to search through it.

"Ah, here we are," Jack said. "I've had it on me for the last two weeks. Louisa Burt asked me to give it to you."

Paul's haunted gaze rested on the dirty envelope which the waiter extended towards him, and imperceptibly the current of his blood moved faster. He stretched out his hand and accepted it. Jack was looking at him with a sharper curiosity.

"We don't see you around much lately."

"No," Paul answered. "Not much."

"Down on your luck, eh?"

"I'm all right." Paul spoke in an automatic tone, his eyes still resting on the envelope, a queer, unformed premonition stirring within him.

There was a silence. The waiter shifted his feet.

"Well," he said at last, "I have to be going. All the best."

He shot a final inquisitive glance at Paul then he shrugged his shoulders, turned and made off down the street.

As the waiter disappeared from sight Paul was still standing in the dreary twilight, motionless. He passed his tongue over

189

his pale lips. With the soiled paper tightly in his hand he hurried towards the nearest lamp-post and tore open the envelope. Holding up the letter to the flickering light he read:

DEAR MR. SMARTY,

Seeing as how you thought you'd make a monkey out of me, as I've since been tipped off, I'd like fer you to know for your own information that I am going to be married, proper, in church, and don't need your attentions nor promises no more, fine sir. Arrangements has been made by Mr. Oswald fer me and my husbant to sail to New Zealand next month just like he done fer my friend Ed Collins what was here before me, who I expects to renew my acquaintance with when I arrives. So you can think on me in comfort and lucksury in a new land and I wish it makes you choke.

Yours,

LOUISA BURT

P.S. You didn't never kid me. I pity you.

Slowly, Paul lifted his disillusioned eyes. After all, it was nothing. And yet, strange thoughts were rising in his mind like mist above a sluggish pond. With a kind of aching wonder he floated in the twilight between reality and illusion. The street swam vaguely before him. There was a humming, a buzzing in his head. Then, as though his mind, dormant for these past weeks, had, in repose, gathered all its forces, he experienced a blaze of lucid power. Slowly the veils parted.

One shoulder dropping, an arm extended, towards the windblown light, he re-read the letter, so spiteful and stupid, so reeking with a cheap, offended vanity. That one phrase — vital, significant and terrible — stood out as though written in letters of fire: *my friend Ed Collins . . . here before me. . . .* His face wore, in the half light, an unnatural rigidity. But his eyes were glittering, and the pulse in his temple was beating fast.

190

Still holding the letter he hung on to the lamp standard as though crushed by an overwhelming weight. Why had he never dreamed of this before? While his brain still reeled he fought for calmness, fought to recollect his dizzy thoughts.

Louisa Burt had been in service with the Oswalds for twelve years — that in itself, though remarkable, was an innocuous fact. But this fact became at once exceptional and unique when coupled with the fact that Burt's co-servant in the household had been Edward Collins.

Ah, yes, how had it come about that these two young persons, the vital witnesses in the Mathry case, had both found positions with the Oswald family. Philanthropy might explain this. Yet it was a peculiar good heartedness which, as its ultimate manifestation, sought to marry off each of the two servants, and to ship them away to the furthest corner of the globe.

Paul felt his nerves vibrate and upon the screen of his sight there came a sudden vision of Enoch Oswald — tall and craggy of figure, his massive head sunk into those high, angular shoulders, the dark eyes glowing benevolently beneath their silvery brows. Could it be that this good man was involved, in some manner, in the case?

The tentacles of Paul's thought reached out, flickering and questing, keyed to an unnatural alertness. Why it should be so he could not tell but, at this precise moment, his whole consciousness seemed drawn and directed towards one extraordinary recollection — the sound of the voice of the man who had spoken with Albert Prusty on the dark stair landing that afternoon of the snowstorm, the landlord of Ushaw Terrace.

Like a beam from the darkness, fresh suspicion struck at Paul. He straightened in growing excitement. Since this was Thursday, the tobacconist's day of early closing, Prusty would almost certainly be at home. It was not yet five o'clock. Impulsively he squared his shoulders and set off through the rain.

191

# Chapter 5

TWENTY minutes later he was rattling upon the second-floor door of 52 Ushaw Terrace. At first there was no response, but after repeated knockings, the letter slot swung back and Prusty's voice came through.

"Who is it? I can't see anyone."

Quickly, Paul bent down and revealed himself.

"I have asthma," Prusty complained. "And I'm just turning in. Come back tomorrow."

"No, no . . . I must see you now . . . I must."

Paul was not to be denied and finally, after much grumbling, the tobacconist opened the door and admitted him to the hall, which was very hot and filled with the pungent aroma of burning stramonium powder. Wearing only shirt and trousers, Prusty wheezed spasmodically as he gazed at Paul, his cheeks slightly congested, his expression justifiably incensed.

"What the devil do you want?"

"I won't keep you a minute." Paul spoke hurriedly. "I only wanted to ask you . . ." his mouth suddenly was parched, he swallowed dryly, "who is the landlord of this house?"

In the close and overheated passage, Prusty's irritable wheezing seemed almost stifled by surprise. He peered at his visitor.

"Why, you heard me talking to him that afternoon. It's Mr. Enoch Oswald."

Again Paul felt weak, as though struck by a hammer of ice. He supported himself against the lobby wall.

"I didn't realize it was Mr. Oswald."

"Well it was . . . and it is. He owns all the Terrace . . . like his father did before him. He's one of the biggest property owners, and one of the best, in Wortley. He's not raised the rent on me once in ten years. And he's kept my flat in nice repair."

"And the flat upstairs," Paul said in a strange, suppressed tone, "he's kept that nice too?"

"Of course he has," Prusty answered warmly. "The man has a sense of decency and respect. What the devil has got into you?"

"I don't know. Have you still got the key?"

"Yes, I have. And I have the asthma too. You'll have to go. I can't stand here in my shirt tails any longer."

He began to press Paul towards the doorway.

"Just a minute. You remember you promised I could look at the flat upstairs. Well, give me the key."

Prusty's face was a study in annoyance. He seemed about to refuse. Yet he did not wish to go back on his word and he wanted to be rid of Paul. Abruptly he went into the kitchen and returned with the key.

"Here!" he exclaimed, curtly. "Now leave me in peace."

He banged the door shut.

On the landing Paul stood, in the half darkness, hearing Prusty draw the bolt behind the oak panels. His eyes were tensely raised towards the flight of stairs which led dimly to the flat above. But as he took the first step upwards, a better, and more immediate course of action flashed across the screen of his mind. He checked himself, reflected further, then slipped the key into his pocket. Not yet, he thought. He swung round sharply and went down.

Outside, he turned up the collar of his coat against the bitter wind, and hurried off. A dreadful suspicion was forming steadily in his throbbing head. In his calmer moments he would have dismissed it as sheer insanity. But now he was driven beyond all calmness, and this thought, this thing within him, grew from nothing, grew with an urgency beyond his control, until it filled and suffocatingly possessed him. Enoch Oswald . . . it was he who owned the flat which Mona Spurling had occupied. Since he conducted his business personally he must have seen her at least every month when he collected his rents. And if he had called upon her oftener, who would question his comings and goings? He was the landlord, free of the common entry, a person no more noticeable than the postman, or the grocer who delivered her daily stores. If Mona Spurling had been this man's mistress who would have suspected it? If he had murdered her . . .

A shuddering convulsion swept over Paul. This was lunacy perhaps, yet his tortured mind would not, could not, let it go, but kept piecing together, like links in a preposterous chain, the singular actions of this man of property. Even his public benefactions now seemed a sham, or at best, a form of atonement exacted by an unconquerable sense of guilt.

Almost running now, Paul reached the centre of the city and, breathlessly, entered the reference department of the Leonard Library, that dim and musty room where, months before, his first groping and uncertain strivings had begun.

Mark was no longer behind the counter, a young woman was in attendance, and in response to his pressing request served him with intelligent civility. Bearing the load of books she gave him to a remote corner table, he applied himself with feverish energy to a rapid perusal of their pages.

The first volume, the national *Who's Who*, contained no more than a few lines of condensed information relating to the parentage, official titles, and present address of Enoch Oswald. Two others were equally brief, equally useless for his purpose. A fourth gave no more than a lengthy list of the charitable foundations supported by the Oswald family. But finally, in a local publication issued in paper covers by a firm of Wortley printers, entitled *Wortley and its Notables*, Paul, with a gasp of satisfaction, came upon a full biography of the city's most prominent philanthropist. Avidly, with the speed of lightning, his gaze flashed across the conventional and flattering paragraphs.

Enoch Oswald, born 13 November 1891, only child of Saul Oswald and Martha Cleghorn. . . . Educated Wortley Grammar School and Nottingham University. . . . At first was intended for a professional career but owing to ill health, after two years at St. Mary's Hospital, abandoned his studies as a medical student. . . .

A thrill passed over Paul as he realized the significance of these last two words. Scarcely breathing, he read on:

Thereafter . . . entered his father's business . . . prosperous and old-established . . . extensive property holdings in Eldon . . . began in exemplary fashion, at the lowest rung of the ladder, collecting weekly and monthly rents. . . .

Despite recurrent attacks or indisposition young Oswald was no milksop . . . an interest in outdoor sports . . . in particular cycling . . . and for some months . . . was an active member of the short-lived Grasshoppers' Club. . . .

The screed continued, but now the ill-set lines of print were blurred and twisted, Paul could no longer read them. He lay back, overcome. Amidst the grim reflections that poured like a torrent through his brain, Paul became conscious of what he must do next. With this supreme objective looming before him there was no time for hesitation or compunction. Charged again with preternatural energy, he pushed back his chair with a clatter and, leaving the books littered on the table, dashed from the room.

Ten minutes later he entered Ware Place, ran up the steps to the door of Mrs. Hanley's house. It was Lena herself who answered his knock. Then, even as she welcomed him, he said in a tone which startled her:

"Lena . . . I want your help . . . now, at once."

# Chapter 6

STANDING in the hallway, heedless of her questions, and of the solicitous glances which she cast upon him, he outlined in detail what he wanted. His words were so laboured, his air so unnatural, she wondered if he had not momentarily been thrown off balance. Despite her anxiety, and the apparent absurdity of his requests, there was in his manner something deep and terrible which caused her to obey. She went into the kitchen and found a cardboard box, brown paper, string, a stick of sealing wax. From her bedroom she brought an old notebook with some pages still unused.

In the dim hall, her hand pressed against her side, she watched him as, methodically, he wrapped the box in the sheet of brown paper, then tied it up, sealing the string with the red wax.

Next he turned his attention to the slip book, selecting a clean page, filled in the first six lines in pencil with names and addresses.

"Oh, Paul," she exclaimed. "What on earth are you doing?"

He hesitated. Perhaps he had an inkling that his actions verged upon the fantastic. But shock had dulled his mental processes and, having fixed upon this plan, he clung to it tenaciously. One thing more he must discover . . . only one thing more.

"I'll explain later . . . now we have to go out."

She stood beside him, torn by feeling, scarcely knowing whether to obey. Yet perhaps in these trivial, almost senseless preparations, there lay something of importance.

"Don't worry," he said. "It's quite simple."

"Simple or difficult, I'll do it."

He looked across at her. In a suppressed voice he went over what she was to do.

"You understand?"

"I think so. But Paul . . ." her voice shook, "there's nothing in the package."

A queer look came into his eyes.

"Nothing . . . yet everything." He glanced at the hallway clock which indicated a few minutes to nine. "We may as well go now. Are you ready? The whole thing won't take half an hour."

They went out together. They walked in silence along Ware Street in the direction of the Lanes, turned right down Northern Road, then left through the narrow passage known as Weaver's Alley. At the end of the Alley Paul drew up, his gaze searching the open triangle of the Corn Market. The canteen was open, the long line of men was already in motion, and, with a shrinking of all his flesh, he saw that Oswald had arrived. He stood at the tailboard, plainly visible under the hanging electric light, his silver hair gleaming, palely, like a halo, in the dusk.

Instinctively, Paul retreated a step into the deeper shadow of the alley. Deep in his mind lay the conviction that Oswald was aware of his identity. For this reason he had decided to refrain from showing himself lest he impair the validity of this crucial test. For a long time he stood motionless; then, with an imperceptible motion of his arm, he directed Lena towards the canteen.

Steadily, she crossed the street and approached the figure of the Silver King. The dryness in Paul's throat increased. He leaned forward, his eyes starting from their sockets, his whole body rigid. Watching, he saw Lena address the Silver King — he could almost follow the movements of her lips as she spoke.

"Mr. Oswald?"

The tall figure gave Lena his attention, then made a dignified inclination of assent.

"I was asked to deliver this to you, sir."

197

How good, how steady and composed were Lena's actions! Paul ceased to breathe as she passed over the package, held the receipt book open, offered the pencil stub to Oswald.

"Sign here, sir, please."

The pencil was now in Oswald's hand. The moment was prolonged beyond endurance, the silence grew so rigid and unnatural it seemed to crack Paul's eardrums. Then Oswald signed the book. A long sigh, a slow expulsion of breath came from Paul. Lena was on her way back, still walking steadily, unhurried and composed. Now she had joined him. Without a word he turned. Their retreating footsteps were muffled in the thick darkness of the deserted alley.

# Chapter 7

PAUL never knew how he got back to Ware Place. On the return journey he did not speak but walked blindly, with lowered head, on the verge of physical collapse. When they reached No. 61, he sat down, dominated by a single thought. A hard pain kept beating behind his forehead, and chill, shivering waves swept over him. Oswald was left-handed. Enoch Oswald, ex-student of anatomy, member of the Grasshoppers' Club, collector of rents, owner of 52 Ushaw Terrace, was the man. The revelation suffocated him, dazed him by its blinding light. He could not, by himself, sustain it. Leaning his elbows on the table, he supported his head, with both hands.

"Lena," he muttered. "There's something I must tell you."

"Not yet, Paul." She was very pale, but her expression was firm. From the pot simmering on the stove she poured a cup of soup and, with an insistence not to be denied, forced him to drink it.

198

When he had finished she sat down opposite him.

"Now, Paul," she said quietly.

There was a pause. Then, raising his head, he began to speak and, while she listened intently, he told her everything. Although his voice was low and tremulous, his manner held a seething bitterness as he concluded:

"So now I know. I know it all. And what can I do? Nothing. Whom can I go to? Nobody. When they wouldn't listen to me before, what do you think they'd do — Sprott, or Dale, or even Birley — if I went to them with this? There's no justice. So long as people are comfortable themselves, with plenty to eat and drink, spending money in their pockets and a roof over their heads, they don't care a damn about right and wrong. The whole world's rotten to the core."

There was a rigid silence. Deeply moved, she shook her head slowly.

"No. If people only knew about this . . . they wouldn't allow it. Ordinary people are honest . . . and kind."

He looked at her with disbelief.

"Does your experience prove that?"

She coloured slightly, started to speak, then as though unsure of his meaning, was silent. But in a moment she took a deep breath.

"Paul! I'm not clever. Yet I think I know what you should do."

He stared at her.

"Yes," she said earnestly. "There is someone you should go to."

Incredulously, he repeated her words. Then he added:

"Who?"

"Well," she hesitated, her face flushed and confused, "it is a friend of mine."

"A friend of yours? A friend of . . ." As he echoed the words they sounded so inept, so preposterous, in the face of his terrible dilemma that a pained and twisted smile distorted his cheek.

199

A friend of Lena's! After all his efforts, all that he had tried to do, this naïve solution seemed so ridiculous that, without warning, in a fit of sheer hysteria, he began to laugh. Try as he might, he could not stop laughing and before he knew what was happening, all the rending anguish in his breast flowed over in a burst of choking sobs. She had risen to her feet and was gazing at him, deeply troubled, but afraid even to lay a hand upon his shoulder. When at last the spasm was over she said:

"You must get some rest now. We'll talk it over tomorrow."

"Tomorrow," he echoed, in a strange, savage tone. "Yes . . . lots of things will happen tomorrow."

Alone, in the spare room he had occupied the night before, Paul sat down on the edge of the bed. His head felt hot and his feet were cold. He sensed vaguely that he had caught a chill, but this seemed to him of no importance whatsoever. Indeed, the more his physical discomfort grew, the more dazzlingly acute his mind became. He saw, clear and vivid, the picture of his futile strivings, saw, too, that he might continue in futility unless once and for all he could force the matter to a crisis. The need for open and decisive action swelled within him like a great river about to burst its banks. In this strange urgency of his mood, his natural balance and good sense were gone, supplanted by a frantic recklessness. He wanted to stand in the market place, to reach out his hands and shout of this iniquity to the four winds of heaven.

At that thought, a gleam that was in part irrational lit up his eyes. Presently, he rose and, first reassuring himself that the door was locked, went over to the wooden writing desk which stood in the corner. Here, he took out the few sheets of white shelf paper which had been used to line the drawers. He laid the paper on the floor; then, taking pen and ink, he knelt down and began to block out certain letters in big capitals. He had always had a special talent for printing and in about an hour, although his hand shook slightly and his vision was not quite clear, he had finished. He left the papers on the floor to dry and lay down, fully dressed, upon the bed.

Despite the burning project that filled his mind, he slept, but restively, and always with that same sense of fever gathering in his veins. About seven o'clock he awoke with a start. His headache was worse, a splitting frontal pain, but this merely strengthened his intention. He picked up the paper sheets from the floor, rolled them into a long cylinder and, treading warily as he passed Lena's door, went out.

The rain had quite gone as he hurried down Ware Street, the morning was clear and fresh with the softness of dawn. At the cabman's shelter opposite Duke's Court he stopped, and finding some coins in his pocket, ordered a mug of coffee and a thick slice of margarined bread. The food made him feel less ill, but he had not gone half way up Duke's Row before a rush of sickness came over him. He leaned over the gutter in a fit of nausea.

At the end of the Row, Duke's Yard, the premises of the Lanes Billboard Company, at this early hour, were still deserted. He squeezed through a gap in the rotting wooden fence, against which, awaiting his turn, he had so often stood in line with the other sandwichmen. Inside, the double posterboards, scores of them, were packed in a long open corrugated iron shed. Paul selected the newest he could find, and using one of the many "brush-pots" standing in the shed, pasted on his printed sheets. He was about to sling on the boards when his eye was caught by a rusty heap in the corner of the shed. He recognized the iron chains which had been used as an advertising feature during the recent visit to the Palace Theatre of the illusionist, Houdini. Without hesitation, for he was now completely possessed, he went forward and, after some searching, found a sound thin chain and a serviceable padlock. Five minutes later, with the chain round his body and wearing the sandwich boards, he left the yard.

The cathedral clock was striking eight as he came back into Ware Street and started his march towards the centre of the city. Already the bustle of the day had begun. People were swarming from the buses and subway exits. But as they hurried towards their places of business, only a few directed curious glances to wards the young man bearing on his back the notice:

## MURDER: THE INNOCENT CONVICTED.

And on his chest:

## MURDER: THE GUILTY FREE.

If any of them gave the matter a second thought it was to class it as part of an astute advertising campaign — one of these eye-catching slogans which intrigued the public for weeks before the date of disclosure.

Nine o'clock came and Paul still plodded along the gutters, gazing straight ahead, with an expressionless face, clutching the heavy boards with rigid hands. Since he wished as long as possible to avoid the attentions of the police, he kept away from the main intersections, at each of which an officer was on point duty. Once or twice he was conscious of a sharp scrutiny, but for once fortune seemed upon his side — no one stopped him.

As the forenoon advanced Paul began to feel faint, but with the real part of his purpose still unaccomplished — this parade was merely the prelude to his main intention — he would not give up. Deafened by the noise of the traffic, splashed with mud from the grinding wheels, he still kept on. Yet he could not altogether master his increasing weakness: several times he swayed uncertainly.

Towards noon a curious crowd had begun to follow him. For the most part it was made up of loafers and out-of-works, the idle riff-raff of the city, augmented by a few errand boys and a mangy, barking dog. At first Paul had been a target for some vulgar jeers, but as he gave no answer, the crowd attended him in silence, mystified perhaps, yet now, by instinct, more than ever certain of reward. Shortly after one o'clock the procession reached Leonard Square and here, at last, under the statue of Robert Greenwood, first Lord Mayor of Wortley, Paul halted. He took off his boards and stood them on the pavement; then, first twisting the chain tightly round his wrist, he padlocked himself to the iron railings at the statue's base. A gasp of bated anticipation went up from the onlookers and immediately, since it was now the lunch hour, the press of people round about increased. When Paul turned and faced the assembly he had an audience of almost a hundred people.

With his free hand he unloosened his necktie — it seemed to be strangling him. He was conscious of no fear, no excitement, only of a desperate urgency to put his case before these citizens of Wortley. Now was his chance, they were waiting on him to speak; Lena had said that ordinary people were kind, he could never have a better, a fairer opportunity to convince them. If only his head had not ached so frightfully. Worse than that was the sickness, and the sense of unreality which pervaded him, as though his feet were mounted on balloons which floated dizzily through the air. He moistened his cracked lips.

"Friends," he began, "I've come here because I've something to tell you . . . something you should know. My name is Mathry and my father is in prison. . . ."

"You'll be there yourself, chum, if you don't watch out!"

The interruption from the back produced a laugh. Paul waited till it died out.

"He's been in prison fifteen years and all for a crime he didn't commit."

"Ah! Tell that to the marines!" shouted another voice from

the back. Again the general laugh, followed this time by shouts of "Shut up!" "Fair play," "Give the poor b—— a chance!"

"I have proof that my father is innocent but no one will hear me. . . ."

"We can't hear you either, chum, unless you speak up."

"That's right. Speak up. Speak up," cried several others in the crowd.

Paul swallowed dryly. He realized dimly, that although he was straining his throat to the utmost, his voice was emerging faint and cracked. He made a superhuman effort.

"Fifteen years ago on circumstantial evidence my father was convicted of murder. But he did not commit the crime. . . ."

The mongrel dog, which had followed Paul persistently, suddenly began to bark.

"I repeat . . . he did not commit the crime . . . in proof of which . . ."

But the dog was now barking so loudly, snarling and snapping at Paul's feet, that he could not make himself heard. Then, while he paused, the hound, encouraged no doubt by the approbation of the onlookers, unexpectedly jumped up on him. Paul staggered and almost fell. As he clutched dazedly at the sandwich boards a murmur grew amongst the mob.

"He's drunk."

"Does he think he can make a mug of us!"

"Paste the young soak."

A banana skin flew through the air and pulped against Paul's cheek. It was the signal for a fusillade of bread crusts and unwanted food from people eating their lunch in the crowd. A few apple cores followed by way of variety. At that moment two policemen pushed their way through the closely packed crowd. One was a young constable, the other was Sergeant Jupp.

"What's all this? D'you know you're creating a disturbance."

Paul gazed at the two blurred figures in blue, vaguely recognizing Jupp. He had reached the end of his resources. He opened his mouth to speak but no words came out. The crush around him increased.

"He's tight, Sergeant," a sycophantic voice suggested from the front rank. "Been talkin' a lot of rot."

"You've really done it this time. I've been waiting for it. Come along with us." The sergeant took Paul and tried to pull him through the crowd. Meeting with resistance he pulled violently, almost dislocating Paul's wrist, before he noticed the presence of the chain. His muscular neck turned dark red.

He muttered to his companion.

"He's padlocked himself. We'll need the wagon."

The two policemen struggled angrily to free the chain, tugging Paul this way and that, while the crowd pressed and milled around them. Another policeman arrived, then hurried off, blowing his whistle. Everyone seemed to push and shout at once, the traffic was held up, there was a general commotion. This was the moment which Paul had foreseen as the climax of his resistance, the crisis when he would deliver his most impassioned address.

"Friends," he tried to shout, "I'm only asking for justice. An innocent man . . ."

But the younger policeman had smashed the padlock with a blow of his truncheon, Paul was bundled into the waiting police wagon, and whirled off to the station. Half insensible he scarcely knew what was happening to him until he was flung forward into a cell. His brow hit the cement floor with stunning force. This made no difference to the splitting pain permanently established within his head, rather it seemed to shock him out of the stupor into which he had fallen. At least, he groaned. This groan had a bad effect on the three policemen who stood watching him, and who were already considerably annoyed by the trouble he had caused them.

"The young swine," remarked the first. "He's coming out of his drunk."

"No," said Sergeant Jupp, "it's not drink."

The third officer, a stout figure, was still red and fuming — in the struggle someone had kicked him in the stomach.

"Whatever it is, he's not going to muck me about and get away with it."

He bent forward, caught Paul by the scruff of the neck and dragged him upright, like a sack of flour. Then, clenching his fist, he struck him between the eyes. Blood spurted from Paul's nose. He dropped in a heap and lay still.

"You shouldn't do that," Jupp said coldly. "He'll get enough . . . and soon."

As the cell door clanged on the silent huddled form the youngest of the policemen laughed uncomfortably.

"Anyway," he said, as though salving his conscience, "he asked for it."

# Chapter 8

IT was late afternoon when, in an uncertain fashion, Paul again became conscious of his surroundings. He lay for a long time staring up at the single armoured light in the roof of his cell. Then, he got on his hands and knees and crawled to the ewer standing at one end of the wooden plank bed. Tilting the ewer, he took a drink, then dabbed his swollen features. The water was cool and refreshing, but almost at once his face began to burn.

Carefully, he pulled himself up and sat down on the plank. His head did not ache so much now. But to his surprise, he was finding it difficult to breathe — at every inspiration he felt a cut-

206

ting pain in his left side. Presently he discovered that the way to avoid this, or at least to diminish the intensity of the pain, was to breathe less deeply, to take, in fact, only half a breath. Naturally he was obliged to make these shallow respirations faster, but this did not greatly inconvenience him.

Suddenly, as he sat there, accommodating himself to this new symptom, the cell door opened and a man came in. Paul peered up through his swollen eyes, recognising the Chief Constable of Wortley.

Dale stood staring down at him silently for a long time, as though examining every detail of his condition. In contrast with their previous meeting, his demeanour was aloof, his expression strangely sombre. When he spoke, his voice was quiet and restrained.

"So you didn't take my advice after all. If I remember right, I told you to go home. But no, that wasn't good enough for you. You preferred to stop on and stir up trouble. So here you are, just like I told you, only worse, far worse."

There was another pause.

"No doubt you thought you were mighty smart. Defying my sergeant and getting away with it. Hanging around all these weeks without being picked up. Don't deceive yourself, my friend. All the time you were living on my bounty. I could have hauled you in at a moment's notice. But somehow, against my better judgment, I wanted to give you an extra chance. And you didn't take it."

Dale's lips drew back over his strong teeth.

"So now you're in a pretty poor state, by the looks of you. Maybe my chaps used you a bit rough. But, tut, tut — you mustn't mind. That's what happens when you resist an officer in the execution of his duty. Nobody to blame but yourself."

Again a silence. It seemed as though the Chief Constable were inviting Paul to speak, even hoping that he might do so, might commit himself through some ill-chosen word. But from the moment Dale had entered his cell Paul had resolved to say nothing. His chance would come later, in court. He listened, with a queer sense of detachment, as the Chief resumed:

"And what do you think will happen to you now? Maybe you imagine you'll be let off with a caution and some more good advice. Somehow I don't think so. Somehow I think the day for advice is past. You had your chance and you didn't take it. And now you've been worming your way into things that don't concern you, working against the community, bothering decent citizens, pestering law officials, yes, even annoying Members of the House of Parliament. Besides that," the voice became low, "you've been annoying me. Not that it makes any odds — I'm sure of my ground — it's solid rock. Nevertheless I resent it, I resent your persistence, your imputation that I've done wrong. And now I've a curious feeling that you're going to suffer for it. Now it's you that's done wrong. You'll be up before the magistrate first thing tomorrow. It wouldn't surprise me if he took a serious view of the case and fixed bail pretty high — say fifty pounds. Now you'd have no manner of means of raising a sum like fifty pounds, would you? No, I was afraid not." He shook his head in silent satire. "That means you'll be remanded, back here to us. Well, it's a nice cosy cell you have . . . not much outlook to be sure . . . but every convenience. I hope you like it, for it looks as though you might be in it for quite some time to come."

For a moment longer, his narrowed scrutiny lingered, bore down on Paul, then he swung round and went out.

But as soon as Dale was out of the cell his expression altered. He frowned heavily. He had not been himself in there. He was like an actor who had given a bad performance and was now disgusted with himself. Yet what else, in the devil's name, could he have done? He had received an urgent message asking him to telephone Sir Matthew at the Law Courts. Before he did so he must be in a position to state that he had seen the prisoner.

As he entered his private office and sat down at his desk the cloud upon his brow deepened. Hardened though he was to all sorts of "messes," the sordid tangling of human affairs, which resulted from lives of crime, he did not like this affair that was back again upon his hands, it gave him a queer sensation in his stomach. He wished to God the crazy young fool had taken advantage of his leniency and cleared out during these past weeks. And again that tormenting question flickered out from the back of his mind, less a question than a whisper, a whisper of uncertainty: "Is there something in it . . . after all?"

He jerked his head back, angrily, like a goaded bull. No, by God, so far as he was concerned, there was nothing in it. He knew himself too well. He could produce a record of downright honesty, of unblemished integrity that would stand the closest scrutiny. He wasn't like some others he could mention who compromised with their consciences. His motto had always been: *You cannot touch pitch and not be defiled.* His hands were clean.

Yet he stared at the telephone a long time before he could bring himself to unhook the receiver. And he dialed the number slowly, as though in doubt. It was Burr, the clerk, who answered, but almost at once Sprott came on the line.

"Hello! Hello! Is that you Sir Matthew?"

Immediately, Dale heard the click signifying that Sprott had pulled the switch which cut all extraneous connections and made the wire private. Then the prosecutor's voice came over, not this time suave and friendly, but full of anger.

"What's the reason of this new blunder?"

"Blunder, Sir Matthew?" repeated Dale, doggedly.

"You know perfectly well what I mean. This thing today, in the square. Didn't I give you specific instructions regarding that individual?"

"Your instructions were carried out."

209

"Then why has this occurred . . . this public pantomime . . . the very thing I was seeking to avoid? You ought to be able to use a little intelligent anticipation, once in a while."

The Chief Constable tried to steady himself. He could not afford to lose his temper. He answered:

"It wasn't easy for us, Sir Matthew. Who was to know what this young idiot was going to be up to? We watched him the best we could. I detailed one of my best men. But we didn't lay our hands on him since you told us not to be harsh. However, he has gone over the score this time. He ought to get six months easily for this."

"Don't be a fool."

There was an odd silence. When Sir Matthew resumed his tone was milder, full of reason.

"Look here, Dale. You were nearer the mark when you used the word idiot. There seems no doubt now but that this young man is a psychopathic case."

The Chief Constable, to control himself, had been drawing patterns on his blotter. But he stopped now, suddenly, and fixed his eyes on the blank wall before him.

"If that is so," Sprott's voice went on, reasoning mildly, "he becomes immediately a subject, not for judicial examination and punishment, but for medical treatment in one of our institutions dedicated to the therapy of aberrations of the mind."

"An asylum?" Dale interjected.

Sprott gave back a pained exclamation.

"My dear Dale, don't you realize that such objectionable terms as 'asylum' and 'lunatic' have passed out of civilized speech. To so describe our admirable poor-law institution at Dreem is in my opinion a most unwarrantable slur."

"Ah!" the Chief Constable murmured, in an indescribable tone. "Dreem!"

"Naturally, to certify him," Sir Matthew threw back, "one would require some data. Tell me something of him, Adam. Is he wild in his manner?"

"Yes," Dale admitted. "You could call it wild."

"And his friends? He has no one to take care of him?"

"He has a mother . . . and a girl in Belfast, but they seem more or less to have given him up. He's been living on the streets until lately . . . quite alone."

"Poor young man." Sprott spoke with a note of pity. "Everything points to the need for institutional care. He'll come up before the police magistrate tomorrow morning I presume?"

"Yes," Dale answered in a hard voice. "There is no way out of that."

This time the prosecutor's tone was not pained. The mellow unctuousness dropped from him and his answer went through the Chief Constable like a knife.

"I am not seeking a way out. Unless it be for both of us."

Now there was no doubt as to which was the stronger personality. In a quieter manner the prosecutor resumed.

"I think Mr. Battersby, the magistrate, is a very sound man."

"He is," Dale said, in that same slightly unnatural tone. "If he fixes bail high enough we're sure of a remand."

"I do not ask you to press the matter in any venal or questionable sense," Sprott said directly. "But it might be well for you to have a word with him, explaining the psychopathic aspects of the case, indicating that a remand would give us time to arrange a competent medical examination which, after all, would be in the young man's best interests."

"Yes," Dale said.

"Very well, then," Sprott said. Then he added with great distinctness, "Make no mistake this time."

He rang off.

A full minute later, and slowly, the Chief Constable hung up the receiver.

# Chapter 9

THE police court opened next morning at ten o'clock. The courtroom, on the first floor, was lofty but quite small and informal, with a mahogany dais for the magistrate underneath the window, a row of chairs for the public on either side and, at the end, a wooden bench for the prisoners. It was a draughty chamber and a folding leather screen had been placed between the dais and the window, cutting off a good deal of the light. On the ceiling was a fresco of the city arms — two archers with drawn bows against an oak tree vert — which no one ever saw.

The red-necked officer took Paul upstairs. He did not seem a bad sort this morning — his breath smelled as though he had just enjoyed an after-breakfast pipe. As they left the cell he glanced meaningly at Paul's bruised and swollen eyes.

"Nasty fall you had yesterday, cully. Take care you don't slip up this morning. You follow me?"

Paul did not answer. Towards the early morning he had actually slept for several hours, a pained uneasy oblivion into which as into a dark pit, he had dropped from utter exhaustion. But this rest had not revived him. He could not understand why he felt so weak; even to breathe demanded an effort; and his side hurt him so badly he had to keep his left arm pressed hard against it in an effort to control the pain. But, in contrast, his mind was again keyed to that pitch of feverish sharpness which had characterized all his mental processes since memory had been restored to him. He saw everything with a bright, unnatural lucidity. And he was firmly determined that he would speak out, reveal everything. Yes, this time nothing would deter him.

When he was escorted through the side door and shown his place on the prisoner's bench the court was already in session and the magistrate, Mr. Battersby, a thin middle-aged man with a kindly yet careworn appearance, had begun to deal expertly with the usual run of misdemeanours. Paul studied him as he rapidly disposed of three elderly drunks, a youth caught collecting betting slips, a street hawker who had traded without a license, an old musician accused of begging, a tramp apprehended for being "without visible means of support."

The magistrate's lips were thin, moulded by his office to an apparent severity, but his eyes were wise and humane. He never smiled at the blandishments, the cajoling pleas of the old "lags" who stood before him. Yet none of his sentences were severe, several first offenders he merely bound over, and a young girl charged with petty theft he turned over, without comment, to the representative of the Salvation Army. To himself, Paul said: "This is a man who will listen to me."

Suddenly, while he studied Mr. Battersby, he became aware that he himself was the object of a steady and compelling inspection. He looked towards the public seats and immediately saw Lena. She was not alone. Beside her sat a complete stranger to Paul, a man of about forty, very bulky and unwieldy, wearing a flannel suit, a carelessly knotted tie, and a creased tweed overcoat which had seen much service. His battered soft hat was pushed back on his head, exposing a round bald brow. All his face was round and chubby, presenting, despite the frankly unshaven jowls, a curious nakedness which the pale-lashed eyes made a great effort to conceal by assuming a look of boredom. He had apparently for some minutes been contemplating Paul with this disillusioned detachment, but now, although his expression did not alter, he raised his forefinger and laid it against his lips. It was a trivial, short-lived gesture yet somehow its significance was overpowering. Paul glanced quickly at Lena, read

213

the appeal in her eyes, then returned his gaze to the corpulent stranger, who nodded once, slightly, but again with irresistible meaning, before tilting back his chair and examining his finger nails with the air of one to whom the proceedings had no further interest.

At that moment Paul's case was called. He had barely time to think as he stood up, dizzily, listening to the charge rattled out against him. He observed that, for the first time, the Chief Constable had entered the court and taken a seat near the dais with his back to the body of the court.

"Well, what have you to say for yourself?"

The magistrate looked down at Paul with an attention far less perfunctory than that bestowed by him on the earlier cases. There was a short pause. The flood of words was ready, ready to gush forth but somehow, for some reason which ran contrary to his own will, it would not come. He did not even dare to look at the public seats towards Lena, or the stranger who had given that singular, compelling signal. But suddenly, irrespective of his own volition, he hung his head and, in a tone of simulated contrition, copied fairly well from the old hands who had gone before him he muttered:

"I'm sorry, your honour. Perhaps I'd had a little too much to drink."

There was a short but complete silence. Paul could see the Chief Constable straighten himself in his chair. Mr. Battersby cleared his throat.

"You were intoxicated? At your age that's a positive disgrace."

"Yes, your honour."

"Aren't you ashamed to admit it?"

"Yes, your honour."

There was a submissive note in Paul's voice which made the magistrate frown in perplexity. He examined some notes on the desk before him then leaned forward.

"Why did you make this demonstration . . . chaining yourself in the most public place in the city?"

"I've told you, your honour. I'd had one too many. I must have wanted to show off."

"Can you explain the . . . the monstrous poster that you displayed?"

"No, your honour. I meant no harm. When people have had a glass . . . you know they do silly things."

Although Paul did not see it, a faint flicker, which might have been a smile, twitched the lips of the man who, having abandoned the inspection of his finger nails, seemed now bent on trying to decipher the murky coat of arms on the roof. The Chief Constable, sitting up stiffly, had half turned in his place, exhibiting his hard profile to the court. The magistrate glanced imperceptibly in his direction before putting his next question to Paul.

"You have never made a demonstration of this kind before?"

"No, your honour."

"But you have suffered at times from nervous attacks?"

"I don't think so, your honour."

A pause.

"What are your political opinions?"

"I have none."

Again the magistrate hesitated, redirecting his gaze, in undecided fashion, towards the impenetrable figure of the Chief Constable. At last he seemed to make up his mind.

"Young man, in the ordinary way I should fine you two guineas and costs and dismiss you with a caution. But from responsible representations made to me I am of the opinion that your case may be more serious than is presently indicated. I shall therefore fix bail at fifty pounds. Failing this you will be remanded in custody, to enable the police to collect further evidence."

As this judgement was pronounced the stranger in the public seats forgot to register detachment. He seemed neither indignant nor surprised, but a peculiar interest stirred in his bilious eyes. On Lena's face there was a look of startled concern.

"Can you find bail in the amount of fifty pounds?" The clerk of the court was asking Paul, in a sing-song voice.

"No."

"Can you name any person who will guarantee the amount?"

Paul had begun to shake his head when the stranger rose.

"I am prepared to put up bail."

Paul stood perfectly still, his hot hands locked together.

Meanwhile, the Chief Constable had swung round, his expression of surprise and chagrin turning to sudden anger.

"I protest. I want to know where this money comes from."

"It comes from me — L. A. Dunn, of 15 Grant Street, in this noble and historic city. I have it here, in my pocket."

"I protest."

"Silence in court."

"Your honour." The Chief Constable persisted. He was on his feet now, his jaw hard and grim. "I protest that the bail set is insufficient. I request that the amount be raised to a more substantial sum."

"Silence in court."

The magistrate waited stiffly, refusing to proceed until the Chief Constable had resumed his seat. Then, in a seriously provoked tone, he announced:

"This court wishes to make it quite clear that it is not subject to influence or suggestions from the police or from any quarter whatsoever. It sees no reason to reverse its present decision. Bail will therefore be accepted in the amount of fifty pounds. Next case."

As Paul quitted the court he was conscious of a scene of some confusion, of Dale arguing with the magistrate, then abruptly turning away through the private side door. Nevertheless, fifteen minutes later, having submitted to the formalities conducted by the clerk of the court in his chamber, Paul walked out, free.

He came into the open street, where the brightness of the day struck at him like a shining spear and made him sway. Then he saw Lena and her companion, standing together on the pavement, not ten yards away. The sight of Lena brought a strange solace to his lacerated heart. She did not move. It was the big flabby man who approached, his overcoat flapping open, his hands in his pockets, hat more than ever on the back of his head.

"Excuse me," he said. "My name's Dunn. I'm a friend of Miss Andersen's. We were waiting to take you back to Ware Place."

"Why have you done this for me?" Paul said.

"Why shouldn't we do it?" Dunn smiled absently. "When a man's as sick as you, he needs a little help."

There was a tingling silence. Paul's gaze wavered away towards Lena whose anxious eyes had never left his face.

"I feel badly about this," he muttered, through the drumming in his ears. "Bringing you into it."

"Don't worry, Son. We'll survive it."

Dunn put two fingers in his mouth and whistled piercingly: the cab that was passing drew up at the curb. Dunn helped Paul in, then Lena and he followed. They drove to Ware Place.

Half an hour later Paul was undressed and in the spare bed, washed, propped up on two pillows, with a cold vinegar compress on his bruised, burning forehead and a hot-water bottle at his icy feet. He had managed to swallow and keep down the glass of milk which Lena had brought him. That infernal pain still stabbed at his left side but this was far outweighed by the relief of being out of the cell and back in this peaceful room.

Wedged in the narrow wicker chair, still encumbered by the eternal hat and coat — the impression grew that he slept in them — Dunn had not once taken his eyes off Paul.

"Feel better?" he inquired.

"Much," Paul gasped.

Dunn made no comment — perhaps he had his own views upon the matter. Once again he studied his bitten finger nails, for which he seemed to have a profound admiration. Then he said:

"Look here, son. I don't want to worry you when you're sick. But I understand you've something on your mind. I've heard about it from Lena, who incidentally is quite an old friend of mine. But if you care to get it off your chest, yourself . . ." He made an expressive gesture with his shoulders.

"Are you a lawyer?"

"Holy Church forbid."

Lena had been downstairs, but now she came back to the room, and seated herself on a low stool behind Dunn.

Both figures were in the direct range of Paul's vision, he could view them without the fatigue of turning his head. He began to speak, his gaze resting upon them, stopping occasionally to regain his breath, feeling, in Dunn's silent attention, in Lena's absolute immobility, an encouragement to unburden himself, of everything that lay upon his soul.

When he finished there was a long silence. Dunn who, during the hearing, had sunk lower and lower into the chair, slowly prized himself loose. He yawned and stretched himself, pulled the curtain aside and looked out of the window.

"It's raining again . . . what a goddam climate." He yawned again and turned to Lena. "Look after him. We have five weeks before he surrenders to his bail."

He leaned against the door for a few seconds, took a cigarette from his overcoat, placed it unlighted between his lips. There was a sleepy look in his eyes. Suddenly he rolled his bulky frame round and, without a word, went out.

# Chapter 10

THIS man, Dunn, with the bored eyes and close-bitten nails, was a product of Wortley city and of certain odd hereditary circumstances. His full name, Luther Aloysius Dunn — which he concealed like a crime, making deadly enemies of those who dared to use it — affords the first indication of his origin, for he had come to being as the result of a "mixed" marriage, which, in contrast to many such unions where mutual tolerance and understanding are achieved, had been a most unhappy one. His Calvinistic mother and Catholic father had warred fiercely and continually. The child's life was a misery, torn, as it were, between Chapel and Church — later he confided to his intimates that he had been baptised in both places, and he grew up with a nervous antipathy for organised religion.

When the boy reached the age of fourteen his father was killed in a street accident — he went out after a hearty breakfast, reviling John Knox, and came back before lunch, on a stretcher, dead. A just retribution! But the widow, after a period of blankness, was inconsolable — discovering too late her dependence upon this stiff-necked upholder of Papal Infallibility and, incredible as it may appear, she reversed the whole current of her life. Her own strivings are unimportant — but they had at least one consequence for her son — she removed him from the public school and sent him to the Jesuit college on Hassock Hill.

Here he was treated by the fathers with the most prudent consideration — on his admission the wise old director of studies had blinkingly surveyed him, then remarked to his colleagues: "Now for God's sake leave that boy alone." Nothing could have surpassed the unobtrusive encouragement he received, but he was now fifteen and the damage had been done. He never felt himself part of the corporate life of the college. He kept to himself, went alone to football matches in remote parts of the city, stole down to the billiard saloon at the foot of Hassock Hill where he would sit for hours — his interested, serious face a pale moon in the smoky air — quietly watching the green cloth. He loved games, although he never played them, and his knowledge of the records and achievements in every branch of sport was quite encyclopaedic. Since he had a certain talent for composition, Father Marchant, his English master, encouraged him to write little pieces relating to athletics for the college magazine. And when, at eighteen, he graduated — a silent, slightly downcast youth — he obtained through the intervention of the Director of Studies, a position in the office of the Wortley *Chronicle*, a daily paper of limited circulation but independently owned, and of high reputation.

For the next few years his life continued wholly uneventful. He ran errands, cut and pasted, and, on rare occasions, went out to report the most minor of local sport events. His first contribution to the *Chronicle*, which he cut out and carefully preserved, filled the tag end of a column.

Later, however, they began to send him on less trivial assignments, water polo games in the Corporation Baths, boxing contests at Blakely's Arena, and it was seen, recognised at the main desk, though not of course disclosed, that he was good, vivid in his appraisals, graphic in his descriptions. On New Year's Day, when he was only twenty-five, he was given, without warning, the choicest of all sporting assignments — the local senior league football game, which draws annually a frenzied multitude and sends two thirds of Wortley raving mad. From the press-box Dunn dictated two columns straight over the private wire; then, next morning, he turned in a feature article. This feature article did not describe the game at all, but dealt simply with a single incident which had occurred during its progress.

On that same afternoon James McEvoy, the editor of the *Chronicle*, who was also its owner, came wandering out of his office with the article in his hand. It was characteristic of McEvoy that he never "sent" for anyone. He sat down beside Dunn's small desk.

"What does this mean?" he inquired, tapping the article with his pince-nez. "I ask you to report a football match. You give me a story on a young half-back accidentally kicked on the head. While he's unconscious, you show me thirty thousand human beings yelling for his blood. Then you show me another thirty thousand equally ready to destroy the opposing centre. You describe the shouts, the abuse, the partisan fights, the bottles thrown at the players, the gashed cheek suffered by the referee . . . in a word, you give me a picture of jungle sportsmanship, of racial and religious intolerance which would make an Esquimo . . . sitting in his igloo . . . blush."

"I'm sorry," Dunn mumbled. "I started the machine and that's what came out."

McEvoy was silent, reflecting on the queer contradiction: that this heavy and embarrassed young man, with not a word to say for himself in conversation, who probably couldn't tell an after-dinner story to save his life, should be, on paper, a very lion of verbosity, a spouting geyser, a volcano in eruption, with a flow of sentient expression which swept away the ordinary reader, tugged at the heartstrings, made him laugh and weep.

McEvoy stood up.

"It's the worst story I've had in a twelvemonth. But tomorrow it's going on the front page." While Dunn gazed at him in a muddled manner, he smiled. "I want you to come to supper at my house on Sunday evening."

That was the end of Luther Aloysius Dunn's connection with the world of sport and the real beginning of his career. McEvoy sent him first to the police courts, which yielded much of that human incident so particularly suited to his pen. Then he began to move about the country and to do regular half-page feature articles. Since the comedy of his names was now no secret to McEvoy, the editor had hit upon an excellent pseudonym for his leading reporter. Henceforth Dunn's articles were always signed: "The Heretic." And the series which he produced, entitled: "Burning Questions," followed by: "Further Burnings at the Stake," attracted wide attention — besides evoking two libel actions which the paper successfully defended. The circulation of the *Chronicle* spasmodically increased, as did the friendship between the Heretic and his editor, a relationship which was strengthened in 1929, when McEvoy's tall and rather stately sister Eva, who had for a long time bent her limpid eyes modestly towards Dunn, finally took possession of him.

The marriage, though it did not cure Dunn of his fondness for beer and old clothes, was a steady success and produced two little girls who were secretly doted upon by their father. Eva was a nice swan-like woman, with a fondness for ivory beads, lavender sachets and long drop earrings. Dunn allowed his wife to manage everything and since she was sincerely religious, he accompanied her to Mass with the children in orthodox fashion. They were, indeed, often publicly held up in the parish of St. Joseph as an exemplary family. But Dunn's heart was not in it, something had happened to him, inside, when he was a child. He set little store upon outward form, holding of greater importance what lay in the heart of every man. If he had a motto it was: "Live and let live," and in his own life he was always eager to redress a wrong, always ready to champion the underdog.

Such inherent sentimentality made him highly vulnerable, especially to himself, for even at the age of forty his nature was still essentially as retiring, as sensitive as in his adolescence. He could not endure to be regarded even remotely as a spiritual "uplifter," a reformer with a message. He was simply a newspaper man doing his job. Therefore he developed and covered himself with a protective veneer of melancholy cynicism, the sort of boredom which members of his profession are popularly supposed to acquire. It was a pose, a perpetual act which probably deceived no one but Dunn himself. There were, so to speak, always tender patches of sentiment showing beneath the tough skin grafts, but this good fellow did not see them and, like the ostrich, he felt himself secure.

His contact with Lena has already been recorded. He had kept in touch with her during the past year, often calling in at her counter for coffee and a bun on his way to the *Chronicle* office in Arden Street. Therefore, when she came to him at his house on Hassock Hill, late on the night of Paul's arrest, he did not fail to recognise her distress and listened to her with attention. Nevertheless, on the following morning as he accompanied her to the police court he fancied he was setting out upon a wild goose chase. What he had seen there had shaken this belief. Then had come Paul's narrative, delivered in great distress, unmistakably authentic, without a single false note, complete from first to last.

Dunn had trained himself never to jump to conclusions, but all his instincts told him that he had stumbled upon the one great story of his life. He was a placid man, rendered somewhat lethargic by his girth, but as he walked home that night, a sudden boil of excitement made him step as briskly as a youth.

He said nothing to James McEvoy for a week. During that time, although he did not once appear at the newspaper offices, he was extremely occupied, and took several extensive journeys. Then, after eleven o'clock on the night of the following Thursday he came, noticed only by the night porter, to the *Chronicle* building and locked himself in his office. He was tired and travel-stained but his eyes were bright, no longer bored, as he took off his coat, his jacket and waistcoat, ripped open his collar and sat down in his braces at his desk. He remained in meditation for some time, then slowly, with a rapt expression, he spat on his hands, rubbed them together, and drawing his typewriter towards him, set its keys clicking with his own inimitable blend of sentiment and sensation.

In the damp darkness of the condemned cell, in this great city of Wortley, an innocent man sat waiting to be hanged. Outside, in the prison yard, he could hear the sounds of hammering as they erected the scaffold. In a few hours they would come, pinion his hands behind his back, lead him out into the cold dawn. Then, beneath the gallows the rope would be cast around his neck, the white bag slipped over his head. . . .

Next morning, at nine, he rolled drowsily off the office sofa. Bleary and unshaven, still in his shirtsleeves, he took his typescript into McEvoy.

"Here," he said, "is the first of the new Heretic articles. Also a complete synopsis of the other nine that make up the series. Read it. I'm going out for breakfast."

Half an hour later when Dunn returned, the editor was at his desk, so immobilized by thought he did not immediately stir. Then he turned his head slowly. He was a neat, spare man in a blue business suit, thin-faced, his dark hair greying at the temples, parted precisely in the middle, wearing rimless pince-nez and a white pique piping to his waistcoat. He prided himself upon his imperturbability. But now he was labouring under stress. In fact, though he tried not to show it, he was staggered.

"How in the name of God Almighty did you get this?"

"I didn't get it."

"Then who did?"

"Mathry's son. He got it all."

"Where is he now?"

"Out on bail, in bed, and damnably ill."

"Are you sure it's right?"

224

"Positive. I've checked everything I've written."

McEvoy rubbed his thin jaw. He was worried, undecided, and deeply excited.

"Can we print it?"

Dunn shrugged. "Please yourself."

"But, Almighty God, it goes right through the top judiciary to the Secretary of State. And how about . . . how about Mr. O.? We can't come out with that. What about libel? We'll be sued for a certainty."

"Not a chance. Don't you see how I've planned it? We save him till the end. We don't particularize. We simply say Mr. O. — or better still Mr. X. Then we sit tight and watch what happens. Oh, God, it's terrific. It's the biggest thing that's ever come our way. Think of it . . . here's a man, fifteen years in Stoneheath . . . and for nothing."

"Maybe he d-did it?" In his excitement the precise McEvoy actually stuttered.

"No, I'll swear he's innocent."

"They'll never admit that, never."

"We'll make them." Dunn began to walk up and down the room. "We'll show them the power of a free press. And the strength of public opinion. I'm going to launch such an attack that the parties concerned will be shamed out of their official defences. We'll make them re-open this case. We'll force them to hold an inquiry. For months young Mathry has been battering at their doors and they haven't opened up an inch. Why? Because they know they've made a mistake. And they're trying to keep it stowed away down in the cellar. What the hell's the good of calling ourselves a democracy if we let ourselves be dragooned by a lot of bureaucrats. From that it's only one step on to communism. If we want to keep our democracy we've got to put our house in order. We've got to have progress and orderly advancement. If we clamp the lid down even on one case of injustice, if we suppress free speech even for a second, then we're done for. The weevils will burrow into us and destroy us. Look what nearly happened to this young Mathry. With a little help — he nearly went over the edge, and he may still go. And why? Because everything that was done to him suppressed his right to be heard. If we are a free country, and want to stay free, a man must be able to raise his voice. . . ."

"All right, all right," McEvoy said sourly. "Don't quote the whole article. We'll print it, if it ruins us. And it will!" With sudden determination he pressed the bell on his desk.

Dunn went back to his office, put on his jacket and waistcoat, his hat, his overcoat. Down below, the presses were beginning to run, a heavy thrumming note which vibrated through all the building. He rubbed his hand reflectively across his rough chin — Evie was always worrying him about his appearance — he had better get a shave. It would freshen him up. He was thirsty too. His eyes brightened: it was nearly eleven, he would drop in at Hannigan's for a beer.

# Chapter 11

ON the previous Wednesday afternoon, when Dunn left Ware Place, Lena saw that Paul had fallen back on his pillow and was asleep.

Gazing at him with a furrowed brow, she was forced to admit that he looked ill, quite ill, in fact. Nevertheless, a strange feeling, which she could not restrain, made her want to keep him here, in this refuge, quiet and secure, beside her. At least she would try. Her nature, crushed by the brutality that had made her shrink from the very thought of love, was now fully awakened, stirred to the depths by an emotion she had believed herself incapable of experiencing. How little had she imagined, as she strode through life, a sad young Juno, hurt and solitary, shunning all men with nun-like misgiving, that love would come to her, and come like this, transforming her, filling her heart with sweetness and anguish. Yet this pain gave her strength.

She sat down on a chair by the bed, her eyes not moving from his face. At intervals she rose and wiped the heavy perspiration that gathered on his brow. She took this to be a sign that the fever had broken and was partly reassured. Towards evening she gave him some hot milk and a beaten egg. As she left him for the night she felt hopeful that she might go to work next day. She did not wish to lose her job at the Bonanza.

On the following morning when she roused him, Paul told her that he felt better and could look after himself, but when she was dressed for the street and had put some soup on the stove for his lunch, she suddenly felt his hand. It was burning. Her expression did not change, but she felt in her breast a sharp sinking of dismay. She stood in her beret and raincoat, one hand on the door.

"Perhaps I should stay home, after all?"

He shook his head.

"I'll be all right."

"You're sure?"

"Yes."

She went reluctantly, and all day, as she moved about behind the counter, her thoughts were bent uneasily upon him. At four o'clock she brought herself to ask Harris if, as a favour, she might go. His brows lifted, and he smiled at her in his offensive style, but he raised no objection. She hurried out of the store, and paused at a greengrocer's to buy some stores. As she came up the stairs she felt a most unusual oppression in her throat — it was the surging of her own strong heart.

Paul was sitting up in bed, with the pillow wedged behind him, staring out through the window at the rows of roof-tops. His face lost its distant and harassed expression, and cleared faintly as she entered. Nevertheless, her immediate glance told her that the symptom which had alarmed her was, if anything, worse. On each of his cheekbones there was a bright round flush. He greeted her with a catch in his breath.

"Surely you're early?"

"We had a slack day." She took off her raincoat slowly. "Shouldn't you be lying down?"

"I feel better propped up."

"Did you take your soup?"

"I drank a cupful."

She straightened out the coverlet, trying to hide her anxiety.

"I brought you a sponge cake . . . and fruit. Would you like some lemonade?"

"Very much." He suppressed a cough. "I'm thirsty. But I couldn't eat a thing."

All at once her breast gave a great heave.

"Paul," she said. "I think I'll fetch the doctor."

"No," he protested. "I'd rather be left alone. If you only knew . . . after everything . . . just to be left alone. . . ."

She looked at him in strained indecision, torn between her sound common sense and her own aching desire to be with him, undisturbed. For his sake she did not welcome the thought of outside interference which might place him in fresh difficulty, even land him back in the hands of the police. Oh, what was she to do?

Still irresolute, she lit the gas and pulled the curtain across the window. He watched her with a detachment that made her movements oddly unreal. He had dozed, off and on, all day, and in between, his thoughts had been of Dunn. He had little hope that this newcomer would help him. Indeed, as he reviewed his

228

own strivings during the past months the conviction settled upon him that it was all quite useless. He had reached the end. He could do no more.

In this mood of unutterable despair he had thought, with unexpected pain, of Lena. Her close friendship with Dunn and the obvious understanding existing between them left little doubt in his mind as to their relationship. He acknowledged to himself that this unobtrusive, middle-aged, married man was the father of her child and still undoubtedly her protector. It was a conclusion which made him wince, caused him an actual physical distress, that somehow intensified the sharp stab that came with every respiration. A compelling desire to seek further hurt drove him to speak.

"Lena . . ."

"Yes?"

"You've done a lot for me. I keep asking myself why?"

She turned away abruptly.

"Why does one do anything? I just did it."

"I'd like you to know that I'm grateful."

"It was nothing."

A brief silence fell.

"I suppose you've known Dunn for some time."

"About three years."

"He's been good to you?"

"Yes. I owe everything to him."

"I see."

He seemed to read a challenge in her proud sad eyes. Yet at the same time her pinched features expressed so mysterious a resignation he was overcome with a sort of terror. He turned his face to the wall.

"Anyhow," he said, "it makes no difference. I knew already."

She started and turned pale, made as though to speak, while her eyes questioned him with a miserable smile that unconsciously implored him. It was her only moment of weakness. Firmly she closed her lips.

There was a longer silence. He closed his eyes, suppressed a short throaty cough.

"I'm afraid I do feel rather seedy."

Now she did not hesitate. Without a word, she hurried into the hall, put on her raincoat and went out.

Doctor Kerr's surgery was the nearest, only two hundred yards along Ware Street. He was a young man, not long qualified, who had recently put up his plate and was trying to build up a practice in the district. She had heard that he was pleasant and competent.

When she reached the surgery it was closed, but on the door was a printed notice giving the telephone number at which Dr. Kerr might be called. She went into the public booth at the street corner and dialed that number. It was a woman who answered. She told Lena that the doctor was out at an urgent case, but she promised to give him the message whenever he returned.

Lena came out of the booth with a white and anguished face. Had she done right in leaving the call on such an indefinite basis? Should she not rather have sought out another doctor in the neighbourhood? After her procrastination, for which she bitterly blamed herself, it now seemed imperative to have medical advice without a second's delay.

Back in the room, she found Paul apparently asleep. She waited in unbearable suspense, straining her ears for the sound of the doctor's approach. Shortly after eleven o'clock when she had almost reached the breaking point, he arrived. She saw that he was tired — his sharp features were peaked, his questions to her abrupt — but he gave Paul a careful examination. When he had finished he withdrew from the bedside and looked at his watch.

"What is it, Doctor?" She could barely articulate the words. "Is it serious?"

His day had been hard and he had missed his dinner, but he answered with exemplary patience.

"He's had a dry pleurisy — that was the pain. Then came the exudate — lots of fluid pressing on the lung."

"Pleurisy?" It did not sound so bad.

But he gave her a quick look then glanced away.

"I'm afraid there may be pus there. Empyema. That means hospital."

Her colour changed. She pressed her hand against her side. "You couldn't treat him here?"

"Good heavens, no. This requires a rib resection. The whole cavity must be drained. A six weeks' job. Have you a telephone in the house?"

"Yes. In the hall."

He went clattering downstairs. She could hear him telephoning, stressing the gravity and urgency of the case. Palely, she followed him down.

The doctor was having great difficulty in finding a vacant bed: many of the free hospitals were full, and, since he was not yet properly established in the district, he received scant consideration from most of the receptionists. But, at last, he was successful, and after making the arrangements, he turned from the phone with a sigh of relief.

"They'll take him at St. Elizabeth's Home. It's three miles out on the Oakdene Road . . . a small place but quite good. They're sending for him now."

The ambulance came in a quarter of an hour. Ten minutes later it had gone.

Still labouring under an undiminished sense of strain, confused and exhausted, beaten down by her own emotions, Lena came back upstairs. The little flat felt hot and stuffy. She turned out the gas fire. Going to the window she threw it up, drew in deep breaths of the damp night air, then moving away, began, from habit, to tidy up the room.

His threadbare suit, which he had worn through all that troubled time when he slept beneath the Arches, lay folded upon a chair beside the bed. She took it up, meaning to place it on a hanger in the cupboard. As she did so, Paul's battered old wallet dropped from the inside pocket, hit upon its edge, and spilled its contents, mainly a number of loose papers, upon the floor.

Lena bent to pick up the papers, notes that Paul had made relating to the case, and which she restored piecemeal to his pocket. Suddenly, amongst the sheets, her fingers came upon a small, cut-out photograph and, instinctively, she looked at it. It was a studio portrait of Ella Fleming, done in sepia and extremely flattering — Ella had seen to that — and beneath was written a tender message of scriptural endearment. This was in fact a souvenir that Ella had presented to Paul upon his nineteenth birthday and which, indeed, with a glance of meaningful sweetness, she had personally inserted in his wallet, with the hope that he would wear it next his heart.

Paul had long since forgotten that he possessed the photograph. But to Lena, the pretty features, the appealing eyes, the softly waved hair, shattered above all, by the fondly possessive superscription, it became, immediately, his most cherished treasure.

Not even a sigh broke from her, but in her motionless figure and fixed expression, frozen, but for the faintest trembling at the corners of her mouth, there was hidden an unfathomable anguish. At last she straightened from her kneeling position, returned the photograph to the wallet, and the wallet to the inside pocket. She hung the suit upon the hanger, placed it in the cupboard, went into the kitchen. Here, leaning against the mantel, she half-closed her eyes and turned away her head, a prey to a terrible revulsion of feeling which she could not stifle.

All along she had struggled against the fear that she was creating for herself an impossible situation. But never had she imagined this contingency — so ordinary yet so unexpected — which had exposed the enormity of her presumption. She shivered at the thought of her needless struggle with herself, and of her pitiable, her abject surrender. In her stupidity, mistaking gratitude for affection, she had almost brought herself to the point of exposing the tragedy of her life, of blindly making herself the instrument of his disenchantment. She could never tell him now. Never. Utterly abased, she shut her eyes, possessed again by those familiar devils of self-hatred and shame. Contrasting herself, who had been dragged in filth, with this angelic creature who was pledged to him, she wished she might die, now, at this moment; she longed for the pain that was crushing her breast to be the final pang of dissolution.

How long she stood there in anguish she did not know. At last, with sudden energy she freed herself, pushed back her hair from her forehead, sat down upon a low stool. Dry-eyed, her lips compressed in a firm line which foreswore all leniency towards herself, she forced herself to think. Minutes passed, then, through the confusion of her mind there came to her the remedy she sought — it seemed indeed her sole recourse. No matter how difficult, she must do it. All she wanted was to escape, lose herself, stamp out the memory of this supreme act of folly. Crouched on the stool, she began to make her plans.

# Chapter 12

ON the morning of Monday, February twenty-first the Wortley *Chronicle* carried on its front page the first of Dunn's series on the Mathry case.

Contrary to his habit, for he was a late and sluggish riser, Dunn walked down early to the *Chronicle* building. On the pavements the newsboys were shouting the headlines, carrying the special posters which McEvoy had printed. As he heard the boys calling and saw in huge letters the name MATHRY fluttering in the breeze, a slow thrill of exultation went through Dunn. He was not a vain man and had few illusions regarding his profession. But he believed passionately in the freedom of the press and in the power for good of a well-conducted paper. "It's out in the open now," he reflected tensely. "This will shake them up."

When he reached the office McEvoy had arrived — they had agreed to sit out the series in the office, together — and he could not resist communicating his thought to the editor.

"I'd like to have seen Sprott's face, and Dale's — when they found what was being served for breakfast."

McEvoy was less inclined to enthuse. He shrugged his shoulders a trifle grimly.

"We're into this now, up to the eyebrows. Let's pray to God nothing goes wrong."

During that day no event of any great importance occurred. Several of the distributors phoned in for extra hundreds of the paper. There were no returns. When he went out for lunch Dunn saw people on the street, in the trams, in the restaurant he frequented, reading the article. Everything was calm — the lull, he told himself, before the storm.

On the next day, about eleven o'clock in the forenoon the telephone rang. The second article, much stronger than the first — which merely outlined the main features of the case — had laid a definite charge of error against the police. When McEvoy put the receiver to his ear his eyes rested on Dunn, then he nodded meaningly and his lips silently shaped the name: "Dale."

"Yes," he said. "This is the editor of the *Chronicle*. Oh, good morning, Chief. I hope you're well."

There was a pause. Since the office lacked an extension, Dunn had no telephone. He heard one side of the conversation and watched McEvoy's face for the other.

"I'm sorry about that, Chief. Now to which article do you refer? Oh, the Mathry case. Dear, dear, I hope that isn't causing you any great anxiety."

The editor's expression remained bland.

"Well, really, I don't see what you can object to. It's our job to print the facts. And that's all we're doing. What's that? No, we haven't any doubts. But we've got some interesting evidence."

A longer interval followed. McEvoy's answer was less amiable.

"We're not afraid of libel, or of any other action that may be brought against us. We believe that the public should know about this case. And by the Almighty we're going to see that they do know."

A final pause. The editor's eyes glinted behind his pince-nez.

"I wouldn't do that if I were you, Dale. You see, the minute you close us up, we'll syndicate the rest of the series in the Howard Thomson chain. That's five provincial newspapers and a daily in London. We have a standing offer on Dunn's material. No, I wouldn't if I were you. And try to keep your temper. You'll need all your self-control before you're finished. By the bye, if you'd like to read Detective Inspector Swann's deposition, that's the next article. You'll find it in the *Chronicle* tomorrow."

McEvoy was slightly flushed as he replaced the receiver. He lit a cigarette to calm himself.

"He's angry. And badly worried. Threatened to suppress the paper. I thought it best to take a strong line with him."

"Dale isn't a bad sort," Dunn said. "Fundamentally honest. It's the man above who's pushing him. But he can't do anything."

"He could," McEvoy answered. "But he won't. If they cracked down on us it would be practically an admission of guilt. They're up against it. I'll bet you a drink that tomorrow or the next day we have a visit from the head man." He picked up a slip which had just been brought in to his desk. In a matter-of-fact tone he added: "It's all good for business. We printed an extra twenty thousand today. Every one of them has gone out."

On the following morning it was evident that people were beginning to talk about the case. The mail brought a sack of letters from readers of the *Chronicle* and several other newspapers devoted space to comment upon the Heretic's series. Most of the paragraphs were cautious, and the Blankshire *Guardian* took occasion to rebuke Dunn: "We are afraid that in his mission to reform the universe on this occasion our esteemed colleague is going a little too far." However, the London *Tribune,* a liberal paper of the highest standing, actually had a leader on the subject which began: "Allegations of a most serious nature are being made in the Wortley *Chronicle* which, if they are true, will shock the entire country," and which ended: "As in all previous contributions from the Heretic's gifted pen, every word has the ring of genuine conviction. We await, with the greatest interest, the remaining articles of this remarkable series."

"It's begun." McEvoy handed the clippings over to Dunn. "Wait till they see what you say about Swann. Incidentally . . . if I were you I shouldn't stay out too late at night."

"Good God! They wouldn't try anything like that."

"No," the editor said in a queer voice. "But you might catch cold."

There was a knock upon the door. A young man, McEvoy's secretary, came in.

"Excuse me, sir. Sir Matthew Sprott's clerk is on the telephone. Sir Matthew would be much obliged if sometime this afternoon you would come over to see him."

Dunn and McEvoy exchanged a glance. McEvoy stretched his legs out under the desk.

"Tell Sir Matthew's clerk we're sorry not to be able to step

over. Tell him we're extremely busy. On the other hand, if Sir
Matthew should care to come here, say that we'd be perfectly
happy to see him."

"Very good, sir." The secretary went out.

"He'll never come," said Dunn.

"Perhaps not." McEvoy shrugged. "But for the past fifteen
years he's been frightening people. It's about time somebody
started to frighten him."

The next two articles dealt, in no uncertain manner, with the
suppression of the date of pregnancy, and with the peculiar
manner in which the witnesses had been handled by the police.
And now, indeed, the avalanche was under way. Sacks of mail
kept arriving at the *Chronicle* building, and so many telegrams
poured in that McEvoy arranged for a special group of sorters to
work in the adjoining room while Dunn and he, in their shirtsleeves, stood by in their office. Some of the telegrams were from
cranks, from societies for the abolition of this, that, and the
other, some were abusive, protesting that the articles were under-
mining the forces of law and order, but in the main the messages,
from every corner of the country, were warmly congratulatory.
Amongst the chaff, were a number of mealy grains.

From the Reverend Foster Bowles, the sensational publicist
and preacher of the London City Temple, this:

WARMEST FELICITATIONS ON YOUR MAGNIFICENT CAMPAIGN.
I AM PREACHING ON THE MATHRY CASE NEXT SUNDAY EVENING.
GOD BLESS YOU, BROTHERS. BOWLES.

"Why does he want to butt in?" asked Dunn a trifle jealously.
"He's nothing but a slick windbag."

McEvoy shook his head in mock reproval. "Where's your
brotherly love, brother? Bowles is the man we need. He over-
flows the Temple, and beyond. He'll knock 'em by the thousand
in the old Kent Road."

He took up the next wire. "Listen to this:

> INTENSELY APPROVE YOUR CONTINUANCE OF MATTER RAISED
> BY ME IN HOUSE NOVEMBEF 19TH. IN VIEW IMPENDING ELEC-
> TION SHOULD APPRECIATE YOUR ACKNOWLEDGMENT MY EF-
> FORTS. AFTER ALL I WAS FIRST. WILL CONTINUE TO SEEK JUS-
> TICE. SINCERELY GEORGE BIRLEY. M.P.

"Good old George," Dunn said, unsmilingly. "He wants to climb on to the wagon."

"And to slap back at the Ancasters. They spanked him so hard he almost went off his golf game. 'Will continue to seek justice' is nice." The editor took up another slip, studied it, then passed it across the desk to Dunn. "What do you think?"

Dunn read the telegram with a frown. It was personal, from the editor of the London *Tribune*.

> DEAR MC EVOY. IN VIEW GREAT INTEREST HERE MATHRY CASE
> OFFER RUN HERETIC ARTICLES IMMEDIATELY YOUR PRICE.
> CORDIALLY LLOYD BENNETT.

For a moment there was silence in the office. As newspaper men, both were thinking the same thing . . . McEvoy doodled on his blotter, then suddenly looked up.

"I know how you feel. You're fishing, and you've found a wonderful pool, all to yourself, then somebody else pops up, on the opposite bank, and says, 'let me have a go!' Of course, it's a great compliment . . . the *Tribune* . . . Lloyd Bennett's a pretty good angler . . . if you follow me. . . ."

Dunn got up, and went over to the window and stood with his back to the editor.

"This thing is bigger than personal vanity," he said at last. "We'd better accept."

"Good," McEvoy said briskly. "I thought you'd agree. We'll ask a whale of a price."

"Oh, shut up, Jimmy." Dunn still stood at the window. "This thing doesn't belong to either of us. Here we are, like a couple of bloody bookies, punting on the big race, getting all the thrills . . . and the lad that really did the work, the poor plucky youngster who fought like hell to string it all together is stuck in a hospital bed, with two ribs missing and a hole in his lung. It's all wrong."

"He's still pretty sick?"

"Damn bad." Dunn nodded. "But they give him a slim chance. If only he could read my articles. They'd do him more good than medicine."

"Hm! What a scoop . . . it would be." The editor could not refrain from meditating aloud. "I mean . . . at the psychological moment . . . if he *did* pass out. . . ."

As Dunn swung round, with much profanity, McEvoy hastily recollected himself and apologetically pressed the bell.

"You just can't help thinking these things . . . it's in the blood. I'll wire Lloyd Bennett straight away."

On the following morning the London *Tribune* carried a one-page supplement containing the first three articles of the series. The next day it brought itself in line with the *Chronicle* by printing another three. The seventh article appeared simultaneously in both newspapers. Late that evening, when Dunn and McEvoy were preparing to go home, a boy brought in a teletype flash.

IN THE HOUSE OF COMMONS MR. DOUGLAS GIBSON (L) MEM-
BER FOR NEWTOWN, ROSE TO ASK IF, IN VIEW OF RECENT DE-
VELOPMENTS IN THE PRESS AND ELSEWHERE, THE SECRETARY FOR
STATE WAS NOT PREPARED TO RECONSIDER HIS PREVIOUS DE-
CISION IN RESPECT OF THE MATHRY CASE.

REPLYING, THE SECRETARY FOR STATE, SIR WALTER HAMIL-
TON, SAID HE WOULD REQUIRE NOTICE OF THE QUESTION IN
WRITING.

In the office, the two men looked at each other, in electric silence. It had been a wearing day, without much to show for it, and the strain was beginning to tell on both of them.

"Notice of the question in writing," McEvoy said at last, with a queer cracked lift to his voice. "No point-blank refusal now. They want time to think. The wires to Wortley will be red hot tonight. Tomorrow we may have a visitor."

They shook hands, silently, yet spontaneously, then took their hats and went out.

The following day was Tuesday, and towards four o'clock, that hour when the *Chronicle* management usually refreshed itself with strong tea, brewed by the office boy and served in thick, chipped china cups, a knock sounded on the door.

"Come in."

It was not the tea tray, but McEvoy's secretary, Jed Smith, looking nervous, and directly behind him, entering the room, was Sir Matthew Sprott. The prosecutor, who was extremely well groomed, gave, in his manner, no sign of anything unusual. His features, exhibiting his usual expression of dignified aloofness, were perfectly composed.

There was a slight pause.

"Won't you sit down," said the editor.

"Thank you." Sir Matthew took a chair. "You are difficult to get hold of these days, Mr. McEvoy. I happened to be passing and thought I would take my chance by looking in. Of course, quite unofficially."

"Quite," said McEvoy, his eyes empty of expression, but fixed on the other's face. "Can I offer you a cigarette?"

"No thank you." Sprott waved aside the silver box. "I am fortunate in finding you here also, Mr. Dunn. My remarks to some extent concern you."

There was a longer pause. The prosecutor was completely self-assured, decided in his mind, betraying no disquiet. He even smiled slightly to show that he was completely at his ease.

"Gentlemen," he said, "I have not come here to engage in dialectic. The matter is too trivial. Besides, I acknowledge that you are entitled to conduct your own newspaper in your own way. Nevertheless, I must tell you that your current series of articles is somewhat embarrassing His Majesty's Government."

A silence. Both McEvoy and Dunn were looking at Sprott. Behind his pompous arrogance there was a faint anxiety which he could not quite conceal. When he spoke again it was with unnatural heartiness.

"We are men of the world, gentlemen. I am sure we all three appreciate the difficulties of running the country in these uncertain times. The elections will be upon us in a matter of three months. I make no deduction from these points, I merely ask you to bear them in mind. Now there is no question whatsoever but that His Majesty's Government is entirely sympathetic towards this matter you have raised."

"Indeed?" said the editor.

"I can assure you of the fact." Sir Matthew nodded impressively. "I talked by telephone for an hour last night with His Majesty's Secretary for State." Unseen by the prosecutor, McEvoy darted a swift glance at Dunn. "And I reiterate, dogmatically, that Sir Walter, who is a most enlightened man, wishes to behave with complete humanity in this strange and perplexing affair."

"Ah!"

Sir Matthew surveyed them with an intensification of his genial smile.

"As I informed you, gentlemen, I am here unofficially — how, in my position, could it be otherwise. But frankly, though in absolute confidence, I am here to put before you an offer, a generous, nay, a magnanimous offer which should, I think, once and for all resolve this business and bring it to a just conclusion."

241

The prosecutor moistened his lips and leaned forward.

"I am empowered to state that, if you will cease publication of these articles — which in the circumstances will be no longer necessary — Sir Walter will consent to pardon the prisoner Mathry, and release him immediately from Stoneheath Prison."

The prosecutor's altruistic smile seemed fixed upon his face. Dunn and McEvoy had not even exchanged a glance.

"Well, gentlemen, do you accept?"

"No. We refuse."

Slowly, Sprott took out his handkerchief and wiped the palms of his hands. His smile was gone. He was finding it impossible to hold it.

"You refuse? You surprise me greatly. May I ask your reasons?"

The editor never took his eyes off him.

"In the first place it would be a betrayal of the *Chronicle's* integrity if we compromised at this point. And in the second, one does not pardon an innocent man."

Silence again. Sprott carefully restored his handkerchief to his breast pocket.

"You say 'at this point.' What, may I inquire, is your ultimate objective?"

McEvoy answered in a level voice:

"To obtain the unconditional release of the prisoner Mathry. To secure a full, open, and impartial inquiry into the circumstances of his conviction . . . and if there has been a miscarriage of justice . . . to procure ample and satisfactory damages for the horrible injury done to an innocent man."

Elevating his eyebrows, the prosecutor smiled. At least he attempted to smile, in a careless fashion, but his facial muscles refused to carry out the task. They broke down, midway, and remained fixed, in a contorted grimace. Hurriedly, he raised his hand to the lower part of his face. He kept it there for a moment, immobile, like a man suffering a severe neuralgic spasm.

Then, with a great effort he got to his feet. He said coldly:

"I can only hope, gentlemen, that you will not regret the line of conduct you have chosen to pursue. Needless to say, I shall oppose you to the limit of my powers. And I may remind you that it is a costly business to fight the Crown."

He was too experienced, too skilled in performing before the public eye, not to preserve his self-control. He inclined his head towards each, in turn, and calmly left the room. But there was a grey look about his face. And he walked like an infirm man.

At the end of that week McEvoy, looking ahead, opened the Mathry Legal Fighting Fund in the columns of the *Chronicle*. Contributions came in from all over the kingdom. Rubbing his hands, the editor remarked, with nervous intensity:

"It's a national issue. And it's coming to a head."

In a free country, where public opinion is neither regimented nor suppressed, there arises, in certain instances, when the feelings of the people are deeply stirred, a great roaring wind of protest. It may begin only as a faint whisper, an individual murmur. But it grows, travels, and expands with unbelievable rapidity and strength, until it reaches hurricane force. When such a tornado occurs, it is useless for those in power to attempt to stand against it. They must bend or be broken. Then it is that government by the people, for the people, is given its true effect.

And thus it was, in the present instance, with the case of Rees Mathry. At the time of the trial, this case had achieved only regional significance and, soon forgotten, it had lapsed into obscurity for fifteen years. Now, in McEvoy's phrase, it was a national issue. One after another the newspapers of the great cities fell into line in demanding an impartial investigation of the facts. Millions of words passed through the sweating linotype machines in the cause of Mathry. Writers and politicians, preachers of every denomination, publicists, lecturers, college professors, trade-union leaders, eminent scientists, leading actors, prominent physicians, all joined their voices to the prevailing clamour. "Rees Mathry" societies were formed in various centres. Mathry buttons were manufactured and sold all over the country. School children, who had not been born when the prisoner was convicted, walked in procession with banners: *Release Mathry.* Flesh and blood, still less a tottering government, could not stand against this outcry.

One wet and dreary afternoon towards the end of the month, as McEvoy and Dunn sat in the office, restless and uncommunicative, worn ragged by the continuous tension of the preceding days, they heard suddenly, a burst of shouting in the corridor outside. A moment later, Smith, the secretary, came into the room followed by the other members of the editor's office staff.

Excitedly, he held out a teletype strip.

"It's just come through, sir."

From below, on the compositors' floor, and from the basement beneath, there ascended sounds of further demonstrations.

"Read it then for God's sake," McEvoy said.

In a high voice Smith read out:

AT FIVE O'CLOCK IN THE HOUSE OF COMMONS THE SECRETARY FOR STATE ROSE TO ANNOUNCE THAT REES MATHRY WILL BE UNCONDITIONALLY RELEASED FROM STONEHEATH PRISON ON THE LAST DAY OF THIS MONTH AND THAT A PUBLIC INQUIRY WILL BE HELD AT THE WORTLEY HIGH COURT WITHIN FOUR WEEKS' TIME. THE ANNOUNCEMENT WAS GREETED WITH PROLONGED APPLAUSE.

As though to point these final words another explosive cheer sounded in the building. The editor gazed at the little group clustered in the doorway. In his own overwrought state he was surprised at the delight and excitement on the faces before him. He felt obliged to make some appropriate remark.

"You've all done a great job," he said, conventionally, trying to summon a show of satisfaction. "And now we have the good

244

news I want to thank you for your support. There'll be a nice bonus for every member of the staff the day Mathry is free."

When he had dismissed them he turned to Dunn, who sat back, examining his nails. He felt flat and stale, caught in the backwash of reaction.

"Well, we've done it," he said. "And I'm damned tired. I'm going home."

He began slowly to pull on his jacket.

"I'd like a short editorial for tomorrow's edition. You know, cracking up the parliamentary institution, the power of *vox populi,* and so on. Will you do it?"

"All right."

"Thanks. Then bring Eva round to supper. We'll have something to cheer us up." He picked up his overcoat, paused. "We've won, haven't we? We ought to be shaking hands and dancing the fandango. What the hell's wrong with us?"

"Reaction, I guess. We've been pretty hard at it. But Mathry's free . . . we've brought him back to life."

"I wonder . . . I wonder how Lazarus felt when he came back from the tomb." With these cryptic words, McEvoy shook his head, then departed.

Dunn finished the editorial in fifteen minutes. He pressed the bell, gave the typescript to Smith, then went into his own room. He meant to call the hospital to give Paul the good news — this was a treat which he had looked forward to for a long time. But a thought restrained him. He smiled to himself with that strain of sentiment he could never stamp out, flung his hat on the back of his head, and left the office.

At No. 61 Ware Place he found Mrs. Hanley returned from her trip to London, busy ironing a pile of laundry by the kitchen fire.

"Mrs. Hanley," Dunn said. "Paul's father is going to be released. It's definite and official. I want Lena to go round right away to the hospital and give him the good news. I have a feeling she'll do the job much better than me. Hurry now, and call her downstairs."

Mrs. Hanley did not move. Her lips drew together as she looked at him.

"Lena's no longer here. When I got back last week I found her rooms empty. She left a note to say she'd gone for good."

# Chapter 13

THE morning of March 2nd dawned clear and soft, with a chirping of sparrows among the yellow crocuses which dotted the strip of lawn outside St. Elizabeth's Home. It was perfect spring weather — the sun held its first real warmth, sap was running in the elms which fringed the short entrance drive, and feathery sprays of a delicate green were breaking from the topmost branches. The moist earth, murmuring with unseen rivulets, seemed bursting into life.

It was the day of Paul's discharge from the hospital.

Long before noon, the hour when Dunn had promised to call for him, he was ready, sitting in the St. Elizabeth's parlour, his round of goodbyes made — with an extra word of gratitude, a special pressure of the hand for the buxom, red-cheeked, and perpetually cheerful Sister Margaret who had been his nurse. He had been acutely ill, but the rib was healed, the lung expanded, his cough gone. Now, although his strength had not fully returned and he still showed the marks of debility, he was pronounced organically sound.

Punctually, Dunn arrived in a taxi. After a longish scene in the parlour — it appeared that Dunn was highly esteemed by the good sisters, and he had to evade with all his skill the pressing hospitality of Reverend Mother, who proffered a select refreshment of sherry and biscuits — they at last got away. As they drove towards the city, with the balmy air streaming in through the open windows, Paul experienced all at once a burst of thrilling anticipation, born of what lay immediately before him. This, after all, was what he had worked, and suffered, for all these weary months.

"I've taken rooms for you at the Windsor." Dunn broke the silence. "It's not much of a hotel but it's quiet. Not a bad place to get your bearings."

With a grateful glance, Paul indicated his readiness to fall in with all the arrangements which Dunn might make for him.

"In fact," the other went on, "when your mother arrives tomorrow you might all stay there, till the inquiry is over. The *Chronicle* will take care of the expenses. No, don't thank me. It's our show. And by the same token, here's thirty pounds. You take charge of it. You'll have to buy your father some clothes and things. You can settle up if you want to when the indemnity is paid."

"What indemnity?"

Dunn gave him a sidelong look.

"It looks like your father will have a claim against the government. In the opinion of counsel, up to five thousand pounds."

Paul received this wholly unexpected news in silence. Although, in his present mood, the prospect of such compensation seemed to him relatively unimportant, it did enable him to accept, with less compunction, the bundle of pound notes extended to him by his companion. It would be good to use them as Dunn had indicated. And, reflecting on that impending pleasure, somehow he felt especially glad that he would have this whole day alone with his father before his mother arrived from Belfast next morning.

"You've seen him?" he asked, after a silence.

Dunn nodded. "He's at the hotel. Smith, one of our staff, is with him."

"You think of everything."

"I wish I did," Dunn answered shortly. His manner, while perfectly considerate, held a certain brusqueness and, after a pause, he changed the subject.

"Have you seen Lena lately?"

"No." Paul's face altered. "Not since the night she got me into hospital."

"You don't know about Lena," Dunn said abruptly. "It's about time you did." And, looking straight ahead, in a few curt phrases, he communicated the facts to Paul, sparing nothing.

Dazed and shaken, Paul felt his throat constrict. How he had misjudged her! What a fool . . . what a blind, insufferable prig he had been! The recollection of her face, with its expression of sadness and sincerity, haunted him. When he could control his voice he said:

"I must see her."

"She's gone."

"Gone?"

"She gave up her job," Dunn seemed to derive an acrid satisfaction from his reply, "and disappeared."

"But why?"

"How should I know?"

"At least you know where she's gone?"

"We didn't . . . but we do now." Dunn stole a side glance at his companion. "She's working as a waitress in a cheap restaurant in Sheffield."

"You have her address?"

"If I have, it's not for publication." Dunn spoke with a reticence that closed the subject.

The taxi had detoured the business centre of Wortley, and having crossed the Nottingham Road Bridge was now threading the southern suburbs. Many of the streets which they traversed had been tramped by Paul during the period of his misery when life had held nothing but hopelessness. But presently they reached the Fairhall district and drew up at the Windsor, a rambling, rough-cast building, with wooden balconies, several turrets and a red tiled roof. It was a hotel of the residential type, constructed a decade previously on a grandiose scale, which had never really paid its way and which had lapsed gradually into a semi-commercial establishment, respectable enough, but always half empty, a trifle fly-blown. As they went through the revolving door, ascended the green carpeted staircase and paused momentarily outside the entrance to a first-floor suite, Paul felt Dunn looking at him as though about to speak. But now he could not wait. Trembling with expectation, he pushed forward, through the doorway.

In the sitting room, at the window table, watched from a distant seat by McEvoy's secretary, an elderly man was eating a meal of ham and eggs. He was about sixty, of heavy and ungainly build, with a thick-set torso and muscular arms. His head, partly bald, covered behind the protruding ears by cropped dirty grey hair, was round as a cannon ball, cemented into the bowed and thickened shoulders. The skin of his neck was parchment yellow, baggy and thickened, seamed with scar-like wrinkles, pitted with tiny bluish stains. Dressed in a shiny brown suit bursting at the seams, old-fashioned in cut and grotesquely small for him, he looked like a broken-down navvy out for the day.

Then, as Paul stood arrested, with beating heart, this total stranger raised his cropped head and, wrinkling up his brows, still chewing with his strong discoloured teeth, stared back at him with stony, hostile eyes. For an agonizing moment Paul could not speak. A thousand times, and in a thousand different ways, he had foreseen the meeting, the quick recognition, the warm embrace, the pardonable tears — ah, how tenderly had he embellished the reunion with the beloved father of his childhood. Prepared though he had been for changes brought by the years, in all his imaginings he had pictured nothing remotely resembling this devastating transformation. With an effort he took control of himself, advanced, and held out his hand. The fingers that met his own, after a moment's hesitation, were broad and calloused, hard as horn, with split and yellowish nails.

"Well, sir," Dunn exclaimed, with a note of heartiness, forced, and so unnatural, so out of key with his recent mood of reticence, it grated on Paul's ears. "I hope they're looking after you all right."

The man at the table switched his eyes towards Dunn. He did not answer but went on chewing, as though bent, grimly, on extracting the full flavour from the food.

Dunn saved the situation by turning to Smith.

"You've seen to everything, Jed?"

"Yes, I have, Mr. Dunn," Smith answered.

"You didn't let the reporters bother Mr. Mathry too much?"

"No, sir, I didn't . . . I handed out our prepared statement."

"Good."

There was a pause. The secretary picked up his hat, which lay on the floor at his feet.

"Well!" Dunn exclaimed, shifting his feet. "You two haven't seen each other for some time. Smith and I don't want to intrude. We'll look in tomorrow. Call me if you want anything."

A wave of actual fright went over Paul. He would have given anything to detain the two others, but he could not. He saw that they were anxious to go.

When the door closed behind them he stood for a minute in complete silence, then he took a chair and sat down at the table. The stranger, this Rees Mathry who was his father, was still eating, bent close over his plate, aiding the food into his mouth with quick thrustings of his thumb, and from time to time sending out that mask-like glance, in a kind of blank inquiry. Paul could bear it no longer. In desperation, almost incoherently, in slow and jerky phrases he began.

250

"I can't tell you how glad I am . . . to see you again, Father. It means a lot to me. Of course, after all these years . . . it's difficult for us both. I daresay you feel as awkward as I do. There's so much to say, I hardly know where to begin. And so much to do, for that matter. The first thing is to get you some decent clothes. When you finish your lunch . . . we ought to drive round and visit the shops. . . ."

His remarks, which sounded so inadequate in his ears, gradually tailed off into silence. He was both startled and relieved when the other spoke.

"Have you any brass?"

Although chilled, slightly, by the crudeness of the question, Paul responded willingly.

"Enough to go on with."

"I couldn't get a stiver out of that Dunn." Then, as though thinking aloud, "I'm going to get money. I'll make them pay for what they done to me."

The voice itself was rough, and hoarse, like an instrument seldom used, but worse than that tonal coarseness was the frightful bitterness, the dark and brooding rancour which pervaded it. Paul felt a further sinking of his heart.

"Have you a cigarette?"

"I'm sorry." Paul shook his head. "I've been off smoking for a bit."

Mathry studied him, beneath those mask-like brows, as though to discover if he were speaking the truth. Then, reluctantly, he produced a packet of cigarettes which Paul recognised as the brand used by Dunn. Selecting one, he cowered suddenly, as though to escape observation, and lit it. With the cigarette concealed in the cup of his hand he smoked rapidly, secretly, absorbing the smoke into his system. As Paul watched the intent brooding face he saw for the first time, almost with horror, its stony quality. The mouth, especially, was hard as flint, and shut like a

251

trap beneath the long, raw, badly shaven upper lip. Suddenly, and without warning, Mathry killed the glowing end of his cigarette and placed the stub in his waistcoat pocket.

"What time is it?"

As Paul consulted his silver watch he felt the other watching him with a strange covetousness. Indeed, almost at once, Mathry said:

"I haven't got a watch."

Paul slowly unfastened the catch from his buttonhole, handed over both watch and chain.

"You can use mine. Until you get a better one."

No word of thanks. Mathry weighed the watch and chain, up and down, in hollowed hand, then, with that swift movement of concealment which characterized most of his actions, he slipped them into his inside pocket.

At this point there was a knock at the door and a maid entered to clear the table.

Paul stood up. He knew there were excuses for his father, yet he felt sick at heart. In a scarcely audible tone he said:

"We'd better go out now . . . and do your shopping."

"Yes," said Mathry. "I want good duds."

They went out, into the bland spring sunshine, proceeding by taxicab to Leonard Street, where they entered Dron's, one of the largest outfitters in the city. If Paul had hoped for some relief in this distraction he was rudely disappointed. The afternoon, as it progressed, became for him a torturing nightmare. His father's uncouth appearance caused people to stare after them. His rough manner on one occasion brought the young woman who served them to the verge of tears. But worse than that was the truculent perversity with which he selected the most unsuitable clothes. The suit he insisted on having was of check material, made for a much younger man, the shirt was of vivid artificial silk, the tie a loud yellow, the shoes pointed and brown. He hung about the jewelry department for nearly an hour, fascinated by the bright glitter of the show cases, and Paul could only get him away by purchasing him a signet ring.

When they got back to the Windsor at six o'clock Paul, tired and dejected, sank into a chair in the sitting room. Mathry took his parcels, which he had carried jealously, into his bedroom. He was absent for twenty minutes. Then he came back, fully arrayed in his new garments, wearing the watch and chain, the signet ring, and an air of dogged vanity.

"You see," he exclaimed, "I'm not finished yet — in spite of them. I wish some of these swine could see me now — Hicks particularly. We ought to go out, have a spread and take in a theatre."

"We've only just come in," Paul said quickly. "We'll have dinner up here tonight."

Mathry looked at him, wrinkling the parchment brow.

"We'll have something to drink."

"Yes, of course," Paul agreed. "What would you like?"

"Whiskey."

Mathry stretched himself on the couch and opened the evening paper which he had made Paul purchase on the way back.

"I ought to be in there. They took photographs. I'm going to make them pay me for everything they print."

Paul pressed the bell and in a few moments a maid appeared, the same who had cleared the table earlier that afternoon. As Paul gave the order for dinner and a bottle of whiskey, Mathry, on the couch, in his new clothes, kept glancing at her over the top of the newspaper. She was a tall, foolish-looking girl with hollow cheeks, and this attention from one so prominent in the public eye made her blush and simper.

"She knows who I am," Mathry boasted, as she went out.

When dinner came Paul could scarcely touch it. Mathry, on the other hand, ate with voracity, and without speaking a single word. When he had finished he drew the cork from the bottle of whiskey

253

and poured himself a stiff glass. He carried this and the bottle across the room and took his place in a high-backed chair which stood against the wall. He sat there erect, in absolute silence, staring straight ahead at nothing, with a lowering intensity of vision which was terrifying. From time to time he replenished his glass. Occasionally his lips moved, as though he were talking to himself. He seemed utterly oblivious to Paul's presence, and when the maid came to remove the cloth, to her manifest disappointment, he took no notice of her whatsoever.

As the silence continued, Paul gazed almost with panic at the grotesque and brooding figure of his father. How could this be the man, so gentle and elegant, who had led him by the hand to sail paper boats on Jesmond Dene, taken infinite trouble to amuse him by sketching and cutting out silhouettes, who never failed at the weekend to bring him some little toy, whose every action had bespoken love and consideration. What frightful process of brutalization had changed him, brought him to this state? As Paul strove to envisage all the grinding miseries of these fifteen years — the close confinement of the narrow cell, the prison garb and wretched food, the iron bars, the hours of solitary darkness, the cries and stenches of the herd, the constant surveillance, the perpetual, back-breaking toil in summer and winter, in sunshine and snow, the joyless days and never-ending nights, a faint spark of pity strove, it seemed, to kindle itself within his breast. But it was stifled instantly by the awful reality of the physical presence, erect and staring, in the hard chair across the room.

Suddenly, almost caressingly, Mathry took out his watch. He looked at it a long time. Then he began to speak.

"Nine o'clock. They're all in the dark now . . . on their nice plank beds. They've been in the quarry, sweating their guts out, in the rain. There was watery soup for supper . . . lucky if they got a bit of gristle in it . . . and spuds . . . spuds that taste like soap. Always these spuds, grey lumpy spuds . . . that turn your insides sour. It's all dark . . . but they can hear *him* outside in the gallery . . . up and down, up and down, looking in at them through the spy-holes. Maybe it's Hicks on duty . . . they'll know all right if it's him. They all watch out for Warder Hicks.

"Some of them have smashed their fingers in the quarry, some have blisters and backache . . . they all have the rheumatism that goes with the infernal mist. But that don't matter beside what they're thinking. They're all thinking about the outside . . . lying on their planks trying to remember what it was like over the high walls, thinking about the good times they had, and a soft bed, and a steak dinner, and other things. The old lags are tapping on the walls, tapping the news . . . who got the cat, who's coming in, who's going out. But the most of them know they're never going out. They're in there for life. They have nothing to look forward to . . . they're just buried alive.

"But maybe they're not so cosy, maybe they're not in their nice little cell. Suppose they made a mistake, did something wrong. Then they're in solitary, eight by six, down below, in the basement. It's black as pitch down there. And not even lumpy spuds. Bread and water . . . dry bread and water. Not even room to turn round . . . just two steps and you bang your skull against the concrete. That's where you really start to think . . . to wonder who you are . . . and where you are . . . and what the hell you've done to get there. That's where you tell yourself that if the walls split open, you'll get your own back . . . make somebody pay for what you've suffered . . . hate the whole cursed world . . . grab everything for yourself . . . if only the walls split open.

"Well, by God, they split open for me. So now you can guess what I'm out to do."

When he had finished he stood up and, without saying goodnight, not even looking at Paul, went out of the room. His heavy tread was audible as he tramped along the corridor to his bedroom. There was a short silence. Then Paul heard the faint buzz of a bell followed by the sound of lighter footsteps traversing the corridor. Although he tried to break his rigid attitude, he could not do so, he listened, listened with straining ears. The footsteps did not return.

A groan broke from Paul's lips. He dared not venture to the other door to confirm his suspicions but, by some subconscious process of association, his mind flashed back to a moment, late that afternoon when, as they left Dron's, his father had knocked against him in the crowd. Instinctively his hand flew to his inside pocket. All that remained of the money, some fifteen pounds, was gone.

# Chapter 14

NEXT day, the same brilliant weather prevailed and in the clear morning light the outlook seemed less sombre. Contrary to his expectations, Paul had slept well, and when he awoke he was ready to face his difficulties with new determination. His mother was due to arrive from Belfast at eleven o'clock, and as he shaved and dressed he felt hopeful that this additional support would materially improve the situation. After all, it was inevitable that prison should have changed his father — only his natural eagerness had made him overlook that fact! — but time and kindness and family affection must soften and regenerate the hardest heart.

He took breakfast downstairs in the restaurant, alone, then went up and along the corridor to the other bedroom where, not without some recurrence of his misgiving, he tried the door. It opened easily and, relieved, he entered. Mathry was still asleep, lying as though dead, his dirty grey head buried in his arm, the sheets rumpled and disordered, the pillows discarded, on the floor.

With a fresh stab of pity, Paul gazed at the huddled figure of his father, so defenceless in this oblivion. He decided not to rouse him. Taking a sheet of the hotel notepaper from the bureau in the corner he wrote out a message: *I have gone to meet the train. Hope you will be ready when we arrive. Paul.* He placed this conspicuously upon the chair on which were draped the new clothes. Then he went out.

On the way to the city it was fresh and invigorating — his road lay along the canal, a lively scene, with a string of cargo barges loading at the quay and actually a little pleasure launch preparing for departure. At the station the express was late, but at twenty-five minutes past the hour, the engine came steaming round the bend, drew up at the main platform. And there, leaving the foremost compartment, was a little group — his mother, Ella, and Emmanuel Fleming.

Paul started perceptibly — he had not expected to see the pastor and his daughter, indeed they had been so long absent from his thoughts he felt embarrassed and ill at ease. But he had no time for reflection, they had already seen him — Fleming had his arm upraised and Ella was fluttering her small white handkerchief. In a few moments they had passed the barrier and were pressing close to him, greeting him with enthusiasm, all speaking at once, in a confusion of disjointed phrases. His mother's eyes were moist, Ella seemed loath to remove her gloved hand from his, while the minister, standing somewhat in the background, smiled at him with understanding and approval.

As they set off along the street to the tramway stop, Fleming and his mother led the way while, as seemed expected of him, he followed behind with Ella. An excited colour tinged her wax-clear complexion, her short glossy hair had been recently shampooed and curled. She wore a new dove-grey costume and a neat little grey hat beneath which her eyes gleamed. She began, immediately, in a confident tone, taking his arm.

"Well, I must say, Paul, we owe you an abject apology. We ought to go down on our bended knees to you. And we will, too, if you like. At least, I will." She gave him a bright, intimate glance. "Of course we had no idea, or it would naturally have been quite different. We thought you were just ruining your splendid career and blighting your life all for nothing. And to those of us who love you that was the worst thing possible. We felt if we helped or encouraged you it would only make things worse. As I say we never dreamed. . . . And then, look what happened, yes, just look what you did, you wonderful person. When the news came out I nearly fainted, with joy, I mean. I was in the kitchen, making some cocoa, when Father came in from the district and told me. I had to lie down. Oh, Paul dear, I must tell you I haven't been at all well myself, I nearly had a breakdown through worrying about you, and the disgrace, and everything. But I don't want to talk about poor little me, though I suffered too in my own quiet way. It's you, Paul, you're the great wonderful person. If you only read the Belfast papers, and I'm sure they're the same here, you'd see what people think of you. All over the country, your name is on everyone's lips. Naturally one wouldn't wish to be vulgar or sensational at a time like this, I was really glad there were no photographers at the train, though I must say I expected them. Do you like my new costume, dear? I think it's spring-like, but subdued and appropriate to the occasion. As I was saying, it's your triumph, Paul, and I want you to enjoy it to the full. Naturally prayer must have been responsible, too, we both know that, and never a night passed but I made supplication for you to the Throne." Her gaze grew fonder and — as always happened when she spoke of religion — the clear greenish whites of her eyes turned up.

"It's so wonderful, Paul, that we're together again, with all our future before us. Of course in all the joy of our reunion we mustn't forget your father. The poor, poor man. My heart just bleeds for him. It's hard for us to understand how such a thing should be permitted to happen. But I suppose certain things are sent from on High to test and try us, to refine and purify our spirit. I can scarcely wait to meet him to express my sympathy and sorrow. And I want to assure you, Paul, that if there is anything I can do in any way, to help him, you have only to command."

She broke off, with another upturned glance, as they joined the others at the tramcar. He bit his lip at this prolonged possessive monologue, so vain and shallow, so indicative of a cheap and petty nature. Was he really as deeply committed to her as she made out? It amazed him that he could ever have cared for her — how greatly he had changed. He thought of Lena and his heart sank. When they had all four seated themselves, outside, on the upper deck of the tram, he felt he must at least inform them of the change which had taken place in Mathry. The pastor, more reserved than usual, staring out of the window as though debating some question in his mind, and frowning slightly as Ella resumed her flow of gossip, seemed alone to harbour a secret doubt. But the two women were, as he himself had been, obviously unprepared. It was his duty to warn them. Yet, as the tram lumbered forward, bringing them every minute nearer to the hotel, he remained stiffly silent. There was in Ella's facile enthusiasm, even in the primly nervous anticipation that he discerned in his mother, who was also dressed in her best, with even a touch of matronly coquetry, a quality which, in some peculiar fashion, antagonized him and aligned him, not on their side, but with that dulled and brutalized man who awaited them at the hotel. Yes, they must find out for themselves.

When they dismounted at the Windsor, he led the way into the hotel without a word. Upstairs, with a compression of his lips that was almost satiric, he threw open the door of the sitting room and ushered them in.

Mathry had finished his breakfast and was smoking a cigarette.

Clad in trousers and braces, his shirt unfastened at the neck, his new brown shoes, unlaced for comfort, gaping wide on his feet, he sat at the table which was still covered with soiled dishes. His expression, as he turned slowly to face the newcomers, was more inscrutable than ever. Watching them, he raised his coffee cup. His wrinkled navvy's throat worked up and down as he swallowed the dregs. Then setting down the cup, he turned to Paul, as the one person he recognised and tolerated.

"What do they want?"

Thus appealed to, Paul sought for an answer which would not provoke an outburst.

"You know, Father . . . they want to be with you."

"I don't want to be with them. You at least did something. They did nothing. They left me to rot for years. And now I'm out, they want to crawl back to lick my boots and see what they can get."

The pastor took a step forward. He was pale, yet he seemed less discomposed than the others by this reception — perhaps, as Paul had surmised, he had anticipated it. In a low persuasive voice he said:

"You have every reason to reproach us. We can only throw ourselves upon your mercy and ask you to forgive us."

Mathry bent his forbidding gaze on Fleming.

"You haven't changed . . . I remember you quite well. I want none of your mealy-mouthed slush. I put up with so much of it in the old days. Forgiveness!" His chapped lips drew back in a kind of snarl. "There was a warder in there by the name of Hicks. One day we were at the quarries. It was my first month, I was green at the work, and it was half killing me. But Hicks was there, right beside me, driving me on. The sweat was running into my eyes, I could scarcely see. As I swung my pick it shot off the granite and went into his boot. It never even scratched him, it only cut the uppers of his boot. Did he forgive me? He swore I'd tried to kill him. He had me before the governor. Even then he wasn't satisfied. He kicked and bullied me, spat in my skilly, got me solitary, watched me at every turn, for fifteen years he made my life a hell. And you talk to me about forgiveness."

"I know you've suffered," Fleming said weakly. "You've suffered horribly. All the more reason why we should help you to reestablish yourself, to find peace, back in the bosom of your own family."

"I have other ideas." Mathry's face assumed the same dogged insistence which had stamped it when he was selecting his new clothes. "I'm not done yet. I'm going to enjoy my life."

"How?"

"You just wait and see, you bleating hypocrite. They've had their fun with me. Now it's my turn."

Drawn up short, Fleming gazed almost helplessly at Paul's mother who, with parted lips, and an aghast expression, was staring at Mathry. So far she had not said a word. She was indeed, incapable of speech. But now, compelled by an unknown emotion, perhaps by some prompting from the distant past, she gave a quivering cry and held out her hands.

"Rees . . . let us try to start over again."

His look repulsed her even before she advanced.

"None of that." He struck the table with his fist. "It's all finished between us. I want somebody younger, with some blood in them." His eyes roved towards Ella, who blushed shamefully, then he returned his gaze to his wife, his lips drawn in a broken bitterness. "In any case, you were always snivelling, whining after me to go to meeting when all I wanted was to have my pals in for a glass of beer. I wouldn't come near you now if you were the last woman in the world."

She sank down on the edge of a chair, humiliated to the heart, her head bowed, tears streaming from her eyes. Ella ran to her, knelt beside her and began to whimper in sympathy. Mr. Fleming still stood silent, his eyes bent upon the carpet. Paul glanced at the bent figure of his mother. But he did not move towards her — it was almost as though, once again, he felt drawn, in sympathy, to his father.

At the table Mathry remained for some moments immobile, with wrinkled brow and drooping lids, as though, in some fashion, he had retreated into himself. But now he got heavily to his feet and moved to the door. Before he went out he swept them with his pallid eyes.

"Thirty strokes of the cat," he muttered. "That would make you blubber. That's what they served out to me."

The door slammed behind him, leaving nothing but the sound of sobs. Fleming moved to the window and looked out grimly.

"Oh dear, oh dear," Paul's mother moaned. "I wish I were dead."

Ella was crying in a frightened manner. "I don't understand. I don't understand. I thought it would be nice, like they said in the papers. I want to go home."

Paul's mother uttered a sob of assent. "We should never have come. We must leave at once."

Pastor Fleming, at the window, swung round slowly.

"No," he said, in a choked yet forbearing voice. "We must remain for the inquiry. We failed him once. We cannot do so again. It may not be too late. If we hope and pray we may save him yet."

# Chapter 15

AT ten o'clock on Monday the twenty-fifth of March, a warm and humid morning, the High Court of Justiciary was filled to suffocation, had overflowed to the pavements of the street outside. In the public gallery the spectators were wedged together on the benches, packed on the steps of the passage ways, their excited faces rising, tier upon tier, to the roof. The well of the court was equally congested. On the left an army of reporters was already busy with pens and paper. On the right there was grouped a privileged audience of Wortley notables and national personalities. In the centre sat the Attorney-General, with the instructing Crown Agent, Sir Matthew Sprott, Lord Oman, and other high officials of the Crown. Immediately behind were counsel for the appellant, Mr. Nigel Grahame, K.C., his junior, and the instructing solicitor. Then came Paul and his mother, Ella and Pastor Fleming, Dunn, McEvoy, and a number of their friends. On the front bench, where, against the wishes of his counsel, he had chosen to sit, in full view of everyone, biting at his lip as he broodingly surveyed the scene, was the former prisoner, the fifteen-year convict from Stoneheath, Rees Mathry.

Suddenly the expectant buzz of conversation was stilled and, when perfect silence had been attained, a door swung open. Everyone stood up as the five lords of appeal, led by the Lord Chief Justice, filed into court, solemn and imposing in their flowing robes. Until they had taken their places upon the bench the hush deepened. Then, with a rustle, the court reseated itself. A moment later a voice was heard:

"Call the appeal of Rees Mathry against His Majesty's Crown."

Cramped and tense in his place, Paul drew a sharp, painful breath. Day by day, living upon his nerves, he had followed the painstaking preparation of the case by Nigel Grahame. He could scarcely believe that now, at last, the inquiry had begun. He felt his eyes cloud as Grahame rose quietly. Tall, erect, and perfectly composed, one hand clasping his lapel in the traditional attitude, the young advocate addressed himself to the bench. His tone, like his manner, was quite informal, utterly devoid of rhetoric, almost conversational.

"My lords, on December 15, 1921, and subsequent days. Rees

263

Mathry, your petitioner, was tried at the Wortley Assizes on an indictment at the instance of Mr. Matthew Sprott, His Majesty's Prosecuting Counsel, the charge being that he did assault one Mona Spurling and did wound her with a razor and did murder her. Your petitioner having pleaded not guilty, the trial proceeded before a jury presided over by the Honourable Lord Oman, who, on December 23, 1921, sentenced him to be executed in Wortley Jail. Subsequently, the sentence of death passed upon your petitioner was committed to penal servitude for life, whereupon the petitioner was removed to His Majesty's prison at Stoneheath, where he was detained for fifteen years. The petitioner desires now to avail himself of the statutory provisions of the Criminal Appeal Act with a view to proving that he is innocent of the charge contained in the said indictment, that his conviction thereof was most erroneous and unjust, and constituted a grave miscarriage of justice."

Surreptitiously, Paul observed the three agents of the law who sat so near to him that he could have leaned sideways and touched each upon the shoulder. Chief Constable Dale's profile was stolidly impassive, Oman wore a haughty and absent air, Sprott, slightly sprawling in his seat, was flushed but his look was firm, determinedly indifferent. From these Paul's glance turned to the lonely and ungainly figure of his father, suffering again the ordeal of a public court, and, all at once, his heart began to beat with suffocating violence. Surely, at last, there would be vindication for this man. Quickly, lest he should break down, he turned his eyes away.

Grahame, having completed his reading of the petition, had paused for a moment, permitting his eyes to rest, gravely, upon the bench. Now, in that same controlled manner, he began his opening address.

"My lords, twelve months ago, the case of Rees Mathry was buried in the dusty archives of the Department of State. For fifteen years it had been forgotten, the convicted murderer was serving his life, or should I say his death, sentence in His Majesty's prison, all was well with the world.

"Then, by the merest chance, the son of that convicted murderer, from whom all knowledge of the crime had been concealed, discovered, suddenly, the odium, the frightful stain of guilt which lay upon his father and which, of course, in some measure descended like a blight, upon himself. Overcome, he nevertheless trusted the forces of the law, and in trembling horror, accepted the shameful fact that this parent was a murderer. Yet, out of his deep love and affection, he was constrained, almost against his will, to seek out the awful circumstances which had led his father to do this deed. He set forth and, through months of suffering and the cruellest opposition, he uncovered, step by step, the full facts of the forgotten case. My lords, it is because of these efforts, and the results which have attended them, that we are gathered here, in this court, today."

Grahame's opening words and the quiet solemnity with which he uttered them produced a profound sensation. Paul kept his eyes fixed upon the floor. He felt himself trembling inside as, after a due pause, Grahame resumed his address, and, from time to time consulting the papers before him, proceeded to define and analyse the facts of the apprehension, the trial, and the conviction of Rees Mathry in December 1921. Familiar though he was with these searing events, Paul could not restrain a hot surge of feeling as, point by point, in unfaltering sequence, Grahame calmly took up and logically set down the details of the circumstantial evidence which had enmeshed his father.

The brilliant and masterly speech lasted, with an interval for lunch, for nearly four hours. And, at the end of it, before its manifest effect could subside, Grahame tranquilly pushed on. Unstudied and restrained, showing no signs of fatigue, he bowed to the bench, and indicated that he desired to call his witnesses.

"My lords," he declared. "I propose in the first instance to call the appellant himself. At the trial, because of the unparalleled attack upon his character made by the counsel for the Crown, Rees Mathry was not afforded full opportunity to defend himself. But he will now give evidence denying all knowledge of the crime, and answering any questions relative to the charge."

Immediately, the Attorney-General rose in protest. All through Grahame's address he had remained chafing and helpless in his seat. Now he exclaimed:

"My lords, I am anxious, nay eager, to assist legitimate inquiry in this appeal. But there must be no attempt to re-try the case. I strenuously oppose the motion that the accused be allowed to give evidence."

A stir of excitement went round the court. Paul saw his father sit up, and turn his grey face strainingly towards Grahame. Their lordships, upon the bench, had bent their heads in consultation. And presently the Lord Justice General announced their decision.

"With reference to the appellant, this court is of the opinion that his evidence would amount to no more than a repetition of his plea of not guilty. In these circumstances it would be quite unreasonable to spend time over his examination now. The court therefore is not prepared to allow his evidence to be received."

Leaning forward, Mathry had followed his lordship's words with increasing agitation. And now, amidst the buzz which arose, he jumped suddenly to his feet, his heavy figure, ludicrously garbed, trembling all over. To Paul's horror he shook his fist at the bench and shouted, in hoarse tones:

"It's not right. I ought to have my say. I have everything to tell. I want you all to hear it. How I was done down. How they treated me in quod for fifteen years." His voice rose to breaking point. "You can't shut me up now . . . like they did before. I want to be heard. I want justice . . . justice."

Gesticulating wildly, Mathry was at last forced back into his seat by Grahame and several attendants of the court who had hastened to restrain him. For some minutes there was a great commotion, followed by a sense of consternation, then by absolute silence. Shrunk into himself, Paul became aware that Ella and his mother, beside him, were in tears. Further along, Dunn and McEvoy exchanged an anxious look. Sprott and Dale, manifesting emotion for the first time, seemed grimly pleased.

Then, with great severity, the Lord Chief Justice bent his brows upon Mathry.

"We are prepared to make great allowances. But I must advise the appellant that such conduct is not calculated to improve this court's opinion of his case. Furthermore, if it is repeated, I must warn him that he will be held in the most serious charge of contempt of court."

Grahame, back in his place, deftly interposed.

"My lords, on behalf of the petitioner, I offer sincere apologies to the court for this regrettable, but perhaps understandable outburst. And now, with your lordships' permission I will call my first witness, the eminent Home Office expert, Sir Malcolm Garrison."

Again the Attorney-General got quickly to his feet.

"My lords, once more I object. Further expert opinion is not admissible unless it arises out of fresh facts."

The Lord Chief Justice, by an inclination of his head, indicated assent.

"On what grounds, Mr. Grahame, do you desire to lead the evidence of Sir Malcolm Garrison?"

"My lords," Grahame replied, "Sir Malcolm, as you know, is our foremost criminologist. He has had a description of the injuries sustained by the murdered woman. He has seen photographs of the body taken at the time, also the razor presumed by the Crown to have been the lethal weapon, and he is definitely of the opinion that this instrument had nothing whatsoever to do with the crime."

The Lord Chief Justice frowned and took consultation with his colleagues. A few moments later he returned his beetling gaze to Grahame.

"The court must support the contention of the Attorney-General. Sir Malcolm Garrison did not view the body. Therefore, his evidence cannot be received."

Paul grew hot, then cold, with indignation. Were they to be obstructed at every turn? But Nigel Grahame merely bowed, accepting the decision of the court with perfect equanimity.

"My lords, I perceive it is your intention to limit as far as possible the number of witnesses and for that reason I shall call only five, to whom you cannot possibly take exception. Touching the question you have raised of those who saw the body, you will recollect, my lords, from your reading of the case, that Dr. Tuke, the physician who viewed the murdered woman immediately she had expired, was not summoned to give evidence at the trial. My lords, in all your experience, you cannot name one case in which the doctor who first examined the body was not asked to testify. Why, then, in this instance was this crucial witness ignored? Dr. Tuke is now dead, but his widow is here today to answer that very pertinent question."

A ripple went through the court as Mrs. Tuke's name was called, and a moment later she went into the witness box, a staid, elderly figure in black, a woman upon whose plain, lined face honesty and respectability were unmistakably written. She took the oath intelligently, then turned towards Grahame, who began his interrogation in an easy tone.

"You are the widow of Dr. Tuke, who died in 1933, and for a number of years prior to his death carried on practice in the Eldon district of Wortley?"

"That is correct, sir."

"You know that your husband was called to Miss Spurling's house on the night of the murder?"

"I do."

"Did he say anything to you regarding it?"

"Oh, yes, it was such a terrible event, we talked it over together on many occasions."

"Did your husband at any time express surprise to you that he had not been called as a witness at the trial?"

"Indeed he did. He said it was most remarkable. He said . . ." She broke off with a timorous glance towards the bench.

"Do not be afraid, Mrs. Tuke. The object of this court is to obtain, not to suppress, your evidence. What did he say?"

"He said the prosecutor did not regard his opinion as relevant."

Again a wave of interest went through the court and for the first time the attention of the spectators was directed towards Sir Matthew Sprott. Although Paul knew the facts so well he felt himself carried away by the rising current of excitement in the air.

"Tell us, Mrs. Tuke," Grahame resumed, "in your own words, the views which your husband expressed to you in the many conversations which you had with him upon the subject."

There was a pause. The witness sipped from the glass of water before her.

"Well, sir," she began, "Dr. Tuke always believed that the murder could not have been committed by a razor. In his opinion the instrument was quite different — sharp-pointed and piercing, more like a surgeon's scalpel than anything else."

"How did he reach that conclusion?"

"From a careful examination of the injuries. You see, sir, he found a deep penetrating wound at the right side of the neck, then a great slash, tapering away to the left ear."

"So he concluded that a pointed, thin-bladed weapon had first been thrust deeply into the great vessels of the neck, before the secondary slash?"

"Yes sir."

269

"And a razor, with its round, blunt end, could never have achieved such a result."

"That is just what he said, sir. He also believed that the assault was committed by someone very powerful, and violent. Moreover, from the disposition of the wounds, and the way the blood had splashed the rug near the body, he believed, indeed he told me he was sure, that the knife had been wielded by a left-handed man."

"A left-handed man," repeated Grahame with peculiar emphasis, and he gazed at his witness with a hint of severity. "Your recollection of that is quite clear and distinct?"

"Quite clear." The widow's lips trembled slightly. She answered with touching dignity. "Dr. Tuke was a good husband to me, sir. I respect his memory. Do you think I would put words in his mouth I believed to be untrue?"

"Not for an instant. I wished merely to make your good faith indisputably apparent to all the court."

As though sensing a challenge in these words and in the momentary glance that Grahame directed towards him, the Attorney-General responded testily.

"I am quite in the dark as to the purpose for which this witness is being examined at such length. In the meantime I have no questions."

"That will be all, then, Mrs. Tuke. We are much indebted to you. And now I ask my next witness to appear."

At a sign from Mr. Grahame the old lady stepped down, and the name of Professor Valentine was called out in court.

The individual who now stepped forward was a short and officious man aged about fifty, dressed very professionally in a slightly seedy frock coat with satin lapels, high white collar and black tie. His complexion was sallow and from his high forehead there arose a bush of black hair which, worn long at the back, gave him the air of a second-rate impresario. When he had taken

270

the oath he struck an attitude, one hand on his hip and the other on the ledge of the box before him, head thrown back, ready, it seemed, for every eventuality.

"Mr. Valentine," Grahame began, mildly, "you have, I understand, some knowledge of handwriting?"

"I am a professor of paleography," Valentine stated, with dignity. "I possess the diploma D.P.W. And I think I may say that my reputation as an expert is universally known."

"Excellent. At the trial I believe you testified that the note of assignation found in the murdered woman's flat had been written by Rees Mathry?"

"I did, sir . . . I was called in specially by the prosecution."

"You realized at that time, I am sure, the gravity and importance of your opinion and you were perfectly convinced, I presume, that it was correct?"

"Indubitably correct, sir. I have had great experience in attesting the validity of private and public documents in cases of the most vital importance."

"Then would you tell us Mr. — I beg your pardon — Professor Valentine, how you arrived at such a very positive conclusion?"

"By the use of the magnifying glass, sir, upon the document in question and by enlarged photographs of the calligraphy, which I compared with the specimen of the prisoner's handwriting — as manifest in the post card admittedly written by the prisoner — I was able, owing to my expert knowledge, to reach the definite conclusion that the note had likewise been written, in a disguised manner, by Mathry."

"In what manner disguised?"

"By the simple and extremely common expedient of taking the pen in the left hand."

"Ah! So the note of assignation was written left-handed?"

"Indubitably. And by the prisoner, Mathry."

"And by Mathry." Grahame smiled agreeably. "Such conviction is very reassuring. I am ill-qualified, Professor, to plumb the mysteries of your art. Nevertheless, it would appear, from the highest authorities upon the subject, that evidence of this kind, based on opinion and theory, cannot always be implicitly relied upon. You have heard, perhaps, of the case of Adolf Beck?"

The Professor did not answer, but his air became loftier.

"In that case, Professor, a handwriting expert of acknowledged reputation swore upon oath that certain letters had been written by a man named Adolf Bcck who, on the strength of this evidence, was sentenced to five-years penal servitude. At the end of which time, after this long sentence had been fully served, it was proved beyond all shadow of doubt that he had not written the letters, that he was completely innocent, and that the handwriting expert had made a ghastly, unspeakable blunder which condemned a blameless fellow creature to five years of ruinous misery."

Valentine threw back his hair with an outraged air.

"I had nothing to do with the Beck case."

"Of course not, Professor. Your case was the Mathry case and that is what immediately concerns us. Now, in your opinion there were three distinct points. First, that the writing was left-handed, secondly, that it was disguised, thirdly, that it was by Mathry. Would you tell us which of these findings you base upon fact and which upon personal deduction?"

The Professor now looked thoroughly put out, and he answered somewhat heatedly.

"The merest novice, sir, could tell from the slope and configuration of the letters that the note in question was written disguised and left-handed. The third point, however, involves skilled technical knowledge of a high order . . . one might even use the word intuition . . . a sort of sixth sense which enables the expert to recognise a specific calligraphy amongst a host of others."

"Thank you, Professor," Grahame said quietly. "That is precisely what I wished to know. In point of fact, with all your senses you affirm that the note was written disguised and left-handed. With your sixth sense, your intuition, you opine that it was written by Mathry. That is all."

The Professor, more ruffled than ever, opened his mouth as though about to speak. But he seemed to judge it wiser to say nothing. As he stepped down, Mr. Grahame turned to the bench.

"My lords, with your permission I will call Police-Surgeon Dobson."

Again, the Attorney-General, despite his bulk, was swiftly on his feet.

"My lords, I must strenuously object. You have agreed that we are not here to re-try the case. The police-surgeon was heard in full at the original trial. Further evidence from him is not admissible."

"Unless," Grahame interposed calmly, "as you yourself have stated, it arises out of fresh facts."

A moment of tension followed, a silent conflict of wills, broken by the voice of the Lord Chief Justice.

"You wish to call the surgeon upon these grounds?"

"If it please your lordships."

A motion of assent was made following which a spry dark-haired man, dressed in a navy-blue suit, with an athletic figure and an agreeable, virile face bustled across the court and, with the composure of one who has often occupied that position, took up his place in the box.

"Dr. Dobson," Grahame began, in his most winning manner, "you have heard the theories of Dr. Tuke relating to the murdered woman's injuries, given to the court concisely and most lucidly by his widow. What do you think of them?"

"Rubbish."

The word, not uttered contemptuously, but with a disarming

smile, sent a murmur of amusement through the gallery. Although it was at once suppressed, Mathry ground his teeth and glared at the offenders.

"Rubbish, Doctor? A strong term, is it not?"

"You asked for my opinion. I have given it."

Paul caught his breath sharply. He doubted the wisdom of calling the police-surgeon and feared that Grahame would fare badly against this confident, determined witness. But unruffled and undeterred, the young barrister went on.

"Perhaps in general you are opposed to theories."

"When I find a woman with her throat cut and her head virtually severed from her body I find little need for theoretical speculation."

"I see. You conclude immediately that the lethal weapon was the obvious one—a razor."

"I did not once mention the word razor."

"But the prosecution in its most damning indictment produced a razor as the actual fatal instrument."

"That is not my department."

"Then let us return, if we may, to your department. Theorizing apart, what was your conclusion, if any, in respect to the weapon?"

"That the injuries were occasioned by an extremely sharp instrument."

The surgeon, justifiably but mistakenly, was growing angry. Grahame smiled at him gently.

"So, as Dr. Tuke contended, the murderer could have used a thin, sharp blade, such as a scalpel."

Annoyance and honesty contended openly in the surgeon's face.

"Yes," he declared at length, "I suppose he could. Provided he had some knowledge of anatomy."

"Some knowledge of anatomy." Grahame, despite his quiet tone, gave the phrase a thrilling significance. "Thank you, Doctor . . . thank you, very much. And now, you performed an autopsy upon the murdered woman."

"Naturally."

"You found that she was pregnant."

"I stated the fact in my report."

"Did you state the term of pregnancy?"

"Of course," the police-surgeon answered warmly. "Are you suggesting that I was remiss in my duty?"

"Far from it, Doctor. However much we may differ on the question of metaphysics I am convinced of your absolute integrity. How long had the murdered woman been pregnant?"

"Three months."

"You are sure?"

"As sure as I'm standing in this box I reported that she was three months gone . . . perhaps a day or two over."

"And your report was sent to the prosecuting counsel?"

"Of course."

"Thank you, Doctor. That will be all." Grahame, with a pleasant smile, dismissed Dobson then turned to the bench.

"My lords, with your consent I will call my fourth witness."

A weedy little man came forward, thin-faced, bald, prematurely aged, dressed in a check suit too large for his wizened frame.

"What is your name?"

"Harry Rocca."

"Your present occupation?"

"Stableman . . . at the Nottingham Race Course."

"It was you who, fifteen years ago, disclosed to the police the false alibi which Mathry attempted to arrange."

"Yes."

"You knew Mathry well?"

"We knocked around together."

"Where did you meet him?"

"In the Sherwood Pool Rooms . . . around January 1921."

"And later on you introduced him to the Spurling woman?"

"That's right, sir."

"Can you recollect precisely when this introduction took place?"

"Very well. It was the day of the big July Handicap at Catterick. I recall it quite clear because I had five quid on the winner . . . Warminster."

"You say the July Handicap?"

"Yes, sir. Run the fourteenth of July."

"Did you mention the exact day to the authorities?"

There was a pause. Rocca lowered his head.

"I don't remember. . . ."

"In the light of the medical evidence, this date, which showed that Mathry had known Spurling for only seven weeks, was of the utmost significance. Were you not questioned about it at headquarters?"

"I don't remember."

"Try to refresh your memory."

"No." Rocca shook his head persistently. "I don't remember. They wasn't much interested . . . didn't seem to think it was important."

"I see. It was not important to prove that the most odious slur, the most damning link in all the evidence against Mathry was, in point of time, an absolute impossibility. That will do, thank you."

As Rocca left the box, Grahame gazed mildly toward the bench.

"My lords, my next witness is Louisa Burt."

Permission being granted, one of the court attendants went into an adjoining anteroom and, a moment later, returned with Burt.

She came in jauntily enough, with only a glint of uneasiness in the corner of her eye, and having taken her place on the stand, she preened herself, then gazed round the court with that affected air which Paul knew so well. She had not seen him, nor

276

did she once glance in the direction of Mathry who, from the instant she entered, glared at her with blazing hatred.

"You are Louisa Burt?" When she had taken the oath Grahame addressed her in his most courteous manner.

"Yes, sir. At least I was." She bridled consciously. "As you probly know, I just recently got married."

"May we congratulate you. We are indebted to you for your appearance here, especially at such a time."

"I must say it was a suprise when we was detained at the boat. But I'm only too willing to oblige, sir."

"Thank you. I can assure you that you have not been summoned without due cause. You realise, I am sure, that the evidence which you gave at the trial fifteen years ago was of vital importance and was, indeed, probably instrumental in securing the conviction of the prisoner."

"I done my best, sir," Burt answered modestly. "More nor that I cannot say."

"Now, the night of the murder was, I believe, dark and rainy."

"Yes, sir. I remember it like it was yesterday."

"And the fugitive who came from 52 Ushaw Terrace was running very fast."

"He was indeed, sir."

"So fast, indeed, that he flashed past you in a second."

"I suppose he did, sir." Burt spoke thoughtfully.

"Yet you obtained a very clear and complete picture of this man. He wore, you said, a fawn waterproof, a check cap, and brown boots. Tell us now, how, in an instant, and in the darkness, did you secure so comprehensive a description?"

"Well, you see, sir," Burt answered with confidence, "he run under the street lamp. And the light shone full on him."

"The time being twenty minutes to eight."

"Exactly, sir. I left the laundry with my frient at half-past seven, and it's less than a ten-minute walk to number 52."

"So you are absolutely certain of the time?"

"I'll take my oath, sir. In fact I've already took it."

"In that case, how could you have observed the fugitive by lamp light? In the district of Eldon, under a municipal ordinance in force in 1921 the street lighting was not turned on until eight P.M."

For the first time Burt appeared taken aback and, in a furtive fashion, her eyes sought out Dale, who sat in the well of the court deliberately averting his gaze from the witness box.

"It seemed like the lamp was on, sir," Burt asserted, at last. "I took it all in very quick, it just burned itself into my brain."

"Then why does this burned-in description differ materially from the final deposition which you signed after repeated questionings at the police station?"

Burt hung her head sulkily, and was completely silent.

"Could it be that you received certain promptings from the voice of authority?"

"I object, my lords," the Attorney-General started up violently, "to that unwarranted and unpardonable imputation."

"Let us leave it, then," Grahame agreed, reasonably. "If I am right, you said the running man was clean-shaven."

"Yes," Burt replied after some delay.

"You made that outright statement, it was published in the press and, unless you were to be completely discredited, it could not be retracted." Grahame paused. "Yet Mathry, the man whom you identified at Liverpool as being the fugitive, had a moustache which, in fact, he had worn for the previous six years."

"I can't help that," Burt retorted sullenly. "On second thoughts it seemed like he had the moustache. I told you I done my best."

"Of course," replied Grahame soothingly. "That is becoming increasingly evident. Well, we will leave those trifles of the unlit lamp, the moustache, the altered description of the clothing, and pass to an even more singular matter."

There was a strained silence. Burt's composure had gone. She kept searching for some encouragement from Sprott, then from the Chief Constable, and when both grimly refused to look at her, her gaze circled the court in desperation. Suddenly she saw Paul. She started. Her eyes widened and a livid colour spread over her pale, plump cheeks.

"It is," Grahame continued, "the question of your association with Edward Collins. Were you very friendly with Edward?"

Burt burst into tears. She clutched at the ledge of the box in front of her.

"I feel bad," she whimpered. "I can't go on. I need to lie down. I'm just recently a bride."

The Lord Chief Justice frowned, suppressing the faint titter which expressed the tension of the court.

"Are you ill?" he queried.

"Yes, sir, yes, your lordship, I must have a rest."

"My lords," Grahame said reasonably, "with your permission, I am quite agreeable that the witness should be accorded some respite. But I must recall her thereafter, with reference to another matter of the utmost importance, upon which I wish to lead proof."

After consultation, the judges consented. As Burt was assisted from the witness stand, the Lord Chief Justice viewed the courtroom clock which showed five minutes to four o'clock. Whereupon, in a curt voice, he adjourned the inquiry until the following morning.

# Chapter 16

IMMEDIATELY their lordships rose, Sprott, who had been on edge, awaiting the closure, made his way swiftly from the court, through his deserted robing room, and out by the private side entrance. He was determined not to be harried by reporters or detained in idle conversation, and had ordered his car for four o'clock. It was there, and as he hurried across the pavement towards it the accumulated aggravation of his mood was lightened by a throb of pleasure, when he perceived that his wife was in the back seat. He flung himself into the shelter of the car, and having ordered Banks to drive home, he turned the handle which raised the glass partition, lay back on the soft grey upholstery, and took her hand.

The day had been torture to his domineering spirit. Grahame's address, in particular, had put him on the rack. Moreover, his professional instinct warned him there was worse to come. He winced at the thought of Burt, and what Grahame might draw from her tomorrow. Closing his eyes, for a moment, he was content to rest in silence. Then he said:

"It was like you to come, Catharine. I knew I could depend on you."

She made no answer.

Half raising his jaded lids, he noticed that she seemed unusually pale and that, instead of an afternoon silk frock, she wore a plain tweed coat with a soft felt hat pulled down over her eyes. Presently, she withdrew her hand.

He sat up.

"It went not badly, considering." He spoke to reassure himself, as well as her. "Of course, Grahame was sensational — as we expected. He dug into the muck and slung it at us all — the cheap hound."

"Don't, Matt."

He bent towards her in surprised inquiry.

"What's the matter?"

She averted her white face and, with her slender neck arched against the light, gazed through the wide window of the car. At last, she said:

"I don't think Mr. Grahame is cheap."

"What!"

"I think he's honest and sincere."

His florid face grew brick red.

"You wouldn't say that if you had heard him today."

"I did hear him." She turned from the window, supporting one cheek with her long, delicate fingers and, for the first time, looked at him with her pained and shadowed eyes. "I was in the gallery, in the back seat. I had to go. I went to support you, to sustain you with my love, to hear you cleared of those vile insinuations. And instead . . ."

Startled, he stared at her, while the blood left his face. That she should have been there, to hear everything — it was the last thing he had wanted.

"You should have kept away." He spoke angrily. "I told you to. That court was no place for a woman. Didn't I explain it all beforehand. Every public official has to swallow a dose of bitter medicine once in a lifetime. But that's no reason why his wife should watch him take it."

"I had to go," she repeated in a lifeless voice. "Something made me do so."

There was a pause. He curbed his temper. He loved her.

"Well, never mind." He attempted to regain possession of her hand. "It will soon be over. They'll throw some kind of sop to this Mathry creature. Then it will all be finished and forgotten."

"Will it, Matt?" she answered, with that same strange apathy.

Her manner, the tone of her voice, struck him like a blow. He could have cursed out loud, but at that moment they swung off Park Quadrant into the driveway and drew up at the front portico of their home. Catharine immediately hurried into the house.

"Shall you want the car again tonight, sir?" Banks asked him as he stepped out.

"No, damn it," Sprott answered viciously.

Was there a strange glint in the man's obsequious eye? The prosecutor could not tell. In any case, he did not care. He hurried in after his wife and caught up with her in the inner hall.

"Wait, Catharine," he cried. "I must talk to you."

She paused listlessly, her head drooping upon her soft and slender breast. Wrung by her attitude, by her extraordinary pallor, he hesitated, and instead of importuning her, he asked:

"Where are the children?"

"I sent them to Mother's. I thought you would wish them to miss the publicity of this . . . calamity."

He knew that she had acted wisely, that he himself had sanctioned this step, nevertheless, he longed for the warm and affectionate greeting of his daughters. After a brief silence, he stole a look at her.

"This isn't a very gay homecoming for a man who's been badgered all day. Can't we cheer up, Catharine, and have some dinner together?"

"I have ordered dinner for you, Matt. But you must excuse me. I don't feel well."

Again, the blood rushed into his face, he glared at her with a red, dejected eye.

"What the devil's wrong with you?"

She answered brokenly:

"Can't you guess?"

"No, I can't. And I see no reason why in my own house I should be treated like a leper."

She placed one hand on the balustrade of the staircase and half turned away.

"Forgive me, Matt. I must go and lie down."

"No," he almost shouted. "Not before you give me some explanation."

There was a long pause; then, still supporting herself upon the banister with one foot on the lowest step, she lifted her head and gazed at him, like a wounded bird.

"I thought . . . you might have understood . . . what a shock this has been to me. All these years when I overheard people running you down . . . saying things against you . . . I simply laughed. I refused to believe it. I was your wife. I trusted you. But now . . . now I see . . . something of what they meant. Today, in court, Grahame was not throwing mud at you. He was telling the truth, Matt. You sentenced a man to death, and to worse than death, for your own ambition, simply to get yourself on." She passed her thin hand in anguish over her forehead. "Oh, how could you? How could you? It was horrible, just to look at that poor wretch and see what he had suffered."

"Catharine," he exclaimed, coming nearer to her, "you don't know what you are saying. It's my duty to secure a conviction."

"No, no," she cried. "It's your duty to see justice done."

"But, my dear," he persisted, thickly, "I *am* the instrument of justice. When a criminal is clearly guilty I am compelled to bring him to book."

"Even at the cost of suppressing evidence?"

"Presentation of the prisoner's case is incumbent on his counsel."

"While you employ every means to entrap and condemn him. You are . . . you are what they call the devil's advocate."

"Catharine! Because you are overwrought, you must not be unreasonable. You saw today what Mathry is."

"I saw what he had become. And with it all, he did not look like a murderer. He looked . . . he looked as though someone had murdered him."

"Don't be hysterical," he said harshly. "He has not been exonerated yet."

"But he will be," she whispered.

"That remains to be seen."

Although her lips trembled, she gave him a long intense look. "Matt, you know — have you not always known? — that he is innocent."

At that word "innocent," which he had heard so often from the dock, but which, now, uttered by his wife, assumed a terrifying significance, a sudden sweep of emotion flooded over him, a strange commingling of anger and desire, a wish to hurt, yet to console her, and through it all, an abject longing to lay his head upon her breast and weep. He came close to her and tried to put his arm about her waist, but with a nervous spasm she recoiled.

"Don't touch me."

The exclamation froze him; and in her face, ravaged as it was by grief and suffering, there was something he had never seen before, a look, almost of hostility, and what was worse, of fear. He watched her as she turned and went slowly up the stairs.

The gong sounded for dinner.

He went in alone to the dining room where the table was laid for one. In silence, the maid brought in the soup. It was his favourite dinner — oxtail soup, grilled sole, a tournedos of good red meat, apple charlotte, and a savoury of Stilton cheese. But the food was tasteless in his mouth, he ate in grinding abstraction, a core of anger burning within the misery of his soul. Once or twice, as the service door swung open, he could hear from behind the draught screen the rustle of a newspaper and the murmur of voices in the kitchen. His temper flared suddenly, and in an overbearing tone he abused the elderly maid for serving him so ill.

When he had done, he flung away from the table and entered his study. Here, driven by necessity and the tortured condition of his nerves, he broke from his rule and mixed himself a large whiskey and water, then threw himself into his chair. The turmoil in his mind was something he had never experienced before, and yet, with it there was a kind of emptiness, a cruel vacuum in which he felt himself lost. He dreaded what might happen next day, yet he barely considered it. He was like a man brought down by a stroke of apoplexy — confused and muddled, striving unsuccessfully to find his bearings. All that he had sought for and achieved, his rich belongings which surrounded him, his finely bound books, his beautiful pictures, seemed suddenly to have no meaning. He could think of nothing but Catharine, and in the silent house he strained his ears for some sound of her upstairs.

He took another drink and gradually his senses warmed, things looked altogether less dark. Catharine was a highly strung creature, a perfect thoroughbred, but she would get over this unlucky business. After all, had she not shared in his rise, his prosperity. He would go to her presently. Yes, more than ever he had need of her. His pulse beat faster as he dwelt upon her gentle, obedient, loving favours, her fastidiousness, her inveterate kindness to him.

It was now eleven o'clock, the servants had gone to bed and the house was completely still. He got up, switched off the lights and softly tip-toed his way upstairs.

Outside his wife's bedroom he paused with thudding heart, a fountain of desire, a craving for sympathy welling within him. He placed his fingers on the handle of the door and gently turned it. It was locked. Dismayed, he called to Catharine in a low voice . . . then louder. There was no answer. Again he tried and again, twisting the handle violently, with his shoulder pressed against the panels. But the door was firmly secured. For a moment his thick body drew together in a paroxysm, as though to batter down the barrier, then, gradually, grew slack. The prosecutor swung round and, with drooping lip, groped his way to his own room.

# Chapter 17

THAT same evening, as the long hours passed, a singular compulsion grew on Paul. His mother and Pastor Fleming had gone out to seek consolation at the eight-o'clock service in the nearby Gospel Hall, and although they had pressed him, he had flatly refused to accompany them. Ella, in a fit of sulks, had retired to her room. Mathry, under strict instructions from Dunn and McEvoy, was already in bed. Paul sat alone in the living room at the Windsor, quite alone, caught in the backwash of the day's emotions, a prey to a strange and complex despondency, and to a premonition he could not dismiss.

Several newspapers lay scattered at his feet. Rumours of Oswald's involvement had multiplied rapidly and now the headlines proclaimed the latest sensation of the Mathry case. From his chair the black banner type was clearly visible.

## WHERE IS ENOCH OSWALD? MYSTERIOUS DISAPPEARANCE OF THE SILVER KING

As, once again, he read these words, the impulse to act swelled within him, took stronger shape and form, until it proved irresistible. It was not yet nine o'clock. He rose from his chair, put on his coat and hat, and went out of the hotel. His premonition was now so intense it seemed a certainty.

Earlier, a heavy dew had damped the pavements and this, in turn, had yielded to a cold grey mist which, although it was not yet quite dark, swathed and blanketed the streets. He had turned his steps in the direction of Eldon. And now it became apparent that his destination was Ushaw Terrace. Presently he entered number 52. As he began, a shadowy figure, to climb the stairs, passing Prusty's flat, the muffled stillness pressed upon his eardrums. With a calm forehead, but fast beating pulse, he mounted to the top landing, paused, then deliberately knocked upon the door of the fatal apartment.

There was no answer. Could he have been mistaken? Impulsively, taking from his pocket the key which Prusty had given him, he inserted it in the lock. It turned easily. Then, at last, he was inside and had closed the door behind him.

In a firm voice he said:

"Is anyone there?"

There was no reply.

No lights were showing. He stood motionless in the tenebrous hallway, conscious of the surrounding silence, the deadened silence of the fog, making more complete the cold stillness of the unused flat. Yet the place did not seem neglected — there was neither mustiness nor smell of damp. He found a box of matches in his coat and cautiously struck a flare. The linoleum floor was clean, the solid mahogany hat-stand free of dust. As the match flickered he saw the open door leading to the living room. He took three paces forward and went in.

Once more he called:

"Is anyone there?"

Again there was no answer. Perhaps, after all, he was alone in the flat.

He lit the gas in the pink frosted globe. Up until that moment he had been moderately calm, his nerves congealed by the courage which had brought him here. But now, as he viewed the dreaded room wherein had taken place the tragedy which was to affect so many lives, his flesh seemed to melt upon his bones. The terrifying quality of the room, revealed by the faded gaslight, was its complete normality. There stood the round oak table beneath the brass chandelier. Two plush arm chairs flanked the hearth where, behind a paper fan, the fire was neatly laid. The andirons and fender, the mirror and ornaments above the mantel, all were clean and polished, the clock indicated the correct time.

All at once Paul sharply caught his breath. Suddenly, from the bedroom beyond, came the creaking of a board — a sound which, though faint, rang through the muted house like the crack of doom. He started, and his eyes darted towards the bedroom door. He had to summon all his manhood to fight down a desire to turn and bolt as, a moment later, he heard a dragging tread upon the floor. Although he had expected this, although it was the very reason of his coming, he stood rooted when, presently, the bedroom door opened and Enoch Oswald appeared, dressed in his usual sober black, but dishevelled, with his tie undone, his face pallid, his hair streaked upon his brow, his eyes hollow and heavy as though he had arisen from sleep. Like an apparition he came slowly towards Paul, stared deeply into his face.

"It is you," he said at last. His voice was deep and weary, charged with a harsh resonance which matched his gaunt, ungainly frame. "I felt you might visit me. I knew you had the key."

He lowered himself into a chair at the table and, with a measured gesture, indicated the place beside him.

"I regret that I cannot offer you refreshment. I moved in here only yesterday, on an impulse, one might even say, a whim. So far I have not troubled about food." While he spoke Oswald's eyeballs rolled round their sockets in a blank survey of the room, then rested upon Paul. "Tell me . . . why you have come?"

Paul felt his mouth go dry. How could he explain what was in his mind? He tried to find his voice, strove to keep it even.

"I guessed you'd be here. I've come . . . to tell you to clear out . . . to get away at once."

There was a strange pause. Through his lethargy, that leaden heaviness which lay upon him, Oswald beamed a sudden glance at Paul.

"You surprise me, young man. You surprise me greatly. I am

not unaware of your activities during these last months. I fancied you were not particularly . . . well-disposed . . . towards me."

"I feel different now," Paul answered in a low voice. "What I've been through, what I saw in court today, what I've learned of the machinery of the law . . . has changed my ideas. There's been enough suffering and wretchedness over this case. They gave my father fifteen years of misery. What good will it do if they start all over again on you? So go away, while you can. At the very earliest, they won't issue a warrant until tomorrow night. You have twenty-four hours to leave the country. At least it gives you a chance."

"A chance," Oswald echoed in an indescribable tone. "A chance." He was in a kind of rapture, his long upper lip quivering, his ivory skin suffused with colour, his great eyes rolling, humidly, beneath their silver brows. "Young man," he cried suddenly, in a loud, fervent voice, "there is still hope for humanity. Oh, now I am sure . . . sure that my Redeemer liveth!"

Unable to restrain himself, he got to his feet and began rapidly to pace the room, cracking the joints of his fingers, lifting up his head from time to time, as though in thanksgiving. At last, with an effort to master his emotion, he resumed his seat, and gripped Paul tightly by the arm.

"My dear young man, besides my gratitude, I owe you an explanation. It is only your due that you should hear the whole tragic story."

Still holding Paul in that iron grasp he stared into his eyes and, after a silence, hoarsely began, in a manner so archaic, so scriptural in tone, it crossed the borderline of reason.

"Young man," he said, "I have all my life endured a visitation from above. From my earliest childhood, I have been an epileptic." He paused to draw a deep sigh, then went on. "My parents were elderly . . . I was their only son. Under these circumstances

I was brought up in a sheltered manner, plucked from the local school to be educated by a tutor, indulged in every way.

"I was late to develop, but since my tastes lay towards medicine I was sent at the age of nineteen to the university, thence to St. Mary's Hospital. Alas, my disorder interrupted, finally cut short my medical studies. I was forced to return home. Yet gradually, when I had passed my twenty-fifth year, my nervous attacks diminished and almost disappeared, and I was able to take my place in my father's extensive business and to assume the manifold responsibilities to which I was heir. When I attained the age of thirty I became engaged to a lady of fine character whose family, of a standing equal to my own, consented that our marriage should take place if, after a probationary period, it was finally evident that my disability had been cured."

Oswald paused, and another sigh racked his chest.

"Unhappily, during this period, I became acquainted with the woman Spurling who, as you know, worked in a florist's into which, by sheer chance, I had gone to order some flowers for my fiancée. I shall not dwell upon the triviality of that first encounter, nor upon the insidious manner in which our liaison developed from it. I accept full blame for my weakness and sinfulness. Nevertheless, I can affirm that in my downfall I received every assistance from my paramour. Never, my young friend, allow yourself to become ensnared by a vain, demanding woman. Mona exacted everything from me — clothes, jewelry, money, an apartment — and when, in the last resort, I offered to make full provision for her and the child she was expecting, she refused, in the most offensive terms. Marriage alone would satisfy her.

"At that precise moment my father died. Driven frantic by grief and worry, I experienced a sharp recurrence of my epileptic seizures. After one particularly violent fit I went by arrangement to interview the woman Spurling. Ah, my dear young man, you cannot realise how painful and dangerous is the post-epileptic state. After one rises from the ground, pale and livid, with bitten tongue and frothing lips, the mind remains in a deep narcosis, a sort of oblivion, but the passions, as though still convulsed, are violent and excited. It was in this condition that, goaded beyond endurance, I lost myself utterly, and did the murder."

A long pause followed and the wild disorder of Oswald's features altered to a pallid smile — a look so secret, so expressive of a warped and twisted mind, that Paul gripped the sides of his chair.

"My immediate impulse was to give myself up. Then, for the first time, the Inner Voice spoke to me. One word. 'Refrain.' It was not that I feared the consequences of my crime, but simply that I perceived stretching before me, like a great and holy landscape, what I might do, in reparation and atonement, if I were free." Oswald's manner suddenly grew lofty, suffused by dignity. "Thereupon, I dedicated my life to the service of mankind. Aloud I cried: 'I will care for the poor, the maimed, the lame, the blind. And I shall be blessed, for recompense shall be made me at the resurrection of the just!'"

"But what . . ." Paul interposed, "what about the man who was condemned?"

"Ah!" breathed Oswald in a tone of profound regret. "That was the one flaw in my scheme of reclamation. But it was so ordained. I will not deny that, several times, I was tempted to surrender myself. But the Voice spoke again, and again, more imperiously, in the dark stillness of the night. 'What! Art thou like unto the man that began to build a house and was not able to finish? Give thyself up and, under the law, all thy goods will be forfeit to the state. Refrain!' Ah, yes, my dear young man, I was deeply contrite. Yet what could I do? We are all the instruments of a Higher Power. Suffering is our lot. The end justifies the means." Again that bleak and twisted smile spread, almost slyly, over Oswald's marbled face. "The Inner Voice even suggested steps, precautions to ensure my safety, so that my great work might go forward. There were those, as you know, who sought to profit by a vague suspicion of my guilt. Although I imposed my will upon them, took them into my house, moulded them as the potter does the clay, they remained a source of anxiety. Ah, do not imagine that my life was one of ease. On the contrary, I subjected myself, continually, to the most rigorous austerities. The nervous malady which had plagued me from my youth was now a constant affliction — in prostrating seizures twice and even three times a week I endured its crushing embrace. And, above all, this most oppressive and difficult of all my undertakings, was the constant guard I was obliged to keep upon myself, holding my inspired actions within the mundane limits of convention so that all those outside prying eyes might not read my secret."

Excited by his own words, Oswald got up again, and began restively to tread the floor, with hunched shoulders and pale, swinging hands, reasoning with himself, in a loud and agitated tone.

A shiver went through Paul as he watched Oswald's agitation — a dark and tortured misery which grew with every passing instant. The wreckage of this human soul was horrible to witness, yet its desolation awoke in Paul a greater pity. He saw plainly that the man was out of his mind.

Suddenly from the mist outside, doubtless from the distant canal, there came the faint note of a boat's fog horn. This unearthly sound, like the plaint of a tormented spirit, seemed to pierce Oswald to the heart. A groan broke from his lips, he drew up stiffly, and with staring eyes and head stretched back, he exclaimed:

"The hour approaches. Sanctify thy servant."

On the final words, Oswald's voice broke. His features turned grey, his outstretched arms grew rigid, he stood like a man possessed. But gradually, after a few minutes, he relaxed, looked about him, came back slowly. Steadying himself against the edge of the table, he drew a handkerchief from his pocket and wiped his forehead. Then, wanly, he smiled at Paul.

"My dear young man, again I thank you for your kind attentions. I shall be all right now, if you wish to leave me."

Paul hesitated, that strange glow of pity still unquenched within his breast.

"You promise me to go away?"

"I shall go away." Oswald smiled again and nodded, placing his arm upon the other's shoulder. "This has not been unforeseen. I have resources at my command. Goodbye and God bless you."

The pressure of his hand was icy. He opened the door for Paul to depart.

# Chapter 18

NEXT morning, when the court opened, the atmosphere was electric. The crowd, compressed more tightly, overfilling the already sultry courtroom, spoke only in undertones. Strange whisperings were in the air. When it was seen that Sir Matthew was not in his place, curious rumours flew, barely stifled when he arrived, late, hastening to his seat with a haggard, unslept look, and a gash upon his chin, where he had cut himself while shaving.

When their lordships had seated themselves upon the bench, Nigel Grahame stood up, restrained as ever, yet with a new coldness in his manner.

"My lords," he announced, "with your permission I wish to resume my examination of the witness Louisa Burt."

A brief pause ensued while the requisite formalities were completed, then Burt appeared and took her place upon the stand.

"I trust," Grahame began, courteously but with a frigid note, "that you have had the opportunity to compose yourself overnight."

"I'm all right." Burt spoke without her ingratiating coyness, almost rudely. Her hesitation of the previous day was gone as though, in the intervening period, she had been admonished and fortified. She stood up in the box and boldly returned Grahame's gaze.

"We were speaking," said Grahame, "of your acquaintance with Edward Collins, the youth who brought the laundry to the murdered woman. You saw a good deal of him before, and during the trial?"

"How could I help it, we was together most of the time."

"Ah! You were together. Then you talked over the case with him pretty frequently?"

"No," Burt said quickly. "We never mentioned it once."

Grahame raised his brows slightly and glanced towards the Lord Chief Justice before remarking:

"That is a most surprising statement. However, we shall let it pass. Did you discuss the case with Collins *after* the trial?"

"No," Burt answered flatly.

"I must warn you," Grahame said steadily, "that you are upon oath and that the penalties for perjury are exceedingly severe."

"My lords, I protest against that insinuation." The Attorney-General half rose. "It is calculated to intimidate the witness."

"Did you and Collins *never* talk about the case?" Grahame insisted.

"Well," for the first time Burt dropped her eyes, "I don't properly remember. I suppose we might have."

"In other words, you did?"

"Perhaps."

"And often?"

"Yes."

Grahame drew a long breath.

"On the night of the murder, when the man rushed past Edward Collins on the landing, he did not, even faintly, recognize him?"

"No," Burt answered loudly.

"And you? He was a total stranger to you?"

"Yes."

"You never told Collins that you felt you had seen the man before?"

"Never."

"You did not, in confidence, in a whisper, suggest a name to him?"

"No."

There was a fateful pause.

"To return to your own observations on that momentous evening . . . even if the street lamp was not lit . . . even if you could not clearly discern the features of the fugitive, at least you saw what he was doing. He was running?"

"Yes. I've said so till I'm tired."

"Forgive me if I fatigue you unduly. Did the man run all the way?"

"All what way?"

"To the end of the street."

"Yes, I naturally suppose he did."

"You suppose so? He did not by any chance mount a bicycle, a green bicycle, that lay against the railings, and pedal out of sight?"

"No."

Grahame looked gravely at the witness.

"In the light of certain information now in our possession I must again caution you to be careful. I repeat — did he not dash off on a green bicycle?"

Burt was shaken. She muttered.

"I've told you 'No.' I can't do no more." And she began to snivel into her handkerchief.

Once more the Attorney-General protested.

"My lords, I strenuously object to the means being employed to intimidate this witness."

A faint flush rose to Grahame's cheek. He answered spiritedly:

"Perhaps the Attorney-General feels that I am usurping his prerogative. There have been days, in this very court, when I have heard an agent of the Crown using witnesses as a terrier might use a rat, reducing them to such a state of agitation and confusion they simply did not know what they were saying. If only for that reason I am endeavouring to afford this witness the utmost consideration and I can assure your lordships that she will need it."

Dead silence followed these words. Sir Matthew Sprott glanced towards the bench, but for once the Lord Chief Justice did not intervene.

Grahame waited until Burt had dried her eyes.

"When the trial was over you came with Edward Collins to the Central Police Station to receive your joint reward of five hundred pounds."

"Yes we did, and you can't make no harm out of that."

"Of course not. When you arrived at headquarters you were asked to wait while the necessary formalities were completed."

"That's correct. We was always treated nice by the police, which is more nor I can say for you."

"Once again I must ask you to bear with me, and to turn your thoughts back to that half hour when you sat with Collins in the police waiting room. No doubt the trial had been a strain for both of you. Perhaps you were a trifle on edge, nervous and uncertain, which may have accounted for the conversation that took place between you."

"What conversation?"

"Don't you remember?"

"No, I don't."

"Then perhaps I can refresh your memory." Grahame picked up a slip from the sheaf of papers before him. "I suggest that the exchanges between Collins and yourself went like this:

COLLINS: Well, it's about over now, and I'm not sorry, it's really got me down.

BURT: Don't worry, Ted. You know we acted right and proper.

COLLINS: Yes, I daresay. All the same . . .

BURT: All the same what?

COLLINS: Oh, you know, Louisa. Why didn't you tell about . . . you know what?

BURT: Because they never asked me, stupid.

COLLINS: I suppose not. Will we . . . will we get the reward?

BURT: We'll get it, Ed, don't worry. We might do even better.

COLLINS: What do you mean?

BURT: You just wait and see. I've got something up my sleeve.

COLLINS: Mathry was the man, wasn't he, Louisa?

BURT: Shut up, will you. It's too late to back down now. We didn't do no harm. With all that evidence they would have done for Mathry anyhow. And after all, he didn't get hung. Don't you understand, you fool, it don't pay to go against the police. Besides, things may come out of this better than you ever dreamed. I'll live like a lady yet before I'm through."

When Grahame finished reading, and before the Crown could interpose, he turned sternly towards the witness.

"Do you deny that this conversation, which was overheard and transcribed, actually took place?"

"I don't know. I can't remember. I'm not responsible for what

297

Ted Collins said." Fearfully discomposed, Burt gave her answer in a flustered voice.

"When you had been paid the money by the police, what did you do?"

"I forget exactly."

"Did you not go off on a holiday to Margate with Edward Collins?"

"I believe I did."

"Did you and he occupy the same room at the Beach Hotel?"

"Certainly not. And I didn't come here to be insulted."

"Then perhaps you would rather I did not show the court the hotel register of that date."

"My lords," again the Attorney-General interposed, "I must protest these irrelevant allegations against the moral character of the witness."

"Yet when more damaging and less true allegations were made fifteen years ago against my client's morals the Crown raised no objection."

There was a silence. Grahame turned to Burt.

"When this vacation was over you returned to Wortley. You discovered that the atmosphere had changed and chilled. You were scarcely the popular heroine you had imagined you might be. Work was difficult to find. Yet it was precisely at this juncture that both Edward Collins and yourself were offered excellent situations, which you accepted, in a superior private house in Wortley. Is that correct?"

"Yes."

"Who was the owner of that house?"

Burt's defiance was gone. She darted a furtive look at Paul. For a long moment it seemed to stick in her throat. Then, amidst complete silence, she brought out the name.

"Mr. Enoch Oswald."

"Am I correct in asserting that Mr. Oswald behaved with remarkable kindness towards Collins, married him to his head parlourmaid, then shipped him off to New Zealand?"

"I think he treated Ted handsome," Burt mumbled.

"And you?" queried Grahame suavely. "Were you not treated by him more firmly perhaps, yet with equal consideration? Given a good position in his household, then, in the fulness of time, married off and almost, but not quite, despatched, carriage paid, to that same remote continent?"

As Burt muttered a crushed assent a further stir passed through the court, a tightening of interest already stretched to breaking point. Every eye was fixed on Grahame as he put his next question.

"Can you account for the remarkable interest shown by Mr. Oswald in you and Collins, the two key witnesses of the Mathry case?"

Burt shook her head dumbly.

"Could it be, in any way connected with the fact . . ." Grahame queried temperately, "that Enoch Oswald was the landlord of the flat occupied by Mona Spurling, the woman who was murdered?"

Again Burt gave no answer. There was a mortal stillness in the court.

"Mr. Oswald was fairly regular in his calls at the flat, coming no doubt in the way of business, to collect his monthly rent, to see to the comfort of his tenant. Since he came of an evening, he might well have been noticed, vaguely, by Collins, who was frequently on the street at that hour."

"I . . . I suppose so."

Then, like a knife thrust:

"Did Oswald use a bicycle to make these visits?"

"What if he did . . . and a green bike at that!" Burt moaned. "It had nothing to do with me."

Sensation in court.

"One last question," Grahame said casually, as a kind of afterthought. "We have heard considerable mention, yesterday and today, of a left-handed man. Is Mr. Oswald left-handed?"

A bated hush fell upon the court. Burt was at the end of her resources. She looked about her wildly and let out a gasp of terror.

"Yes, he is," she screamed. "And I don't care who knows it."

After that she went into hysterics. Immediately, the court seethed with excitement. Several of the reporters picked up their papers and hurried towards the telephones outside.

When Burt had been assisted from the stand there was a dramatic pause, then Grahame turned towards the bench to deliver his final address. His voice, which had for the most part been temperate and quiet, now took on a note of burning sincerity.

"I must thank this court for its indulgence in bearing with me so long. Now I shall be brief. My lords, we, in our judicial system, pride ourselves upon the principles that any man is presumed innocent until he is found guilty. A person may be suspected, but the burden of proof rests upon the Crown.

"But what, my lords, if the Crown should fail to fulfill its function honestly! What if the officers of the law, having apprehended a suspected individual, should use every trick of the statutes, every device of oratory, every subtle and secret persuasion, every method of pressure and persecution, to show that they are right, that they have, in truth, brought to book the guilty party.

"The Crown, my lords, has great resources at its command — brains, money, and unquestioned authority. Its agents, being human, are anxious — not only to justify their legitimate suspicions — but to advance themselves, and to stand well in the public eye. The experts whom it engages, men of the highest quality, may nevertheless be influenced by the prevailing mood. The Chief of the Police Department, believing that he holds the guilty man, moves heaven and earth to secure a conviction. The police doctors, asked by the Crown to examine a knife, hammer or bludgeon, rarely say outright: 'There is no blood upon this weapon. But rather: 'The material was inadequate for conclusive tests.' Or even: 'There were traces of a substance which might have been blood.' In short, my lords, once an unhappy wretch has become suspect, or by his own actions has made himself so, unconsciously, a biased attitude of mind develops, almost instinctively, an attitude hostile and prejudicial to the accused man.

"Consider the case of this ordinary citizen, not a strong character, a trifle irresponsible, inclined perhaps to vanity, but on the whole neither better nor worse than his fellows. Unhappy at home, chilled by the air of conjugal austerity, he understandably lets his eye wander in the hope of lighting on a more sympathetic face. At this juncture he is introduced by a friend to an attractive young woman, he flirts with her a little, and, after some weeks, while alone in a dingy commercial hotel in a distant city, sends her a post card — upon which, since he has a talent for drawing, he had sketched a rustic scene — asking her to dinner. Then, to his horror, only a few days later, he discovers, from the screaming headlines of the evening press, that the woman has been brutally murdered, that the police are seeking high and low for the sender of the post card, a replica of which is blazoned in every paper in the country.

"What on earth is he to do? He knows he ought to come forward and make a voluntary admission to the police. But the thought of the publicity, the dread of involving himself, perhaps quite needlessly, holds him back. Besides, there is one question they are sure to ask him. Where was he between eight and nine on the evening of September eighth? Casting back anxiously he remembers he had gone to the cinema, alone, and had, in fact, fallen asleep during the performance. What a useless alibi! Who could have seen him, sitting there in the dark? Moreover, as he entered the girl in the box-office had not even raised her head to look at him, and there was no one who could vouch for him at the fatal hour.

"Badly frightened, he loses his head and, instead of going to the authorities, in a moment of wild stupidity he cooks up an alibi with his friend. Presently he is discovered as the writer of the post card. He offers his alibi and it is proved to be false. From that instant he is ensnared — *falsus in uno falsus in omnibus*. A structure of damning evidence rises against him. But in the erection of that edifice certain discrepancies come to light — a peculiar money bag found beside the body, a green bicycle that might well have been used by the murderer, neither of which can in any way be identified with the prisoner. Yet these discrepancies are treated as irrelevant, ignored, squeezed out of the general incriminating pattern. They do not fit, therefore they are discarded. And when the prosecution rises in court, filled with the righteous lust for justice, they are not even mentioned.

"My lords, it is my contention that the Crown's conduct of the case against Rees Mathry was calculated to prevent, and did prevent, a fair trial. Inadequate as has been my outline of the facts, your lordships cannot but conclude from it that there were serious omissions of evidence. Moreover, prejudicial suggestions of the gravest kind were made by the prosecutor in the course of the trial, and in particular in his speech to the jury.

"The whole speech, indeed, was theatrically loaded with prejudicial hints deliberately and subtly calculated to influence the jury and force a verdict of guilty.

"My lords, when a man's life hangs in the balance, is it not time that we had done with this type of oratory which works, not upon the minds, but upon the feelings of the jury, inducing in them not the clear calm light of logic but the most violent emotions of horror, anger, repulsion, and revenge. Oratory which, indeed, is further debased by a form of play-acting wherein learned counsel will produce a weapon, fling it to the floor, even enact the fatal blow, and all with a kind of morbid melodrama that turns a solemn court of justice into a penny peep show. In my opinion the speech delivered by the Crown against Rees Mathry, and the manner of its delivery, strikes at the very root of our criminal administration, and I trust the court will not hesitate to say so."

As Grahame paused, Paul, tense with excitement, threw a quick glance towards Sprott. The prosecutor's ruddy face had turned pale as death, his lips were pressed tightly against his teeth. What were his thoughts? Of his present humiliation? Of a career, broken short and shattered . . . of political ambitions finally blasted?

"It is, moreover, my submission," Grahame resumed, "that the presiding judge at the trial, in charging the jury, misdirected them in law — his charge, in fact, was inaccurate, inadequate, and misleading. As though taking his tone from the prosecutor he animadverted on the character of the prisoner to his extreme prejudice, and failed to direct the attention of the jury to the grave irregularities attending the alleged identification. As to the police, while doubtless they acted in good faith, according to their lights, the fact remains that they vitiated the crucial issue of identification. And it is quite clear that evidence in their possession, favourable to your petitioner, but unknown to him or his legal advisors, was deliberately withheld, to the grave prejudice of the prisoner."

Grahame, with his one gesture of the day, suddenly extended his right hand towards the bench.

"My lords, Mathry did not do the murder. From our investigation and analysis of the trial it is crystal clear that he is innocent, the victim of a terrible, a ghastly travesty of justice. The witness Burt now stands before you a self-convicted perjurer and, driven from her morass of lies, she has indicated only too plainly the real perpetrator of the crime.

"My lords, I am not an agent of the police, nor is it part of my duty to hail the guilty party before this court, but I have led evidence of sufficient weight to enable me to name that party. Let the authorities seek out that man and the last shadow of doubt will be removed. My lords, by all the sacred tenets of justice I entreat you to redress this awful wrong, to admit the culpability of the Crown, and to proclaim to the world the innocence of Rees Mathry."

Grahame sat down amidst intense silence, then the hush was broken by a storm of cheering. Only by threatening to clear the court was the uproar finally stilled. There were tears in Paul's eyes, he had never heard anything so moving as Grahame's final appeal. Carried away, he glanced from the quiet figure of the young advocate to his father, who sat, confused, as though unable to understand that the same public, which fifteen years ago had execrated him, now cheered him to the echo.

When at last order was restored the Attorney-General, having completed a long consultation with his colleagues, got reluctantly to his feet for the Crown. Although his expression was dignified and calm it was plain he did not relish his task, yet was constrained to put as good a face on it as possible. He spoke for barely an hour, a strain of moderation running through his tempered phrases. By contrast with Grahame's prolonged and masterly address, it was, perhaps by design, an unimpassioned effort. When he sat down the Lord Chief Justice immediately adjourned the court so that their lordships might confer before announcing their decision.

It was four o'clock before their lordships returned to the court. Then, amidst a bated hush, the Lord Chief Justice, dignified and impenetrable, delivered the verdict.

"The case," he announced, "is one of great difficulty, presenting

304

an unusually complex issue upon which the balance of judgment might easily be influenced."

There was a long pause. Paul's heart was pounding like a sledgehammer. He looked at his father who, with twitching cheek, his ear cupped in his hand, was listening with a kind of painful desperation. The judge continued:

"However, the court is of the opinion that the instructions given in the charge by both the prosecutor and presiding judge amounted to misdirections in law. We believe also that the new facts here disclosed are material to the issue."

An even longer pause, during which Paul could scarcely breathe.

"We announce, therefore, that the judgment of the court before whom the appellant was convicted should be set aside."

Pandemonium . . . hats in the air . . . wild and unrestrained cheering. Dunn and McEvoy smiling, shaking hands with each other, with Nigel Grahame, with Paul. People crowding round to pat Paul on the back. Why, here was old Prusty, wheezily embracing him. Ella Fleming, and his mother, close together, bewildered, and still ashamed. The pastor, his eyes closed, as if in prayer. Dale, more than ever stony-faced, Sprott pressing towards the exit, dazed by the blow. A vision, in the gallery, of a slight gesticulating figure . . . could it be Mark Boulia?

Then he swung round and moved to where was seated, amidst the hubbub, bowed, as though not yet comprehending, that broken man, whom they would no longer call a murderer.

# Chapter 19

PAUL got back to the Windsor at four o'clock. They had won . . . not all the circumlocution of the verdict, the legal phrases and formal manner of the judges, the cold aloof precision of the court, could flatten out the triumph of this final victory. Yet his nerves were still overcharged, he felt himself in a state of strange unreality, faced with a future that remained undetermined and precarious.

As he came along the corridor leading to the end wing of the hotel he saw Ella's luggage standing strapped and labelled, while through the half-open door he made out his mother, engaged in packing, in her room. This, in a sense, prepared him. When he entered the sitting room he found Ella, seated there, wearing her hat and gloves, and that determined air which in the past presaged a fixed course of action for them both.

The sight of her seemed to crystallize all his uncertainty. He went to the sideboard and took a drink of water from the carafe, all the time feeling her eyes upon him.

"Well, it's all over now."

"I should hope so." Sitting very erect, with her lips drawn down, she gave her head a sharp toss. "And not before time either."

"I know it hasn't been pleasant, Ella," he said reasonably. "But we had to go through with it."

"Oh, we had, had we? That's what you think. But I don't. I think it's all been completely unnecessary. More than that. Completely useless. And it's all been your doing. You started it. You went on with it. In spite of everybody. And what have you got out of it? Nothing. Absolutely nothing."

"Surely it's something to have won our case."

"What good will that do you? You heard how they wrapped it up — they all stick together, these lawyers. You'll have to go to Parliament to get any money. And even if they grant it *you'll* never touch it."

He flushed indignantly but forced himself to answer without rancour.

"I'm not interested in the money. I never even thought of it. All I wanted was to vindicate my father. And I've done it."

"That's a fat lot of good. The way he's been carrying on, you'd have been better if you'd left him where he was, if you're so concerned about his reputation. He's just shown up for what he is . . . a drunken, disgusting old man."

"Ella! The prison did it. . . . He wasn't always that way."

"Well, he's that way now. And I've more than had enough of it. It was bad enough when he was a convict. But at least he was out of the way then. People never saw him, never even knew about him. Why, even in the court he had to make an exhibition of himself. That's why the judges treated us like we were dirt. I was never so ashamed and humiliated in my life, to think that nice people would know I was even remotely connected with such a person. I tell you straight, if it hadn't been for you, I'd have picked up my things and left."

He saw that she was quite incapable of grasping the real issues involved. Nor had she the least consideration for the sacrifices he had made, the struggle that had been waged. She took into account only the damage to that gentility she perpetually craved, the loss suffered by her vanity and self-esteem. And because of that she threw at him complaints and reproaches which were more petty because she felt them to be justified. How could he ever have been so foolish as to entertain that weak infatuation for her pretty face, hallowed by her sickly religious sentiment?

A silence had fallen which, in the light of past experience, she interpreted as an indication of his submission. Mollified by this, and by his failure to "answer back," she spoke in a milder tone, the martyred accents of one who, though deeply injured, is prepared by a Christian effort to forgive.

"Come along, then. Get your things packed."

"What for?"

"Because we're leaving, silly. There's nothing to wait for. Mr. Dunn has settled up the hotel bill — and well he might, seeing what his paper's made out of us. We're taking the seven-o'clock boat from Holyhead."

"I can't leave him, Ella."

She looked at him, amazed, and then aghast.

"I never heard such nonsense in my life. You don't want him, and he doesn't want you. The minute he came out of the court he slunk off to some low pub. Well, let him stick there. When he comes back here he'll find we've all gone. . . ."

He shook his head.

"I'm not coming."

The blood mounted to her forehead. Her eyes flashed.

"If you don't, Paul, I warn you, you'll be sorry. I've put up with a good deal for your sake because of our love. But I can go so far, and no further. . . ."

While she continued to upbraid him the door opened, Mr. Fleming and Paul's mother came into the room. Both were dressed for the journey. The minister glanced from Paul to his daughter.

"What is the matter?" he asked.

"Oh, it's everything," Ella cried. "After all that we've done for him here, Paul has the nerve to pretend he isn't coming back with us."

A troubled expression came into Fleming's eyes. During these last weeks he had suffered considerably, victim of a constant warring within himself. He had hoped to regenerate Mathry, and despite all his efforts, all his prayers, he had failed. The defeat weighed upon him, pressed on the roots of his belief. And now his daughter and Paul — the situation left him troubled and at a loss. He temporized, in well-worn phrases he had almost come to despise.

"Don't you think you have done enough, my boy? You have worked so . . . so nobly."

"Oh, yes, Paul." His mother pleaded in a subdued voice. "You must come with us."

"After all, from the moral point of view, you have no obligation to remain." Fleming considered, then compromised again. "Or perhaps . . . if we go now . . . you may return later."

"If he doesn't come now," Ella broke in, "he'll bitterly regret it."

"Be quiet, Ella." Fleming rebuked her with a touch of anger. "Is there no end to your selfishness?"

But, breaking into angry tears, she was not to be restrained.

"So far as I'm concerned, it is the end. It means he cares more for that wicked old man than he does for me. I'll never, never speak to him again."

Pale and frowning slightly, Fleming made an effort to gather up the strands of his thought, to pacify his daughter. But it was useless. Ella was too far gone in temper and vexation to heed his words. And Paul's mother, completely stricken by her recent trials, was now too cast down to aid him. She desired nothing but immediate escape.

At last the minister gave it up, salved his conscience and saved his dignity in part by approaching Paul and communing with him in a long and silent handclasp.

A few minutes later they were gone.

Paul could scarcely believe it. A load seemed to be lifted from his mind. Alone in the room, he sank into a chair with a sigh of weary relief. His resolution to remain had not been premeditated. But he knew that because of it, he would never see Ella again. He felt free.

As he sat there, not moving, he heard a heavy step in the passage. After a pause the door opened, and, slowly, Mathry came into the room.

Paul gazed at his father in surprise — usually it was after midnight when he found his way back, uncertainly, to the hotel

Mathry was quite sober; but he seemed tired and out of sorts, slower in his movements, wearing, in the face of his vindication, a strangely disheartened air. His shoddy suit, which had not worn well, was burst under the armpit, and spotted on the lapels. A mud stain on his knee, where at one time he had fallen, was only partly brushed off. He advanced sluggishly to a chair, sat down, and darted a glance at Paul from beneath his ragged brows. He seemed to wait for the other to address him, but when Paul said nothing, after a moment he asked, heavily:

"Have they cleared out?"

"Yes."

"Good riddance." Then, with a touch of his usual ungraciousness, he added: "What keeps you hanging around? I suppose you want some of my cash when I get it?"

"That's it," Paul agreed calmly. He had found this the best way of dealing with his father's sardonic thrusts. And indeed, the answer silenced Mathry. But, from time to time, he darted these queer glances at his son, biting on his chapped upper lip, again almost as though he hoped that Paul would speak to him.

"Lost your voice?" Almost in desperation Mathry threw the question.

"No."

"Had your supper?"

"I was just going to order something."

"Then order for me as well."

Paul went to the room telephone and asked them to send up the table d'hôte dinner for two. Deliberately, he made no comment to Mathry, but took up a book again while the table was being set.

Presently the meal arrived — soup, roast mutton served with peas and potatoes, apple pie, all kept hot under double covers — and they sat down to it in silence. Mathry ate with less than his usual appetite, and after a while his efforts seemed to flag. Without finishing his dessert, he stood up and went over to the arm-chair where he slowly filled and lit the pipe which he had recently adopted. His lumpy figure sagged into the weak chair springs. He looked a spent old man.

"Aren't you wondering why I'm in tonight?" he inquired, at length. "Now the show's over, I ought to be out on the skite."

"Nothing you do surprises me," Paul said.

While he continued to use that indifferent tone which he knew would most provoke Mathry to continue, he got up from the table and took a chair on the opposite side of the fireplace.

"I'm sick of that gang I've been running around with." Mathry spoke with sudden bitterness. "All they're doing is making a mug of me. They keep telling me what a great man I am, then they order the drinks and let me pay for them. Dirty lot of spongers. The women are the worst. What do they care? Not a cursed thing. They'd take my last bob, and laugh at me. And you know for why. Because I'm no good at all now . . . not a stricken bit of use."

There was a painful pause, then, not looking at his son, Mathry resumed in a lifeless voice.

"Can you guess what it's like in chokey . . . hundreds of men . . . strong men in their prime . . . cut off from women. Not nice to think about, eh? Sex is dirty when it's to do with convicts. The prison visiting committee . . . sanctimonious bastards . . . don't even give it a thought. But they would all right, by God, if they were in there. Day and night, week after week, month after month, it works on you till you think you're going crazy. You can't help human nature. You lie there in your cell at night and think . . . imagine a woman waiting for you outside . . . beautiful, young, wanting you . . . waiting . . . until you're ready to smash the walls down with your bare fists in an effort to get out. And now I do come out . . . what a hellish joke . . . I find it's all dead and gone forever."

Suddenly, to Paul's concern and distress, Mathry's chest gave a great convulsive heave, his stiff face began, under its mask, to work pitiably.

"Everything goes wrong for me. Every blasted thing. Even the re-trial. What a washout it was today. I got no satisfaction. All these dressed-up bastards of lawyers with their fancy talk. Why don't they do something for a change? Why wouldn't they let me speak? They were only laughing up their sleeves at me. I'm a freak . . . don't fit in anywhere. I'll never be any good. I'm finished and done for. I never done no murder. It's them that has murdered me."

His pipe had gone out, his face was grey, his whole body shook with anguish.

Paul felt his heart melt. But this weakness in his father, this unexpected gleam of hope was too precious to be wasted by an equal weakness, an answering show of feeling. While his breast throbbed, he steeled himself to answer coldly.

"You're certainly not done for." He waited long enough for this to sink in. "What you've had to go through has changed you a lot. But as far as years go, you're not an old man. It's up to you to readjust your ideas and go in for what really suits you."

"Nothing suits me," Mathry muttered. "I've a good mind to finish myself. Coming by the canal bridge tonight I stood looking over . . . and very near threw myself in."

"That would be an excellent way to repay me for all that I've done for you."

Mathry raised his grey head, which was bowed upon his chest, and stole a look at his son.

"Yes," he muttered. "You've been good to me, you have."

"Drown yourself, if you want to," Paul continued in a cutting tone. "Get out of your troubles the easy way. But it seems to me there's a slightly more sensible idea. You'll be getting a lump sum soon. Oh, yes you will, in spite of what you think. Why don't you buy yourself a little farm in the country . . . get out in the fresh air, have your own place, your own chickens and eggs . . . forget about hating people. . . . You'll get your health back in the country . . . feel younger in mind and body." Paul's voice rose suddenly. "I got you out, didn't I? At least make the most of the years I've given you."

"I couldn't do it," Mathry said in a husky voice.

"Yes, you could," Paul exclaimed. "And I'll help you. I'll try and get a school near you. Be on hand if you need me."

"No . . . you wouldn't do that? Or would you?"

"Yes."

Mathry again stole that shrinking look at Paul. His chapped lips trembled.

"I'm all in," he muttered. "I think I'll go to bed."

Paul felt his heart lift, as at a great victory. What had caused Mathry to break down in this fashion he could not guess — he had not dared to hope for it. But in this crumbling front he saw a future for both of them, a final justification snatched in the moment of defeat. He was glad he had decided to wait on.

He looked straight at his father, keeping his voice under control. "You'll feel better after a good sleep."

Mathry got to his feet.

"In the country . . ." he muttered. "With chickens and a cow . . . it would be fine . . . but could I . . . ?"

"Yes," Paul said again, more firmly.

There was a moment's hesitation.

"All right," Mathry said in a queer hoarse tone. He opened his mouth, closed it again. "Now I'll go and turn in." Suddenly he paused, as though struck by something, lifted his head and looked into the distance. His voice took on a different quality — remote, human, and strangely timorous.

"Do you remember . . . Paul . . . on Jesmond Dene . . . when we used to sail the paper boats?"

He gave his son a shamed, contorted look and, brushing his hand across his inflamed and watery eyes, shambled out of the room.

# Chapter 20

FOR a long time Paul remained in the sitting room. Now, after all, he could carry out his plan. It was not the idyllic vision he might once have entertained of a rose-embowered cottage set on a hill above green meadows in the deep countryside. This new maturity that had replaced his sentimental adolescence had made him soberly practical, wary of rash enthusiasms. He must complete his teacher's course, not in Belfast — that was now unthinkable — but at one of the smaller English provincial universities, Durham perhaps, where the fees were moderate and the tuition excellent. In the suburbs of this Northern cathedral city he would surely find some sort of dwelling, no matter how primitive, to house them both, with an allotment garden in which Mathry might find the incentive to work out his salvation. Could this regeneration be achieved? Paul did not know. He had heard of cases where men, released after long terms of penal servitude, fifteen, twenty, even thirty years, had managed to resume an existence of complete normality, to lose themselves in the crowd, achieve a tranquil and hum-drum old age. But they, of course, had not been wrongfully imprisoned.

Quickly, before the throb of injustice could start in him again, Paul got to his feet. He wished nothing to disturb that new sense of peace, almost of placidity, which had replaced his violent rage against the law. It was not late and before retiring he decided to take a walk. Switching out the light and moving quietly along the corridor so that he might not disturb Mathry, he went down-stairs.

The evenings were lengthening and, outside, the last of the day-light lingered, as though reluctant to depart. The air was warm, luminous, and still. Stirred by the beauty of the twilight he strolled away from the hotel.

He had meant to walk at random, yet though his route was cir-cuitous, he evinced no surprise when, half an hour later, he found himself in the familiar precincts of Ware Place. Outside Lena's lodging he drew up, and from the opposite side of the street, rest-ing against the iron railings, he gazed upwards at the blank, unlit windows of the untenanted upper storey.

The days of stifling uncertainty were over, his nerves were no longer on the rack. Liberated from his obsession, he was at last free to appreciate all that Lena had done for him. Now he real-ized that without her help his father would still be in Stoneheath and he, almost certainly, would not have survived. A pang of regret for his insensitiveness, his lack of gratitude, stung him, to-gether with a sudden longing, that was almost unbearable, to see her again. If only she might appear, at this instant, from the shadows, bareheaded, wearing her old raincoat buttoned up at the neck, hollow-cheeked and pensive, so generous and humble, so heedless of herself, yet exhaling that northern freshness which lay on her like dew.

How puerile had been his attitude towards her, how immature his recoil from the outrage that had flawed her virginity. Now he could think calmly of that act of defilement, the details of which had previously caused him a sick, insensate rage. Now, indeed, because of that violation, he felt for her a greater tenderness.

From the Ware steeple came eleven slow strokes, the crescent moon sank down, and still he did not stir but remained looking upwards at those three blank windows, while across the screen of his sight there passed image after image. Although she was not there, never had he seen her so clearly as during that solitary hour. And more and more the presentiment grew that he would soon be with her again. He rejected the impulse to seek out Mrs. Hanley, whom he would find too eager for confidences. Instead, he would go to Dunn, tomorrow, and obtain the address from him. In a single sweeping act of vision he foresaw the circumstances which would enable him to find her and, as though that moment had already come, he was filled with happiness.

At last he turned slowly away. In the main thoroughfare the traffic was stilled, the shops had long since been closed, but at the street corners a few newsboys remained, calling the final edition. Dimly, throughout the evening, Paul had been conscious of their shouts but, sick to death of sensation, he had ignored them. Now however, his eye was caught in passing by a placard waved by a ragged urchin beneath a street lamp. Arrested, he took a few steps backwards, handed over a coin, and held the copy of the *Chronicle* to the flickering light. And there, in the stop press, were three blurred lines of print. The police had broken into the flat at Ushaw Terrace and found Enoch Oswald. He had hanged himself from the gaselier.

Paul slowly recovered himself.

"Poor devil," he murmured at last. "He promised he would go away, and this is what he intended to do!"

And with that exclamation, uttered in sorrow and compassion, all bitterness, the last shreds of hatred, seemed purged from him. He drew a long deep breath. The night air was damp and cool. From a nearby basement bakehouse, where the men were already at work, came the fragrance of new bread. There was no moon but through the roof-tops a few clear stars looked down upon the city as it settled at last to silence. Insensibly, Paul's heart lifted. His step quickened as he set out for the hotel. For the first time in many months he felt the sweet savour of life, and the promise of the morning.

316